A KINGDOM RESTORED

THE VAZULA CHRONICLES BOOK FOUR

DEBORAH GRACE WHITE

LUMINANT PUBLICATIONS

A KINGDOM RESTORED

By Deborah Grace White

A Kingdom Restored
The Vazula Chronicles Book Four

Copyright © 2022 by Deborah Grace White

First edition (v1.0) published in 2022
by Luminant Publications

ISBN: 978-1-922636-24-9

Luminant Publications
PO Box 305
Greenacres, South Australia 5086

http://www.deborahgracewhite.com

Cover Design by Karri Klawiter
Map illustration by Rebecca E. Paavo

For Berri,
The best sister marriage could buy.

KYONA
GREAT RIVER
LOCH ARINE
VALORIA
BASAL HEADLANDS
VAZULA
BRYFORD
WYVERN ISLANDS
BERLEY MANOR
TRIPLE KINGDOMS
KELP FARMS
TILSSTED
SKULSSTED
HEMSSTED
CENTER OF CULTURE
OYSTER FARMS
E
S

FAMILY TREE OF KYONAN CROWN   FAMILY TREE OF VALORIAN CROWN

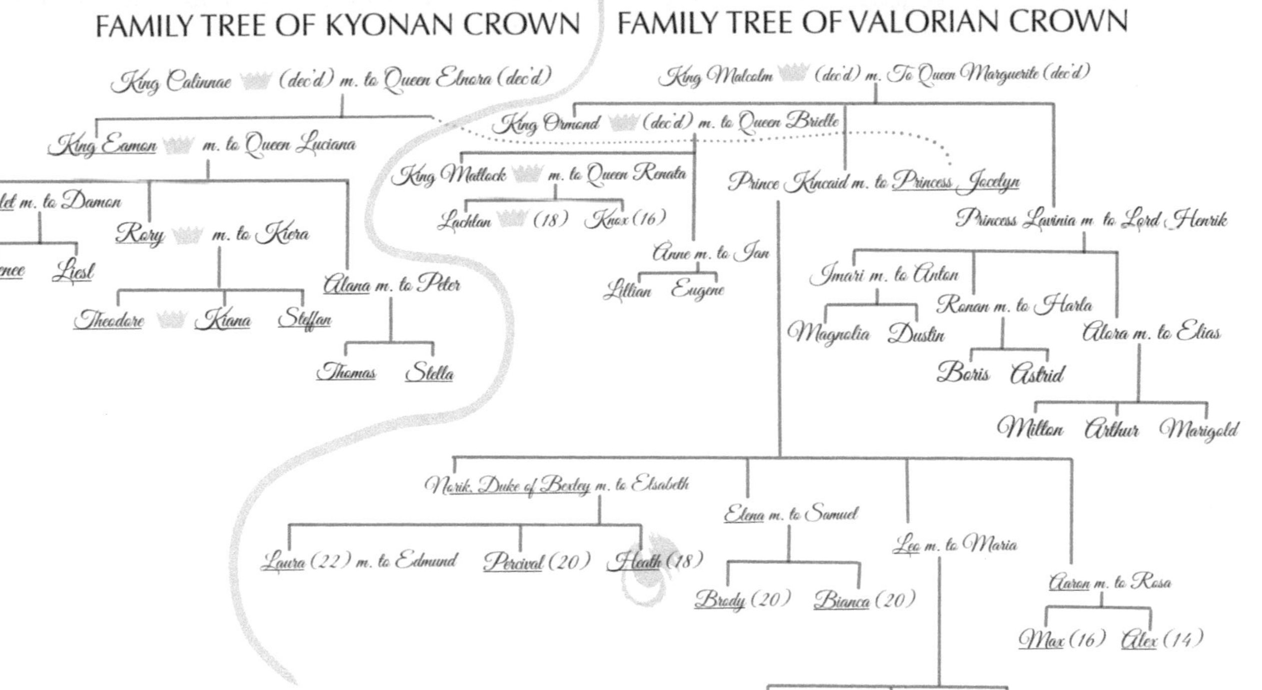

CHAPTER ONE

Merletta

Merletta drew in a slow steadying pull of cold water, letting a shudder run over her. She knew it was foolish to be nervous—these were her friends. But the news she had to tell them this time was enough to turn the closest ally into an enemy.

"It will be all right, Merletta." Sage's gentle voice just sent guilt shooting though Merletta. Her friend knew what was coming, and she hadn't leveled a single reproach.

A quiet knock sounded on the door, and Sage hastened to let the visitor in. It was Emil.

He shot a quick look around Sage's small living space, his brow furrowed slightly. "It's a bit irregular, you know, inviting Andre and me in here."

Sage actually rolled her eyes. "Everything we do is irregular, Emil. Don't be so stiff."

Merletta gave an incredulous chuckle at her friend's bluntness. Even more surprising was that Emil didn't look offended. In fact, unless Merletta was mistaken, there was even a hint of amusement in the long-suffering look he threw toward Sage.

Well, at least that was progressing reasonably well.

Merletta's stomach felt suddenly hollow. Not that it would matter if they were all about to be wiped from the ocean.

"Sorry I'm late." Andre's cheerful voice announced his arrival, as he swam through the doorway behind Emil.

The older merman frowned slightly. "Keep your voice down, Andre."

"All right, all right," Andre said soothingly. "Keep your scales on. So what are we here for?"

They all looked expectantly at Merletta, who struggled for a moment to find words. When she'd joined the program—a reviled outsider—she'd truly never expected friends like these. Seeing how their friendships had not only continued but grown closer in the months of her unplanned absence in Valoria warmed her heart. How could she tell them what she'd brought on them all?

"Just say it, Merletta," Sage advised her. "You'll feel better when it's out."

Merletta nodded, her throat tight. "You're right. Emil and Andre, as you may know, I'm starting my studies again tomorrow, even though it's only been two weeks since my test. The instructors agreed to let me waive my extra weeks of break."

"That's probably the first time anyone's ever requested that," Andre chuckled.

Merletta gave a perfunctory smile. "Anyway, I'll have to move back into the trainees' barracks, and I expect to be closely watched. My best guess is that's why the instructors are eager to see me back in classes. The point is, it may not be so easy to speak privately together like this. Meaning it's time—well past time, really—for me to tell you something."

"If the straight-shooting Merletta is struggling this much to get it out, it must be bad," Andre said in light-hearted dismay.

"It is bad," Merletta told him. "Worse than you can imagine. I told you I spent some months on land with Heath, in his kingdom." A shudder passed over her. "What I didn't tell you is that I went to Rekavidur's dragon colony while I was there. Which was a terrible mistake."

Emil had gone still in the water, his gaze sharp on her. "Why?"

Merletta forced herself to meet his eyes. "The dragons have a legend from their history about fish who were warped into some kind of magical sea monsters. They say it happened when they received magic from dragons who wanted to relinquish their core magic so as to...well, kill themselves." She gestured between herself and her friends. "The dragons believe that's what we are—descendants of those warped creatures. Heath and I—and his dragon friend, Reka—don't think that's true. I'm fairly certain our origins aren't what the Center has taught us, but the dragons' tale doesn't make sense either."

"I hope you're right," Andre said. "I don't like the idea that we're descended from some kind of suicidal dragon frenzy."

"Neither do I," Merletta agreed. "But unfortunately, it matters very little whether I'm right. The point is, the dragons believe that's where we came from. And they, well..." She hesitated, but there was no gentle way to say it. "They have a law regarding such creatures—abominations, they call them. And that law is—"

"To destroy them." There was no emotion in Emil's guess. He spoke the words calmly, albeit a little grimly.

Merletta nodded. "I'm afraid so," she whispered. "They don't know where the triple kingdoms are yet, but they're determined to find us, and wipe us all out."

Andre's eyes were wide with horror, and even Sage, who'd already known, had gone pale at this reminder of what was at stake. Merletta saw Emil's eyes flick to Sage, clearly taking in her lack of surprise, before returning to Merletta.

"I'm so sorry," Merletta told them. "It's my fault. I had no idea about those old legends, and neither did Heath. Even Rekavidur didn't know them when we first met, which is why he had no particular reaction to my mermaid form. Based on my experience of Rekavidur, I never took the warnings about dragons seriously. If I hadn't approached the dragons in their colony, they may never have figured out that I had a tail, and put it all together."

"It's not your fault, Merletta," Sage contradicted softly. "If the Center hadn't been actively promoting lies in almost every other area, you wouldn't have disbelieved them about dragons. How were you to know it was the one thing they were truthful about?"

"Not entirely truthful," Merletta said. "Reka insists that dragons aren't aggressive by nature. Usually they would live and let live. Just not with...abominations. He also insists that although they might kill us to satisfy their laws, they would never eat us, any more than they'd eat a human."

"What can we do?" Emil's calm voice seemed to help center them all in the midst of the terrifying revelation.

Everyone's backs straightened a little, but although it was Emil who had steadied them, they all looked to Merletta for an answer.

"I don't know," she said helplessly. "There's nothing I can think of. I mean, how do we defend against dragons?"

"There must be some ways to fight them," Andre said, like the son of a guard he was. "We're not entirely defenseless."

"They're just so powerful, though," Sage said. "And Merletta says it's true that they can't be killed."

Merletta nodded. "The ones who choose to have offspring rather than live forever will die, but they can't be killed by violence. They just expire when their time comes, from what Heath tells me. Forfeiting their magic in the way I mentioned is the only way an immortal dragon can die. And it's absolutely reviled by their kind."

"What would make an immortal dragon want to die?" Andre asked, sounding awed. "When they could live forever at full strength and power?"

"I don't know, and that's not my concern right now," Merletta said.

"What does this Heath say about it?" Emil asked.

"That he's ready to do anything he can to help us," Merletta responded. "But he doesn't have any bright ideas, either. Reka's parents are more sympathetic than the other dragons. But their attempts to talk the rest around haven't been successful so far."

"We need to find a way to convince them that we're not what they think we are," Sage chimed in.

Emil frowned thoughtfully at her. "That will be difficult, given we can't really be sure we're not."

"We're not," Merletta said firmly. "Our history is tied to Vazula, and perhaps the dragon colony that once lived there. I'm sure of it. It's not tied to the rogue dragons of Heath's land who once forfeited their magic."

She ran a hand through her hair. "If only it was easier for me to get safely to the island without being seen. We never found anything very informative there in the past, but we weren't looking that hard, really. We were always distracted by each other."

"Unfortunate," Emil said dryly.

"You're one to talk," Merletta shot at him, and he actually looked a little self-conscious. Merletta had the impression he was very deliberately not looking in Sage's direction.

Sage looked bewildered, but didn't get drawn into the petty exchange. "Can't Heath and the dragon search the island for some evidence of our origins?"

Merletta shook her head. "Dragons have this magic called farsight. It allows them to follow others from afar, watch them across space. It works particularly with those they know well. Reka and Heath took a great risk in coming to the island a week ago to tell me all this. They think it's too dangerous to come back, for fear the other dragons will follow Reka in their minds, and see where the island is. From there it wouldn't be difficult to find us here. I've got Paul and Griffin scouring the island, but to be honest, I don't have much hope that they'll find anything useful."

"Then we need to look for answers on our end," Emil said firmly. "I'm the most senior amongst us in the Center hierarchy. I'll lose my junior status soon, and be a full record holder. I'll see whether some surreptitious inquiry can uncover anything about our origins beyond the story of the three brothers who came from the deep ocean."

"Thank you," Merletta said fervently. She looked around at the others, too. "And...and thank you all for not...you know, hating me."

"Merletta." Andre's expression was fierce. "None of us would deny that since the moment you started the program, you've been swept up into a maelstrom. But it's not of your making. The fact that your willingness to call out the Center's lies has put a target on your back doesn't make you responsible for their tyranny."

Merletta smiled faintly. "Thank you, Andre," she said. "But it's not the Center threatening to kill us all. It's the dragons. And it's thanks to me that they even know about us."

"That is unfortunate," Emil said gravely, and Merletta's heart grew heavier. "But I agree with Andre," he continued. "It's not a problem of your making. The only way for these issues not to come to a head would be for the Center's rigid control to continue unchecked. And I can see more and more clearly that such a situation is untenable."

Merletta blinked, surprised but no less touched by Emil's more measured support. "Well," she said, her throat once again tight with emotion, "all I know is that I don't deserve such loyal friends as you. But I'm so glad I have you."

Sage gave her a quick hug, and Andre thumped her on the back in a brotherly way. But Emil's mind was already back on practical things.

"Do we know how long we have?"

Merletta shook her head. "Heath says dragons are strange about time. It could be tomorrow that they come looking for us. It could be years from now."

"It would help us prepare if we had more of an idea," Andre mused.

Merletta nodded. "That's what August said. He and Eloise are leaving tonight. They're going to the island, then onward in the morning. They're planning to return to Heath's kingdom, to try to find out more." Her voice was sober. "It's a very dangerous mission. If the dragons see them, they'll certainly kill them."

Andre frowned. "I'll go see them today," he said. "Wish them luck." His tail swished in frustration as he stared out Sage's tiny window. "I wish I could go with them. If we're all going to die soon, I'd like to see more of the ocean than this bubble first. Not to mention try out my legs."

"They'll travel fastest alone," Merletta said, a twinge of alarm for her friend shooting through her. The triple kingdoms weren't necessarily safe, but proximity to the dragon colony was definitely dangerous. "August is very experienced in the open ocean. He'll know how to lose any pursuers, and—"

"It's all right," Andre assured her with a wry smile. "I know I can't go. We all have our part to play here in the Center." His expression grew more serious. "Plus, if there's danger coming for us, the last thing I would do is abandon my family to it while I swam away."

"That's a very real possibility, though," Emil said thoughtfully. His eyes were again on Sage. "We could try to establish a safe base somewhere outside the triple kingdoms. I assume we'd be harder to find without the magical barrier calling the dragons to us."

Sage was nodding thoughtfully, but she suddenly seemed to realize Emil's eyes were on her. "I suppose you'd be part of this group fleeing to the safe base, would you?" she asked innocently.

"Me?" Emil looked startled. "Of course not. I'm going to stay here and try to help find a way to save the whole triple kingdoms."

"Well," Sage said, her voice a little too sweet, "then I doubt there's much point in a safe base. Since everyone in this room is equally determined to stay and help, and no one outside it is likely to believe us about the need to flee elsewhere."

Emil lowered his voice, his tone growing urgent. "Sage, there's nothing wrong with choosing to be safe."

"I'm not swimming away like a frightened fish, Emil."

Sage's tone was final, and Emil didn't respond. It was clear to Merletta that what she'd just witnessed was the continuation of an earlier discussion, one that would likely be resurrected again in the future.

"Well," she said into the slightly awkward silence. "Obviously I wish we could all flee to safety, but I can't really see any course that's free of risk from here. And I for one won't be going anywhere while the rest of my civilization is at risk of death because of me."

She looked around at them all. "I'll be going to Vazula as often as I can, to see Tish, and to find out whether the others have discovered anything useful. But to be honest, I don't expect that'll be all that often. Otherwise, for the moment I think we just need to wait for August and Eloise to come back."

She nodded at Emil. "And for the results of your search, of course."

The group nodded, sobered and silent. The sight of their grim but determined faces tugged at Merletta's heart. She appreciated their presence enormously. But she was under no illusions—they had no more solutions than she did.

Merletta left Sage's tiny record holder room for the trainee barracks that evening. It was a little surreal, on entering the bustling, noisy mermaids' room, to remember her first days in the program. Then, it had been just her, Sage, and Ileana, the former trainee who'd failed third year and become a guard. And who, in spite of hating Merletta since the moment they met, had recently announced that she *wanted in* on Merletta's supposed uprising.

Merletta pushed the thought to the side. She still had no idea what to do with Ileana's offer, and she had bigger problems at the moment.

At any rate, the barracks were a different place, now. Merletta had been told more than once that she was responsible for the sudden influx of aspiring trainees, having given the program a certain buzz. Whether that was true, she didn't know. But the fact that there were now a dozen mermaids in the female barracks—most of them first or second years—and as many in the male barracks suggested that something had changed.

Merletta was the only fourth year trainee, however, and Lorraine was the only third year among the mermaids, having just returned from break after passing her own test. Andre's test was nearly upon him, but Merletta didn't doubt that he'd pass and join Lorraine in third year. He'd shown no sign of struggling to keep up, the way both Ileana and Jacobi had before their failures. It was strange to think he'd then be the most senior merman in the program.

Of course, there was also Indigo in the mermaid barracks. She was still in first year, studying for her upcoming second year test. Merletta had expected hostility from Andre's pale-haired cousin, given Indigo had seemed so shameless in acknowledging to Andre that she'd been spying on Merletta at the direction of a senior Center guard. Merletta knew that Andre had barely spoken to his cousin in months as a result.

But Indigo showed no sign of anger or resentment. Her eyes darted quickly over when Merletta entered the room, then quickly away. She looked troubled, if anything.

Merletta made no attempt to grapple with the mystery. She had enough unanswered questions in her own life. She felt no need to delve into Indigo's.

If it was strange to move back into the barracks, it was even stranger swimming into class the following morning. Wivell's cool greeting gave no recognition to their last real conversation, in which he'd lamented her chosen course. He'd told Merletta that her defiance was a waste of one of the most promising minds he'd seen in a generation.

He'd even said that he truly believed she could have risen all the way to Record Master one day, if she'd been *more teachable*. It was a startling statement from a senior merman within the program, someone whom others might even consider in line for the position in the future. It was impossible to imagine anyone like Wivell ever taking Merletta on to train as their replacement. She'd concluded that his words had been meant to sting rather than being sincere. After all, succeeding in the program and proving herself had been her dearest ambition when she'd joined, and she'd made no secret of it. Somehow, none of that seemed important anymore, little as Wivell might realize it.

Soon enough, Merletta had been given some basic memory refreshing exercises to complete, peeling off from the gaggle of first and second years to work with Andre and Lorraine. It wasn't especially interesting or challenging, a fact Lorraine had clearly also noted. Merletta ignored her regular grumbling.

During her history classes, Ibsen literally never looked at Merletta, let alone spoke to her. There was absolutely no question of him actually teaching her anything. His offense at her continued presence in the program was clear in the tilt of his head and the stiffness of his speech. She didn't let it bother her. The only real reason for being here now was the access it gave her. She had no expectation of lasting long enough to take her fourth year test, let alone pass it.

As always, her training days with Agner at the end of the week were a much-needed release. On the first morning, the instructor set all the other trainees to their tasks, then pulled Merletta aside, where they could watch the first years' clumsy warm up exercises but not be overheard.

"Merletta," he said with a smile. "Welcome back." His voice was as jovial as ever, just as if they weren't in the midst of the tensest crisis the triple kingdoms had seen in generations. And that was without even taking the dragons into account.

"I'm glad you decided to return early," Agner went on. "It's boring without you around. Never so when you're here, though." He chuckled, then leaned close and gave her a wink. "I have to keep an eye out for you, after all, now that we're co-conspirators."

Merletta couldn't help smiling at this reference to Agner's role in authorizing the exemption that allowed her to sit her third year test in spite of missing months of classes.

"I never guessed you had such a rebellious streak, Instructor," she said lightly.

He chuckled again. "It's not called rebellion when you're in a position of power. If you can just keep your head down a little more, Merletta, you can find that out for yourself soon enough."

"I've never been good at keeping my head down," Merletta told him frankly. "It's usually so far up it breaks the surface."

Agner shot her a sharp look, seeming to hesitate over his next words. But if he recognized that there was genuine meaning behind the expression, he didn't call her out on it.

"That's what I thought," he said instead. "In which case, you're going to need my training most. Records learning won't help you stay alive. I prefer not to get involved in that aspect of things, but this is where my part comes in." He waved his hand around the training square. "I'm going to work you harder, teach you how to defend yourself."

"Last year's training wasn't as hard as you can go?" Merletta asked dryly.

Agner just grinned.

"But seriously," Merletta pressed, recognizing that careful dancing with words was out of place with Agner, especially now. At his level of seniority, he must have a pretty good idea of what was going on. "If you know my life is at risk for not keeping my head down, how can you be part of all this?"

There was no offense in Agner's smile, but perhaps the tiniest hint of sadness. "It's like a guard formation, Merletta. We can't see the full picture from where we float in our position. But the one coordinating the squad can. We may not always know the reasons—and we may not always like the methods. But you can be certain there *are* reasons."

"That's not answer enough to satisfy me," Merletta told him bluntly.

His smile was back. "Which is what has always made both your potential and your threat so high. But I'm not interested in the politics. I'm interested in seeing your spear work."

Responding to his gesture, Merletta followed him across the

square as the instructor's eyes roved over his options.

"I think we'll get you to spar with—"

"I can spar with Merletta, Instructor Agner." Ileana's voice cut across him, the green-tailed mermaid appearing from a group of guards in full training mode.

"Ileana." Agner looked faintly surprised. "Don't you have other duties?"

She shook her head. "My squad isn't on patrol today. I'm here to train in my own time."

"Well, then," Agner said, his ready smile growing. "Excellent. I'll leave Merletta in your capable hands for the moment." And with that, he swam off toward the bumbling first years.

Merletta regarded Ileana warily. "What do you want, Ileana? Is this some kind of trick?"

"Of course not," Ileana said impatiently. "I'm trying to help you."

Merletta raised a skeptical eyebrow, and Ileana's cheeks reddened in anger.

"I'm better at combat than you are, I always have been," she insisted. "I'm trying to help you stay alive. You won't get anywhere training with that useless lot." She gestured toward the first years.

"I'm not disputing your prowess," Merletta said mildly. "Just your intentions. Why would you want to help me?"

"Did you get hit in the head?" Ileana snapped. "For a fourth year, your memory is atrocious. I told you a couple weeks ago." Her voice dropped. "I want to help you bring down the Center and expose their lies. You can't do that if you're not even able to stay alive."

Merletta considered her. "All right," she said, raising the new spear she'd been issued upon starting fourth year. She'd yet to find an opportunity to return Griffin's to him. "You want to fight? Let's fight."

Heath

Heath strode down the corridor, blind to the stone walls and tapestries around him. He remembered in a detached way that he'd once found the castle beautiful. Now it was a place of fear and urgency, every feature drawing his attention down to the dungeons beneath, where Percival was still imprisoned.

At the thought, his power flared out without his permission, pulling into his mind an image of Percival at that moment, sitting still and sober on a straw mattress in a corner of his cell. Heath yanked his thoughts back into his own control. Sometimes his extra sight was a very mixed blessing. It wouldn't help quell the rising panic to watch his brother wait in a cell for his execution date to be set.

No, Heath reminded himself firmly. *That's not going to happen. I'm not going to let it happen.*

Not that he could claim any success. His efforts to prove to King Matlock that Percival hadn't been behind the attempt on his life had so far been fruitless. He'd done little else—with the exception of his visit to Vazula a week before to warn Merletta of the dragons' intentions—but there was simply nothing new to find. The king had launched an official investigation as well, his guards crawling all over the site of the fire, but that had also turned up nothing. A fact which clearly neither surprised nor concerned King Matlock.

"Lady Leonora." The gruff voice up ahead sounded uncomfortable. "I must ask you to desist."

"She's not hurting anyone," someone responded angrily.

Heath sped up slightly, recognizing Jasmine's voice. It couldn't be a good sign if two of his cousins were arguing with someone official. He rounded the corner to see the two girls—once both quiet and biddable—facing off against a pair of guards.

"King's orders," the second guard said, sounding no more comfortable than the first at being required to sanction two high-born ladies.

"It's hot in here," said Leonora in a hard voice.

Now he was close, Heath could feel Leonora's power curling out from her. She had the ability to control the temperature, at least within her immediate area. She seemed to be doing nothing more objectionable than cooling down the air around her and Jasmine.

"Regardless, My Lady," the guard started, but Jasmine cut him off.

"If His Majesty can't keep his castle at a livable temperature, then he should expect that we're going to do what we can to make ourselves more comfortable. Any of his subjects would do the same."

"But, Lady Jasmine," the guard said helplessly. "You know the law says that you're not to exercise your powers except under the king's direction."

"What are you going to do?" Jasmine challenged him. "Lock her up in the dungeons and execute her, too? Just for cooling down the air?"

Heath deemed it time to intervene. "Is there a problem here?" he asked mildly, stepping up behind his cousins.

"Lord Heath." One of the guards gave him a small, stiff bow. "Lady Leonora was breaching the king's orders, and we—"

"Was she?" Heath raised an eyebrow. "How would you know, given only power-wielders can sense power?" He leaned close, furrowing his brow as if in conspiracy. "You're not hiding forbidden magic, are you?"

"Of course not." The guard looked irritated. "But our orders are to—"

"Report any unsanctioned use of power, I'm guessing," Heath finished for him. "But how you can be sure magic was at work here rather than just an errant breeze, I can't imagine." He looked at Leonora, who was petite, and looked younger than her nineteen years. "If you're comfortable condemning her to a night in the dungeons based on a mere suspicion..."

The guards exchanged a glance, then gave stiff bows. "As you say, My Lord," one of them told Heath. "Perhaps we misunderstood."

They marched off down the corridor, leaving the sisters to stare suspiciously at Heath.

"Why did you say it wasn't magic?" Jasmine challenged.

"Yeah," Leonora agreed with a frown. "We're not trying to hide it."

"Don't worry," Heath told them. "They knew it was magic. They just took the offered way out of having to actually punish you for it. Couldn't you see how uncomfortable they were? They didn't want to lock you up for something so trivial."

"I didn't see any discomfort," said Leonora. "But if being locked in the dungeons is what it takes to show the king that we won't let our magic be stamped out, then I'll gladly do it."

Heath suspected that she might feel differently had she

spent as much time in the dungeons as he had since Percival's imprisonment. But he refrained from saying so.

"Don't you think beating the heat of the day is a bit of a flimsy thing to take such a stand on?"

"It's not about the heat," said Jasmine, scowling. "It's the principle."

Heath ran a hand through his hair. He understood exactly what she meant, but he'd been getting a pretty close view of what Percival was experiencing, locked in the filth-strewn dungeons for weeks now, uncertain of how many more days he had left to his short life. He didn't want to see his gentle cousin experience any part of that.

"When did you two stop being the easygoing peacemaking ones?" he asked ruefully.

"When our cousin was sentenced to death for a weak excuse!" Leonora said passionately. "We all know the king just wants to be rid of him because of his magic. How can you act so casual, Heath? He's your brother!"

"And if you think I'm not doing everything in my power to get him out of this fix, you don't know me!" Heath burst out.

"We didn't mean that," said Jasmine quickly. "We know you're upset, too. It's just..."

She hesitated, and Heath raised an expectant eyebrow.

"Well, no offense," she said quickly. "But it's hard to know if you're really quite as invested as we are. Given, you know..."

"My lack of power?" Heath said dryly.

It was all so ridiculous, given the breadth and strength of his late-developing magic. But the fact that his uncertain power made his family question his loyalty caused him to be stubbornly persistent in his reluctance to tell everyone what he was learning to do.

"Percival is my brother," Heath said flatly. "And I won't let him be killed for a crime he didn't commit." He considered his two cousins, frowning slightly. "But you're wrong if you think it's just a weak excuse. I was there when King Matlock almost died, and I've been trying exhaustively since then to prove who was behind the attack. I know for a fact it's not Percival. But even I have to admit it looks that way. I have no doubt King Matlock genuinely believes it."

He strode off, leaving Jasmine and Leonora to wrestle with that thought however they chose. Much as Jasmine had tried to take it back, he was still stung by Leonora's suggestion that he didn't care sufficiently about Percival's fate. It was all he cared about.

His magic rose up at once to contradict the false assertion. Unbidden, his connection with Merletta activated itself, and he saw her face as it currently was. She was underwater, of course, and for a moment panic flared within him as he realized she was fighting with her spear. He forced his vision outward with an effort—he still struggled to see her wider surroundings most times—and was relieved to see what appeared to be a training yard.

Not a literal tussle to the death, then.

Letting the image shrink back to the edge of his mind—where it remained ever-present—Heath covered the last distance to the crown prince's study. The guards gave him a curt nod, and he knocked.

"Enter," came Lachlan's weary voice.

Heath walked into the room, noting that his second cousin looked as worn as he felt.

"Heath," said Lachlan, gesturing him into a chair. "I'm sorry, I forgot we were supposed to meet now." He looked up distractedly from the pile of reports in front of him.

"I won't waste your time, then," Heath said. "I don't have anything new."

He squirmed slightly inside, thinking of the one suspicion

he hadn't told Lachlan. But it was probably an absurd thought—surely the faint trace of power he'd felt when Percival was attacked, and indeed when Heath was almost killed by a collapsing chimney, couldn't have belonged to merpeople wandering around Valoria with legs. Merletta had told him time and again how big a shock it was to discover that leaving the water led not to death as she'd been taught but to transformation to human form. So far she hadn't encountered anyone else who seemed to know about it.

And the interaction between Heath and Merletta had occurred by chance, far away from Valoria's shores. There was no reason to think that anyone else from her world even knew about Valoria, let alone had been there. And if they had, why would they want to attack Percival? Besides, he argued with himself, he hadn't sensed that power at the fire. Whoever had set the blaze had been long gone by the time he arrived. So there was nothing concrete to connect it with the previous attacks.

None of that was the reason Heath had kept this vague fear to himself, however. The reason was that he couldn't reveal the possibility—the very faint, unlikely possibility—without exposing Merletta's secrets, and endangering her civilization even more than he'd already done.

But what if it was enough to save Percival?

The thought niggled uncomfortably in Heath's mind, causing him to shift in his seat. The last thing he wanted to do was be forced to choose between his brother's safety and Merletta's. Perhaps, if things came to a true crisis point...if a date was actually set for Percival's execution...

Well, he'd have to reassess if that day ever came. And in the meantime, he was going to try not to allow it to reach that pass.

"I don't have anything new either," Lachlan told him. "I wish I could tell you that my father's anger is cooling. But I can't honestly say it is. At least he's made no mention of setting an execution date. He appears to still be honoring his promise to wait until the formal investigation is complete. But he's not allowing me any involvement in that investigation."

"You do believe my father, don't you?" Heath said. "That there's no deception in Percival's words when he says he had no role in the attack on your father?"

"I do," Lachlan assured him gravely. "Honestly, I think that's why my father won't let me near the investigation." He paused for a moment, then laid down his quill. "To be frank, Heath, I wouldn't have been entirely surprised if your brother had attacked my father. He's seemed angry enough to do it many times. But I don't doubt your father's assurances. Besides which, I have the honesty to acknowledge that it's not in Percival's style to knock guards out from behind and lock someone in a burning building. If he was to lose control, I think he'd attack openly."

"Yes," Heath agreed ruefully. "Although I truly don't think he'd ever actually hurt the king."

Lachlan nodded, his hand straying back toward his quill.

"I'll leave you," said Heath quickly. "You know where to reach me if anything new comes up."

He slipped from the study, his thoughts troubled as he made for a back stairway. He knew his mother would be waiting hopefully for news, but he couldn't bring himself to leave the castle without speaking to Percival. He'd almost reached the top of the stairs when two familiar figures emerged from the stairwell.

"Heath!" Bianca said, looking surprised.

"Hi Bianca, Brody," Heath said. The castle seemed to be crawling with his cousins today. "Have you been to see Percival?"

They nodded, expressions sober.

"Is that where you're going?" Brody asked. He frowned slightly. "What brings you this way?" He cast his eyes up the corridor behind Heath, and his eyes narrowed. "Been holed up with the prince, haven't you?"

"Brody," Bianca sighed.

"Are you really going to pretend you're fine with it?" her twin demanded.

"Don't start, Brody," Heath said shortly. "I've already had an earful from Jasmine and Leonora about how I'm apparently not taking Percival's plight enough to heart, and how my lack of magic means I'm not a true part of the family."

"I doubt that's quite what they said, and we don't think those things are true either," said Bianca firmly. She glared at Brody. "Do we?"

Her brother's brow was still heavy. "No. It's not your magic that's the problem. It's your loyalty. How you can be working with the crown prince when—"

"Lachlan's not the one who locked Percival away," Heath said, exasperated. "He believes Father that Percival's telling the truth."

"But what?" Brody challenged. "He's just a bit too busy to tell the king that?"

Heath sighed. Glancing around, he said quietly, "He doesn't have as much influence as you think. King Matlock makes his own decisions."

"And he seems to have decided that he trusts you," Brody said cuttingly. "It was quite a moving public announcement last week, about your service to the crown when you saved the king from your brother's dastardly scheme. What was that order you were awarded again?"

"You know I didn't ask for that," Heath snapped. "And I didn't want it. I think he only did it to try to make up for the flogging he ordered when I refused my loyalty ceremony."

"And apparently it has made up for it," Brody shot back. "Since you're back working with the crown prince, and the king treats you like an actual human being now, instead of power-wielding scum."

"What do you want from me, Brody?" Heath demanded. "It's not like I've forgotten being publicly flogged. But what is there to gain from staying angry about it? Did you really expect me to hang on to my own wounds when my brother is on the brink of execution?"

"Of course not," said Bianca softly. "We know you better than that. Don't listen to Brody, he's just upset. We all are." She searched Heath's face. "The king understands, doesn't he? That we're not going to just let this go? If he executes Percival, he'll have a full uprising on his hands."

"I don't know what he understands," Heath said wearily. "Whatever you seem to think about my loyalties, his decisions make no sense to me. If he doesn't believe his own son's view of it all, do you think he confides in me, or listens to my advice?"

"He should listen to his own cousin," Brody growled, in reference to Heath's father. "Especially when that cousin has the magic ability to detect deception, and can guarantee that Percival is telling the truth."

Heath said nothing. He wished the king would believe his father as well, but he wasn't really surprised King Matlock doubted the duke. Not with Percival's life on the line. He started to step around his cousins, making for the stairwell again. Bianca's hand on his arm stopped him.

"Take care of yourself, Heath," she said, her eyes searching his in concern.

"I don't care what happens to me," said Heath simply. "And I don't especially care what you all think of my loyalties or motivation. What I care about is making sure Percival and Merletta aren't killed. I'm not going to let it happen."

"Merletta?" Bianca repeated, her grip tightening on his arm. "What does she have to do with it? I thought she went home."

"Nothing," Heath said quickly, shrugging off her hold. "She did go home, and her danger has nothing to do with Percival's." His thoughts flickered uneasily to his absurd suspicions about the nature of the power he'd sensed at more than one suspicious attack. "At least I hope not," he muttered.

"What are you talking about?" Brody demanded.

"Never mind," said Heath. "I'm going to see Percival."

Without another word he plunged down the steps, not stopping until he'd descended three floors and crossed a corridor. His steps slowed as he approached the door where a guard stood sentinel, barring the entrance to the dungeons. The guard sighed at sight of Heath.

"It's not a guest suite," he muttered, "where he can receive visitors at will."

"Really?" Heath challenged him dryly.

The guard was familiar to him. He wasn't one of Percival's close friends, but Heath knew they often sparred together. Or they had, before Percival was locked up in a filthy cell.

The guard just sighed again as he waved Heath through. Heath might have pretended to be irritated, but he was actually relieved that a sympathetic guard was on duty. King Matlock likely didn't realize how popular Percival was with the city guards. Most of them were willing to turn a blind eye to visits that would boost Percival's morale. And Heath wasn't worried they'd report on such trivialities to the king. Just like the guards who'd stopped Leonora and Jasmine were unlikely to inform the king of the suspected use of magic. If they did, they'd have to admit to letting themselves be talked out of cracking down on it. Much safer and more comfortable for everyone to pretend it hadn't happened.

And that, Heath reflected in irritation as he moved through the doorway into the dungeon, was the kind of disorder that arose in a kingdom when the king began making decisions that were unduly harsh and not based on any publicly recognized logic.

Percival was sitting just where Heath's earlier vision had shown, in the corner of the cell. He rose to his feet when he saw his brother, an unconvincing smile on his face.

"Heath, you surely have better things to do than visit me in my lovely home so often," he said.

Heath wrinkled his nose, fighting the nausea brought on by the smell of human waste and mold.

"Don't put on a show for me, Percival, I don't have the patience for it," he said. "I've just had the pleasure of being lectured about family loyalty by Brody, not to mention talking Leonora out of getting herself thrown in the dungeon as some kind of misguided statement."

"Leonora?" Percival repeated, startled. He looked around and gave a shudder. "Let's not let that happen." He frowned at Heath. "Why is Brody hassling you?"

"No real reason," said Heath placatingly. "Everyone's just a bit worked up, and fair enough."

Percival's frown grew. "But surely no one thinks this is your fault. I don't like the idea of you bearing the brunt of any of this."

"I'm fine, Perce, don't worry about it," Heath said, regretting his words already. "You're the one we need to worry about."

Percival was silent, leaning his elbow on the cross bars as he considered Heath, his face still marred by a thoughtful frown. "That's not how it's supposed to be," he said softly. "I'm the big brother. I should be worrying about you."

He ran a hand down his face, over the uneven beard that had grown during the weeks of his imprisonment.

"I'm sorry you had to be the bigger brother," Percival went on. "I know you tried to warn me lots of times, and I know I never listened. I guess it took me being thrown in with the rats to realize the danger you were really trying to warn me about." He chewed his lip. "Does it really seem like I'm guilty?" he asked softly. "I mean, I know you believe me that I'm not. But does it look from the outside like I am? Does King Matlock genuinely believe it?"

Heath nodded, a lump in his throat. "So many little things, Perce. The timing of it, when you were known to be riding out to confront the king in a rage. The impossibly heavy bar over the door of the grain house. The way the guards were felled with a single blow. All things that are possible to happen without you... but seem designed to make you look guilty."

"It must have been designed, then," Percival said simply. "The question is, who tried to frame me for killing the king? And why?"

"Those are most definitely the questions," Heath agreed fervently.

A few short weeks ago, he would have been thrilled by his brother's malleable mood, and his willingness to believe that the king was genuinely suspicious of him rather than trying to set him up. But knowing what had brought about the change in Percival's attitude, Heath could take no joy from it.

He let out a sigh. "I just wish I had answers to them. But I can't find anything that would be likely to convince the king."

"Heath," Percival said, "I appreciate what you're trying to do for me, but I want you to step back from it."

"What are you talking about?" Heath demanded.

Percival gestured around him. "Look where my defiance landed me, Heath. If I'm going to be executed, the last thing I want is for you to get yourself killed over it, too."

"You're not going to be executed," Heath said hotly. "We're not going to let that happen."

Percival said nothing, and Heath could feel panic rising

inside him. If the indomitable Percival gave up, he didn't know what he'd do.

With a glance around, he lowered his voice. "Could you break out of the cell if you tried?" he asked softly.

Percival hesitated, his hand tightening and loosening on the bars. "I don't know," he admitted. "I'm afraid to try. Afraid I can't trust myself." His eyes met Heath's. "I wouldn't run away, Heath, even if I could. Not when I know the deal Father made with King Matlock. If I escaped, he'd execute Father instead. And I'd rather die than live with that knowledge."

Heath was silent, a sense of helplessness overtaking him. He understood. He'd feel the same way. But for all his brother's hotheaded, irritating ways, the idea of Percival being executed for a treasonous crime he didn't commit was unendurable.

He would clear Percival's name openly, and in good faith. There had to be a way.

CHAPTER THREE

Rekavidur

Rekavidur flew low over the water, his tail flicking in irritation. They excluded him, did they? Shut him out, left him voiceless in the discussion, in spite of the fact that he was most closely enmeshed in the situation, and had the most accurate information to offer.

The elders didn't trust his information. That was the truth of it, and it stung. They would be able to tell if he lied, but apparently that wasn't enough. They must suspect that he would withhold information, or perhaps that he believed what he said, but had been deceived himself.

He sighed, smoke issuing from his nostrils only to be whipped away as he sped through the air. Bypassing the largest of the rocky islands sticking out of the water, he made for one right next to it.

Like most of the masses that formed Wyvern Islands, it looked from the outside like a barren rocky crag, with nothing but gray stone and sharp edges all the way to its peak. But once he reached the summit, a very different landscape was revealed. The rocky crags formed an outer ring, but inside it there were two lower levels. The outer of the two was made up of pebbles, a patchy array of black, white, and gray. A second rocky ring encased the lowest inner level, this ring of rock glinting all over with pale purple crystals, each of them thoroughly imbued with the dragon magic that permeated the very air of the dragons' realm.

Inside this ring, the lowest level of flat ground was grassy and pleasant, several dragons lounging on the soft turf. Reka landed beside them, moving swiftly toward one of the many chasms in the rock. His family's home was within, and although he knew his father wasn't there, he expected to find his mother.

Sure enough, the yellow dragon—her scales not as bright as his hide, and missing the purple tint around the edges of his own scales—was curled inside, her tail draped partially up one wall. Her attention was on a cluster of crystals that sprouted from the base of the wall, and into which she was pouring magic. But at Rekavidur's approach, she looked up. Her eyes glinted in the light of the crystals, the magic that constantly poured off the dragons causing them to glow in a myriad of colors that danced across the cave.

"Rekavidur, my son," Raqisa said solemnly. "Welcome home."

"My bearer," he responded. "Greetings."

She straightened, leaving her task for the moment. "You are troubled," she commented, the words not a question. "Are you distressed regarding the meeting of the elders currently taking place?"

"Distressed is too strong for my current state," Rekavidur responded evenly. "But I am displeased at my exclusion."

"You are not an elder," she pointed out unarguably.

Rekavidur let out another smoke-filled sigh. "Naturally I am aware of that fact. But I have the most information regarding current events."

"It was a concession to allow your father to attend the elders' convocation," his mother reminded him. "He knows all you have told him, and will speak for you."

"I would prefer to speak for myself," Rekavidur said, not softened by this reminder.

"I believe it," his mother responded. "I suspect, however, that your words would not be entirely trusted. Lies are not the only form of deception, Rekavidur. Keeping crucial information secret is taken almost as seriously by many of our kind."

"Perhaps they have reason to accuse me of withholding information," Rekavidur acknowledged. "But can they really blame me, given the haste and violence with which they responded when Merletta's presence was revealed? If I was confident I would be fully heard, and wisdom and moderation would reign in the response, perhaps I would share all I know."

His mother's yellow eyes rested calmly on him as she responded. "Wisdom and moderation are generally the way of dragons," she acknowledged. "But even our kind have our sensitivities and our fears. And the history of the abominations is perhaps our weakest point."

She curled her tail around on the stony floor, touching it to his front talons in a gesture of connection.

"I know it feels extreme to you. But I remember well the consequences the last time a dragon used his magic to create an abomination. They were catastrophic. And not just for the dragons. Many humans suffered as well."

Rekavidur turned her words over in his mind, some prickle of emotion digging at him from beneath his logical thoughts. It was irritating and inconvenient, the sensitivity to emotion his interactions with Heath and Merletta had given him. The thought created the necessary link for his mind, and he was able to give shape to the emotion he was unwillingly feeling.

"Heath will suffer," he said, the words drawn reluctantly

from him. "If Merletta is killed, along with her kind, he will suffer a devastation from which I do not think he would recover. And I would share that pain with him, at least to an extent."

"I know you would," his mother agreed. A glint of amusement lit her eyes as she considered him. "It is not a weakness, Rekavidur. Feeling emotions as the humans do is a beautiful experience, and is one of the chief benefits to forming close friendships with humans, as you have done, and as your father did before you. If more dragons allowed themselves to be soft enough to be capable of it, they would learn what a treasure it is."

"It is utterly inconvenient," Rekavidur said, knowing he sounded like a petulant dragonling.

His mother was saved the necessity of replying by the familiar signature they both felt approaching. Rekavidur looked up eagerly, watching his father descend alongside his mother.

"Raqisa, my heartsong," the older dragon greeted his pair calmly.

"Elddreki." She snaked her head forward, and they brushed necks, their scales tinkling with the familiar greeting.

Rekavidur's father turned next to him, inclining his head in a casual but less intimate greeting.

"Rekavidur."

"My sire," Rekavidur responded gravely. He was eager to hear his father's report on the meeting, but he felt no impatience at the necessary formalities that must precede it. Greetings were important.

"The elders have heard the account you gave me, Rekavidur," Elddreki said. His rapidity in getting to the point alerted Rekavidur that there was some time pressure associated with his words. "They wish to speak with you."

Rekavidur blinked slowly, surprised by his father's announcement. He was to be included in the meeting after all?

"Do they await us now?"

His father nodded. "Indeed."

The two dragons made their way out of the cave, taking quickly to the air. Within moments they were descending into the center of the largest island. It was much like the island of Rekavidur's home, with its dual rings of rock and its pulsing crystals. The convocation could be seen from the air, the elders forming a ring from which many dark scales glinted in the sunlight.

"Rekavidur," one said gravely once the pair had landed in the circle's center and the appropriate greetings had been exchanged. "Your sire has reported your testimony to us. We wish to ask you some questions."

"I am at your disposal, my elders," Rekavidur said respectfully.

"You are undoubtedly aware that the purpose of this convocation is to discuss the discovery of sea-bound abominations that survived the purge of our ancestors."

Rekavidur's voice was even and unemotional as he responded. "I am indeed aware of the purpose of the convocation," he said. "But I dispute the conclusion that the creatures in question are abominations, and I respectfully remind the elders that the one who approached these islands—Merletta, by name —is not sea-bound. She has the capacity to transform into human form when on land."

"A capacity undoubtedly resulting from magic," growled one of the elders.

"Peace," the first dragon told the speaker.

He turned his vast head to Rekavidur, studying him in silence for a moment. The dragon was much larger than Rekavidur, his burgundy scales so dark their color was in danger of being lost. But Rekavidur did not feel intimidated. He was confident of the truth of his testimony, and more sure of his course than he had been in many months.

"Your objections are noted," the elder told Rekavidur gravely. "We called you here to discuss your claims. You have told us, through your father, that you have reason to believe that a colony of dragons once dwelt in close proximity to the home of these sea-dwellers, and that you believe these other dragons may have been connected somehow with the creatures' origins."

"That's right," Rekavidur said eagerly.

"What difference does it make whether the abominations were created by our colony or another?" a third dragon interjected.

"It makes all the difference," argued Rekavidur. "It would be unfounded speculation to assume another colony created abominations. I do not believe Merletta's kind are abominations."

"They are," grunted the same dragon. "I saw the beast myself. She had a strange kind of magic lingering around her. One that was utterly unlike that of the power-wielding humans."

"But you also saw her human intelligence," Rekavidur insisted. "That is surely beyond the extent that magic could warp a fish, even forfeited magic from a powerful dragon. We do not create sentience in other creatures, any more than we can create life beyond our own dragonlings."

"I have given testimony on this matter."

The dragon who spoke was enormous, and his scales were so dark their original color wasn't discernible. His voice sounded weary rather than angry.

"I remember the abominations. Their development certainly astonished us, which only reinforced our conviction that they must be destroyed before they could advance into something more powerful, and potentially more sinister. They began merely as enhanced fish, able to survive above water for long periods—although they could not actually come onto land —and to move through the water with impossible speed. We thought we'd gotten them all, but we were wrong. They retreated into the depths of the ocean, and when they resurfaced, they had developed beyond all expectation. Even then they did not ascend onto the land and gain legs, I will acknowledge. But they did bear the partial appearance of humans, and they had the capacity for speech. I assume the ability to gain legs is a new stage of development which has occurred in the many generations since that time."

Rekavidur was silent for a moment. This information was new to him, and most unwelcome. It helped him understand the attitude of the elders, however. They were not stubbornly refusing to listen to the information he considered compelling. They had another source which, in their minds, overrode his own observations.

"With respect, Elder," he said, dipping his head, "I am still not convinced of that explanation. The leap from an enhanced fish to a half-fish half-human with the capacity to assume fully human form seems like something beyond our magic."

"You underestimate the strength of our magic," said another elder coldly. "Your excess of time with human power-wielders has made you think that all magic is as weak as theirs."

"The decision has been made," a further dragon said, sounding weary. "They must be destroyed. Why do we continue to discuss it?"

"There is no great harm in delaying long enough to learn all the information," said the dragon who had initially invited Rekavidur to speak. He returned his attention to Rekavidur again. "Do you have evidence to support your perception?"

"I do not," Rekavidur admitted.

"Where is this former dragon colony?" the other dragon pressed. "That we may consider it ourselves."

"I cannot tell you that," Rekavidur told him. "Not while the attitude of the elders is for total annihilation of the merpeople."

"That is a name created by humans, a bedtime story," one of the dragons huffed. "These creatures are abominations, not merpeople."

"I maintain that you are wrong," Rekavidur said calmly. "And while you are unwilling to consider that possibility, I will not knowingly lead you to those you would make the victims of your violence."

"You dare to deceive us?" demanded one of the elders, a very dark green female. "To brazenly conceal information from us?"

"I take no joy from it," Rekavidur told her. "But I feel I must."

"That is not our way." The main elder spoke in a deep, reverberating voice that sent a chill down Rekavidur's tail. "You will tell us what you know."

"With respect, Elder, I will not," Rekavidur said.

"Then you are not welcome on the lands of our colony," the dragon said simply.

"Wait!" Rekavidur's father shifted forward. "He is young. You would banish him for concealing information to save life?"

"It need not be permanent," the elder said. "When he is ready to speak freely to his elders, he may return."

Rekavidur made no attempt to argue. He didn't even feel any great sense of grief at his sudden exile. That it would distress his parents, he knew, and for that alone it was a sadness. But for himself, he felt mainly relief. No longer would he be pulled constantly in two directions, flying through the colony with the burden of his secrets weighing him down and separating him from others of his kind.

It wasn't as though he had nowhere to go. As incomprehensible as it might be to these elders, he had a true friend among the humans. Heath would give him sanctuary.

Pausing only to take respectful leave of his father, Rekavidur took to the sky, winging away from his colony without a backward glance.

CHAPTER FOUR

Merletta

Merletta grunted as the heavy end of Ileana's spear thudded into her tail. If she had the chance to transform any time soon, she would find a bruise on her leg, no doubt about it.

"It's just like old times, really, isn't it? I've missed pummeling you."

Ileana may have declared her intention to be part of Merletta's team, but it seemed she still couldn't resist making the odd snide remark.

Merletta just grunted again, too experienced a fighter now to let a taunt disrupt her focus. She swung her spear at Ileana in a feint, waiting until the other mermaid's weapon was outstretched before propelling herself up and over the top of Ileana's head, coming down with her spear extended into Ileana's back.

"Not bad," Ileana admitted grudgingly. "You've definitely improved since first year."

Merletta grinned, pulling her spear back as Ileana turned in the water to face her.

"Careful, Ileana. That almost sounded like a compliment. I'd hate to be forced to say that *you've* improved as well. You know, in your personality."

Ileana scowled, but she had no opportunity to respond. Agner was swimming toward them, beaming from ear to ear.

"Excellent bout, ladies! Very good form from both of you."

He stopped alongside them, grinning from one mermaid to the other. "It does my heart good to see my two favorite trainees going head to head."

"I'm not a trainee anymore, Instructor," Ileana reminded him.

"You may be a guard now, Ileana, but your training is far from complete," he informed her. He looked indulgently between them. "I've been looking forward to this day for years. I could see from the start that Merletta was the trainee to challenge you, Ileana. You're both fighters to your very core, which makes you each other's absolute best training resource."

"That's one way of looking at it," Ileana said dryly, as Merletta gave him a skeptical look.

Agner chuckled, undeterred by their lack of enthusiasm.

"I know you didn't get on very well when you were studying together, but the line between bitter rivalry and the type of cooperation that helpfully challenges one another is finer than you realize."

"If you say so," Merletta said, unconvinced. She twisted her spear in her hand. "Ileana certainly never gives me a hit for free, that much I'll acknowledge."

"I can practically see each of you improve as you fight one another," Agner agreed. He turned to Ileana, starting in on his favorite topic. "Don't you think Merletta would make an excellent guard, Ileana? It's not too late for her to drop out of the program and join our number."

"No, actually, Instructor," Ileana said curtly. "I think that would be an anti-climactic end to Merletta's fascinating career."

She spoke with an edge of mockery, but Merletta sensed the truth beneath her words. Ileana wasn't kidding about wanting to see Merletta bring down the Center's lies. Merletta shook her head slightly as she stowed her weapon against her back, sliding it through the strap of her satchel. If Ileana wasn't careful, her desire for vengeance would destroy her.

"Off to lunch then, both of you," Agner said. "But I expect you back afterward, Merletta. I'd like to see you train with the slings for a while." He looked questioningly at Ileana, who shook her head.

"I'll be on patrol this afternoon."

"I went on patrols a lot last year," Merletta commented to Ileana, as Agner drifted away. "But no one's offered me that option this year. I suppose it's because the squad I trained with got disbanded."

She frowned, still feeling guilty that the squad leader, Freja, had been demoted for helping Merletta. She'd seen the older mermaid around, completing simple training exercises for younger guards, and other tasks well below her experience level. She'd made no attempt to approach Merletta, and Merletta had followed her lead.

She pulled her thoughts from the unpleasant topic, glancing at Ileana. "Where is your squad patrolling?"

"Where do you think?" Ileana asked tartly. "Eighty percent of patrols are in Tilssted now."

Merletta looked at her, startled. "That many?"

"Of course." Ileana sounded impatient. "That's where the fighting is. That's the reason you're not allowed to go anymore, of course. They're not about to send trainees into actual armed conflict. No outsiders go into the city anymore, other than guards."

"Actual armed conflict?" Merletta repeated. "You mean

you're fighting Tilssted residents when you go on patrol—*killing* them?"

"There haven't been many deaths yet," Ileana told her, in the tone she might use on an overemotional merchild. "We don't really need to use that much force to keep them in line, to be honest. They're poorly organized and generally not armed."

Merletta narrowed her eyes, unimpressed by the way Ileana was speaking, but the other mermaid had lost interest. With only a grunt of farewell, she swam away toward the dining hall, her pace clearly showing that she didn't want Merletta to travel with her.

Merletta was quiet throughout lunch, enough so that Andre commented on it from where he sat beside her. Sage and Emil were nearby, at a table with other record holders. There was no longer space for them to sit with the trainees, as Emil had often done previously. There were simply too many first years for that to be possible.

"I'm sorry," Merletta told Andre. "I'm not very good company. I'm just worried about Tilssted."

Andre sobered. "From what my father says, things are getting pretty bad there."

Merletta looked up, remembering that Andre's father was a Skulssted guard. "Has your father been doing patrols there, too? I thought it was just Center guards."

Andre shook his head. "No, there are Skulssted squads as well, and Hemssted ones. Apparently the Tilssted guards have been more or less disbanded. I mean," he shrugged, "I suppose they're still there somewhere. But they're not allowed to do any patrols outside their own city anymore, and they're not numerous enough, or well enough trained, to take on the other guards. Father told me that the regent of Tilssted told them to stop operations and await further orders."

"That sounds about right," growled Merletta.

Tilssted's regent was unpopular in the city, notorious for being the compliant puppet of his wealthier and more influential counterparts in the other cities. She played with her squid rings for a minute, deep in thought.

"I'm going there," she announced. "After lunch. I want to see it for myself."

"Are you sure that's the best idea?" Andre asked.

Merletta just shrugged.

"I'll come with you," her friend declared loyally. "If Agner's going to rake you down for skipping training, he may as well expand the performance for two."

"Andre, I don't want to get you in trouble or put you in danger," Merletta started.

"Save it, Merletta," the young merman said shortly. "We're past that, remember?"

For the next few minutes they watched Ileana across the dining hall, noting when she slipped out after shoveling down a quick meal. Merletta intended to follow Ileana's patrol, and to that end she trailed the other mermaid back to the training yard, at an inconspicuous distance.

The patrol didn't take long to get themselves organized and take off toward the drop off. Merletta and Andre followed, much too far back to hear any conversation. No one stopped them as they left the Center and swam through the northern part of Skulssted. When they approached Tilssted, however, it was a different matter.

"How long has the boundary between the two cities been monitored like this?" Merletta asked Andre, as they watched the patrol being cleared for entry by a Center guard.

"I don't know," said Andre grimly. "I've never seen it this way."

They swam forward once the patrol had passed, Merletta trying her best to look confident.

"What's your business?" the guard asked.

"We're with that patrol," Merletta told him, gesturing after them.

"Doesn't look that way to me," he grunted.

"It's all right, I've got this." The familiar voice made Merletta turn, her heart lurching a little as Freja swam into view. "Isn't your shift finished now?"

"Not for another half an hour," the merman told her.

"Well, I'll start a little early if you like," said the older mermaid calmly.

The guard gave a shrug, clearly not caring enough to argue about it, then swam away, back the way Merletta and Andre had come.

"What are you up to, Merletta?" Freja asked.

Merletta opened her mouth, not sure how to express her remorse over Freja's demotion. But before she could speak, the other mermaid gave a sudden, flickering smile.

"Never mind, I don't really want to know. I've got your back, anyway. Go on through."

Merletta closed her mouth foolishly, gratitude rushing over her. "Thanks, Freja," she said softly. "And I'm sorry for—"

"No, no, none of that," the other mermaid said gruffly. "Now get on with you."

Merletta and Andre took her advice, swimming swiftly across the boundary and into Tilssted. Merletta couldn't help letting out a little gasp at the debris that surrounded them. The familiar stretch had once been lined with a row of multi-story buildings, almost as high as Tish's shellsmith tower, all packed in together and crowded with more merpeople than could comfortably fit. All those structures were gone, with building having commenced on several spacious, single-story homes. The forcible expansion of Skulssted into Tilssted had already progressed so much further than the last time she'd been into the city. And where the residents of the demolished buildings were supposed to go, Merletta couldn't imagine.

When they neared the city's central square, Merletta forgot the expansion tension in her horror at the sight before her eyes. Ileana hadn't been exaggerating when she called it armed conflict. Everywhere Merletta looked, squads of guards were steadily patrolling the streets, with regular scuffles breaking out as they encountered groups of merpeople armed with crude weapons.

"What are the residents trying to do?" Andre asked. "I mean, what are the guards trying to stop them from doing?"

"Merletta!" The hiss made them both turn, to see Ileana approaching in evident anger. "What are you doing here?"

"I wanted to see for myself," Merletta told her. "What's going on? What do the guards think they're doing? Why was the border manned?"

"Why do you think?" Ileana said impatiently. "Residents from Tilssted aren't supposed to leave without legitimate reason. They've given too much cause to suggest they're going to make trouble in the other cities. It's stretching us thin, too. What with having to permanently man the Tilssted section of the barrier as well."

"But that's criminal!" Merletta protested. "They're being trapped inside the city? It sounds like they're being rounded up for a massacre."

"There's the overblown drama you're addicted to," Ileana said, rolling her eyes.

"But is it overblown?" Andre interjected. "My father's been a guard for twenty-five years, and he's never had to patrol another city like this."

"Center guards is one thing," Merletta agreed. "If there really was unrest, they would be the obvious choice to help manage it. But sending guards from other cities—the very cities that are expanding into Tilssted—is only going to agitate the conflict! It's just like when they sent teams from the other cities to clear the farms, when Tilssted workers could just as easily have done the work."

"Haven't you figured it out by now?" Ileana said pityingly. "That's the Center's way. The whole point is to create division, to encourage everyone to think in terms of us and them."

"And Tilssted is *them*," Andre said grimly.

"Of course it is," Merletta growled.

"I have to get back to my patrol," said Ileana. "You shouldn't be here. You can't overturn the Center if you're dead because you wandered through a war zone alone."

"Overturn it?" Merletta repeated. "Listen to yourself, Ileana. You can't claim to want some kind of revolution, and then do the Center's dirty work against so-called rabble-rousers whose only crime is not to take the Center's words as absolute truth."

She turned to Andre, jerking her head back toward the Center.

"Come on." Throwing a last glance over her shoulder, she added, "You have to decide, Ileana. Which side are you on?"

She didn't wait for an answer.

The days passed at a painfully slow pace as Merletta waited for August and Eloise to return from Valoria. She had no doubt their absence had been noted by those in charge, but it seemed they'd managed to at least make it out of the triple kingdoms without detection.

On her rest day, Merletta attended breakfast with no great enthusiasm for the day. From the moment she'd left the trainees' barracks, she'd felt the phantom sensation of eyes on her back. It wasn't the first time since her return, either. She couldn't identify who was watching her—it was possible she was just imagining it, although it wouldn't exactly be surprising to learn she was being scrutinized.

But even without the reminder, she'd already decided it was too risky to try to go to Vazula. And since she'd been given no substantial course work to occupy her, that left her at a loose end. She swirled a chunk of salted cod around her basin. A day of inactivity wasn't likely to do her any good.

"Merletta."

Emil's quiet voice startled her from her thoughts. Record holders shared a rest day with trainees. Sage—still estranged from her mother—was probably still sleeping in her little room. But Andre had gone home to his family—taking a rare break from his grueling training for his upcoming second year test— and she'd assumed Emil had done the same.

"Is everything all right?" she asked.

He nodded. "I've been waiting for a chance to speak with you privately," he said. "And for things to settle down."

He slid into the empty place beside her—alone of the trainees she had no family to spend rest days with.

"Have you found information about our origins already?" Merletta asked, impressed.

He shook his head. "I've only made the most discreet of inquiries, and so far they've yielded nothing. I'm here about something else. I'm sure you remember the research you asked me to do on your behalf last Founders' Day."

Merletta straightened in her seat. She certainly did remember. She wasn't likely to forget asking Emil to search for information about her parents, according to the names on the scroll she'd accessed at the end of her second year test. Although more dramatic events since had driven the search from her priorities.

"Did you find anything?" she asked eagerly. "About an Elric and Elminia from Hemssted?"

Emil made a non-committal noise. "Possibly. The census records in the restricted records room were mainly from generations past. Nothing that related to anyone our age, for example. But I did find accounts tracing the major families of Hemssted, in light of what we learned from Oliver about family names."

"And?" Merletta pressed.

"Well, there's a family line by the name of El which was highly influential, at least at the time of the most recent census. Your father's supposed name, Elric, could come from that family."

"I wonder if the family is still around," Merletta said, a shudder running over her. The idea of finding her family was as terrifying as it was tantalizing.

"They are," Emil said. "I did some digging."

She stared at him. "How likely do you think it is that my father came from that family?"

He shrugged. "I would have said it's just as likely that it's a name from a family not high-born enough to have a true family name, except for your mother's name. Unless she had a name starting with El by coincidence, her name being recorded as Elminia suggests Elric came of a family with sufficient standing to claim the name for those who marry into it."

"And my mother's family?" Merletta swallowed. "By Oliver's description, a son would be named with El for his father's family, but a daughter would be named for her mother's family."

"Meaning your mother was Merminia before her marriage," Emil nodded. "I didn't find her specifically mentioned, but I did find a family line of Mer. It was listed some way below the El family, suggesting it was of inferior status to them, although presumably still quite prestigious in the scheme of Hemssted society, to be recorded among the high-born families at all."

"And are they still living?" Merletta asked.

Emil shrugged. "I couldn't find anything definitive about that. The family record I examined in the census section suggested that the Mer family was dwindling over the generations rather than growing."

Merletta ran a hand over her braid. It was a lot to take in.

"Thank you, Emil," she said softly. "I hope you know how much I appreciate the risk you took in investigating the matter for me."

"I was glad to do it," Emil said, in his usual grave way. "Safer for me to ask those questions than for you to do it." He paused. "And I sympathize with your situation," he added unexpectedly. "You are remarkably self-possessed for one your age, in your position. But much as you might know who you are and where you wish to go, there is great value in knowing where you come from. It would be foolish to deny it."

"I don't deny it," Merletta agreed softly.

She didn't try to articulate the complicated tangle of thoughts that hid behind the simple words. Recognizing the relevance of her origins was one thing—but which origins really mattered? The world she'd been born into, or the one in which she'd grown up? She was fairly sure she knew which one had shaped her more, and colored all her experiences.

"I can see you need time to process it all," said Emil. "I certainly have no desire to press you. But if you wish at any time for assistance in locating the living members of either the El or the Mer families of Hemssted, you know where to find me."

"Thank you," said Merletta earnestly.

She sat for several long minutes after Emil swam away, her thoughts scattered. Eventually she rose, drifting from the dining hall with a destination in mind.

She wasn't ready to seek answers from any living merpeople yet. But she'd rarely even entered Hemssted, and that felt wrong all of a sudden, given how much her thoughts were centered on the place.

Perhaps her rest day would be well used in wandering its streets, trying to understand not just where she came from, but where she might have come from, if the ebb and flow of the tides had carried her to a different fate.

CHAPTER FIVE

Rekavidur

Rekavidur stretched out across the edge of the rocky clifftop, his tail dangling down the sharp drop. He felt...not impatient, exactly. That was much too human an emotion—not befitting a dragon within reach of immortality. But restless, perhaps. He hadn't doubted Heath would offer him sanctuary after his elders exiled him—he didn't doubt it still. But he hadn't anticipated Heath's absence from his family's seaside manor being so prolonged. With the use of his farsight, Rekavidur could see that his human friend remained in Bryford still, showing little sign of leaving. He was no doubt worrying about the fate of that headstrong, foolish brother of his.

Percival really was incredibly tiresome. Would it truly trouble Heath's family so much if his life were to be cut short by a few paltry decades?

Rekavidur found it incomprehensible, but it was clear that Heath felt strongly about the matter. Human emotion was blinding, it seemed.

It was also mildly inconvenient for Rekavidur, who had not expected to have to spend his isolation from his kind in true solitary state. But he had no interest in hanging around the capital while Heath sorted out his affairs. He would await his human friend near the manor, and hope the months didn't drag too tediously.

Rekavidur shuffled his head forward on the rocks, so his snout hung over the edge. It was, after all, a pleasant place to wait. He liked to smell the salt of the sea in his nostrils.

Suddenly another scent trickled in, and he narrowed his eyes. What was that faint, strange magic? He'd felt it before.

He lifted his head, sniffing the air more deeply. It was familiar, no question. Was it the power of Merletta's kind? But surely she hadn't returned. He and Heath had been very clear about the danger when they'd spoken on Vazula.

Rekavidur slipped forward, his body sliding sleekly off the cliff face and plummeting downward. He pushed against the rock with his back talons to put some distance between him and the cliff, then snapped his wings out to turn the fall into a controlled flight.

As he caught the wind, he rose back up, hovering in place halfway up the cliff as he sought the source of the magic.

There. In the water below, the faint flash of scales.

He could see at a glance that it wasn't Merletta, but he was still certain he'd sensed the precise power before. Curious, he angled himself downward, reaching the water in less than a second. He entered it smoothly, his wings folded back and his eyes searching the gloom.

"Ah," he said, pulling up.

Pleased to have the mystery solved, he regarded the two merpeople who were blinking back at him in evident astonishment. He gave the mermaid only a brief moment of attention before focusing on the merman beside her.

"I've seen you before. That's why your signature is familiar."

The merman stared back at him, perhaps surprised by the ease with which Rekavidur could speak under the water.

"Greetings, Dragon," he said, in an imperfect imitation of the proper address used by humans when greeting the magical creatures. "I am August, and this is my wife, Eloise. You saw me when I ascended onto the land with Merletta, during her visit to this kingdom."

"Yes, I recall," Rekavidur remarked. "Has Merletta not communicated to you what occurred after your departure? It is not safe for you to be here."

"She told us," August said. "That's why we're here. She explained why you can't come to the island anymore, to give us updates. We understand the risks of coming here ourselves. But she led us to believe that the annihilation of our kind is almost inevitable, and staying away can achieve nothing more than delaying it."

"That is likely true," Rekavidur agreed.

He felt a flash of appreciation for the merman's ability to discuss the imminent destruction of his civilization without descending into impractical and unpleasant displays of extreme emotion. This conversation would probably be tedious with a less collected member of the species.

Rekavidur's own thoughts caught at his mind. When he'd thought of *the species*, he'd been picturing humans, and their emotional tendencies. It wasn't the first time he'd conflated merkind with humans in his thinking. In fact, Merletta had seemed human to him from the first time he'd seen her. Human but with modifications.

Rekavidur had the sense that Heath and Merletta saw the differences between their kinds, not to mention the gulf between their worlds, as a nearly insurmountable barrier. He couldn't see it, himself. Human kingdoms had cultural differences, and yet managed to communicate with passable success.

Merletta's behavior, speech, attitude to the world...all of it seemed indistinguishable from any human's, as far as Rekavidur was concerned.

It was all just more reason to think that his speculation was correct—that the mermaids were not descended from abominations that had been transformed from regular fish into something more by forfeited dragon magic. The other abominations —such as the horned horses, or the oversized, savage wolves— had not undergone such dramatic transformations. They had been merely warped versions of their kind. They hadn't become human in appearance or intelligence.

Rekavidur didn't feel entirely comfortable with the idea that he was right about something that all the elders of his colony had wrong. But he felt even less comfortable with the thought of standing passively aside while they annihilated an entire intelligent species on the basis of what he was sure was a misconception.

All of this passed through his mind in a matter of seconds, doing nothing to disrupt the flow of his conversation with the two merpeople in front of him.

"What did you hope to achieve by coming here?" he asked August.

"First, I wanted to confirm whether Merletta's understanding is correct. Is there truly so little hope that the dragons will leave us be?"

"Very little," Rekavidur said matter-of-factly. "The elders met recently to discuss the matter, and they emerged from their convocation determined to act."

August's wife looked at her husband, but the merman kept his eyes on Rekavidur.

"What about timing, then? How long do you think we have to prepare ourselves?"

"That is difficult to predict," Rekavidur informed him. "I

suspect that they do not take my initial refusal seriously, and expect that I will in time tell them the whereabouts of your kingdoms. It is rare for dragons to deceive one another, even through omission."

He lifted his wings, flapping them gently to keep himself in his desired position under the water.

"They will eventually discover that I am set on my course, however," he went on. "And I imagine that at that time they will discuss a new approach, most likely deciding to send out scouts to scour the ocean from above. That process will not happen in a day, but it could happen very quickly if they decide the matter is urgent. Once scouts go out, I anticipate your cities will be quickly found."

"Will they decide it's urgent?" August demanded.

"I cannot see the future," Rekavidur said, flicking his tail in irritation.

"I didn't think you could," August said. "But your experience and knowledge regarding dragon attitudes and decision-making must put you in an infinitely better position than us to speculate as to what they will do."

"True," Rekavidur acknowledged, struck by the simple good sense of August's point. He considered the matter. "I do not think they will decide it is urgent. They are unaware that you have been warned so specifically. Their total confidence in their ability to find and destroy you all will influence them against rushing the process."

"How reassuring," said Eloise faintly.

Rekavidur looked at her, mildly surprised by that sentiment given the context, but August spoke before he could comment.

"Merletta seemed hopeful that it might be ten or twenty years before the dragons act."

Rekavidur shook his head slowly from side to side, water flowing pleasantly past his scales.

"That is unlikely, I would say. They may not consider the matter urgent, but it is of grave significance to them."

August's tail was swishing slowly back and forth, apparently signifying that he was deep in thought. His eyes passed over Rekavidur's form.

"Clearly it would be pointless to hope that dragons would be unable to follow us into deep water."

"Pointless indeed," Rekavidur agreed.

"And we will not be able to match their force, or injure them sufficiently to stop them," August said.

The words were not a question, and Rekavidur didn't bother to respond.

"What do you think is our best chance of survival?" August asked.

Rekavidur considered the matter. "Your best chance of individual survival would probably be to scatter across the ocean. It would then be a long and arduous task for the dragons to track you down, and it is conceivable that some might escape. That is, after all, what the colony believes happened in the purge that occurred long ago."

The couple exchanged heavy looks.

"That's not a realistic option," said August.

Rekavidur gave a rippling shrug. "I do not know what else to suggest. It is hard for me to see a way to preserve your cities from destruction once an entire dragon colony becomes focused on removing them from existence."

"What about the barrier?" Eloise asked. "We have a magical barrier around our territory. It keeps out dangerous creatures, such as sharks or poisonous jellyfish. We've always been taught that it would keep dragons out as well."

Rekavidur frowned. "I doubt that very much," he said. "I do not believe such a barrier could be the work of any creatures but dragons. There is a similar one around my own dragon colony.

Only humans with magic can cross it—which appears to include you, given that Merletta entered our waters without difficulty when she so foolishly approached the colony."

"You think dragons created our barrier?" August repeated, stunned. "But our history says it was put in place by our founders."

"If your founders had such magic, where is it now?" Rekavidur challenged.

August looked at his wife, bemused.

"I suppose...I suppose it died out of the bloodline," Eloise said.

Rekavidur shook his head. "Magic does not work that way. Certainly not in dragons. And what we are seeing from the human power-wielders of Valoria supports the same conclusion —if anything, the magic is growing stronger with each generation, in spite of so far always coming from only one parent. Once the seed is there in the bloodline, it continues to grow."

"But why would dragons put a barrier around an underwater area?" August demanded.

Rekavidur gazed into the murky gloom as he pondered the question. "It is curious," he acknowledged. "No doubt the answer is to be found in the hidden history regarding the origin of your civilization. There is, I suppose, a slim possibility that the dragons of my colony might pause to ask the same question when they come to destroy your cities and sense the barrier for themselves. But I would not pin any hopes on such a course, not without some external and objective evidence of the history of the barrier. They would be more likely to trust the known accounts of elders who were actually present when the sea-dwelling abominations were destroyed. Which," he added, "given the way your leaders bend and distort history, is not unreasonable."

"You don't offer us much hope," August said grimly.

"I don't offer you anything," Rekavidur responded. "You came to seek something from me. And I thought you sought information, not hope."

"Well, we optimistically thought some hope might linger within the information you provided," said Eloise, looking weary.

For the first time, Rekavidur wondered how long they'd traveled to reach Valoria.

"I intend to do what I can," he volunteered. "As does Heath. But how much assistance we can provide is impossible for me to predict. If you wish for my advice, I would say your best hope is to find verifiable information on how your civilization came to be—trusting that it provides an account that will contradict what the elders of my colony have concluded as to your origins."

"Yes, that's what my remaining patrol members are currently seeking on Vazula, but so far without success," said August softly. "I imagine Merletta is looking within the triple kingdoms as well. But to tell the truth..." His voice became heavier. "After the things I've learned from Merletta, I don't know that any record in our entire kingdoms could truly be considered verifiable."

"Well, that I cannot help you with," Rekavidur told them.

"We wouldn't expect you to," said Eloise. "Thank you for the time you have given us, and the information."

Rekavidur inclined his head in acknowledgment. "Will you return now to your home? I have formed the impression you do not intend to flee the destruction yourself."

August nodded. "We will live or die with our kin," he said simply.

Rekavidur remained silent. He could appreciate that attitude.

"I wish you safety on your journey," he said, already starting to propel himself up toward the surface.

He could sense the faint signature of magic as the two merpeople moved away, but he didn't waste thought on the details of their journey. He hoped none of his kind had witnessed the exchange with their farsight. He didn't think so. They must know from their observations so far that he spent the entirety of his time lying around on the cliffs doing and saying nothing worth observing. It was unlikely that anyone was watching him very closely while he remained in Valoria.

But there was someone else who would be very interested to learn of the visit. Perhaps it was time to pursue Heath to Bryford after all.

CHAPTER SIX

Heath let the arrow fly, his attention too distracted to even notice as it buried itself into the dead center of the target. Training in archery was the last thing he cared about at this moment. Why had Brody insisted they meet in the training yard?

"Nice form, Lord Heath."

The friendly voice was a little too loud, and Heath glanced over to see one of the city guards, bow in hand. Heath recognized the man—he was one of Percival's particular friends. And not at all the archery type, from what Heath knew of him.

The guard selected an arrow from a mounted quiver nearby, but didn't actually attempt to fit it to his bow. He just tested the fletching with his hand, his eyes on the weapon as he spoke, this time fast and low.

"A group of us are meeting to discuss Percival's situation," he muttered. "Your cousin asked me to show you where to go."

Heath selected another arrow himself, stalling for time as he called on his power in the way Reka had taught him. He was getting better. It responded instantly to him this time, darting out and testing his companion. Heath could find no flavor of ulterior motive beneath the man's words. It was hardly conclusive evidence, but it was probably as good a guarantee as he would get.

"Brody sent you?" he asked, fitting the arrow to the bow and lifting it to eye level.

The guard grunted an acknowledgment, finally copying the gesture himself. He let his arrow fly clumsily, and it clattered to the ground well short of the target.

"Guess archery isn't for me," he said cheerfully, his voice once again not quite natural.

"Yes," Heath agreed. "I think I've had enough for the day myself." He returned the borrowed bow slowly as the other man strode from the practice yard. Hesitating for only a moment, Heath followed at a discreet distance.

The guard exited the training yard not onto the street, as Heath expected, but into the small courtyard that attached it to the guards' barracks. Heath continued to trail him as he walked briskly down a maze of covered outdoor corridors. Several other guards crossed Heath's path as he went deeper into the guards' area, but none did more than glance fleetingly at him.

When his guide disappeared around a distant corner, Heath sped up slightly, knowing he was hopelessly lost inside the labyrinth. Rounding the corner, he found the corridor deserted. But as he hesitated, unsure which way to go, a hiss drew his attention to a door to his left, standing slightly ajar. Heath slipped inside it, blinking in surprise at the crowd crammed inside.

Scanning the group, he realized crowd was an exaggeration, but the dozen people seemed like more, squished as they were into what appeared to be a sparse sleeping space designed for two.

"Heath, you made it." Brody stepped forward, rubbing his hands together. "Good. We can start."

"Start what?" Heath asked.

"Planning Percival's rescue," Brody said, as if the question was idiotic.

Bianca nodded from behind him. Even Jasmine was present, her fierce expression transforming her normally gentle face.

"Start?" Heath repeated, exasperated. "What do you think I've been trying to do since he got thrown in there?"

"You're the only one with any faith in diplomatic solutions, Heath," Brody said impatiently. "The rest of us want a real plan."

Heath glanced around at the others, all of whom seemed to be guards. It wasn't a surprise. Percival had many friends among the city guards. Heath sent his power out in a targeted exploration, relieved to find no sense of deception or hidden agendas in the cramped room. That was a mercy, at least.

He saw Bianca looking at him curiously, and wondered if she'd caught the use of his magic. It would make sense—his power was certainly getting stronger.

"What do you have in mind?" he asked Brody.

"We're going to break him out," Brody said simply. He jerked his head toward the several guards sitting knee to knee on one of the simple sleeping pallets. "A few of these fine gentlemen are on the guard rotation for the dungeons, which will be a considerable help."

Heath raised an eyebrow at the men in question. "You're ready to be hanged in his place? That's presumably what would happen if you unlocked his cell and let him walk out."

"Give us a little credit, Heath," Bianca said impatiently. "We weren't planning to unlock the cell. We just want guards we can count on not to notice any unusual noises and the like."

Heath frowned, looking between them all. "Well?" he prompted impatiently, when no one explained.

"There's a wisteria vine growing not far from the dungeons,"

Brody said meaningfully. "With branches strong enough to climb down."

Heath considered him thoughtfully, his thoughts flying to the many occasions when he'd seen his cousin use the magic with which he'd been born. It allowed him to manipulate plants in all kinds of ways.

"You mean branches strong enough to rip apart iron bars, with the right super-strengthened encouragement, you mean."

"That's precisely what I mean," Brody said approvingly.

"The bars will have a little assistance in moving, hopefully," Jasmine said.

Heath raised an eyebrow at her. Her strength had grown if she was expecting to move iron. Last he'd seen, her ability to move things with her magic had been limited to small items within her immediate environment. It seemed he hadn't been the only one who'd been spurred on by the king's restrictions to secretly develop and hone his magic.

Ironic, really.

"Where's Leonora?" he asked. "Doesn't she approve of this?"

"I didn't want to drag her into it," Jasmine said, with a touch of defensiveness. "Besides, it's not like she could help much by cooling or heating the air."

"And when is this marvelous rescue happening?" Heath asked.

"The first even vaguely stormy night," Bianca informed him brightly. She gave him the ghost of a grin. "You won't believe the racket the wind can make, and the things that kind of noise can cover up."

Clearly she had figured out how her ability to control weather could help.

"Are we sure we can trust him?" The muttered aside from one of the guards was easily audible in the enclosed space. "He's practically the crown prince's lackey."

"Percival is Heath's *brother*," Bianca said fiercely, turning to the man who'd spoken. "He'd never let the king kill him." She looked back at Heath. "Right, Heath?"

"Of course I won't," he said firmly. "But the situation isn't desperate yet."

"Not desperate?" exploded Brody. "Heath, the whole city is waiting with bated breath for the king to announce an execution date any minute."

"But he hasn't announced one, has he?" Heath said patiently. "The formal investigation is still ongoing." He held up his hands to stop Brody's rising retort. "Don't get me wrong, I'm glad you're not willing to let Percival die for a crime he didn't commit. But I don't think you've really thought this all through. If we bust him out, he'll be a fugitive for the rest of his life. He'll have to flee the kingdom, and never look back." He glanced around the room. "As will any of us implicated in his escape."

"It's worth it," Jasmine said, a slight quaver in her voice.

"Wasn't your father considering moving your whole family to Kyona anyway?" Bianca asked earnestly. "When the king announced he was going to take Laura's babies away from her for testing?"

Heath ran a hand through his hair. "Yes, he was," he acknowledged. "But all that went out the window when Percival got arrested. Of course none of us would dream of leaving with him trapped in the dungeons. Besides, the king personally told me that he would reconsider the plan regarding Laura's children."

"And you're ready to take his word for it?" Brody demanded. He stepped forward in the cramped space, his eyes fierce as they rested on his cousin. "Heath, I'm starting to wonder if Percival was right about you forgetting where your loyalty belongs."

"Save the dramatics," said Heath tartly. "I haven't forgotten anything. I have no more intention than you do of letting

Percival be hanged. But I don't plan to condemn him to a life on the run unless it's truly necessary. I haven't given up on changing King Matlock's mind openly."

"And when will you give up on that?" one of the guards challenged. "When the noose is around your brother's neck?"

Heath met the man's eyes squarely. "Well before that," he assured him. "If King Matlock sets a date for the execution, I'll coordinate the rescue myself."

"I suppose that's as good as we'll get from you," muttered Brody, disgruntled at Heath's calm response.

"For the moment," Heath acknowledged unashamedly. He frowned at his cousin. "Heroics are all well and good, Brody. But whatever your thoughts about diplomacy, there's a place for subtlety. Haven't you wondered why Percival hasn't broken out himself? It's well within the realm of possibility that he'd be able to."

"Of course I've wondered," said Brody. "I tried to talk him into it when I visited him, but he just dodged the question. I have no idea why he's being pigheaded when his life is on the line."

"Well, I have a very good idea," Heath said shortly. "There are things at stake that you don't know about. Percival has his reasons for complying." He didn't elaborate. No doubt Brody would pump him for answers later, but Heath had no desire to share his family's personal information with a group of mostly strangers.

"Whatever those reasons are, you'll have a hard time convincing me that they're worth Percival hanging for," Brody shot back. "If his hands are tied from saving himself, it's all the more reason for us to step in."

"I agree," Heath said calmly. "Which is why I said I'll coordinate the rescue myself if it comes to that. Between us I'm sure we can subdue Percival, pigheaded though he is."

The hint of a chuckle went around the room, warming Heath's heart. It was encouraging to be reminded that for all his brother's folly, he had plenty of friends who cared about him, and had his back.

Some of the guards started to slip out in inconspicuous pairs, and soon there were only a few of them left, along with the cousins.

"Where's Laura in all this?" Heath asked Bianca.

She shrugged. "We didn't tell her about the meeting. We weren't sure she could get away. But I was intending to tell her our plan once we had one."

Heath nodded slowly. "I'll do it. I'll fill her in now."

His sister had arrived in the capital a week before, with her family in tow. Heath was sure it couldn't be pleasant, traipsing about the kingdom so often with two babies, but he hadn't commented. With Percival in prison pending execution, no one would actually expect Laura to stay away.

One of the guards guided Heath through the maze of corridors, sending him out of the barracks via a different door from the one through which he'd entered. It took Heath a minute to recognize his surroundings, but soon he was striding toward his family's city manor.

He didn't have to search for Laura. He'd barely made it through the gate when he spotted her, hurrying across the courtyard with little Jacqueline on her hip.

"There you are, Heath!" she called. "Have you been to see Percival?"

Before Heath could respond, he was astonished by the unmistakable rushing that filled the air. He stared upward, amazed to see Rekavidur's familiar form descending into the manor's courtyard.

Laura stepped backward, Jacqueline held protectively against her. Laura would recognize Rekavidur, of course. But

Heath knew that while his family understood his unusual friendship with Reka, even they were often a little overwhelmed by the dragon's presence.

"What is it, Reka?" Heath asked, as soon as the dragon had alighted. "Is something wrong?"

"Greetings, Heath," Reka responded, his tone holding the faint hint of disapproval he always showed when Heath skipped the formalities so valued by his kind. He swiveled his head to face Laura. "Greetings, sister of Heath."

Laura dipped her head in acknowledgment, but Reka's attention had passed to the baby in her arms.

"I assumed this infant was one of your twins," the dragon commented. "But it seems I am mistaken?"

"What?" Laura's awe was already markedly lessened. She sounded a little offended. "Of course this is one of my babies. This is Jacqueline."

"Born of your body?" Reka demanded.

"Yes," she said, still defensive.

"And yet the child has no magic," Reka mused. "How curious. She must be the first one in the bloodline since the birth of your grandmother. And I thought magic was getting stronger with the generations."

"How do you know Jacqueline doesn't have magic?" Laura said, definitely offended now. "I'm sure it's just too early to tell."

Reka shook his head. "The absence of magic in her being is notable," he informed her. He stilled, his gaze suddenly sharp, then lowered his head toward Heath's sister. "But what is this? Your magic is absent as well. Have you somehow lost it? I didn't believe it possible."

"Of course I haven't lost it," said Laura, shifting uncomfortably. "My magic is the same as it ever was."

Rekavidur cocked his head to the side, clearly fascinated by whatever phenomenon he was sensing. "Pass the child to Heath," he instructed Laura.

She looked disgruntled at being ordered what to do with her own daughter, but after a moment she offered Jacqueline to Heath. It seemed she was still a little in awe of Reka. Heath took his niece with a long-suffering sigh. In his opinion, such unquestioning capitulation would only add to Reka's already overdeveloped sense of superiority.

"Hey there, Jacqueline," Heath told the infant quietly, as he clasped her against him in one arm. She nestled in, apparently content with her position.

"Amazing." Reka's eyes were alight with the interest of a scholar, whatever errand had brought him to the capital apparently forgotten. "Heath, your magic is now obscured." His gaze centered on the infant in Heath's arm. "That child has concealment magic. This is...a development."

"What do you mean?" Laura demanded, sounding unnerved as she took Jacqueline back from Heath. "What's concealment magic, and why is it a development?"

"That's a dragon ability," Reka told her simply. His gaze passed to Heath. "A second human with a type of magic that is considered a hallmark of my kind." He fell silent as he thought it over. "I wonder what the colony would make of this information."

"Will they be angry when you tell them?" Laura asked nervously.

"I do not know if I will have the opportunity to tell them," Rekavidur informed her. "Given I have been exiled for the moment."

"What?" Heath demanded. "What do you mean, you've been exiled?"

"Is the meaning of the word unclear?" Reka asked, bewildered.

Heath cast Laura a long-suffering look, ready to silently complain about the obtuseness of dragons, but he found his sister's eyes narrowed on him. It seemed her attention had been caught on a previous point.

She glanced at the dragon. "What do you mean a second human with dragon-specific magic? Are you talking about Heath?"

"About his farsight, yes," Rekavidur answered, tilting his scaled head to more closely examine little Jacqueline. "Her magic must be strong," he murmured. "It is almost impossible to even identify its signature, which means it conceals itself incredibly well for an ability so freshly exposed to the world."

"Heath has farsight?" Laura's eyes were wide, her gaze back on her brother. "As in...proper dragon farsight? He can see things from...wherever he is?"

"Well, he's still developing it, but essentially," Reka confirmed.

"Thanks for sharing that information, Reka," Heath muttered.

"You are welcome," the dragon responded gravely, apparently unaware of the mingled astonishment and reproach Laura was directing toward Heath.

Heath refused to look at her. He would face her questions and reproaches later. For now he wanted answers as to Reka's appearance.

"Why were you exiled?" he asked his friend.

"I refused to tell the elders the location of Vazula," Reka told him. "Or to give them any other clue as to where Merletta and her kind can be found."

"What?" Laura's voice was sharp. "The dragons are riled over Merletta, and wherever she comes from? I thought they were upset about King Matlock's restrictions!"

"Well, I'm sure they're upset about that, too," Heath said evasively.

"Not especially," Reka corrected him. "That minor offense has been put aside in light of the much more troubling appearance of what they believe to be abominations."

"Abominations?" Laura repeated, sounding aghast. "Heath, what exactly have you been dabbling in?"

Heath ignored her. "Thank you," he said to Reka. "For keeping the secret."

Reka gave a rippling shrug. "I do not wish to be an executioner, whatever my elders believe."

Heath nodded, but Reka's expression became stern.

"Do not become complacent, however," Reka warned him. "It will not be difficult for them to find the cities, regardless of my answer. As I told August."

"August?" Heath stared at him. "When did you speak with August?"

"Immediately before coming here," Rekavidur answered. "He and his wife Eloise traveled to Bexley Manor, seeking you. I was there instead, and answered their questions as I was able. I believe they intended to depart immediately for their home again. To live or die with their kin."

Heath was uncomfortably aware of Laura's rapt attention, so he didn't ask Reka for more details of the conversation with August, much as he wanted to know exactly what had been said, and whether they'd mentioned Merletta's current situation.

"Why were you at Bexley Manor?" he asked instead. "You must have known that I was here."

"I was seeking sanctuary, given I have been expelled from my home," Reka explained, without any particular emotion. "I was content to await your return. But I thought you would wish to know of August's visit."

"You were right," Heath assured him. "And you were right

that I'd be glad to offer you a place to settle for as long as you need it. I'll speak to my father about it."

Reka inclined his head in regal acknowledgment. "I think I will return to the manor to await you," he said. "The city is too full of human deception." His face twisted in distaste. "It is unpleasant."

Without another word, he took to the sky, the resultant wind causing Laura to put her arms protectively over Jacqueline's face. Heath watched him disappear, then turned reluctantly to see Laura's accusing expression.

"He's pretty high and mighty about human deception for someone just thrown out of his own colony for refusing to answer their questions," he said, in a lame attempt at deflection.

Laura ignored his words completely. "Answers," she said curtly. "Now."

Heath gave a helpless shrug. "What do you want to know?"

"For starters, what's all this about you having unprecedented dragon magic? When did that happen?"

Heath sighed. "Gradually," he said simply. "Over the last few years. I was as surprised as anyone."

"But why don't we all know about it?" Laura demanded.

"It's...complicated," Heath told her vaguely.

Laura glowered at him for a moment, but as Jacqueline stirred in her arms, her expression softened abruptly.

"Not that complicated," she said, looking down at her daughter in evident unease. "Let's not mention to anyone official about Jacqueline's so-called concealment magic, all right?"

Heath nodded. "Agreed."

Laura gave a small gasp, comprehension crossing her features. "That's why the physicians couldn't tell there were two babies in there!" she said. "She was hidden from them...because of her magic, whatever it even is."

Heath raised an eyebrow. "It was already operating that

strongly before she was even born?" He gave a low whistle. "It must be strong."

Laura clutched Jacqueline a little tighter. "And Germain's is already showing up, too. Edmund thinks I'm just being a fond mother, but it's not that. I can actually feel his magic when I hold him. He...makes things better."

Heath nodded slowly. "I remember," he said. "You made me hold him after I'd fallen from the cliff at Wyvern Islands, and the pain noticeably lessened. I didn't even try to understand it at the time—there was too much going on. But now you say it, it makes sense that it was Germain's magic."

He studied his sister's face. "If Germain has some kind of healing power, why do you look so worried? Isn't that a good thing? Who could argue that was dangerous, or disloyal to the crown?"

"That's not what I'm concerned about," Laura told him. She sighed. "Has it occurred to you that having our magic feared and rejected is only one of two possible extremes, both equally dangerous to us?"

Heath's frown grew as he took her meaning. "You're worried about him being exploited," he guessed. "Used for his magic."

"It sometimes feels like Father has been," Laura muttered. "All his life he's served the crown, identifying threats no one else would have discovered, giving Valoria a formidable reputation in diplomatic negotiations, using his magic for his kingdom without ever asking for anything in return. And this is how the king repays him?"

Heath ran a hand through his hair, suddenly weary. "I'm as upset as you are about Percival's predicament," he told his sister. "But I've seen the evidence, and even I have to admit that he looks guilty. King Matlock is wrong, but he believes what he says. He's not looking for some excuse to kill power-wielders."

"I didn't say he was," Laura responded. "But if we can't

convince him he's wrong, what then? Will we let Percival die for diplomacy?"

"Of course not," Heath said quickly. He glanced around to make sure they were alone, then lowered his voice to tell her about the meeting he'd just attended in the barracks.

Laura listened with furrowed brow, then gave a curt nod of approval. "If it comes to that, we'll be ready," she told him. "We'll all flee to Kyona, so Father won't pay the price for the king's pigheadedness any more than Percival will."

For a moment she was silent, then she cast Heath a sharp glance. "What was all that Rekavidur said about Merletta? I think it's time for you to tell me plainly what her history is."

"Never mind that," said Heath firmly. "You let me worry about Merletta. We've got more than enough to contend with on Percival's account."

"Heath, this isn't something you can brush off with a vague answer," Laura said sternly. "The dragons were angry at the Winter Solstice Festival. They said there would be a reckoning. I have nothing against your Merletta, but is she going to bring dragon fire down on us all?"

"Of course she isn't," Heath protested. "It's her world that's in danger, not ours."

"But you brought her world into ours when you invited her here and paraded her in front of the dragons," Laura pointed out. "Can you really be sure you can control the repercussions?"

Heath rolled his shoulders, feeling much older than his twenty-one years. "I never claimed to be able to do that," he said wearily.

The idea of control was something he'd given up long ago. At this stage, if he could keep both his family and Merletta alive, it would be all the triumph he could hope for.

CHAPTER SEVEN

Merletta cast her eyes around Hemssted's large central square. It was bustling with activity, due to the rest day market that had been set up around the stone sculpture that dominated the space.

She'd been quietly watching the ebb and flow of the crowd for some time. She had once again felt the sensation of being followed as she'd traveled from the Center to Hemssted, but she could see no sign of anyone now. Perhaps it was the hubbub of the market, or perhaps whoever it was really had moved on. It didn't much trouble her either way. It wasn't as though there was really any harm in someone knowing she was wandering Hemssted on her rest day. In fact, it was probably a good thing—less likely to cast suspicious eyes in the direction of Vazula.

Her thoughts strayed to her friends. She knew if she'd asked, any one of them would have come with her on this exploratory trip. But she hadn't been able to face voicing her fears and hopes to anyone. Especially when they all had plenty of problems of their own. Emil had been lecturing Andre just the night before on the second year test that was only days away for the younger trainee. And although Merletta usually considered Emil overly cautious, this time she agreed with him. As capable as Andre was, his life would still be in danger during the test which would lead him to the heart of the maelstrom.

Putting the matter aside for the moment, Merletta returned her attention to the market. Judging by the decorations worn by the various shoppers and the nature of the purchases, there was more variation in affluence than she'd expected. Still, everyone seemed fairly well provided for, the fashions more tasteful in her opinion than the flamboyant style often favored in Skulssted.

Was this the environment she'd been born into? She watched a pair of laughing merchildren darting around the tails of roving merchants, as playful as seal pups. Could she have grown up here, perhaps attended just such markets with her parents, if fate had been kinder?

Her thoughts were inevitably drawn to her actual childhood. With memories of the charity home came an image of Tilssted as she'd last seen it. She felt her brow darken as the pleasant picture before her was soured. It wasn't right that Hemssted continued on in peace and prosperity, while one city away, their neighbors were trapped and beleaguered, their territory being slowly eroded by others from this very group, and their tentative efforts to expand outward crushed by the Center.

Merletta drifted across the square, moving between distracted locals as her eyes fixed on a large residence on the far side. It was as elegantly carved as the Center's receiving hall, and separated from the chaos of the marketplace by a low decorative fence of what appeared to be whalebone.

Expensive, Merletta noted.

"Who lives there?" she asked a passing market-goer.

The mermaid glanced over her shoulder to see where

Merletta was pointing. "That's the residence of the Ol family," she said. "I thought everyone knew that."

Merletta cast another appraising glance at the stately home. So that was where Oliver's family lived. It looked large enough to house several branches of a family, so it was probably the home where he'd grown up. Lorraine hadn't been exaggerating when she jokingly referred to him as *a mighty member of the Ol line.*

"Are you a messenger?" the mermaid asked, eyeing Merletta's armband in confusion. She clearly hadn't noticed her Center-issued spear. "They won't take kindly to strangers knocking on their door out of curiosity."

Merletta shook her head, turning away from the imposing building. She had no desire to run into Oliver on her rest day.

"I'm not going to knock on their door. I have no business with the Ol family. I thought it might have been the residence of the El family, actually."

"The El family?" The other mermaid wrinkled her nose in thought.

"Have you heard of them?" Merletta asked tentatively. Emil had given the impression that they were influential, but he'd only been speculating.

"Of course I've heard of the El family," said the mermaid impatiently, supporting Emil's conclusion. She gestured to a nearby street. "They live down there. It's the big house with the mollusk shell facade, but it's not as grand as the Ol place."

She was off again with the words, clearly intent on whatever errand Merletta had interrupted.

Merletta floated slowly in the direction the other mermaid had pointed, not at all sure of her purpose. How would it help her, really, to see the home of an influential Hemssted family who may or may not be her blood? And yet, she kept swimming forward.

The building in question was as easy to locate as her guide had suggested. It rose above the others around it, the facade glinting green and pearly white. There was no whalebone fence here, but the boundary of the property was clearly marked with a tail-high border of coral, cultivated to grow in a perfect line.

Merletta hovered for a moment, staring at the structure while the flow of passersby continued around her. A number of merpeople, arms full of wares from the market, muttered in irritation as they dodged her, but she ignored them all. As she watched, a middle-aged mermaid with a no-nonsense expression swam briskly past her, swimming up and over the coral edging without a check to her pace. She carried a large basket of woven seaweed, the bundle swaying slightly to her strokes and revealing the fresh goods within.

Without being conscious of her own decision, Merletta found herself following the older mermaid, drifting over the coral with her eyes riveted on the doorway. In response to the mermaid's call, the limestone door—itself a sign of the family's wealth—slid smoothly to one side, revealing a merman who wore no decorations whatsoever.

"Delivery of market wares?" he asked impassively.

The mermaid nodded, her voice louder and less refined than his. "Yes, that's right, but I want the mistress to look over it this time before I leave it. Last week I was accused of selecting undersized mussels, and—"

"The mistress is out at present, but I would be glad to assist." The cool voice belonged to a middle-aged merman who glided up beside the one who'd opened the door.

"My apologies, Master Elfin," said the other merman quickly, inclining his head. "There's no need for you to be troubled."

Merletta stared at the newcomer. Master Elfin? Was he the

master of the house, then? The current patriarch of the El line, perhaps?

"No trouble," he was saying. He floated with his hands behind his back, his long, mostly silver hair drifting out a little in the current. "I daresay I can inspect a mussel as well as my wife."

He waited in austere silence as the mermaid from the market displayed her selection, then approved the goods with a simple nod. Once she'd passed off her basket, she swam briskly away, leaving Merletta hovering several strokes back from the door.

"Can I help you?" asked the silver-haired merman, who hadn't even glanced at her until that moment. Most likely he'd thought she was an assistant to the other mermaid.

"I, uh..." Merletta swallowed, feeling foolish. She hadn't planned any of this, but a direct encounter with the head of the family seemed too good an opportunity to pass up. "I'm looking for Elric, actually. Is there someone by that name in this family?"

The merman's expression changed instantly, shock flitting across his features before his brow lowered.

"Who are you?" he asked.

"I'm..." Merletta hesitated under the strength of his gaze, and he pushed on impatiently.

"What do you want? You're too young to have known Elric. Why would you come asking for him after all these years?"

"So he is dead, then?" Merletta asked, her voice small.

"My brother has been dead for more than eighteen years," Elfin said curtly.

Merletta felt her eyes widen. His brother? Was this merman her uncle? She looked him over surreptitiously. Streaks of dark brown were still visible in his silver hair, not dissimilar to her own hair color. His skin was considerably paler than hers, but that didn't mean much. Perhaps she had her coloring from her mother.

"I...I'm sorry to hear that," she said, belatedly responding to his words.

"Who are you?" he asked again, his eyes narrowed. "Why are you asking about Elric?"

"I'm actually looking for the Mer family," Merletta said, deciding impulsively on a half-truth. "I don't have an official family record, but I believe I'm descended from the Mer line. I'd understood that an Elric of the El line married someone from the Mer family."

Elfin relaxed slightly. His hands, which had been clenched over his elbows, drifted slowly down to his sides as he gave her a critical examination.

"You do have a little of the look of Merminia," he said thoughtfully. "Do you suspect that your mother was a relative of Merminia's?"

Merletta hesitated. "It's possible," she said evasively. It wasn't exactly a lie. She supposed anything was possible.

Elfin let out a slow stream of water. "You're right," he told her, his tone much less combative. "My brother Elric married someone from the Mer family—Merminia was her name, or Elminia as she became known. But I don't think I can help you much. She was among the last of the Mer family. I imagine there are a number of others like yourself out there, carrying the name through the mother's line. But the family no longer exists as a unit."

Merletta nodded slowly, trying to master her disappointment. To have actually come face to face with a living relative of hers on this vague exploratory trip was more than she could have reasonably hoped for. But the El family was intimidatingly exalted. She'd hoped the Mer family, if they could be found, might have been a more approachable avenue for exploring her history.

"Thank you for your answers," she said, through lips that felt a little numb. "I appreciate you speaking with a total stranger."

Elfin inclined his head, his eyes passing over her form again as if not quite satisfied with the conversation.

"I'm sorry I couldn't help you more," he said.

She swallowed. "And this Merminia, or Elminia...is she still living?"

He shook his head regretfully. "My brother and his wife died in the same accident."

It was on the tip of Merletta's tongue to ask if they'd had any children, but her courage failed her. Would he suspect? Did she want him to?

"How...how did they die?" she asked tentatively.

The merman who'd answered the door, and who was still hovering with a disapproving frown, clucked his tongue.

"If it's not too painful a question," Merletta added quickly.

But Elfin didn't seem either angry or emotional. "No, it's all right," he said. "It was many years ago now, and it's not as though it's any secret. In fact," he frowned, "given this recent obsession with adventuring outside the barrier, it's all the more important to talk about it."

Merletta stared at him. "What do you mean?"

"They were outside the barrier when they died," he said heavily. "I didn't even know they intended to join the harvesting expedition, although I can't say it surprised me." He shook his head ruefully. "It was just like Elric...and his wife was no better. Not that they deserved to pay such a price for their recklessness."

"What price?" Merletta pressed urgently.

His eyes, which had seemed to be gazing back across the

years, refocused on her face. "Their lives," he said simply. "They strayed from the harvesting group, and ran afoul of a fever of rays. They were both stung through the heart. I saw the wounds myself."

Merletta ran a shaky hand over her forehead. The last tiny particle of hope drained away—the head of the charity home's assertion that her parents had dried out had just been another lie, it seemed. There was no longer any reason to hope, however foolishly, that they'd found their legs and escaped to safety somewhere on land. It had always been the slimmest of chances.

"How...how awful," she managed. "I'm sorry."

"It was awful," Elfin acknowledged steadily. "But like I said, it was a long time ago." The frown grew on his face again. "But not so long it should be lost to memory. All these young folk, giving weight to the nonsense being talked in Tilssted, acting like no one's ever thought of expanding outside the barrier before. Elric and Merminia were obsessed with the idea, and they weren't the only ones back then. And look where it got them!"

His face had grown angrier as he spoke, and he cut off abruptly, sucking in a mouthful of water.

"My apologies," he said stiffly. "It's just got me frustrated, all this foolish talk. As if no one learned a thing from those deaths twenty years ago—it isn't as though Elric and his wife were the only ones. And when you showed up asking about him, I thought you might have been one of these young rabble-rousers..." He trailed off, inclining his head. "I wish I could help you more, but I don't hold any records pertaining to the Mer line. We didn't keep contact with Merminia's family after her death, I'm afraid."

"It's all right," said Merletta quickly, her own emotions

barely under control. "Thank you for your time, and I'm sorry to trouble you, and to reopen old wounds."

With a respectful nod, she turned, swimming swiftly over the coral barrier and back onto the street. She needed to put some distance between herself and her oblivious uncle before she succumbed to the storm of emotions building inside her.

CHAPTER EIGHT

Merletta

Merletta struggled more than ever to focus on her classes that week. Andre was equally distracted, with his second year test upon him at last. Merletta knew that he and the others thought her own nerves arose mainly from concern for him. And that was part of it, of course. She'd been kept awake at nights by the fear that Andre's open support of her would mean his test ended as hers had been intended to—with masked Center guards waiting to murder him when he emerged from the maelstrom.

But that was only one cause of her abstraction. Elfin's revelations consumed her thoughts so fully, she'd almost stopped looking for August and Eloise's return. The hearty cry she'd had when she reached the privacy of an abandoned back alley after fleeing the El residence had done her good, but she was still struggling to come to terms with all she'd discovered.

If the record of her parentage was accurate—a fairly significant *if*—then she belonged to a wealthy and influential Hemssted family, one with living members within her reach. It was quite an adjustment to think of herself as the daughter of a well-respected couple who died in a tragic accident, leaving behind a family who loved and missed them, even if they considered their recklessness to have led to their deaths. She'd grown up being told that she'd come from disgrace and ignominy.

But if she was truly a daughter of this noble and wealthy house, how had she ended up abandoned in a charity home in the slums of Tilssted? Perhaps it was all some cruel joke of the Center's, intended to rattle and distract her.

But then...Elfin had said she looked a bit like his brother's wife, hadn't he?

"First and second years, divide into groups by city of origin."

Wivell's cool voice broke into Merletta's thoughts. All of the trainees were in together, and the younger ones hastened to split as instructed. The two groups—Hemssted and Skulssted—were fairly even in size. There was no third group.

"You will complete this exercise in teams," Wivell continued. "Each group will be led by a junior record holder." He nodded to the two mermaids floating behind him. "Sage hails from Skulssted, and will lead the Skulssted group. Bridget comes from Hemssted."

Wivell paused, glancing over as if he'd only just remembered the presence of Merletta and Lorraine. Andre wasn't present—it was his test day. His absence brought Merletta's thoughts back to him, her anxiety spiking, along with a dose of guilt that she'd temporarily forgotten where he was.

"Third and fourth years, you may proceed to the scribes' hall. An educator is waiting to instruct you, Lorraine. Merletta..." He hesitated over her name just slightly, as if reluctant to address her. "A record holder will commence your introductory sessions regarding the duties of the position."

Sage sent Merletta a small smile—her own distraction on Andre's behalf evident on her face—as the two older trainees moved toward the door. Merletta returned it, but the expression slipped away as she looked at the two groups of young trainees, eyeing each other calculatingly.

Us and them, Ileana had said. Even with Tilssted out of the picture, the Center—the one place in the triple kingdoms supposedly outside of city loyalty, where everyone was supposed to come together—was still encouraging its trainees to see those from other cities as opponents.

Her thoughts were heavy as she swam to the scribes' hall alongside Lorraine. It was sobering to see so many young trainees, and not a one from Tilssted. She thought of her angry words to Ileana, about the residents of the city being trapped inside as if to subdue them ready for a massacre. Ileana had called it overblown drama, but Merletta wasn't so sure. Tilssted's workshops and homes were being cleared in order to allow expansion by the other cities. Were the merpeople next?

When she reached the scribes' hall, resigned to a morning of unalleviated anxiety as she waited for the record holder who would probably fail to even appear for her lesson, Merletta received a pleasant surprise. Emil was floating inside the doorway, watching the group's approach with his usual calm gaze.

"You're late," he informed Merletta.

"Don't tell me you're my assigned record holder!" she said, not trying to hide her delight.

"It was more a case of volunteering than being assigned," said Emil, with a faint smile.

"I'm surprised they allowed it," Merletta told him frankly.

"The record holder who oversees the group of juniors asked for a volunteer," Emil said. "I don't believe it would have occurred to him to report back to the program's instructors on the identity of the volunteer."

"Well, thank you," said Merletta fervently. "How much can you teach me in one morning? Because it's probably all the education I'll get this year."

Emil was once again smiling faintly. "I think we'll stick to the assigned coursework. I'm to explain to you the basic functions of a record holder."

"I'll take what I can get," Merletta informed him as she followed him into a small study room off the scribes' hall. But in spite of her words, she jumped in as soon as they were settled, cutting off whatever Emil had been going to teach her.

"How do you think Andre's doing?"

The older merman gave a shrug, although the tension in his frame belied his apparent unconcern. "We'll find out soon enough."

Merletta leaned forward, ready to pursue the topic, but at the last moment she changed her mind. Neither of them knew anything. Talking about it would only make them more nervous for their friend than they already were.

"I went to Hemssted last rest day," she said abruptly. "I visited the residence of the El family."

Emil stared at her. "You did? Did you speak to someone?"

She nodded. "The head of the family, I think. He was just going past the door by sheer luck when I arrived."

"And?" Emil prompted.

Merletta lowered her eyes, staring at her fins as she recounted the gist of her conversation with Elfin.

Emil clucked his tongue thoughtfully. "So you didn't tell him who you are...or might be. Are you going to?"

"I don't know," Merletta said. "It didn't sound like he had much opinion either of Tilssted or of anyone interested in going outside the barrier. Which is two counts against me."

"But if you truly are of that family, you're not really from Tilssted," Emil pointed out.

Merletta shook her head slowly. She knew it didn't entirely make sense to Emil—how could it to someone whose birth and upbringing were inextricably intertwined—and she wasn't sure how to explain it to him. But no matter what she could or couldn't prove about her birth, she would never cease to be from Tilssted.

And she didn't want to, she realized with a flash of defiance, picturing again the two groups of trainees. The Center might be eager to push Tilssted out of the program, even to write Tilssted out of the triple kingdoms. But Merletta had no desire to scrub it from her own history.

In defiance of custom, she abandoned the trainees' table at dinnertime, sitting instead with Emil and Sage, among the junior record holders. None of them said much, and all three glanced upward, as if they could see the sun high above through the stone ceiling. They all knew that in order to pass the test, Andre would have needed to return to the Center by sunset.

Although at this point, Merletta didn't care much about whether he passed. She would settle for him surviving.

They didn't have long to wait. Merletta had barely begun to eat when a familiar form burst into the dining hall, crimson tail flicking excitedly.

Sage and Merletta both let out cries of greeting, and even Emil visibly relaxed. There was no need for any of them to ask how Andre had gone. The grin splitting his face was answer enough.

"You did it!" Merletta cried when he'd swum up to them. "Congratulations! We've all been beside ourselves!"

He chuckled. "I'm not surprised. You weren't kidding when you said that test is no joke." Although, judging by his continued beaming, his good cheer remained unimpaired by the ordeal.

"And now you're a third year," said Sage encouragingly. "A senior trainee!"

"I know." Andre's chest seemed to inflate a little.

Merletta caught Indigo watching him avidly from the

trainees' table, her own face light with relief, although a hint of sadness was visible as well. A pang went through Merletta at the sight. Whatever her feelings about Indigo's conduct toward her, she couldn't help but feel responsible for separating the two cousins.

Still, it wasn't a moment for gloominess. It was a moment for celebration. Andre left the Center after dinner, returning to his family's home to commence his month long holiday. But his success lingered behind him, the thought of it bolstering Merletta through the following days of combat training. It helped that in the training yard, she didn't have to try to focus on complicated etymological rules while her mind was mainly occupied with her parentage. She just had to let her body settle into the familiar rhythms of combat, and try not to let Ileana get in under her guard while she was distracted.

She spent much of the last day of the week debating whether to return to the El family residence on rest day, to speak further with Elfin. She was still undecided at dinnertime, when Andre slipped into the seat next to her.

"What are you doing back here?" she demanded. "You're supposed to be on your break." As she took in the expression on his face, her eyes narrowed. "You have news," she said, the words not a question.

Andre gave a surreptitious nod. "August and Eloise are back." His voice was barely more than a whisper. "They got word to my father through some back channels."

"They're here?" Merletta murmured, trying not to let her expression display her astonishment. "I didn't think they'd be able to show their faces in the triple kingdoms after disappearing so suspiciously."

"They're not exactly parading down the streets," Andre said, shoveling food inconspicuously into his mouth for appearance's sake. "They came the long way around, entered through the oyster farms in the south, and they're hiding out at the home of some old allies of August's among the guards."

"What's their news?" Merletta asked.

"I don't know yet," said Andre. "But my father asked me to tell you they want to see you tonight. In the coral garden near my parents' house. I think the idea is for you to pretend you're coming to visit my family with me."

Merletta couldn't finish her food fast enough. She'd been waiting two weeks for August and Eloise to return. Now she knew how close they were, dinner was the last thing on her mind.

She and Andre made what she hoped was a passable attempt at cheerful conversation as they swam from the dining hall a short time later. They traveled through the Center by a roundabout route, and by the time they crossed the drop off, Merletta was reasonably confident they weren't being tailed. Hopefully it wasn't just that she'd become immune to the sensation—she reflected that it was the first time since starting fourth year that she'd left the Center without feeling that inexplicable conviction that she was being followed.

She'd been surprised that August had picked a public location, but when she reached the coral garden, she realized he'd been wise. There was nothing notable about them entering it, and nothing to tie Andre's family to the situation if August and Eloise were detected.

The older couple wasted no time on pleasantries. It was clear they wanted to impart their information and return to whatever safe haven they'd found within the city.

"We made it to Heath's kingdom," August told her curtly.

"Is he all right?" Merletta asked, alarmed by his grave expression.

"I have no reason to think he isn't," August assured her. "But we didn't see him. We spoke with the dragon, Rekavidur."

"Did he have any new information about when the attack might come?" Merletta pressed.

August ran a hand over his chin. "He had no certain information. But he told us his leaders had just met, and he doesn't share your optimism that it will be years before they act. He said the matter is of grave significance to them, and once they decide to act, they will do so quickly. Although he acknowledged that there was no way to be sure when they would make that decision."

"Is there any good news?" Andre demanded, his crimson tail twitching. "What about the barrier?"

"He is of the opinion that the barrier could only have been formed by dragons," August answered. "And that it will therefore be entirely ineffective at keeping them out."

"Formed by dragons?" Merletta repeated, staring at the guard. "Reka said that?"

August nodded, and Merletta fell silent, trying to make sense of the suggestion.

"Did he give you nothing useful?" Andre asked, his voice strained.

August's face was grim. "He didn't give us any reason to hope for the survival of our civilization. His advice was that we scatter across the ocean, make it harder to track us down, with the view that some individuals may survive."

"We can't do that," Merletta protested. "Even if the Center would allow it, most of the triple kingdoms are too afraid of the open ocean."

"I know," August agreed simply. "Neither the Center nor the populace would countenance the idea unless they were aware of —and actually believed—the nature and extent of the threat."

Merletta let his words roll back and forth in her mind, like seaweed tumbled by the waves on Vazula's beach. Her stomach dropped as she grasped the truth behind the simple statement.

She'd hidden her indiscretions too long already. Too many lives were at stake for her to think of her own safety, even from the insidious enemies hidden inside the Center. It was time to give those in power the information they needed to have a fighting chance of surviving the coming attack, and bear the personal consequences that would follow.

"I don't know if it's in my power to make them believe it, but it is in my power to make them aware," she said quietly.

"Merletta," Andre started warningly, but she just shook her head.

August's gaze was shrewd as he studied her face. "I also feel it is time to make that stroke," he told her. "And I'm willing to be the one to carry the news. I believe I can get access through my connections to senior—"

"No." Merletta cut him off uncompromisingly. "This mess is not of your making, and I won't even consider letting anyone else do this."

August was silent for a moment. "It is a one way street, Merletta," he told her quietly.

"I know." She met his eyes calmly. "But I've been living on borrowed time here for a long time already. I think I'd actually rather take decisive action than keep waiting for the blow to fall."

August nodded gravely. "I can respect that. Will you speak to your instructors about the dragons, then?"

Merletta shook her head. "I don't trust the chain of communication. I need to go straight to the top."

"You're going to try to speak to the regents of the cities?" Andre said blankly. "How will you get access to any of them? Well," he amended, "maybe the Tilssted one, since you're sort of famous there, but the others—"

"Andre." Merletta cut him off with a look. "However the governing of the triple kingdoms theoretically works, everyone here knows the truth of who's in control. And it's not the regents of the cities. I'll go to the central spire tomorrow and see if I can speak to the Record Master himself."

Andre bit his lip, but didn't attempt to argue. "I can come with you," he said staunchly.

"Thank you, but no," Merletta responded. "I started this, and I'll finish it. You should be enjoying your well-earned break. Besides, there's something I need to do first. Something I want to do alone." She looked back at August. "Is there anything else we can do?"

He ran his hand over his spear, the motion seeming unconscious. "The only other advice the dragon gave was to search the island for some clue as to our origins, in the hope that we find information that will convince the rest of his kind that their assumptions regarding our existence are wrong."

Merletta nodded uneasily. "That's what Paul and Griffin are supposed to be doing while waiting for you to come back. Heath and I never found anything much, but it's definitely worth looking harder. It won't be easy for me to get there without attracting notice, though."

"No one is suggesting you do it, Merletta," Eloise said patiently. "We're leaving the triple kingdoms at first light, provided we can get away unnoticed and be sure no one is following us. We intend to remain on the island for the foreseeable future. We will search, along with Paul and Griffin. If there's anything to be found, we'll find it."

Merletta nodded again, although her heart remained heavy. It was, after all, a slim hope on which to base the survival of their entire civilization.

CHAPTER NINE

Merletta

Merletta slept little that night. It wasn't the first time she'd suspected that the following day could be her last—or, at the very least, that her world was about to change dramatically—but this time the sensation was doubled. Not only was she going to approach the formidable Record Master and confess to the devastation she'd brought on their civilization, but she was going to return to the El residence, and tell them who she really was. Or might be, at any rate.

She figured she might not get another opportunity, and it was no time to leave questions unanswered out of fear or embarrassment.

As soon as the first faint hint of light reached the Center's depths, Merletta was out of her hammock and swimming toward the dining hall. She had prepared herself for a solitary meal, knowing that Andre had returned to his home the evening before. So she was stunned to see not only her fellow trainee, but Sage and Emil waiting at the otherwise deserted trainees' table.

"What are you all doing here?" she demanded, sliding into place alongside Sage.

"Refusing to let you be a martyr," Sage told her calmly. "Andre told us what you mean to do."

"I wish I didn't have to do it, too," Merletta assured her. "But to keep what I know secret any longer would be criminal. I appreciate the sentiment, Sage, but you can't talk me out of being a *martyr*, as you put it."

"None of us expect to talk you out of it," said Emil calmly, as he shucked down an oyster.

"Of course not," Sage agreed. "But honestly, Merletta, you must be out of your mind to think we'd all just float idly by and let you go alone."

"I don't want you all mixed up in this," said Merletta desperately. "I can't have that on my conscience."

"We are mixed up in it," Andre told her bluntly. "And it's by our own choice. We're not going to desert you now."

Sage was nodding determinedly, and Merletta took Emil's silence as acquiescence.

"I appreciate it," she told them, genuinely touched. "And I recognize that whatever my own feelings, I don't have the right to exclude you from whatever's going to happen. But I'm not going to the central spire now. There's something else I want to do first. Something more personal that I really do think will be better without a crowd."

Sage frowned suspiciously at her, and Merletta raised her hands in a placating gesture. "I'm telling the truth, I swear. I can meet you all back here at lunch if you're determined to come with me to the spire. This morning I'm going to Hemssted."

Emil looked up sharply, his gaze seeming to lift Merletta's thoughts right out of her head.

"Very well," he said, in a voice of finality. "We will meet you back here at lunch, as you suggest."

Neither Sage nor Andre attempted to contradict him. Merletta felt three pairs of concerned eyes follow her progress across the room as she rose from breakfast a short time later. But she tried to push it all from her mind. The afternoon would be for world-shattering confessions. The morning was for a different kind of confrontation.

The city of Hemssted was well and truly awake by the time Merletta swam once again through the noisy central square. Another rest day meant another market, and the same flurry of activity she'd witnessed the week before.

She ignored all of it, swimming for the El residence with much surer strokes than the previous time. She knocked on the limestone door, trying to calm her nerves as she waited for the disapproving servant to appear.

Sure enough, the door was opened by the same merman she'd seen last time. He frowned slightly as he looked her over, a spark of recognition in his eyes.

"Can I help you?"

"Yes," she said confidently. "I don't know if you remember me, but I was here last week. I need to speak to Elfin on an important matter."

"Appointments can be made with the master's—"

"No." Merletta cut off the slightly pompous words. "This isn't a business matter. It's personal. It relates to his brother, Elric. The one who died outside the barrier. Please tell him I'll wait as long as it takes."

The merman frowned at her, clearly considering dismissing her out of hand.

"I really will wait as long as it takes," she warned him grimly.

With an irritated twitch of his tail, he gave in, waving her through the doorway and into a small alcove just inside the entrance. Merletta sank onto a ledge under a narrow window, trying to calm her nerves.

"I'll see if the master is at home," the merman said sniffily.

Merletta rolled her eyes as he swam away. As if he didn't know exactly where his master was.

She wasn't left in suspense for long. Only a few minutes had passed when she saw the silver-haired Elfin swimming toward her down a broad and well-carved hallway.

"Good morning," he said, his brows lifted slightly in surprise. "I didn't expect to meet you again, uh...?"

"Merletta, sir," Merletta supplied, rising into the water. "My name is Merletta."

One eyebrow went up, and his eyes passed slowly over her. After a prolonged moment, he nodded. "Yes, you said you were descended from the Mer line. Through your mother, then, I take it?"

"I believe so," she said carefully. "Although I can't be sure. In fact, I was hoping you might be able to answer that."

He frowned. "I thought you were here about my brother. I don't know why you would think I could help you with your mother's lineage. I told you, I kept no contact with my sister-in-law's family after her death."

"I am here about your brother," Merletta assured him. "But also about my mother's identity." She took a steadying pull of water, sternly telling herself to pull it together and make a little more sense. "Sir, you said that your brother and his wife both died in the same accident, outside the barrier."

"That's right," he said warily, as if expecting a trap.

"Did they have any children?" Merletta asked, gathering her courage.

His eyes narrowed slightly, and he didn't immediately answer. "You said your name is Merletta?" he pressed at last.

She nodded, her heart pounding.

He regarded her for another moment in silence, then gave his tail a convulsive flick. "Come with me," he said, his voice curt, before turning and swimming back the way he'd come.

Merletta followed as Elfin led her down a series of corridors, past a staggering number of large, well-lit rooms. Finally, he preceded her into a study. Just like the one at Andre's house, this one boasted a large stone slab, almost the size of the far wall.

"Your family record," Merletta murmured.

He nodded. "You'll find my brother's name there."

Following his pointing finger, Merletta swam up to the slab. Her eyes moved slowly, almost fearfully, over the inscribed names. She saw Elfin's name, a line connecting him to the name of a mermaid, and three descendants appearing underneath. One of them even had, so far, one descendant of their own. The names above Elfin's—his parents, presumably—were underlined.

And alongside, in the position of a sibling, was the name *Elric*. It also was underlined, as was the name to which it was connected by a thin line—*Elminia of Mer*. Merletta's eyes moved even more slowly as she followed the markings down, to see one name, again underlined, below the couple.

Merleisha.

She stared at it, her whole frame slumping in disappointment. The nervous energy drained out of her, making her feel like a pufferfish suddenly deflated.

"What..." Her throat was so tight, it took her two attempts to form the words. "What does the underline mean?"

"That the person in question is deceased," Elfin said. "If you look further up, the names are all underlined."

Merletta glanced up to see that he was right, but her eyes flicked immediately back to the names she'd come for. So this Merleisha, whoever she'd been, was as dead as her parents.

"Who are you?" Elfin demanded. "You said your name is Merletta. But where do you come from?"

"I'm..." Merletta swallowed. "I'm an orphan. I grew up in a charity home in Tilssted. I never knew who my parents were. I was told that I was abandoned anonymously at the home. When I reached sixteen, I left Tilssted, and gained a place in the Center's training program. It was my ambition to be a record holder."

Her words were met with silence, and she looked around to see Elfin staring at her, his face showing astonishment and a hint of anger.

"You're the infamous trainee from Tilssted? The one who's been causing all kinds of trouble for the Center?"

She gave a weary smile, too crushed by her disappointment to care what was being said of her around Hemssted.

"Not nearly as much trouble as I'd like, given the things I've discovered about our virtuous Center."

She half expected to be thrown from the house in a rage, but again Elfin was silent. When she raised her eyes to his once more, he was frowning thoughtfully at her.

"Explain that, please."

She shook her head. "I don't think I can. I wouldn't even know where to start, and it doesn't matter, anyway. I've learned what I came to learn." Yet she made no move to leave, her eyes lingering on the names before her. "How did your niece die?" she asked softly.

"With her parents." Elfin's voice was curt. "I regularly offered for them to leave her with our children's nurse, but they were determined to take her with them everywhere they went." He scowled. "Even outside the barrier. Not even a year old, and they took her out into the deep ocean." Abruptly, he ran a hand through his long, brown-streaked hair. "She also was killed by the rays. Although..." His words were suddenly too casual, his demeanor changing as his eyes passed to Merletta, seeming to pierce right through her. "Unlike her parents, her body was lost to the ocean."

Merletta looked up, startled. "You never saw Merleisha's body?"

"That's right," he said, his eyes still keen. "And we didn't call her Merleisha. It was a family name, but Merminia found it too long and formal. In everyday use, she called her daughter what she said she would have liked to name her if conventions gave her total freedom. We all got into the habit as well."

"What...what was the name?" Merletta asked, her lips numb.

"Letta," Elfin said calmly. "She was called Letta."

Merletta passed a hand over her face, trying to master her swirling thoughts.

"Why did you come here?" Elfin asked urgently. "I've been thinking about you all week. I couldn't shake the familiarity of your face. I told you that you had a look of Merminia about you, and it wasn't a lie."

"You...you suspected last week that...?" Merletta couldn't finish the question, but Elfin was already shaking his head.

"I suspected nothing consciously. I just couldn't get our conversation out of my mind. And then when you asked today if my brother had any children...How old are you, Merletta?"

"I turned nineteen not long ago," she said faintly.

Elfin digested this information in silence. "What led you to this house?" he demanded. "What prompted you to ask questions about my brother?"

Merletta found she was shaking, and clasped her hands together to try to still them. "I found a record of my name," she said. "In the Center. It was in a section marked Orphan Records. It had been damaged, so that I couldn't read the details. But it looked like there had been names for my parents, rather than the blank entry there should have been if I truly had been abandoned anonymously. And then, later, I was baited with an undamaged copy of that record. It was designed to rattle me, and I had no way to know if it was accurate—I still don't know.

But it listed my name, alongside the parents Elric and Elminia of Hemssted."

"Who would create a false record like that just to unnerve you?" Elfin demanded, his face pale. "And why would they choose my brother and his wife?"

Merletta gave a hollow laugh. "If you knew as much as I know about the Center, you wouldn't find it hard to believe."

He was still staring at her, and she looked away, unable to withstand the intensity of his expression.

"I would say it's harder to believe that you could be..." He trailed off. "But we all wondered how her body had been lost, when Elric's and Merminia's were recovered." He was whispering now. "But the guard told me himself that he saw her die."

"Who was this guard?" Merletta asked sharply. "Maybe I can speak to him, ask what he remembers."

Elfin shook his head. "He was in his older middle age at the time, and that was nearly two decades ago. I suspect he's gone by now." He frowned slightly. "I did know his name, but it was a long time ago. He was a Center guard, but originally from Hemssted, as I recall. Part of the Den family. Denford, perhaps?"

"Denton?" Merletta asked, another wave of shock washing over her.

"Yes, that's it," Elfin said. He took in her expression. "What is it?"

"I...I knew him," Merletta said disbelievingly. "He volunteered at the charity home. He's the one who taught me to read and write. He's the only reason I made it into the program." She shook her head. "He even told me once that he used to be a guard."

"But...I don't understand," said Elfin.

"I think I do." Merletta's thoughts darkened. "A Center guard, you said? Two adults were one thing, but he couldn't bring himself to murder a baby. Instead he condemned me to a life of cruelty and poverty, assuaging his conscience by teaching me to read."

She ground her teeth together. No wonder he'd taken such an interest in her, going out of his way to teach her to read and write properly. And she'd once thought he was the only one who was kind to her purely for her own sake.

"Murder?" She could hear the hint of unease below Elfin's incredulous words. "My brother and his wife weren't murdered. They were stung by rays."

"Of course they were," said Merletta scornfully. "Just like August's patrol died of land sickness."

Elfin's jaw worked as he scanned her face. "You're speaking about that Skulssted patrol?" he asked. "I've heard about the patrol leader's miraculous survival, of course. He was lucky to make such a recovery."

"Luck had little to do with it," said Merletta curtly. "He was skillful enough to fight off the Center guards who tried to murder him, and wise enough to hide out in the open ocean until the hunt had died down."

"That's not what happened," said Elfin, sounding more uncomfortable than angry. "It can't be."

A shudder went down Merletta's frame as she fought to keep her calm. She found that she wanted Elfin to believe her, not just because she was telling the truth, but because she didn't want him to think her a fool or a troublemaker.

"You said Elric and his wife died on a harvesting expedition you didn't even know they were going on," she began. "I assume Center guards were sent to protect the harvesters? And none of the harvesters saw the accident, right? Your brother and sister-in-law wandered off, and the next thing anyone knew, the guards had found them dead, correct? I'm guessing none of the harvesters even noticed the rays."

Elfin's pale face was devoid of all color now. Merletta had no doubt she'd recreated the circumstances exactly.

"But this is nonsense," he said, clearly rattled. "Why would anyone want to kill them?"

"For the same reason the Center wants to kill me now." Merletta sank wearily onto a stone bench. "You've said yourself that they were obsessed with the idea of expanding beyond the barrier. You even said that they weren't the only ones who were outspoken about the issue, then lost their lives in the open ocean."

"Because it's dangerous out there," Elfin insisted.

Merletta rose back into the water. "Have you ever seen a ray for yourself, Elfin?" she asked softly.

He shook his head.

"I have," Merletta told him. "Let's just say I didn't especially like the charity home where I was dumped, whether by Denton or by nameless parents who didn't want me. I used to escape at every opportunity, and the building was right near the barrier. I've spent more hours in the open ocean than a patrol guard, and it's not what they claim. I've weaved my way through a fever of rays many a time, admiring the sleek grace of them. They can be dangerous if provoked, but they're gentle creatures by nature. It's not as though they're trained killers who would size a mermaid up then take aim and spear through the heart. An unscrupulous Center guard, on the other hand..."

She shook her head. "If you don't want to believe it, nothing I say will change your mind. You have to make the choice. I'm not asking for anything from you. My name isn't even Merleisha. I suppose we'll never know if that history is mine."

"You're generous," Elfin said dryly. "I don't suppose you doubt it any more than I do. It's just a lot to take in." Far from ushering Merletta out the door as she'd expected, he sank into a seat himself. "I suppose if the guard heard your parents calling you Letta, and knew your mother's name, he probably thought your name *was* Merletta, since he was from Hemssted, and familiar with our conventions."

His gaze was a little misty as it passed over her. "You're like them," he murmured. "Not just in that you resemble your mother. But to hear you talk...they were always on a mission as well."

He let out a groan, tinged with humor. "I don't know what I'm struggling to comprehend more—that little Letta is alive, or that she's the troublemaking trainee from Tilssted we've all been hearing so much about."

Since he seemed in no hurry to expel her, Merletta lowered herself to a seated position again.

"I'm not what everyone thinks I am," she told him ruefully. "Neither as impressive as my admirers think, nor as much of a brat as my critics make me out to be."

"Well, it's clear from one conversation with you that you're not quite the uncultured, crass interloper I've heard described," he said. He straightened. "Of course you're not. You're an El. We'll soon set those rumor-mongers straight."

Merletta was shaking her head before her thoughts even caught up. "I'm not asking you to do that," she said quickly.

"I know you're not," Elfin responded. "But a daughter of this house will not be spoken of as some attention-seeking vagabond. You will learn that with the proper connections, and a family to lend you credibility, your influence will be greater through less dramatic means."

"I'm not backing down." Merletta spoke abruptly. "I'm not going to stop pushing back against the Center's lies."

"Merletta...Merleisha...Letta..." He gave her a strained smile. "I don't know what to call you."

"Merletta," she said, pleased with how clear her voice came out now. "My name is Merletta."

"Very well," he said, speaking more calmly as he studied her face. "Merletta. I can understand, given the disadvantages you've suffered—and most unfairly so—your desire to gain attention through—"

"With respect, I don't think you do understand," Merletta cut him off. "It's never been about seeking attention. Maybe I don't value status and reputation the way you do. But I'm not so sure that's a bad thing. Coming from nothing is what's given me the freedom and determination to speak out against what I've seen. Think about it, sir. I've just given you reason to think your brother might have been murdered, and your first thought is to reel me back from embarrassing myself by challenging the very figures who were probably behind his death."

"Hang on," Elfin said defensively. "That's still only speculation. Don't think I won't be investigating what you've said. But what I'm offering you is protection, and standing. I can understand your feelings at the resistance you've faced, and perhaps it is unjust. But look at what's happening in Tilssted right now. You have to acknowledge that there are reasons behind the prejudice against that city. If your instructors knew you weren't from some Tilssted slum, but actually hailed from an influential Hemssted family, don't you think you might be treated differently?"

"Exactly!" Merletta told him seriously. "It was never about me. It was about what their treatment of me has revealed." She shook her head. "You have no concept of how deep the rot goes."

Her thoughts flew to Wivell's lesson, the Hemssted group and the Skulssted group eyeing each other off, no sign that there was even a third city. She was the only spokesperson Tilssted had in the Center, and she was suddenly certain—absolutely certain—that removing even that weak representation was the last thing she wanted to do. She hadn't forgotten the risk she was about to take, and the fact that she might soon be out of the picture anyway. But going down swinging was one thing. Taking an offered exit by way of suddenly acquiring the privilege of one of the wealthy cities was something else entirely. Something she could never do.

"I don't want you to think I don't appreciate your willingness to recognize me," she said quietly. "Because I do—more than you can possibly imagine, most likely. I came here wanting answers for my own sake, and I'm glad to have found them. But I meant it when I said I don't expect anything from you. My past is already set—I can't change that. And I've chosen my course forward as well. I have no desire to turn back. This is who my experiences have shaped me into, and this is who I need to be. But I thank you, from the bottom of my heart, for your answers, and your offer. If we don't meet again, I wish you and all your family well."

And against his protests, she turned and swam for the door, emerging quickly onto the street.

The conversation, while heavy with years of significance, hadn't actually taken long. Merletta found herself wandering dazedly through Hemssted, trying without much success to grapple with all that had just passed. By the time she found her way back to the Center for lunch, she'd almost forgotten about her afternoon's plans.

But the somber presence of Sage, Emil, and Andre soon reminded her.

"Are you sure about this?" Emil asked her.

Merletta nodded, still jittery from her conversation with Elfin. "Yes, I'm sure."

They were a quiet bunch as they swam the short distance to the central spire. No one asked Merletta what she'd been up to that morning, and she was glad of it. She wasn't yet ready to talk about her discoveries.

Upon entering the central spire, the four of them all instinctively glanced up.

"I've only ever seen him descending from up there," Merletta commented. "Is that where I go to find him?"

"I imagine you need to approach him through his personal assistants," Emil said.

He led the way across the open, stories-tall lobby area, staying at seabed level. Following him, Merletta pulled up before a small opening on the far side of the space. She hadn't even noticed it on her previous visits, but she saw now that the gap in the stone—positioned at head height—allowed communication with the merman settled in a seat on the other side of the wall.

"Excuse me," Merletta said through the gap. "How do I go about speaking with the Record Master?"

The merman had been focused on a stack of writing leaves in front of him, but he raised his head at her words, brows quirked.

"You don't. The Record Master doesn't just sit down with anyone who has a fancy to speak to him. You can make a report, or register a request, through me. It will proceed through the appropriate channels."

"Actually," Merletta said evenly, "I think he will want to sit down with me."

The man's expression was scornful. "Do you indeed? And who are you?"

"I'm a fourth year trainee," Merletta informed him. "In fact, I'm the only fourth year trainee."

"And I'm sure all your friends back home are very impressed," he said dryly. He waved an arm vaguely behind her. "But everyone you see has won a place in the Center in one way or another. If you expect the Record Master to be impressed by your position as—"

"I don't expect him to be impressed," Merletta said shortly. "But I do expect him to meet with me." She raised her head slightly, the morning's conversation with Elfin fresh in her mind. "My name is Merletta of Tilssted—I have no doubt he's familiar with it."

The merman's face creased in a frown, his finger tapping on the stone bench in front of him.

"Just a moment," he said curtly.

He swam briskly through a doorway behind him, and Merletta turned to see Sage regarding her with raised brows.

"Going for a bold approach, are we?"

Merletta shrugged. "I'm sick of playing games. There's no way the Record Master doesn't know who I am."

They were left waiting long enough for Merletta to grow antsy. Sage and Andre showed similar signs of strain, although Emil remained his usual unflappable self. At last, however, the merman reappeared, his expression disapproving.

"You have been awarded an appointment with the Record Master. You are to return at this time next rest day."

"Next rest day!" Merletta protested. "That's a whole week away!"

"Your level of education stuns me," the merman said sarcastically. "Did you expect immediate attention? Difficult as you may find it to believe, the Record Master has other matters requiring his focus than the whims of trainees."

"But this matter is urgent," she insisted. "A great deal is at stake!"

"And I'm sure the Record Master will be riveted by the details," the merman said tartly. "This time next week."

Merletta scowled, fully aware that it was useless to argue with this merman, who was nothing but a messenger. She turned away without thanking him, making it halfway across the lobby before Emil spoke.

"It's a power play, Merletta, plain and simple. Nothing to become distressed over."

"I'm not distressed." There was a slight snap to Merletta's voice which she hadn't intended, and she deflated at once. "I'm sorry, I know you're trying to reassure me. But it's easy to think an extra week doesn't matter when you're not the one who's geared yourself up to throw everything into a life-defining gamble."

"If you think we didn't have to gear ourselves up to be here, you must be seriously overestimating our nerve," said Sage mildly. "At least in my case."

Chastened, Merletta begged her pardon. The last thing she wanted was for her friends to think she undervalued the sacrifice they were making for her. And if she was completely honest, she had to admit to feeling some relief at the reprieve. It hadn't escaped her notice that after the interaction with Elfin, she wasn't in the best frame of mind for the coming confrontation.

"It's just hard to do nothing," she said, lowering her voice. "For all we know, the dragons could be planning to attack tomorrow."

"From what we've been told, that's unlikely," Emil said in his calm way. "We'll just have to hope that this Heath of yours finds a way to warn us if things become that desperate. And in the meantime, you're not doing nothing. You've made an appointment with the Record Master."

"I wish there was more I could do," Merletta fretted. "But it seems like our only other hope is finding answers on Vazula. And I think it's too dangerous for me to go there right now."

"Definitely too dangerous," Sage said firmly, as Emil nodded his agreement.

Merletta bit her lip. She would just have to trust August and the others to find anything worth finding. It wasn't easy—she'd never been good at delegating.

As they moved toward the spire's main exit, her eyes were drawn to the restricted records room halfway along one wall of the seabed level. Perhaps there was something more she could do after all. Vazula wasn't the only place where information could theoretically be found about the merpeople's history.

"Emil, have you found anything useful in your inquiries?" Merletta asked.

He shook his head. "Nothing of significance. I haven't searched in there, though," he added, following Merletta's gaze. "I thought you'd scoured it when you were studying for your third year test."

Merletta shook her head. "I did my best to focus on what I thought might be in the test, but I definitely didn't cover everything. There are so many records in there."

Her eyes strayed back to the records room as they exited the building, a tiny measure of the stress of inactivity lifting. Perhaps there was something she could do after all.

CHAPTER TEN

"What are we looking for, Heath?"

Heath didn't turn at the sound of Brody's impatient voice, instead continuing to stare dejectedly at the boarded up remains of a doorway that graced the grain house before him. He had no answers for his cousin.

"Seriously, there's nothing here," Brody pressed.

"I know." With a sigh, Heath turned away from the building at last. "I've been back here three times before now, and I can't find any clues as to who set Percival up. I just keep hoping there's something I missed."

"If there was anything to find, I doubt it's still untouched," Bianca said. "Surely the king's guards have been all over this place as part of their investigation."

"They have," Heath admitted, glancing back at the charred doorway.

In his mind's eye, he could still see the flames licking at the wood, smoke billowing into the sky as a muffled banging announced the presence of the king and his guards, trapped inside. All laid at Percival's door.

"But they can't sense magic," he went on, "so you never know what they might have missed."

"I thought the idea was to prove that Percival and his magical strength *didn't* commit the crime," Brody drawled. He was making no effort to hide his impatience with Heath's continued desire to clear Percival's name properly, instead of spiriting him out of the kingdom.

"I'm not talking about Percival's magic," said Heath shortly.

"Whose, then?" demanded Bianca. "Surely you're not suggesting dragons had anything to do with it? I mean, I know fire is sort of their signature, but I can't imagine them doing anything so underhanded. Why would they need to?"

"Not the dragons," Heath assured her. "No one dreams for a moment they were involved, least of all me."

He bit his lip, the familiar battle raging inside him. Guilt over keeping his wild speculations to himself pitted against fear of betraying Merletta's trust.

"I don't really know how to explain this," he said carefully, "but I've sensed magic that doesn't feel like any of ours. When Percival was attacked on the road, and when that chimney collapsed on me."

Bianca stared at him. "You've kept that quiet!"

"It's complicated." Heath shrugged uncomfortably.

"Did you sense it here?" demanded Brody. "During the fire?"

Heath shook his head. "But it's still possible it was the same person," he said, a touch defensively. "Maybe they'd just left by the time Reka and I arrived."

"But who could it be if it's not one of us?" Bianca demanded. "Do you have any suspicions?"

Heath hesitated. "None I can prove," he said evasively.

Guilt licked at his insides again, but he tried to push it down. His speculation about the faint magic that hovered around Merletta and others like her was nothing more than a stray thought. An absurd thought. One he couldn't voice without revealing the truth of Merletta's mermaid form. Which he'd promised not to do, he reminded himself unnecessarily.

"Heath isn't telling us the full story," said Brody dryly. "How astonishing and unprecedented."

Outwardly, Heath ignored his cousin. Inwardly, the words sent a fresh wave of guilt shooting through him. It wasn't as though his cousins could do anything useful with the information, even if they had it, he argued with himself defensively.

"I think I'll speak to Reka," he said aloud. "Ask him to reconstruct his memory of the incident. Dragon memory is fascinating. They use their magic to form a perfect recreation of any event they personally witnessed."

"That does sound interesting," Bianca acknowledged. "But how will you speak to him? I thought you said he was hiding out near your father's country manor."

"He's got nothing to do," Heath said absently. "I imagine he won't mind coming." He raised his voice slightly, unnecessary though it was. "Reka, do you have a minute? I'm at the site of the fire. Do you mind meeting me here?"

He squinted, focusing on his farsight rather than his normal vision. He could see Reka draped over Heath's own cliff's edge. The dragon had raised his head lazily at Heath's call, and was cocking it to the side. With a sigh, he rolled sideways, straight off the cliff, the fall turning fluidly to flight.

"He's coming," Heath told his cousins. "If he flies at full speed, he should be here within half an hour." He could have just spoken with Reka from a distance, of course. But conversation was more practical and comfortable in person, where possible.

He looked up to find both the twins staring at him.

"What?" he asked defensively.

Bianca shook her head slowly. "I'm not sure you really

understand just how incredible your friendship with Rekavidur is."

Her words sobered Heath at once.

"I do understand," he assured her. "I really do. I just wish I'd grasped sooner how unlike the rest of his kind he is. Then maybe Merletta wouldn't be in such a disastrous situation."

"Merletta?" Brody repeated. "You mean Percival?"

Heath shook his head. "Percival's situation is disastrous as well," he acknowledged. "But it has nothing to do with the dragons."

"What mess is Merletta in?" Bianca demanded. "Is that why she left so suddenly to go home, after you'd claimed she only came here to escape some threat where she's from?"

"Yes, in a nutshell," Heath sighed.

"What do the dragons have to do with it?" Brody pressed.

Heath rolled his shoulders uncomfortably. "It's difficult to explain," he hedged. *At least, difficult to explain without saying too much*, he amended in his mind. "But the dragons sort of want to...well, kill her."

"What?" Bianca was clearly horrified. "Heath, just how many people are you trying to save from violent death by sheer determination?"

Heath grimaced by way of answer.

"Look, I have nothing against Merletta," said Brody curtly. "Although frankly, I don't want to get mixed up in whatever conflict she has with the dragons. And I don't feel a responsibility to keep her safe. But you clearly do, and I don't see how you can possibly focus on Percival's situation if your loyalties are divided. If you let us get him safely out of the kingdom, then you can focus on—"

"Don't lecture me about divided loyalties." Heath's voice came out in a snap. "You've shown no sign of struggling in that area yourself. And I'm sick of you acting like I'm the one who threw Percival in the dungeons."

"Well, you weren't entirely uninvolved, were you?" Brody shot back. He gestured to the burned building beside them. "As I understand it, you're the one who busted the king out of this grain house, and confirmed to him that the door was barred with a beam too heavy for a regular man to lift. *And* made a big deal of Percival being nearby."

"I didn't know Percival was anywhere near here," said Heath, stung. "What should I have done? Left the king to die in there?"

"I never said that," Brody said impatiently. "But you didn't have to make it look so much like Percival was guilty."

"I didn't make it look that way!" Heath protested. "Percival took care of that, openly raging against the king, then riding out here in search of him, making no effort to hide his anger."

"In case you've forgotten, he was angry because the king had you publicly flogged!" Brody retorted furiously.

"I haven't forgotten, thanks," said Heath, his own voice cold. "The scars on my back will make sure I never do." He scowled, wishing Brody's words didn't hit such a nerve. He already felt guilty enough about the series of events that had led Percival to his current situation—having Brody throw it in his face was too much.

"It wasn't just Percival's carelessness," he said, speaking more calmly. "Someone clearly set the whole thing up to look like he did it. And that's exactly why we're here—to try to figure out who it was. So I don't think it's fair to accuse me of not caring enough about Percival just because I dare to be concerned about whether Merletta lives or dies."

"I agree with Heath on this one, Brody," Bianca informed her twin. She frowned at Heath. "I spoke out of concern for you, Heath. You can't hold everything together with your bare hands, you know. We've seen you try to do that before, and it'll rip you apart."

"She's right," said Brody curtly. "If the dragons are determined to kill Merletta, there's nothing you can do to stop them. You may as well give it up now."

Heath turned abruptly from his cousin, swallowing the growl that rose to his throat. There was no point arguing with Brody. It would achieve nothing. Without a word, he stalked across the blackened grass, opting to await Reka's appearance in solitude.

When the dragon arrived, however, Heath's cousins inched back toward him, clearly curious to see the display. Reka was perfectly amenable when Heath asked him to reconstruct the event. But the results were disappointing.

"I can't make anything new appear, you know," the dragon informed him indulgently. "I can't change the fact that we didn't arrive until after the fire was lit, and the culprits had departed. My memory cannot construct information about what occurred prior to our arrival."

"I know," Heath sighed. "But I was hoping there might be some detail we missed at the time."

"More magic, like the other attack, you mean?" Reka frowned in concentration. "The only magic I can sense in the memory—other than yours and mine—is the dormant magic coming from your brother's hiding place. It is faint, suggesting he was already unconscious when we arrived."

"I already know that," muttered Heath. "And I don't think our word is going to convince King Matlock."

"Given that I'm not offering to give testimony to your magic-fearing king, it is a moot point," Reka said, with a touch of coldness.

Heath ignored his friend's offense, his thoughts on his own feeble human attempt to reconstruct the events of that day. But as with all previous attempts, there was nothing new to find. Reka was right. Whoever had lured the king into a trap, and incapacitated Percival nearby, must have already been gone, along with whatever magic they did or didn't possess.

And, he thought chillingly, there was no reason to think that the intent had only been to make King Matlock believe his life was in danger, as Heath had come to suspect was the case in the attack on Percival. This time, he had no doubt that without his intervention, the king would have perished. Two of the king's guards had been knocked unconscious outside the door, in addition to those trapped inside the grain house with their sovereign. Those guards would have survived and would surely have discovered Percival nearby.

And Heath suspected that no amount of growing trust and friendship between him and his cousin would have prevented Lachlan from taking drastic action against not only Percival, but likely all the power-wielders in that event. Who would blame him for responding forcefully if he'd become king at twenty-one due to the murder of his father?

"Is it really so important to solve the mystery?" Reka asked, breaking Heath from his reverie. "I understand that your brother has been unjustly accused, but he has always seemed to me to be more of a nuisance than anything."

"Yes, it's important," said Heath curtly. "It's important to me."

"Well, if it's so important to you, why haven't you made any progress on investigating?" Reka asked reasonably. "You're intelligent and resourceful for a human. I'm surprised you haven't found anything yet. Or are you suffering from the usual human tendency toward distractibility?"

"That's what I said," muttered Brody. "He's too busy thinking about how to protect that girl of his."

"Merletta?" Reka asked, turning his interested gaze on

Brody. "What does protecting her have to do with the plight of Heath's brother?"

"Nothing," said Heath gruffly.

Reka's reptilian head swiveled swiftly back toward Heath, and although his face was unreadable, Heath sensed his increased interest. He couldn't help but wince. The answer hadn't been entirely honest, and Reka could clearly sense it with the irritating talent of dragons.

"Just leave Merletta out of this," Heath told Brody curtly, hoping Reka wouldn't push the matter with the twins present.

He should have known better.

"What is her connection?" Reka asked, his gaze fascinated. "It must be of great concern for you if it has caused you to be deceitful. You are usually very honest."

Brody and Bianca exchanged a glance at this confirmation of Heath's false answer, Brody's brow raised incredulously at the claim that his evasive cousin was usually so honest.

With a sigh, Heath looked up at Reka. "I don't *know* there's a connection between Merletta and Percival's situation. But I've wondered if it's possible that whoever attacked Percival, and me, and presumably King Matlock, could be...from the same place she is." He gave Reka a meaningful look, silently begging the dragon to understand the need for careful speech. "I didn't mention it before because I was afraid of violating Merletta's privacy."

Reka leaned back on his haunches, understanding emanating from him. "I see," he mused slowly. To Heath's relief, he didn't immediately blurt out anything revealing.

"It's an interesting possibility," said Reka thoughtfully. "I hadn't considered that explanation for the power we both sensed at the first attack."

"Hold on." Bianca's voice was sharp. "I thought you said you sensed magic at that attack. Are you saying Merletta is a power-wielder?"

"No," said Heath quickly. "No, she's not a power-wielder. She just...comes from a situation where there's magic. It's not easy to explain."

"It's very easy to explain," Reka contradicted. "But Heath promised Merletta that he wouldn't."

Heath's cousins both glared at him, but Reka ignored all three humans. He closed his eyes, and Heath felt power pulse from him. He suspected Reka was using his magic to reconstruct his memory of that first attack, the one where he'd sensed no power at the time, but had discovered it in his memory later.

"I think it's very possible," the dragon said a moment later, his voice amazed. "It is a similar type of signature, faint and foreign. But if so, it's not any signature I've specifically encountered at any other time."

Heath was silent, his thoughts exploding. He appreciated Reka's restraint in using veiled speech. Heath understood perfectly. Reka agreed that the signature of magic they'd felt at the attack on Percival was akin to the type of power that lingered faintly around Merletta, and others of her kind. But if Reka hadn't felt it elsewhere, then it wasn't Merletta—obviously—or any of the guards from Vazula.

Was somebody else from Merletta's world targeting Valoria?

The thought was absurd...and terrifying. And it placed Heath in an impossible situation. How could he keep Merletta's secret now, without wronging his own people? He'd sworn that in concealing Vazula and the triple kingdoms, he wasn't concealing a threat from his king, and he'd unequivocally believed it. But had he been wrong? Attacking Percival to inflame tensions—even targeting Heath—was one thing. But if someone from the triple kingdoms had tried to murder King Matlock...

But had they? Heath argued desperately with himself. He hadn't sensed power at the fire. Just at the other two attacks.

The argument was weak, even in his own head. He had no real doubt that the same players were behind each of the attacks. Which meant that finding and identifying the true culprit—the only way to clear Percival's name—would mean betraying Merletta's secret and exposing the triple kingdoms.

It made sense, at least partially. Although he still didn't understand why any merperson would want to create tensions in Valorian society, it explained the attack on Heath. If someone underwater had found out about his connection with Merletta, they might wish to remove him in order to protect their secret.

But that meant...

Heath drew in a sharp breath, horrified by the inevitable conclusion. If someone had found out about him, Merletta was in more danger than he was. How was she still alive so long after the attack on Heath?

He remembered that she'd become so visible she wasn't easy to inconspicuously kill, but the thought did little to reassure him.

Heath reached inside himself, teasing out his magic in the way Reka had taught him to do. Perhaps because of the dragon's proximity, his extra vision flared instantly to life, his image of Merletta encompassing not only her, but her surroundings.

She was in a room, the light dim under the water. The walls were made of stone, and stacks of some kind of large leaf were piled onto shelves which were cut into the stone at all levels. Not just within arm's reach of the floor, either—the shelves extended all the way up and out of sight. Of course merpeople weren't restricted to the ground like humans were.

As fascinating as it was to get a glimpse of an underwater building, Heath was more concerned with what Merletta was saying. She was speaking to her companion, the pink-tailed mermaid Heath had seen before.

Sage, her name was. Merletta had spoken of her often.

Right now her face was creased with concern, her dark eyes seeming to bore into Merletta as she listened to her friend.

It will be what it will be, Sage, Merletta was saying. *I don't think there's really anything I can do to change whatever's coming.* She cast a furtive glance around, then continued. *We both know that when I sit down with the Record Master—when I tell him about the dragons—I'll be completely in his power.*

What? Heath's breath caught in his throat, his heart speeding up. Merletta was going to tell the top authority in her world about the threat of the dragon colony? If there was any hope they didn't know about her connection with Heath, it wouldn't survive that meeting. There was no way she could avoid confessing to things which would make them more determined than ever to be rid of her once and for all. A shudder went over Heath as he pictured the retribution that would surely follow. He had to talk her out of it somehow.

But how? He could hear her, but she had no idea he was watching at that moment. There was no way to get a message to her, not when she was deep underwater.

"Reka," he said, pulling his attention back to his surroundings. "It's Merletta."

"What about her?" Brody demanded.

Heath looked at his cousin, vaguely surprised to be reminded of the twins' presence. "We're not finding anything of use to Percival here," he said abruptly. "I have to go now. Will you take my horse back to the city?"

"But, Heath! You can't drop something like that on us, and then just—"

"We'll talk later." Heath cut off Bianca's spluttered protest, turning to Rekavidur. He needed to think, to figure out what to do now Reka had confirmed his vague and absurd suspicions. And more immediately, he needed to know what Merletta was up against.

At a beseeching lift of Heath's eyebrow, Reka clasped his talons around Heath's shoulders, taking at once to the air.

CHAPTER ELEVEN

"Where are we going?" Reka called calmly over the wind, as they streaked up into the sky, Brody and Bianca shrinking to the size of ants below them.

"Somewhere I can think," Heath shouted back. "Where we can talk freely."

Reka said no more, directing his flight southeast, so that they would bypass the capital. Heath didn't try to guess their destination, his focus already back with Merletta.

I'm still not entirely sure what you're hoping to find here, Sage was saying. *Why did we need to come to the restricted records room? I thought Emil already found out about your family.*

Heath locked that information away for later—clearly there had been developments in that area.

He did, Merletta acknowledged. *That's not what I meant when I said I had to know the truth. I was thinking of this section.*

She gestured, and with an effort, Heath stretched his farsight, expanding the vision far enough to see what she was pointing at. It was a section of shelving marked in large letters: *Dragon Aggression.*

I saw records from this section, Merletta went on. *In Tilssted, when they were trying to convince everyone not to leave the barrier. They described our ancestors' attempts to create new settlements outside the barrier. But the records were truncated. There's definitely more to the story, and I need to know what really happened.*

Sage looked troubled. *Why? What will it gain you at this point? And how can we trust any account we find here, given the Center's record with falsifying our history?*

I thought it was all nonsense at first, too, Merletta acknowledged. *Fear-mongering. But now I'm not so sure. I'm starting to suspect that the records in here are real—and that's the reason they're so restricted. There's nothing so dangerous as the truth, at least from the Center's perspective.*

The wind whipped past Heath's face, his clothes flapping wildly around him as Reka flew over farmland. But Heath was aware of none of it, lost deep in Merletta's world.

As for what it will gain, Merletta was adding, *it could be invaluable. Rekavidur thought our best hope was to prove that we don't originate from dragons siphoning off their magic into fish so as to enable themselves to die. Maybe if we find accurate information about encounters between our kind and dragons, it might help answer those questions. And while we can't search the island, you and I—and Emil and Andre—are the only ones who can hunt for whatever answers might be hidden in here.*

Sage didn't look entirely convinced, but she drifted across the space in Merletta's wake, examining the records in the relevant section.

For a considerable space of time, the two mermaids rifled through the waxy leaves in silence, and Reka sped over the Valorian countryside. Heath felt suspended, fully existing in neither world, but painfully aware of both.

Here. Sage's sudden speech was intended for Merletta, but it made Heath lift his head sharply. *This account gives a lot of detail* about the incident you mentioned. She grimaced. *A lot of gruesome detail.*

Merletta hurried to her friend, looking over Sage's shoulder. Heath tried to read the words on the page, but his extra sight wasn't refined enough for that. He had to be satisfied with Merletta's reflections.

They tried to create the new settlements because of overpopulation? Merletta said, sounding uneasy. *But this is generation upon generation ago. If the triple kingdoms were already overflowing back then, how have they managed to stay contained inside the barrier in all the time since?*

I don't know, Sage said thoughtfully. *Is it possible they expanded the barrier somehow?*

I doubt it, Merletta responded. *If that was possible, I'm sure they'd be talking about it now.*

She fell silent again as she continued to read.

This description certainly sounds like it could be near Heath's kingdom, she mused. *They must have known the benefits of settling near land then, even if the information has been forgotten—or obscured—in the time since.* She frowned. *Did you see this part? It says there were only a very few instances of contact with humans as the settlement was being built.*

Sage nodded. *I saw it. And where it says the humans were more inclined to be afraid of the merfolk than aggressive toward them.*

'But then disaster struck,' Merletta read aloud. 'A pair of mermaids strayed further east along the shore of the land, and encountered a dragon. From the accounts of their ancestors, they expected an amicable response, but instead were met with fear and outrage.' *That's...sinister,* Merletta commented, once she'd finished reading aloud. *And fits with my own experience in the same waters.*

Sage nodded again, her expression solemn. *Did you see what comes next? The mermaids thought little of it when they saw no more dragons for a couple of months, then a horde of them descended on the fledgling settlement and attacked.*

Merletta took a moment to reply. *Yes,* she said at last. *I see it. They were absolutely brutal. No wonder the merpeople gave up on the idea of a settlement out that way, and the survivors all retreated back inside the barrier.*

Her eyes scanned the page, then rose up to meet Sage's, her expression stricken. *Are we reading our future, Sage?* she whispered. *These descriptions...diving into the deep, pulling mermaids from the water, spearing them like fish as they swim, with a single talon piercing through the heart...is that what they're going to do to everyone in the triple kingdoms?*

Sage's face was devoid of color. She said nothing, clearly having no answer.

I've brought this on everyone, Merletta murmured, not seeming to expect a response.

To Heath's relief, Sage spoke up, voicing his own thoughts. *You're not responsible for the dragons' reaction, Merletta. And nothing will be gained by beating yourself up.*

You're right about that part, Merletta said, her voice suddenly determined. *What I'd really like to read is the story behind this statement—'From the accounts of their ancestors, they expected an amicable response'. What amicable history is there between our ancestors and dragons? It must not have been with dragons from Rekavidur's colony. It must have been the dragons on Vazula. Clearly they didn't see our kind as offensive or dangerous. If only they were still on the island to speak for us to the rest of their kind.*

The two mermaids spent a considerable period scouring the rest of the records, but they didn't find any reference to friendly interactions between dragons and merpeople. Perhaps not surprising in a section marked *Dragon Aggression*. Heath was dimly aware of Rekavidur setting him down, but he took no stock of his surroundings. He was fully immersed in the underwater room.

Well, Sage said with false cheer, when the pair finally gave up their search, *perhaps August and the others will find something useful on the island.*

We'll probably never know, Merletta said glumly. *Because we'll be unlikely to see them—or anyone—again after the meeting in two days.*

Two days? Heath felt panic stir inside him. It was only two days until Merletta was going to throw herself on the mercy of the Record Master? What could he possibly do in that short time to prevent her taking such drastic action? How could he warn her that someone in her world might know about their connection—might have already started trying to permanently end it?

"You have been watching Merletta, I take it?"

Reka's calm voice grounded Heath, reminding him that he wasn't actually underwater with Merletta. Blinking, he glanced around him, realizing that Reka had brought him to his own clifftop. Bexley Manor was visible a short distance away.

"Yes, I have," he said grimly. "And she's about to throw herself to the wolves." He paused. "Or sharks, I guess."

"I don't know what you mean by that," Reka complained.

Heath explained what he'd witnessed, hardly able to contain his agitation over Merletta's intended course.

"It is a sensible plan," Reka said with maddening unconcern. "Laudable, even. It would not be the path of honor to conceal the coming attack from those in power, however unsavory their behavior might have been."

Heath scowled, irritated rather than softened by the knowledge that Reka was absolutely right. It was easy for the dragon to be so relaxed about it all—it made no significant difference to him whether Merletta lived or died. To Heath, it was everything.

"It is interesting what Merletta and her companion learned about the attempted settlement near Valoria," Rekavidur commented thoughtfully. "Presumably that explains the ruins you and I once found."

Heath nodded distractedly, not caring about the minor point. "I'd figured the same thing."

"It might also explain something the elders said," Reka mused.

Heath sent him a questioning look, and he continued.

"They said that the abominations in the deep started out as nothing more than enhanced fish, and the dragons thought they killed them all. But after some time, they reappeared, and they had advanced beyond recognition, bearing partial human appearance. The dragons who populated my colony at the time concluded that the abominations had retreated into the deeps, and during the period of their absence—which was apparently many generations—had developed far in excess of what any dragon would have expected."

Heath frowned as he thought this tale over. "It sounds to me like the 'abominations' who reappeared bore no true connection to the ones who were initially wiped out," he said. "As in, maybe the dragons really did get them all the first time, and the advanced ones who showed up later were actually merpeople, who'd come into existence through some unrelated process, and had the bad fortune to attempt to settle near a colony of dragons who mistook them for descendants of their own abominations."

Reka nodded serenely. "That is my speculation as well."

Heath let out a frustrated breath. "Merletta's not wrong," he muttered. "What we really need to know is the earlier history— the one about amicable relations between the Vazula dragons and merpeople. Surely that would tell us where Merletta's kind really come from."

"Presumably," Reka agreed.

Heath ran a hand through his short hair. "If only I'd searched more diligently when I was on Vazula all those times. But I was completely distracted by Merletta's presence." He glanced at Reka. "Do you think we could go back there now? We could hunt for answers, and maybe get a message to Merletta."

Reka did his rippling shrug, his yellow scales tinkling with the motion. "We can if you wish. But I consider it highly likely that such a course would precipitate the attack my colony is planning. Remember that if I set out on a journey, I must assume my flight will be followed through someone's farsight. And from the island, it will not be hard for my kind to find the underwater kingdoms."

Heath groaned. "Well, we can't do that, then," he said. He paced up and down across the clifftop, agitation building inside him. "But I can't stand to do nothing!" he burst out.

"I could take this new information to my colony," Reka offered. "I could present to them this alternative history for how the so-called abominations developed such astonishing capacities. I could tell them that I've come across credible evidence of former friendly relations between dragons and merpeople. I doubt they will place much value on the information without actual evidence, but I am willing to try if you wish it."

"Thank you, Reka," Heath said earnestly. "It's asking too much of you, but we can't leave any stone unturned. Not if we're going to save Merletta."

Reka nodded. "Very well. I will attempt to make them listen. Await my news."

Heath barely held in another groan as the dragon took to the air with his usual abruptness. He was truly grateful to Reka for his assistance, but the idea of just waiting around, watching from afar as Merletta put herself once again into danger, was unendurable.

But he had no other option. Merletta had said two days, and

dragons didn't work to human schedules. He was well aware that even if the dragons took Reka's new information seriously—a possibility which was already painfully slim—there was no way anything would change quickly enough to prevent Merletta from placing herself at the mercy of the Center's Record Master.

And with nothing to do to help her, he was left without anything to distract him from the question he least wanted to grapple with—what was he going to do about the secrets he'd sworn to keep, but which might now be condemning Percival to execution?

CHAPTER TWELVE

Merletta

Merletta glanced at her friends' grim faces as the central spire loomed large before them.

"You know, it's really not too late to—"

"Enough, Merletta," said Emil disapprovingly. "We need to keep focus, and going through all this again will just be a distraction. We've all decided to come with you. Show us the courtesy of respecting our decision."

Merletta fell silent, recognizing the uselessness of arguing. Emil had made his position clear, and Sage and Andre were no less determined. Whatever the outcome of this meeting, they were all in it together.

Given she'd expected more power plays, Merletta was pleasantly surprised that they were not kept waiting. As soon as they approached the opening at which she'd made the appointment a week before, a mermaid swam out from a side door and curtly instructed them to follow her.

They all swam straight upward through the center of the spire. Center employees bustled past in all directions, and Merletta caught glimpses through many doorways into various workshops, offices, and storage areas. It would all have been fascinating once, but now she couldn't muster interest in any of it.

She'd been struggling to focus on anything that past week. Even the life-altering revelations about the family she'd come from had paled in significance compared with the looming meeting with the Record Master. Perhaps it was because she'd decided not to claim her birth position and the privileges that came with it.

Or perhaps it was because the Record Master's attempt to rattle her by delaying their meeting had worked perfectly.

Either way, she'd felt like a luminescent jellyfish trapped in a lantern cage all week. She'd had no doubt that once she made her mysterious appointment she would be watched very closely. She hadn't been anywhere but classes, training, the barracks and the dining hall all week. The only exception was her foray into the restricted records room with Sage a couple days before. Not that the trip had yielded anything of much value.

They'd ascended more than halfway up the interior of the spire when their guide directed them through an open doorway to one side. As they floated around the edges of the small room, the mermaid fixed Merletta's friends with a glare.

"The appointment, I believe, is with Trainee Merletta," she said.

"We're here to give our support to Merletta's testimony," Emil replied, before Merletta could speak.

The mermaid was unimpressed. "And you are?"

"My name is Emil, of the Skulssted family Waveracer," he said. "I'm a record holder."

"As am I," Sage chimed in. "My name is Sage, of the Skulssted family Clearfoam."

"And I'm Andre," Andre added. "Of the Skulssted Seawatch family. I'm a trainee in the program."

The mermaid's eyes lingered on each of them in turn, her

expression still disapproving. But it seemed the decision about their inclusion was above her authority, because she just turned away, swimming swiftly up and through an opening in the ceiling above them.

"Seawatch is an interesting name," Merletta commented to Andre as they waited. "I noted it on your family record, but never asked you about it."

Andre nodded. "My father claims that the family have served as guards for as many generations as we know of. And that's why our name is a guardian type name." He wrinkled his nose ruefully. "He likes to bring it up regularly, as his not very subtle protest that I've chosen to pursue the record holder role instead of the noble path of a guard."

"Not always so noble," Merletta muttered. She still felt disillusioned over the realization that Denton's kindness in educating her had been motivated by his guilt over abetting in the murder of her parents, and then abandoning her to the charity home in the first place.

"Are you thinking of the guards who attacked August's patrol?" Andre asked, frowning. "They're Center guards, not Skulssted guards like my father and his line."

"No, I wasn't thinking of that," Merletta said quickly. She flicked her thumb against the scales of her tail in a compulsive gesture. "All the formal introductions just made me think of..." She swallowed, then the words tumbled out in a rush. "I found out who my family is. Where I came from, I mean, before the charity home. I even met my uncle."

Emil had gone still, his gaze piercing as he waited for her to continue. The other two looked stunned and, in Sage's case, excited.

"Who are they?" she asked.

"I come from the El family of Hemssted," Merletta said. "They're a fairly influential family, with a decent amount of wealth, from what I saw. My mother was from the Mer family, also from Hemssted, but they seem to have faded out of existence. I can't prove it for any official purpose, of course, but the head of the family, Elfin, was convinced enough by all the circumstances that he offered me the protection and recognition of the family name."

"Merletta, that's amazing," Sage said. "I can't believe you hadn't told me! Now you can—"

"I told him thank you, but no thank you," Merletta cut her off. "In a clamshell."

Sage closed her mouth, her expression bewildered. "But...why?"

Merletta shrugged. "If I had time on my side, I would be interested in a relationship with them. But I don't want anything from them. It might be who I was born, but it's not who I am. I used to think I needed the validity of a family name, but I see all that differently now." She gave them a tight smile. "I'm not alone —you're all here, risking your lives to float by me, aren't you?"

"Of course we are," Andre said quietly.

"Besides," Merletta's tone turned brisk, "it's not about what I need. I'm all Tilssted has, and they really do need me. I found that when it came down to it, I didn't actually want to disown them."

"Still," Emil mused. "It would make you less vulnerable. And might give you more credibility with those in power at the Center."

Merletta gave him a look. "Do you really think any amount of credibility could make them more cooperative given that my aim is to reveal the truth they've gone to such efforts to conceal?"

"No," Emil admitted. "I don't think anything would make that much difference."

"Exactly," said Merletta. "In fact..." She hesitated, surprised by how hard it was to say the words. "Again, I can't prove it, but I'm pretty sure my parents were murdered by the Center for pushing the idea that we could expand outside the barrier. So the position of privilege clearly wasn't enough to help either them or their cause."

Sage's eyes were wide with horror. "Merletta," she whispered.

Merletta gave a humorless smile. "It's ironic, isn't it? Even though they had no part in raising me, I still managed to grow up obsessed with the very concept which cost them their lives."

There was a moment of silence, no one seeming to know what to say.

"So you're putting all your pearls into the one oyster, embracing the persona of the defiant Tilssted trainee," Emil commented at last. "I can respect that course. But are you honestly claiming you're doing it because that's who you really are at heart?"

Merletta's chuckle was wry. "You're very perceptive, Emil," she acknowledged. "Let's just say that role is who I need to be for the task ahead. That's all that matters."

"Your own feelings matter, too, Merletta," Sage said gently. "Your feelings about who you really are, I mean."

Merletta gazed at her friend, no ready answer rising to her lips. Emil was right that she didn't fully identify with the role she'd grown up in—that of a Tilssted orphan, fighting hard for every scrap of success. But neither could she see herself as a privileged member of high Hemssted society. In fact, even the position of Center trainee, for which she'd fought so hard, felt at heart like a part she was playing, rather than who she really was.

So which version of herself felt real?

Her thoughts floated away from her without her permission, to the place where she'd felt most free, most at peace. Merciless sun beating on her shoulders. The sea sparkling before her, its azure depths beckoning and familiar, and right there, within reach. Wet sand squelching between her toes. Heath's arm firm around her waist, his skin warm against hers, not with the searing heat of his touch on her mermaid form, but with the comfortable familiarity of co-existence.

She pulled herself back to the small waiting room where her friends floated by her side, ready to brave the Center's retribution for the sake of both friendship and truth. Vazula—and especially Vazula with Heath—had been a very agreeable present for a brief spell. But the idea of the island forming her future was no more possible than rewriting her past and giving that to Vazula. For so many reasons—found both in her world and Heath's.

Before she'd decided what, if anything, to say in reply to Sage's words, the mermaid appeared again in the opening above them.

"You may all follow me," she said, her tart voice communicating her disapproval at the inclusion of Merletta's friends.

They swam up two more stories, and were ushered into a simple room, smaller than Merletta had expected. It had two rows of tiered seating along one wall, like a smaller version of their lecture rooms back in the program's complex.

The four of them had barely taken places on the seating when the curtain of fronds which separated the room from one next to it stirred, and a lithe form appeared.

It wasn't the first time Merletta had seen the Record Master up close. He'd approached her and Sage at the Founders' Day feast all the way back in first year, and she'd encountered him more than once since then. But she'd never dared to scrutinize him as closely as she did now.

His figure was lean but strong—it was clear at a glance that anyone would be foolish to underestimate either his intelligence or his capability due to his advanced age. He had an austere presence, swimming with the assurance of someone used to authority. But he was otherwise unimposing. He wore no adornments in his silver hair, and his hands were folded behind his back in a non-threatening gesture.

But his gray eyes were shrewd and careful.

He was followed into the space by his two personal guards—the only ones Merletta had ever seen shadowing him. It seemed when they were otherwise occupied, he preferred to move about unguarded than take on other protectors. Both of them were familiar to Merletta as well, but only because of repeated exposure. She'd noted the first time she saw them that they were unremarkable, their expressions blank, and their coloring such that they blended with the ocean around them. One was weedy, with hair and skin so pale they seemed to fade before her sight, his silvery tail like water made solid. The other was more thickset, but not such that it was notable. His most attention-grabbing feature was his piercing blue eyes. They were the same color as his tail, which—like his companion's—blended seamlessly into the water around him.

The nature of their role and their perfectly crafted weapons made their presence a little menacing by default. But on this occasion they floated casually by the Record Master's sides, showing only the usual alertness one would expect from guards.

"Trainee Merletta." The Record Master's voice was cool and unemotional. "You requested a meeting with me, I understand."

"I did, sir," Merletta responded.

He looked her over in silence, his gaze passing thoughtfully from her golden fins all the way up to her face.

"It is unusual for a trainee to meet directly with the Record Master," he said, his voice and face still conveying no particular emotion.

"I can imagine." Merletta spoke shortly, already losing patience for whatever games he had planned.

"I won't pretend not to know who you are," he went on. "I would not have agreed to meet with any trainee. I accepted the meeting in the hope and expectation that you wished to speak candidly."

"I would like to do so," Merletta agreed.

He raised one silver eyebrow ever so slightly. "I see you have brought companions with you to this candid meeting."

Sage squirmed slightly in her seat at the implied rebuke. But a glance to the side showed Merletta that Andre's brow was creased in a defiant frown, and although Emil's unexpressive face rivaled the Record Master's for calm, his posture was taut and unyielding.

Merletta swallowed the instinct to explain or justify her friends' inclusion. If she wanted to maintain any semblance of control in this conversation, she would do well not to compliantly accept the premise of whatever criticism the Record Master chose to level at her.

"Allow me to introduce my friends," she said instead. "This is—"

"I have been informed of their identities," the Record Master cut her off smoothly. "Greetings, Record Holder Emil Waveracer, Record Holder Sage Clearfoam, and Trainee Andre Seawatch."

Merletta couldn't help glancing again at Sage, to see how she would take this subtle reminder that not only they, but their families had now been noted in the Record Master's mental list of troublemakers. But Sage's expression was steely, her resolve apparently strengthened rather than shaken by the Record Master's attempt to intimidate.

"Since it was you who requested this irregular meeting, Trainee Merletta, I will leave it to you to clarify its purpose." The Record Master's gray eyes bored into Merletta.

She felt an involuntary shudder pass down her scales, but she held her head up. "Of course, sir," she acknowledged. "I regret to say that the circumstances which prompted me to seek an audience with you are dire. So much so that I could see no way forward but to communicate them to you."

The Record Master's face remained blank, giving nothing away.

Refusing to be rattled, Merletta pushed on. "You expressed the hope that I would be frank, so I will. Whatever the official hierarchy of authority, I know as well as you do that the Center actually holds the balance of power in the triple kingdoms."

She paused, but still he gave no response to her words.

"In light of which," Merletta continued, "if I want to report something to the highest authority in our civilization, it seems you are the one to speak to."

"And what is it that you want to report?" he asked calmly.

Merletta shook her head ruefully. "That wasn't entirely candid," she corrected herself. "I don't want to report anything to you. Let me rather say, I feel compelled to report something." She searched his face, wishing she could read the thoughts and secrets behind those inscrutable eyes. "Given I publicly announced as much, I have no doubt you're aware that I've spent a considerable amount of time outside the barrier in my life. That was, in fact, how I first learned about the various lies the Center has propagated, when I experienced how much less hazardous the open ocean is than what we've been indoctrinated to believe."

She felt Sage tense beside her at this aggressively plain speaking, but the Record Master gave no reaction.

"Unfortunately," Merletta went on steadily, "I made the mistake of assuming that everything the Center taught was lies. There's no simple way, you see, for someone discerning enough to recognize the inconsistencies to identify which information can be trusted, and which is pure manipulation."

The blue-tailed guard shifted ever so slightly, but the motion was the only acknowledgment of Merletta's blunt accusations. The Record Master continued to watch her in calm silence.

"It was my mistake to make assumptions about such a potentially dangerous topic," Merletta acknowledged. "And I don't deny it. There are no words for how deeply I regret the calamity I've brought on the triple kingdoms, however unintentionally it was done."

"And what is the potentially dangerous topic about which you made an assumption?" the Record Master asked, when she paused.

Merletta clasped her hands in her lap. "Dragons," she informed him. "I thought the Center's tales of dragon aggression were more lies to keep us away from the surface. I had my own reasons for thinking they couldn't be as vicious as they were painted."

She didn't elaborate on this point. She'd given the matter a great deal of consideration, and had decided that it was too dangerous to tell the Record Master all about the time she'd spent on the island. He must know of the place, but she didn't think he knew the extent of her discoveries there. To reveal that she'd frequently met Heath and Rekavidur there could compromise Heath, and would certainly endanger Tish, Paul, and Griffin, who still lived on the island. So, candid though she might be about the dragons, she wasn't going to mention her discovery of her legs.

The Record Master was still waiting, clearly not intending to give her the satisfaction of asking what she meant, or hurrying her along. He was totally master of both himself and the situation, and it rattled Merletta more than she cared to admit.

"The long and the short of it is, I strayed too far from the triple kingdoms, and I encountered a dragon," she admitted. "Not just one. Several. They attempted to kill me, and I was fortunate to escape with my life. But I have reason to believe that they will not be content to leave the matter there. In fact, I fully expect them to search until they find our civilization, with the intention of destroying us all."

At last, she received a reaction from the Record Master. He blinked, a slow, controlled movement.

"That is certainly a calamity," he said blandly.

Merletta scowled, irked that he was still focused on projecting a masterful image in light of the information she'd just told him.

"I won't pretend to fully understand why they hate us enough to wish to annihilate us," she added. "No doubt you know the answer much better than I do, given you're the primary keeper of our history."

The Record Master drew in an unhurried pull of water, his eyes studying her in apparent fascination.

"I confess myself surprised at your candor," he said at last.

"What?" Merletta's irritation was rising rapidly. She'd braced herself for this conversation, imagining all kinds of dire outcomes and reactions. To have the Record Master treat the information like a barely interesting harvest update was more maddening than anything she'd pictured.

"You have so far been remarkably skilled—or perhaps fortunate—in escaping consequence from more than one potentially incriminating incident," he said.

"I didn't come here to talk about being framed for stealing non-existent records," Merletta said impatiently. "Or being poisoned to look like I had the mythical land sickness. I came here to talk about the absolute disaster which is—"

"It is therefore not logical to me," the Record Master interrupted, as if she hadn't been speaking at all, "that you would choose to share information with me which implicates yourself. You have, in fact, acknowledged that it is you who have brought *calamity* upon us all."

"Are you serious?" Merletta stared at him incredulously. "Did you not hear what I said? A colony of enraged dragons is coming to kill every last one of us, and you're surprised that I'm not trying to keep it secret to save my own skin?"

"Yes," he confirmed. "I am."

She hardly knew how to answer him. "I think you failed in what should be a very basic rule for someone playing at your level—that is, to know your enemy. It seems you don't have much of an idea who I am."

"Evidently you are right," he owned. "I thought you were a survivor first and foremost. But I understand my error now." His eyes scanned the other three. "And you all have played your part in this situation, have you?"

"Their only connection to the whole disaster is me telling them about it," Merletta cut in firmly. "None of them had any hand in alerting the dragons to our presence."

"Hm." The Record Master looked unconvinced, his gaze lingering longest on Sage.

Merletta pushed down the fear and guilt that threatened to claw its way up her throat. This was the Record Master's own game, and he was clearly good at it. More likely than not, his accusations toward her friends were designed primarily to weaken her, not to punish them. But honestly, what power did he think he could exercise over her now? There was a reason she'd spoken so bluntly and forcefully. What did she have to lose—what did any of them have to lose if the dragons were going to wipe them out?

"If you truly don't comprehend why I'm telling you this," Merletta started resolutely, "then I can explain it. As the one in power, you have the best chance of responding effectively. Hopefully of actually preventing the threatened slaughter."

"Do you think so?" he asked, his expression still neutral.

"Of course," Merletta said impatiently. "If you tell everyone they need to flee into the ocean and hide, they'll believe you. If I tell them that, most people will ignore it as the ravings of a brazen trainee with an overinflated ego."

"Would they believe me?" the Record Master asked conversationally. "Faith in the accuracy and integrity of the Center's teachings is a little low lately. Someone seems to have been throwing our work into question."

"If you want me to apologize for that, then you'd better prepare yourself for disappointment," Merletta snapped, losing her cool in the face of his apparent unconcern. "I've acknowledged my role in all this, but the Center is at least as much to blame. If they did what they were intended to do, accurately preserving our history and faithfully communicating the truth to the population, this situation would not have arisen."

Again the thickset guard showed a flicker of emotion, his eyes narrowing as they rested on Merletta. The Record Master gave no such outward sign.

"It's not just about whether everyone would believe you," Merletta pressed on doggedly. "You also need to actually let them out. Everyone will get slaughtered if your guards keep them trapped inside cities which now have a target on them."

"So your solution would be for the population of the triple kingdoms to flee into the deep ocean, scatter in small groups, and hope for the best?" The Record Master's voice held no discernible tone, and yet disdain still managed to drip from every word.

"No," Merletta retorted. "That's a last resort at absolute best. The ideal solution would be to convince the dragons not to attack at all. And from what I understand, we can only do that if we demonstrate to them that they're wrong about our origins. That's another task which I figure the Center would be best placed to carry out, given that it's supposed to have the answers about how our civilization came to be."

The older merman considered her for a long and thoughtful moment. To Merletta's surprise, the silence was broken by Emil.

"In my role as a record holder, I have been researching the question of our origins," he said calmly. "I have been surprised to discover very little information beyond the simple tale told to the masses. Which, as everyone in this room must be aware, is not a very credible one."

The Record Master's scrutiny passed to Emil, and Merletta had to admire the way her friend continued to project total unconcern as the austere leader studied him unabashedly.

"Your understanding of your role appears to be underdeveloped," he said at last. "Record holders are the keepers of our civilization's history. They need not be concerned with what came before our civilization."

Merletta made a noise of disbelief, but he gave her no chance to call him out on the absurd distinction.

"You seem to know a great deal, Trainee Merletta," he said, his attention returning to her. "But to one with experience, your apparent knowledge is nothing more than an illusion. I have been studying dragon lore since before you were born. If you truly think it is possible to talk the beasts down from this course you say they have chosen, then you know nothing of them."

"Dragon lore is one thing," Merletta argued. "But actual dragons are something else altogether. You don't know it's hopeless. Maybe we only need to convince one dragon, or two. Maybe that's all it would take, and they could convince the rest."

"Foolish." The Record Master spoke dismissively, but still without heat. It was almost chilling, how calmly he was taking her pronouncement about the rapidly approaching end of their world.

"Well, what's your plan, then?" Merletta demanded, stung. "How do you propose we avoid detection and death?"

He ignored her question.

"You have made your report," he said. "You may now leave the matter in more capable hands."

Merletta frowned at him. Did that mean he had a solution? A way out of the nightmare? She could only hope so, little as she would normally want this merman's plans to succeed.

"Will you try to reason with the dragons?" she pressed. "Do you want me to tell you how to make contact with the ones I encountered? Because I do know a way. Don't you think that if you tell them the true story of where the triple kingdoms came from, it might change their minds? Surely your secrets aren't worth keeping at such a cost."

She wasn't really surprised when the Record Master failed to answer any of her questions. "As I said," he responded baldly, "you have made your report. Your role is finished."

"So what next for Merletta?" Andre asked bluntly, speaking for the first time since the Record Master had arrived.

The silver-haired merman met the young trainee's eyes blandly. "I believe we may consider our meeting complete," he said, in the same neutral tone. "It was most enlightening to speak with you all."

And without another word, he rose into the water, and straight through the waving fronds into the next room, leaving the four of them in tense—and bewildered—silence.

CHAPTER THIRTEEN

Is Lord Percival still receiving visitors?

The king's voice in his ear caused Heath to still. His eyes became unfocused as he let his actual surroundings—the royal training yard—fade away. He drew on his magic impatiently, and his farsight expanded, showing him King Matlock's grave face as he spoke with the captain of his guard.

That situation cannot be allowed to continue. He is in the dungeons, not an inn.

Yes, Your Majesty, the captain replied.

But Heath was already tuning them out. The conversation was turning to matters of no interest to him.

"Heath, are you even listening?"

"Yes, I'm listening," Heath said, turning his attention back to his cousin, who'd sought him out in the training yard.

Brody stared at him out of narrowed eyes. "Where did you go just now? If you were calling your dragon to come carry you away again, and leave me standing here like a fool—"

"Will you let that go?" Heath interrupted, rolling his eyes. "You had horses—it wasn't like you couldn't get back to the city."

"How did you get back to the city?" Brody asked. "I didn't hear any gossip about a dragon sighting in the town square."

"Reka dropped me off at Bexley Manor," Heath said absently. "I slept there, and rode back yesterday. So what's so important, Brody? What's going on with Max?"

Brody frowned. "He applied for a job as a communications runner for the guards."

"That's..." Heath blinked. "Actually a really good idea."

Max was their cousin, two years younger than Heath, and gifted with the ability to run as fast as a galloping horse.

"It's an excellent idea," Brody drawled. "Which the king has flatly prohibited."

"He has?" Heath frowned. "But it's such a good way for Max to use his power for the benefit of everyone. Surely if he applied to the king for—"

"That's precisely what he didn't do, of course," said Brody. He scowled. "And he shouldn't have to."

"Ah." Heath leaned his bow on the ground as he comprehended it all. "So King Matlock was put in the ridiculous position of having to intervene to prevent something that wasn't harmful at all, just to be consistent with his own regulations." He thought it over. "Which was presumably Max's aim."

"Yes, I think it was," Brody acknowledged. His face creased in another frown. "And if you try to tell me he should have compliantly applied to help the king save face—"

"No, no." Heath waved his hand in protest. "I'm way past that point. King Matlock's had as much of a hand in making this mess as anyone. If he looks foolish because of his own regulations, that's on him."

"Good," said Brody, although the tone of disapproval lingered.

However irritated Heath might feel with his sovereign, King Matlock continued to treat Heath with considerably more respect than the rest of the power-wielders. As a result, most of Heath's cousins—Brody included—still seemed to view him as something of a traitor to the power-wielders.

Heath tried to tell himself it didn't sting.

"It was a clever type of protest by Max," Heath mused. "Much better than Leonora's constant attempts to get herself thrown into the dungeons with Percival."

Brody sighed. "She definitely doesn't understand what she'd be getting herself into. But at least she's trying to do *something*." He glanced at Heath. "You know the king required her father to pay compensation after she froze out the royal wing?"

"Something tells me that tame punishment didn't satisfy her determination to martyr herself," Heath said dryly.

"Not quite," Brody agreed. "But it had the desired effect of causing her parents to keep a tighter hold. Apparently they intervened in a planned stunt by Jasmine and Lucas." He named Leonora's siblings.

Heath ran a hand through his hair. He didn't need Brody to remind him of the escalating situation with his cousins. Leonora's harmless attack against the royals' suites wasn't the first incident to provoke punishment from the king in recent weeks. At least he hadn't flogged anyone since Heath's own experience. If nothing else, that humiliation seemed to have achieved the restoration of some measure of King Matlock's moderation.

"I don't know what you want me to do about Max's situation," he said wearily. "But I have nothing to suggest."

"Never mind about Max," said Brody. "He's fine. But what about Percival? I think it's time to put our plan into action."

Heath shook his head. "King Matlock's official investigation is still being finalized, which means he hasn't set an execution date. We still have time."

"What cloud is your head in, Heath?" Brody said impatiently. "Every day we delay is another day your brother spends in the dungeons."

The thought of having this argument with his cousin yet again made Heath's head hurt. He hadn't even framed a response when his awareness was suddenly pulled toward Merletta. He'd been watching her on and off since the moment he woke, knowing she intended to meet with the Record Master that day. And it looked now as though she was on her way. At least her friends seemed to be with her.

"I have to go," Heath told Brody curtly, making no attempt at politeness. He turned on his heel, but before he could take a step, Brody's hand shot out, gripping his arm.

"No, you don't. Tell me what's going on. It's something to do with Merletta, isn't it?"

"That's none of your business," Heath told him simply.

Brody was unimpressed. "You can't just shrug me off on this, Heath. You told Bianca we'd talk later, but you've been avoiding us ever since. Two days ago you said that whoever's been attacking your family," he lowered his voice as he glanced around, "not to mention possibly trying to kill the king, is someone from Merletta's home. Wherever that is."

"I didn't say that," Heath protested. "I still don't know it for sure."

Brody gave him a look, and Heath scowled.

"Look, I really don't know, all right? What do you want me to say? It's not like I've forgotten about it. I've spent two days trying to figure out what to do, and everywhere I turn, it's disaster for someone."

Brody's brow was creased, but he didn't look angry for a change. "I know Merletta's important to you, Heath. But can protecting her secrets really be worth your brother's life?"

"Percival isn't going to be executed," said Heath. "I'm not

going to let that happen, whether or not I can convince the king of his innocence."

"But it's not just about Percival, is it?" Brody asked, his grave words making a much greater impression than any angry outburst. "If Merletta's people are targeting us...even willing to make an attempt on the life of our king..."

Heath squirmed uncomfortably under his cousin's serious gaze.

"Bianca and I have been talking since the other day," Brody continued. "We're not King Matlock's greatest admirers right now, but we're not sure we can keep this from him in good conscience."

"Neither am I," Heath admitted miserably. "That's the unsolvable problem I've been trying to solve for the last two days." He ran a weary hand over his eyes, checking in on Merletta. She was still swimming.

"And it's my problem to solve, not yours, Brody. What would you tell the king? That Merletta and I once met on an island—which incidentally, is not where she comes from—but if he tried to sail there, he would be prevented from reaching it by the impassable East Seas? And that you don't know where to find the rest of her kind, or what exactly is the nature of the threat? You'd achieve nothing but making the king as suspicious of me as he is of the rest of you. Which might be a worthwhile aim in your mind," he added bitterly, remembering the grief Brody had given him over King Matlock's subtle approval of Heath since he foiled the assassination attempt.

"No, I don't want that," Brody said quietly. "I know I'm usually too stubborn to admit it, but I do actually know that you're our best hope of resolving this mess."

No pressure, Heath thought. The words sounded petulant in his mind, but he was so sick of everyone doing their utmost to inflame tensions, then looking to him to fix an already impossible situation.

"I really do need to go now," he told his cousin. "But I'll decide what I'm doing soon. And then we can talk. I promise."

Brody didn't look satisfied, but he made no further attempt to detain him as Heath strode from the training yard with his bow still in hand, heading toward the castle.

A few minutes later, he was settled in a corner of a public garden that opened onto the castle. It was a large garden, with plenty of quiet spots to hide. Heath had hoped to show Merletta some of the more elaborate garden beds, but her time in Bryford had been too short.

It was always too short. No matter how much time they had together, it never felt like enough. The ache of missing her was a constant discomfort in his gut, like the continuous pinprick of her presence in his mind, thanks to the connection he'd forged with his farsight. It had been so many weeks since he'd seen her.

At least, since he'd seen her in person.

She filled his vision at that moment, her face determined as she moved through dim water. Heath tried to see her companions, but he couldn't. Perhaps it was because he was alone now, without Reka's magic to bolster his, or even the smaller boost provided by Brody's magic. But in his anxiety, he seemed to have regressed, once again only able to see her face, not her surroundings.

He felt a bit guilty for his eavesdropping, but he nevertheless listened avidly as Merletta told her friends what she'd discovered about her family. His hand clenched convulsively on the stone bench beside him. He wished he could be there, his hand on hers while she wrestled with these weighty matters. He knew how much it must mean to her to discover where she'd come from. She'd mentioned something about learning the names of her parents once, but they'd had no time for her to explain it.

He followed with trepidation while Merletta's interview with the Record Master began. To Heath's frustration, his farsight continued to be limited to Merletta's image. No matter how he tried to draw on his magic, he couldn't seem to tease it out enough to show the merman to whom she was speaking.

It didn't surprise him to hear how brazenly she spoke to the leader who undoubtedly held her life in his hands. More than once he let out a small groan, his head dropping into his hands as Merletta spoke. He noted that she made no mention of him, or of finding her legs.

"Good gracious, Heath, who's died?"

The anxious voice made Heath look up, to see his grandmother standing two feet away from him.

He blinked rapidly, emerging from deep water. He needed to work on maintaining awareness of his immediate surroundings while exercising his farsight.

"Grandmother," he said, standing quickly. Merletta's image faded from his mind, although he was still painfully aware of her. "How did you find my hiding place?"

"I followed your signature," said his grandmother, settling onto the seat and gesturing for him to do the same. "I don't know exactly what you were doing, but it was using a lot of magic."

"I was watching Merletta," Heath said simply, as he lowered himself to sit beside her. "And being terrified by her fearlessness."

"I see." She studied him thoughtfully. "She's still alive, then?"

"For the moment," Heath said miserably.

She let out a breath, settling against the back of the bench, her eyes still fixed on his face.

"I've just gone to visit Percival," she said conversationally.

Heath looked up, dismayed. "Grandmother, the dungeons are no place for you."

She gave him an amused smile. "I'm not as delicate as you might think, Heath. I've seen my share of confronting things."

Heath let the matter drop. "How was Percival?" he asked.

"I didn't get to see him," the princess answered. "The guard wouldn't let me in. He said his new instructions are that visits must be authorized by the king."

"Yes." Heath scowled. "I heard King Matlock say as much not long ago."

She raised an eyebrow. "He issued the order in front of you? Was he trying to be inflammatory?"

"Oh, no, he didn't know I could hear," Heath said matter-of-factly.

His grandmother looked confused, so Heath drew on his magic, using more than necessary as he cast his farsight over Percival. His brother was bored, and understandably tense, but otherwise fine.

"Heath!" His grandmother had obviously sensed his use of magic, and grasped what he was trying to say. "You're telling me you listened to the king instructing his guards by way of..." She waved a hand toward the air, as if his magic was a visible substance floating past them.

Heath shrugged, unrepentant. "Should I be apologizing?"

She eyed him shrewdly. "I don't know. Maybe. Surely you comprehend how dangerous that ability could be. How powerful, and in the wrong hands, sinister."

"Of course I do," Heath assured her. "Why do you think I haven't told the king about my talents?"

She still looked troubled, and he turned toward her, speaking more seriously.

"I'm not ordinarily in the habit of surveilling the king," he told her. "I don't want to follow him all the time, and even if I did want to, I don't have the skill. Farsight doesn't let you see anyone and everyone at will. There has to be a connection between you. Even Reka would struggle to just follow King Matlock. But he has no trouble watching me from afar, because of the depth of relationship between us."

"So how did you overhear the king's order?" she asked.

"I've used my farsight to create a limited connection," Heath said, warming to the topic in spite of himself. It had been a complex and difficult task, and he was quite proud of his success. "It's not like the connection I have with Merletta."

"What's that connection like?" his grandmother asked, sounding fascinated.

"I imagine it's a bit like what Reka experiences with me," Heath said. "He doesn't literally watch me all the time, but it's as though we're at opposite ends of a thread, and if I say his name, the thread is tugged, grabbing his attention. For me, I'm constantly aware of Merletta. Usually it's just in the background —I'm so used to it now, I barely notice it most of the time. And if I want to see what she's doing, like I did just now, I don't really have to concentrate in order to connect in."

"Does she know about this connection you've forged?" the princess challenged.

Heath leaned forward, resting his elbows on his knees. "Yes," he said. "I've told her. She says she doesn't mind. Sometimes she uses it, to tell me things. It must be frustrating for her not to be able to see or hear my response, though."

"But the king doesn't know you can watch him," his grandmother pointed out.

"Then I suppose it's a good thing I don't watch him very often," Heath said. "It's a matter of investment—I don't have anything like the personal investment in him that I have in Merletta."

"So how were you able to create a connection, however limited?" pressed the princess.

"It's as much a connection with Percival as it is with the king," Heath explained. "Perce is easy for me to see, and even King Matlock is sufficiently within my circle of concern for me to catch glimpses of him from time to time, when my magic is being most cooperative. With some practice, I've sort of...woven my magic around the king in such a way that any mention he makes of Percival activates my extra sight."

"So your magic—and by extension some corner of your mind—is always listening for a prompt. In addition to watching Merletta half the day, unless I'm much mistaken." She pursed her lips. "That sounds exhausting."

"It is a lot," Heath acknowledged, his weight still resting on his knees.

She laid one wrinkled hand on his arm. "It's too much, Heath. You'll be torn in two if you keep this up much longer."

"I'm fine," Heath told her dismissively. He ran a hand over his chin, feeling the rugged growth there. It had been days since he'd shaved. He'd been too distracted to care about such trivialities.

"Heath." Something in his companion's tone compelled him to look up and meet her eyes. "You're not fine. I don't mean to insult you, but the strain is showing. You look a mess."

"How do you expect me to look, Grandmother?" Heath protested, frustrated. "Percival still has a noose dangling over him, and Merletta has just put her head in the shark's mouth. Should I just be going happily about my life as if everything is normal?"

"I don't blame you for being distressed," she responded. "We all are. But it won't do anyone any good for you to stretch yourself so thin you break."

"My best chance of keeping Percival alive is to be alerted as soon as the king decides to set an execution date," Heath told her. "I can't afford to be taken by surprise."

She was still frowning at him, apparently considering her response, when the sound of approaching wind made them both look up. Reka descended in slow circles, eventually alighting right in the middle of a well-manicured garden bed nearby.

"Greetings, Heath," he said placidly, inclining his head slightly then swiveling to face Heath's grandmother. "Greetings, Princess Jocelyn, dragonfriend of my sire."

"Greetings, Rekavidur," she said softly. "I am glad to see you again."

He inclined his head once more, although his gaze was already traveling back to Heath. "Did I just hear you instructing the princess on the use of farsight? Has she developed a new type of magic so late in life?"

"No, I'm happy to say," Heath's grandmother responded dryly. "It sounds like more responsibility than I think I can handle."

"What a curious perspective," Rekavidur said, sounding intrigued. "Do you consider your own magic more pleasure or responsibility?"

"Let's not get into a discussion of magic lore," Heath interjected quickly. "Reka, you can interrogate my grandmother later."

"I would be wise not to count on that," Reka pointed out. "She is, after all, of an advanced age for a human."

"Watch whose age you're calling advanced," laughed the princess. "I'm not on my deathbed yet."

Reka looked like he was going to give a literal answer, but Heath once again jumped in.

"Did you come with a message, Reka? I know you don't especially like the capital, so I doubt you came just to chat."

"You are correct," Reka acknowledged. "I wished to report to you that I returned to my colony and spoke with the elders as we discussed."

"And?" Heath asked eagerly, hope sprouting inside him.

"And they did not accept my testimony concerning the origins of the settlement we once observed off the coast near your home. As I feared, in the absence of tangible evidence, they were not swayed by our speculation that the more advanced abominations were separate creatures entirely, not returning to the place of their origin, but visiting from a distant home."

Heath slumped back in his chair, the small shoot of hope withering away into nothing. He could sense his grandmother's curiosity beside him, but he didn't have the heart to explain at that moment.

If it came to that, a guilty part of him was relieved by Rekavidur's interruption. Left alone with his grandmother much longer, his conscience would probably have compelled him to tell her what he'd discovered about the possible connection between Merletta's kind and the attacks in Valoria.

"I suppose I shouldn't be surprised that our feeble attempt to stop disaster achieved nothing," he said bitterly.

"I did not say it achieved nothing," Rekavidur said. "In fact, I believe it did spark a reaction, although it certainly wasn't the one we were hoping for."

"What do you mean?" Heath asked ominously.

"The elders did not share their intentions with me," explained Reka. "But I formed the impression that by raising the matter, I may have redirected their focus to the underwater civilization. I expect they will send scouts to hunt for Merletta's home within the week."

Heath let out a groan, his fingers twisting despairingly in his hair. The situation was worse than hopeless.

CHAPTER FOURTEEN

"You're very quiet."

Merletta looked up at Andre's comment, slowing to let a trio of first years speed past them, eager to reach the dining hall for lunch.

Andre's eyes were narrowed in suspicion. "What are you plotting?"

Merletta restrained a smile. Her friends knew her well. But she didn't intend to share her plans with Andre on this occasion.

"I'm thinking about yesterday," she said instead. "It didn't go how I expected."

"I don't think any of us expected to just swim out of there," agreed Andre. "Or for the Record Master to be so unperturbed. Do you think he didn't believe you?"

"He believed me," said Merletta grimly. She shook her head. "I should have learned by now, but it never fails to surprise me how measured the Center's responses are."

It was true. Knowing the unscrupulous lengths to which they were willing to go, she always expected a swift and decisive attack each time she drifted out of line. But they were more careful than that, especially since she'd turned their battle into a public display.

They'd reached the dining hall by this time, and Merletta scanned the room for Sage and Emil. They were both there, sitting at a table with other record holders, but apart a little way, their heads bent together. They had the look of being marked. Merletta found herself hoping the Center would act soon. It had only been a day, and the strain was already unsustainable.

When they all rose from the meal, Emil and Andre drifted out first, deep in conversation about their best guesses as to the Center's next move. Sage lingered behind, swimming more slowly with Merletta.

"Have you been to see your family?" Merletta asked her friend softly. "Given we don't know how much time we have?" She was fairly sure she knew the answer.

Sure enough, Sage shook her head. "I don't have anything to say to my parents, or any interest in anything they might say to me."

"Sage..." Merletta hesitated. "I don't want to be the reason you aren't speaking to your mother."

"You're not," Sage said shortly, her tail flicking. "Her actions are the reason."

"You know what I mean," Merletta said, unimpressed. She followed Sage from the dining hall. "Her actions toward me."

"It wasn't just toward you," Sage said. "She was using me as well, you know. She encouraged me to believe that she was inviting you to stay with us because she wanted to show kindness to my closest friend. And all along she was following orders to spy on you." Sage scowled. "She even put my little sister up to watching you—remember how she used to hang around, and let herself into your room randomly?"

Merletta winced a little as she nodded. She'd already drawn that connection in her mind.

"The worst part of it is she can't see how she did anything wrong by me," Sage burst out. "By either of us. My own mother! Don't you think that shows just how messed up the Center's whole system is?"

"I do," Merletta assured her. "That's exactly what I think. Which seems to me all the more reason not to blame it all on your mother. She was doing what she's been trained to do. I'm sure she even thought it was the right thing."

Sage was silent for a moment. "If that's true," she said quietly, "then I have no idea what I was ever doing here. I don't want to be a record holder if that's what the role is all about." She sent Merletta a pleading look. "You're very generous, Merletta, and I admire that. But the betrayal was more personal for me. I don't know how to get past it. Especially since it's sullied the goal I've dedicated my life to achieving."

Merletta slid her arm through her friend's, giving it a squeeze. "I understand," she told her. "We're all grappling with disillusionment. But..." She hesitated, not wanting to push too hard. She could see now how complex the whole situation was for Sage, personally speaking. "But if the end of our civilization is hanging over us, is it maybe the time to forgive even if it hurts? Even if it's not deserved?"

Sage just flicked a shoulder, and Merletta let the matter drop. It wasn't really her business, after all. They'd almost reached the drop off, and Sage glanced around, confused.

"Where are we going?"

"You're going wherever you want to go—I'm going to the island," Merletta said simply. "I know there's a risk if I'm followed, but who knows if I'll get another chance? I need to see Tish."

She expected her friend to argue. But Sage just looked at her out of thoughtful eyes.

"I'm coming," she said. "It's well past time, and like you said, I don't know if there'll be another chance."

Merletta nodded gratefully. "Since Tilssted is closed off, we'll have to exit the barrier through Hemssted, and go the long way around," she informed her friend. "It will mean a longer swim, but it's probably for the best. The barrier isn't nearly as tightly manned in the other cities as it is in Tilssted."

She glanced back across the drop off. It was empty, but her sense of unease didn't disappear.

"What is it?" Sage asked.

Merletta frowned. "Hopefully nothing. I just feel...conspicuous. Like someone's following us. But I always feel that way these days. It might be just in my head."

Sage glanced back as well, looking unnerved. "I know what you mean," she said. "I often feel like everyone's looking at me, like they somehow know everything I'm hiding. But I don't feel that way any more than usual right now."

Merletta nodded, continuing eastward across the drop off and into Hemssted. She couldn't help casting a glance toward the El residence as they skirted Hemssted's main square. A strange sensation passed over her—like nostalgia, but without the memories to give it solidity. Nostalgia for what might have been, perhaps.

She dismissed it, focusing her attention ahead. The El family had played no significant role in her past—at least, not in her living memory—and there was unlikely to be opportunity for them to play a part in her future.

They passed the barrier without incident, Sage looking impressed by Merletta's stealth and tactics for evasion of the guards patrolling the area. Neither of them spoke until they were well clear of the triple kingdoms.

"It's beautiful out here," Sage said, her voice awed as they wove their way between fronds of coral. "Where are all the terrifying dangers?"

Merletta chuckled. "They're out here. But if we're smart, we can probably avoid them. And if not, we have these." She patted her spear, growing excited by the unexpected chance to show Sage her world. "If you think this is beautiful, wait until we get to the island! It's incredible."

"I'm eager to see it," Sage said. "I'm sorry it's taken me so long to work up the courage to come with you." Her lithe form seemed to deflate a bit. "I guess I'm not as brave as Emil and Andre."

"Of course you are," Merletta protested. She gestured at the empty water around them. "I don't see either of them here. Although now you mention it," she added with a grimace, "Emil will have my hide for taking you outside the barrier without protection."

Sage scowled. "Emil can mind his own business."

Merletta glanced at her friend, eyebrows raised. "Do you really mind his protectiveness so much? He's just worried about your safety."

Sage took a moment to answer. "Yes, he's certainly a worrier. I don't really like the constant reminders that he doesn't think I'm strong enough for the coming fight, though."

"I don't think it's your strength that's the issue," Merletta told her.

"Of course it is," Sage said, trying and failing to speak lightly. "You're in more danger than I am, and he never questions the appropriateness of your involvement. And neither should he," she added hastily, as if worried Merletta would be offended. "You're more than strong enough for all this. He's always admired that about you. That and your determination."

Merletta stared at her. "You can't seriously think that's why he gets all disapproving about you putting yourself in danger, and not me."

Sage didn't seem to be listening. She cleared her throat, not meeting Merletta's eye as she spoke again. "Merletta, do you think Emil fully understands the nature of the connection between you and Heath? When you've mentioned Heath, it doesn't seem to me like he...gets it." She snuck a glance at Merletta's face. "I suppose it's ridiculous to even talk about things like that when we're all under a death order, but I would hate to see him get hurt out of all this."

Merletta didn't know whether to laugh or give her friend a good hard shove. "Sage, I honestly don't know how you could be misreading Emil so hopelessly. He gets stressed about you being in danger because he cares more about you than he does about me."

"That's not true," Sage said, her face heating as she fixed her eyes on a harmless ray making its way across the sand beneath them. "He admires you a lot."

"Admiring someone is not the same thing as caring about them," Merletta retorted. She frowned as she studied her friend's face. It was tempting to give Sage a good hard talking to, but there was every possibility that would do more harm than good. "Just take my word for it, Sage," she said firmly. "There's no kind of romantic interest between Emil and me, in either direction. I doubt he cares what I think of Heath, but either way, I'm confident he's not at risk of being hurt by me. Not like that."

Sage looked unconvinced, but she didn't argue. They'd neared familiar waters now, north of Tilssted. Merletta started pointing out landmarks, telling Sage how she'd used this route for her memory journey, in place of the mind palace the program taught trainees to form in order to store information. Sage was fascinated by it all, and the awkwardness of their earlier conversation soon faded.

When the water began to grow shallow, Merletta could sense Sage's nerves.

"Don't worry," she assured her friend. "You can watch from the water until you're comfortable."

"What?" Sage looked alarmed. "I was planning to stay in the water."

Merletta shook her head. "No way. You've come all the way here—it's time for you to find your legs."

She gave Sage no chance to retort. Her body rippled into motion, her arms at her side as her tail worked up and down, sending her smoothly over the top of the coral ring that surrounded Vazula. When the water was too shallow to swim, she waddled up toward the beach with her hands, flipping her tail around her until she was fully out of the water.

She heard Sage's gasp as the transformation took place. Pushing herself to her feet, Merletta turned to grin at her friend.

"Pretty impressive, right?"

Sage's eyes were unnaturally round as she stared back at Merletta, taking in every inch of her new form.

"I don't think I can do that," she said, sounding slightly queasy.

"Of course you can," said Merletta briskly. "I'll help you, come on." She waded forward into the water, not far enough to trigger the return of her tail, just far enough to reach for Sage. "I can pull you up."

"Are you sure about this?" Sage's voice was nervous, although she swam forward slowly.

"Absolutely sure," Merletta promised. "August, Eloise, Griffin, Paul, and Tish have all done it successfully—I've seen them."

She gripped Sage's trembling hands and tugged, pulling her friend from the water.

"It hurts!" Sage gasped, her voice breathless with fear.

"I know," Merletta told her. "And I'm sorry about that. But it's just because your body isn't used to it. After a few times it will feel quite comfortable."

She hauled Sage up the beach a little, then sat beside her on the sand. The other mermaid flopped onto her back, her breath coming in gasps as her body completed its first, slow transformation. Merletta squeezed her hand reassuringly, remembering her own panic the first time she'd dried out.

"It's working," she assured her friend, watching the scales on Sage's tail ripple frantically. "It will be done soon, and then it won't hurt."

With a last shudder, Sage lay still, her tail gone, and two legs sticking out from underneath the coral-colored scaly skirt she now wore.

"That was terrifying," she whispered. "I thought I was going to die."

"I know," Merletta told her sympathetically. "Maybe I should have given you more time to gear yourself up, but I was worried you would just talk yourself out of it."

"I would have," Sage said fervently. She pushed herself up into a sitting position, her eyes moving so slowly Merletta suspected she wasn't entirely sure she wanted to see her new legs.

It was impossible to miss the moment when she caught sight of them. She stilled completely, her mouth falling comically open.

"It's strange, isn't it?" Merletta said. "But amazing once you learn to use them." She sprung eagerly to her feet, extending a hand. "Come on. Let me show you how."

Sage accepted the offered help, her movements wobbly as she struggled to her feet. She listed immediately to the side, her arms flailing so wildly that she came free of Merletta's grip and fell promptly onto her backside.

"How in the world can you balance without your fins?" she demanded. "Everything feels so...heavy!"

Merletta couldn't help laughing. "It is a bit like that, isn't it? As for balance, you use your feet. Look, you put them forward one at a time, like this." She walked slowly across the sand and back, exaggerating her movements for Sage's benefit. "Now you try."

But before Sage could get up, there was a violent rustling nearby, and someone hurtled out of the jungle.

"Merletta!"

Merletta lowered her weapon, her heart's suddenly escalated beat slowing once more as she took in Griffin's form.

"Griffin, you scared me half to death. What's the matter?"

"What are you doing here?" he demanded, ignoring her reproach. "Surely it's not safe for you to leave the barrier."

Merletta shrugged. "We decided to take the risk."

Griffin's eyes passed to Sage, seeming to see her for the first time. "Who are you?" he asked suspiciously. His expression softened as he watched Sage attempting clumsily to rise. "First time with your legs?"

"Merletta assures me it gets easier, but I'm skeptical," Sage said ruefully.

Griffin laughed. "It does, I promise. I was just as hopeless when I first found my legs."

Merletta noted his change of demeanor with a sigh. Most likely he'd suspected her of bringing another human to the island.

"This is Sage," she told him, waving a hand. "And Sage, this is Griffin, one of the guards from August's patrol."

"Glad to meet you," he said kindly, leaving Merletta to wish he'd show half the same level of politeness to Heath.

She squirmed slightly as she remembered Heath's claim as to the reason for Griffin's behavior. She still found it hard to believe. The irony wasn't lost on her, given the conversation she and Sage had just had.

Another figure stepped out onto the sand, and Merletta smiled at Paul, performing introductions again. She searched the foliage behind the guard.

"Are August and Eloise around? They made it back safely, didn't they?"

Paul nodded. "They made it back fine. They're on the other side of the island at the moment. We're taking turns systematically searching every inch of this place, as instructed."

"And?" Merletta pressed.

He sighed. "Nothing yet. We've found some interesting records, and artifacts from the people who used to live here. But nothing that provides evidence about our own origins."

"We did find some drawings of merpeople," Griffin offered. "Etched into the stone of a cave. We even came across a sketch on paper. But that just suggests that the people here knew about us. It doesn't prove that we somehow came from here."

Merletta bit her lip, unsurprised, but disappointed all the same.

"I think you're the one who should be answering questions. What was so important that you risked your life—and ours—to come here?" Griffin asked, his stern tone seeming to reinforce Merletta's earlier thoughts about attraction and overprotectiveness.

"I need to see Tish," Merletta said. "She must feel like I've abandoned her."

The two guards exchanged a glance that filled Merletta with foreboding, and neither of them immediately answered.

"What is it?" she demanded.

Paul cleared his throat. "She's not here, Merletta."

"What do you mean?" Merletta asked. "Is she still hanging around at the lagoon?"

"No, we mean she's not on the island," Griffin supplied. "She left. Two days ago."

"What do you mean, left?" Merletta said, aghast. "She can't have left!"

Paul scratched the back of his neck uncomfortably. "But she has. There's no reason to think it wasn't voluntary. We've checked everywhere on the island she might plausibly go. She must have returned to the ocean."

"But she's terrified of the open ocean," Merletta protested. "And she's not equipped to survive out there alone."

"We've searched the immediate area multiple times," Paul said quietly. "She's not here. We think she might have returned to the triple kingdoms. Or at least, tried to."

Merletta ran her hands over her face, trying not to panic. If Tish had made it all the way back to the triple kingdoms, she'd done well. But there was no way she would get past the guards at the barrier. She had none of the experience Merletta had in stealth.

"I'm glad you're here, Merletta," Paul said. "We haven't known how to contact you safely. If we had, we would have told you about Letitia leaving. August told us that you intended to notify the Record Master of the threat from the dragons. Did you do that?"

Merletta nodded. "Yesterday. He hasn't done anything about it yet, or at least nothing visible. But I have no doubt he will soon."

Griffin and Paul exchanged another look. "We want to return with you," Paul said.

"What?" Merletta looked between them. "But you're so much safer here."

"We're not hiding here for safety," Griffin said, as if offended by the suggestion. "We were here to protect Letitia, and she obviously didn't want our protection. We have loved ones back in the triple kingdoms, and we haven't seen them for a long time. We don't want to wait out here while destruction races toward our home."

"But someone has to keep searching the island," Merletta said desperately. "We have to find answers."

Neither guard looked excited by the prospect. "We all know we're not likely to find anything," Griffin said impatiently.

"I can't stop you, of course," Merletta said. "But at least tell me you'll talk it over with August."

"We have," Paul said dryly. "He's not convinced."

Merletta looked at him helplessly. "That's between you," she said. "I have to go."

"But you just got here," Griffin protested. "You've barely told us what's going on."

"I have to find Tish," Merletta said. "I got her into this mess, and I can't leave her at the mercy of the open ocean!"

"If she's in the open ocean, you'll never find her," Paul said brutally. "Your best hope is that she made it back to the triple kingdoms."

"Then that's where I have to start," said Merletta firmly. She turned to Sage. "I'm sorry you didn't get to properly see the island, Sage."

Her friend shook her head. "Don't be silly, of course Tish is more important. I'll help you look for her."

With a nod of gratitude, Merletta waded back into the water. Her legs turned sleekly to tail as she dove back under, and in moments she was swimming toward the triple kingdoms, Sage on her fins.

They'd barely cleared the coral when movement caused Merletta to pull up. She peered hopefully through the sparkling waters, willing it to be Tish returning to the island.

But the tail of the mermaid trying unsuccessfully to hide

behind a coral-covered shelf wasn't green like Tish's. It was a pale, shimmering blue.

"Indigo?" The name burst from Sage, her voice aghast. "What are you doing here?"

Indigo floated slowly out from her hiding place, her eyes wide as they flicked between Sage and Merletta.

"Following you," she told Merletta blankly. "Like usual. Did...did you just turn into a human?"

CHAPTER FIFTEEN

Merletta

Merletta's mouth opened and closed twice before she managed to get any words out.

"Did you say you were following me *like usual*?" she said at last, dodging Indigo's question.

The other mermaid shifted uncomfortably, showing none of the brazen confidence she'd had at the previous Founders' Day when she explained to Andre that she'd been instructed to watch Merletta by a senior Center guard.

"I've been following you since you took your third year test," she admitted. "I'm surprised you haven't spotted me."

"I had the feeling someone was tailing me," Merletta told her. "But I'll admit I never saw you. I'm impressed."

Indigo's smile was a little painful. "I spent a lot of time with Andre's family growing up. Most of the brothers didn't want their annoying little cousin yapping at their heels. I used to follow them whenever they tried to ditch me. I got pretty good at it."

"Good at sneaking around," Sage said coldly. "What an admirable skill." She turned to Merletta. "What are we going to do? We can't let her report to the Center guards about the island."

"I'm not here under anyone's instructions," Indigo interjected, her expression defiant.

Merletta raised an eyebrow. "And we're supposed to believe that? We heard you tell Andre you'd been directed to spy on me."

"I was," Indigo acknowledged. "But that was last year. I haven't reported to anyone in months. No one knows I'm here."

"What's changed?" Sage asked suspiciously.

"I have, I suppose." Indigo's honest answer was disarming. "I'm sure you think I'm a traitor, like Andre does. But I never realized I was working against him. I thought he was doing the same as I was."

"Yes, we heard all that," Sage said, her voice still hard. "You thought his friendship with Merletta was a scam, designed to win her trust then betray her to the authorities."

Irritation flickered across Indigo's pale features, and Merletta found herself warming to the other mermaid a little in spite of herself. Indigo's indignation made it easier to believe that she had genuinely thought herself to be doing the right thing.

"My point is, I never meant to betray Andre. He's family. And I know him pretty well, I think—he's not the type either to be easily deceived or to deceive me. I honestly didn't know what to make of it all after you came back from wherever you'd exiled yourself. I would've asked Andre to explain it all better, but he refused to even come near me."

Merletta winced. She couldn't help it. Perhaps it was the absence of a family of her own, but she still felt horribly uncomfortable at the thought that she'd created rifts in the families of two of her closest friends.

"So I went to see August and Eloise," Indigo said matter-of-factly.

Merletta stared at her. "You did?"

The other mermaid nodded. "They told me a very different tale from the official one. And it was pretty hard to dismiss their account as fanciful or exaggerated. I mean, have you met August?"

"He's as credible as they come," Merletta agreed. She studied the other mermaid. "They took a risk, trusting you with the truth."

"Not really," Indigo said. "I think you have the wrong idea about my level of involvement in...whatever all this is. I don't have authority, and I'm not in anyone's ear. I was just told to keep an eye on you, report back about your movements."

Merletta frowned. "But I came here, a week after I passed my test. Does that mean the Center already knows about the others living here?" Fear flashed through her. Was that what happened to Tish? The guards thought she'd left voluntarily, but was it possible someone from the Center had actually gotten her?

But Indigo was shaking her head. "I never followed you outside the barrier. I never even followed you as far as the barrier. I usually just saw what city you were entering. Even if I'd known you were leaving the triple kingdoms, I wouldn't have been brave enough to follow." She glanced at the water around her. "This is the first time I've ever been outside the barrier."

"Why did you follow this time?" Sage demanded.

"Because of you," Indigo told her simply. "I saw you going with Merletta. I've watched her quite a bit, and..." Her gaze flicked to Merletta. "I knew that whatever your politics, you wouldn't choose to endanger a friend. I figured it must be safer than I thought."

For a moment there was silence as the two friends regarded her thoughtfully.

"So is it my turn for some answers?" Indigo asked, her tail flicking slightly.

Merletta couldn't help smiling. It was clear that this forthright manner was more natural to Indigo than her chastened one of earlier, and Merletta found she liked her the better for it.

"Answers about what?" she asked innocently.

Indigo gave her an incredulous look. "What do you think? I just watched you both grow legs!"

"Oh, that," said Merletta casually. "Yes, that's what happens when you dry out. It's probably the Center's biggest lie."

Indigo's eyes were impossibly wide. "But surely they don't know about it," she said. "Surely they'd be as astonished as—"

Her words died away at the pitying look Sage was giving her. Indigo bit her lip, her mind clearly whirling.

"That's what August meant, isn't it?" she whispered. "He accused the Center of systematic deception. He even said they're willing to murder anyone who threatens their lies."

"Did he?" Merletta said, pleased. "Good on him for speaking so plainly."

Indigo was silent for another moment, then her head came slowly up to meet Merletta's eye.

"I'm on your side," she said firmly. "Yours, and Andre's, and August's, and whoever else is trying to expose the truth. I don't want to be part of the Center's lies."

"Just like that?" Merletta let out an incredulous laugh.

Indigo shrugged. "Did you want me to make a blood pact?"

"No, thanks," said Sage dryly. "This may not be my first time outside the barrier, but I don't think I'm quite ready to tangle with a shark."

Merletta was still staring at Indigo. "So you're just...changing sides?"

"Wouldn't you, if you found out you'd unwittingly joined the side of liars and murderers?" Indigo demanded.

"I would," said Merletta unhesitatingly.

"How unwitting was it, though?" Sage challenged, her usually pleasant brow darkened. Like the true friend she was, she was taking Indigo's wrongs toward Merletta much harder than she'd take an offense against herself. "You were told to spy on a fellow trainee—to pretend to befriend her for the purpose of reporting on her without her knowledge. Can you really claim to be astonished to discover you were on the side of liars?"

Shame flitted across Indigo's features. "That's fair," she said quietly. "And I should have known better. But I honestly thought Andre was doing the same. And I assumed that if someone so official was giving the instructions, it must be all right."

Merletta let out a bubbled stream of water. Indigo was hardly the first to fall into that easy trap. Those in authority in the Center were practiced at taking advantage of their position of trust to manipulate well-meaning individuals into doing things they wouldn't otherwise think were acceptable.

"But how can we trust you?" Sage asked.

Indigo gave a helpless shrug. "I don't know. What can I do to prove I'm telling the truth? I suppose you'll figure it out eventually, when I don't report about this to anyone." She gave Merletta a shrewd look. "Because something tells me that whatever the danger to the others on that land, you're not going to make me disappear in order to stop me telling anyone."

"You're right about that," said Merletta, with a touch of humor. "I'm not in the habit of murdering fellow trainees."

"Did they really murder some of August's patrol?" Indigo asked, her voice small again. "It's hard to believe they'd go to those lengths."

"Not so hard to believe," Merletta said absently. "It's nothing new. I'm pretty sure they murdered my parents for a similar reason, and that was almost two decades ago."

"What?" Indigo looked aghast, but Merletta's thoughts were elsewhere.

"Indigo, I don't want to put you in danger, but if you really want a way to show that you—"

"Yes, I do," Indigo cut her off. "I really do want to help."

"Well, in that case, I think you *should* report this. To whoever you used to report to."

"What?" Sage stared at Merletta like she'd lost her mind. "Merletta, what are you talking about?"

"Don't pretend it isn't killing you, Sage, waiting for the blow to fall. I have to know what the Record Master is going to do about our disclosures yesterday. If Indigo goes to her contact to report this outing—or at least, a fictional version of this outing with just enough truth to make it credible—maybe she could get a clue as to what's coming."

"I suppose it might work," said Sage reluctantly.

"I'll do it." Indigo was clearly struggling to fill in the gaps, but what she lacked in comprehension, she made up for in eagerness.

"Can you be convincing enough to fool them?" Merletta asked doubtfully. "I don't want to endanger you by sending you in with a false tale."

"I can do it," Indigo said confidently. "Honestly, the most suspicious part will probably be approaching you to report back. They know I didn't succeed very well in befriending you last year."

Merletta gave her a wry smile. "If you'd been more like this instead of the overly friendly persona you put on every time I came into the room, you probably would have."

Indigo flashed her a grin, then instantly sobered again. "Will you...will you tell Andre about this? Tell him I'm truly trying to help now?"

Merletta took a moment to answer. "I'll tell him what's

happened today. I guess your actions will speak for themselves." She fixed Indigo with a penetrating look. "You're right that there's no way for us to silence you that I'm willing to take. So we're in your hands. Just know that more lives than ours might depend on you keeping the true story of this island to yourself."

"I won't carry tales," Indigo promised. "I don't want blood on my hands. I never did. Just tell me what you want me to say to the guard."

The three of them thrashed out the best story to tell as they swam back toward the triple kingdoms. Merletta felt a pang of unease at the risk to Indigo. But then again, they were all in constant risk now. And she couldn't deny that it lightened her heart to see Andre's cousin come good when confronted with the truth of the Center's tactics. It made her dare to hope that many of those currently carrying out the Center's dirty work would make different choices if they knew what they were really part of.

She and Sage parted ways with Indigo before re-entering the triple kingdoms—Merletta just had to hope the younger trainee wasn't exaggerating about being good at sneaking around, given she would be on her own when it came to getting through the barrier.

As Merletta and Sage approached the barrier together, Merletta caught a flash of movement and pulled her friend back into a clump of seaweed. The fronds waved gently around them, reaching high above their heads as the two of them peered through, toward the patrol paused at the border not far away. They were in conversation with a small group of merpeople on the inside of the barrier, the words too quiet for Merletta and Sage to hear.

"Look," Sage whispered. "That group definitely aren't guards, but the ones on duty are letting them through! Are they opening the barrier because of what you told the Record Master, do you think?"

Merletta frowned, studying the group who were now moving out into the open ocean, thankfully not in their direction.

"I don't know. I'd like to think so, but they didn't look like they were carrying supplies for an extended absence. I caught Center armbands on at least some of them. They must be someone official."

Sage nodded her agreement. "Maybe they're making preparations for setting up a safe base outside the triple kingdoms," she suggested. "Maybe they're going to start relocating everyone, in the hopes of clearing the place before the dragons come."

"Maybe." Merletta wasn't convinced, but she had to assume that the clandestine activity—for the interaction had certainly been furtive—had something to do with the Center's response to the coming crisis.

She was relieved when they finally managed to get past the guards into the city, after almost an hour of tense waiting. Normally Merletta wouldn't travel to Vazula so late in the day— she preferred to avoid shark feeding time. But on the other hand, the near darkness was probably the only thing that allowed them to get through the tightened border security.

"So much for the border not being this closely guarded outside Tilssted," Sage muttered, as soon as they were safely into the streets.

"That was this morning," Merletta said grimly. "Things are going to change pretty quickly from now, I imagine."

Sage frowned. "But what's the point of manning the border? That won't stop dragons."

"Maybe they think it will give us warning of their approach?" Merletta guessed.

She fell silent as a small patrol squad swam past, weapons

gripped tightly and strokes purposeful. They were well above the seabed, and the two mermaids followed their movement as they ascended swiftly.

Merletta heard Sage's quiet gasp when they caught sight of the formation above them, with guards spread evenly but sparsely in a half bubble perhaps half a league above their heads. They hadn't even noticed it before, and Merletta chastised herself for her lack of observation. Most merpeople didn't look up very often, but she knew better.

"Surely there's no reason to guard the barrier upward except for dragons," Sage murmured. "I guess that means the Record Master believed you. That's something, at least."

Merletta nodded slowly. She supposed she should be encouraged. But putting extra guards on patrol—armed with only the usual spears—didn't suggest the Center had any very effective plan for how to hold off a colony of dragons.

"If only he'd take up my offer to get in contact with the dragons," she burst out. "I could speak to Heath right now, and he could tell Reka. I know the dragons tried to kill me on sight, but I'm a random lowly mermaid. Surely it's worth at least *trying* to arrange formal negotiations between them and the leaders of our civilization. There's nothing to lose, so even the slim chance of gaining something seems worth it."

"I'm guessing the Record Master hasn't been in touch since yesterday to take advantage of your offer," Sage said dryly.

Merletta grimaced. "Not exactly."

Sage was frowning. "How could you speak to Heath right now?"

"It's part of his magic," said Merletta. "He can sort of...see me. From anywhere."

Sage raised an eyebrow. "That seems powerful. Is that why the humans in his kingdom are scared of magic? I remember you telling me humans are very particular about their privacy."

Merletta shook her head. "Actually, they don't even know about his magic. He's kept it secret. But you're right. If they did, they'd probably be even more worried."

She glanced upward again, but darkness was falling rapidly, and she could barely see the guards above her now.

"I suppose it's too late to hunt for news of Tish tonight," she said reluctantly. "But I'll make inquiries first thing."

"What about classes?" Sage pressed. "Ibsen will be furious you skipped today."

"Look around you, Sage." Merletta gestured upward, to the no longer visible armed guards crisscrossing the water above them. "Classes are the least of my concerns right now."

True to her word, she rose with the sun, determined to seek news of Tish. Unfortunately, she was unable to sneak into Tilssted—conflict there was raging as hotly as ever, and the boundary was too tightly guarded. But she managed to locate Felix, a friend among the guards. Like many of his fellows, he was posted in the contested city, and he agreed to make inquiries.

With nothing practical to do, Merletta made her way to class after all. The trainees were with Wivell, and if he knew of her truancy the day before, he made no comment on it. He'd always been hard to read, but Merletta thought he was watching her more closely than usual. She couldn't be certain, but she suspected he knew of her report to the Record Master.

Felix sought her out at lunch, but his report wasn't encouraging. He'd gone to the shellsmith tower where Tish had been apprenticed, and spoken with several of her colleagues. No one had seen any sign of her. He'd even visited the charity home where Tish and Merletta had grown up. The windows were boarded against the fighting outside, and if the guard at the door was to be believed, no one but the carers and beneficiaries had gone in or out for weeks.

Reluctantly, Merletta had to acknowledge that she had no idea where else to search. Like Merletta, Tish had no family to retreat to in times of danger or distress.

Some part of Merletta's mind knew it was a very real possibility that Tish was either lost or perished, somewhere out in the open ocean. But somehow she just couldn't believe it. No matter how uncomfortable Tish had been with her legs, and her place in the slowly building rebellion centered on Merletta, it was utterly inconceivable that she would leave the relative safety of the island to venture into the ocean alone.

Still, in spite of her belief that Tish was alive, Merletta remained deeply uneasy over the mystery of her friend's whereabouts.

There was nothing she could do for Tish, however. Nothing she could do at all, except await events, she acknowledged to herself as Felix swam from the dining hall. By the end of the afternoon, during which the Center still gave no sign either of moving against her or seeking to contact the dragons through her, she started to wonder if the waiting might just kill her before the Center could.

She knew conflict was still raging in Tilssted, and Center employees were still carrying out questionable tasks all over the triple kingdoms. But she couldn't even find the heart to pursue her mission to expose the Center's lies to the populace at large. Not when willfully ignoring one of the Center's rare truths had brought the whole triple kingdoms under threat of violent death.

Besides which, as little as she might trust the Record Master, his hierarchy of power surely had a better chance of stopping the dragons than anyone else in the triple kingdoms. Bitter as it tasted, it wasn't the time to stir up rebellion against the Center. It was the time to support whatever efforts were to be taken to fend off the coming attack.

When she drifted into bed, hardly able to believe the Record Master had gone another day without acting, Merletta's thoughts floated to Heath. As she so often had, she wished she could watch him the way he watched her.

At least, she hoped he still watched her. Lying in her hammock, surrounded by whispering and snoring first years, her mind went back to their last meeting, on the island. When he'd kissed her, she'd let herself believe for a moment that things would work out, that they'd somehow find a solution for the various disasters engulfing them. As long as they worked together.

But he was far away, out of her reach, and their separation was eroding away her hope, steadily and mercilessly.

CHAPTER SIXTEEN

Merletta

Merletta rose from her hammock with determination the next morning. During a restless night, she'd come to a conclusion. Whatever the Record Master did or didn't intend, she wasn't going to let another whole day pass without any change.

If it had been a couple days earlier, she would have skipped class and gone straight to the central spire to confront the Record Master. Ibsen had abandoned all pretense of teaching her—no fourth year material had been covered in his class since the commencement of her fourth year studies. But it was an Agner day, and on reflection, Merletta decided it wouldn't be a bad thing to start her day with some physical training, to sharpen up before anything else.

To her own surprise, she found herself looking around for Ileana, not to avoid her, but in hopes of sparring with her. But the young Center guard was nowhere to be seen, presumably out on patrol.

"Merletta." Agner drifted up beside her, his eyes also scanning the training area. "I think Andre is just about the only one who'll really challenge you among this lot, and he's fighting with Lorraine right now."

"I'd like the chance for a bout with a senior trainee."

They both turned at the hopeful voice, to see Indigo floating nearby. Her eyes were a touch too innocent as they rested on Agner, and Merletta felt herself tense, waiting for the instructor to become suspicious.

But Agner just shrugged. "I don't object. Merletta has probably done less than her share of training younger fighters."

The two mermaids started a fairly half-hearted bout, and the moment Agner was out of earshot, Indigo spoke, her words low and urgent.

"I did it. I wasn't able to get access until this morning, but I made the report we talked about, that I'd followed you outside the barrier and seen you searching for a new settlement site. Then I pretended to leave, but doubled back. I know the guard I've been reporting to is someone important. I was hoping he would be senior enough to make a decision about how to respond, and I was right. I heard him give an order to his assistant."

"And?" Merletta pressed. "What order did he give?"

Indigo bit her lip, her spear movements sluggish. "You're not going to like it. He said, 'Get the shellsmith. It's time to move on the trainee.'"

Merletta stilled, hardly realizing she'd stopped sparring. "So they do have Tish," she whispered, horrified. "They're keeping her captive somewhere."

Panic raced over her. Did that mean they knew about the others on Vazula as well? Or had a scouting patrol found Tish in the water, not realizing about her time on land? It was certainly possible—she spent as little time with legs as she could. Merletta hated to think of leaving August and the others on the island without warning, but there was no question of going to

Vazula. If the Center had kidnapped Tish, she had to be Merletta's first priority.

"Thank you," she muttered, lowering her spear. Agner seemed to have noticed their pathetic bout, and was working his way toward them along the line of clumsy first years. "I know you took a risk, and I'm grateful."

"You understand that they're coming for you, right?" Indigo said earnestly.

Merletta nodded, her thoughts already far from the conversation as she raced through a series of hopeless options.

"Will you flee?" Indigo pressed.

"Flee?" Merletta brought her gaze back to the younger trainee, startled. "And leave Tish at their mercy? Of course not!" She groaned to herself. "They already tried using Tish to get to me. Can't they think of something new?"

"What are you going to do?" Indigo asked.

Merletta's face was grim. "I'm not sure yet. But whatever it is, I'm going to do it today."

She turned away from the other mermaid, intending to leave before Agner reached them. But she'd barely made it half a dozen strokes before a much younger form barred her way, arms crossed.

"What was that about, Merletta?" Andre demanded, his fight with Lorraine apparently over. "Why did Indigo corner you?"

"I told you," Merletta said impatiently. "Indigo is working with us now. She reported to me about—"

"Just because you caught her following you, doesn't mean you can trust her with your secrets," Andre cut her off.

Merletta scowled at him, in no mood for his well-intentioned stubbornness. "You're as bad as Sage. No, you're worse. Indigo isn't an experienced record holder a whole generation above us, like Sage's mother. She's a sixteen-year-old trainee who did what she was told by someone senior. And she's been wrestling with what she did ever since the moment she understood what you thought of her actions. Don't lecture me on trust. I hardly know her—you're the one who should be telling me whether I can trust her. But you can't do that if you refuse to talk to her, and hear her side of the story."

Andre looked a little stunned at these harsh words, but before he could speak, something over Merletta's shoulder caught his eyes, and he tensed.

Merletta swirled around, a shimmer of silver glinting in her vision. She had no difficulty recognizing the two mermen whose entrance had brought an instant check to the motion of the training yard. What underhanded attack were the Record Master's guards going to try this time?

But, once again, the workings of the Center surprised her.

"Trainee Merletta."

It was the blue-tailed, blue-eyed merman who spoke, his eyes hard and unyielding. Merletta remembered how he'd seemed offended when she accused the Record Master to his face.

"You are under arrest."

"Not so underhanded," Merletta murmured, her mind moving rapidly as she tried to catch up with the new direction of the conflict.

"What for?" demanded Andre, shifting protectively in front of Merletta. She floated out from behind him, appreciating the gesture, but in no way intending to hide.

"For consorting with humans and revealing the secrets of our kind to a dragon colony, thus endangering the very existence of our civilization."

For a moment, the silence which met this pronouncement was absolute. Merletta opened her mouth, but no words came. What was there to say? For once, the accusation was entirely truthful. It was a crime to which she herself had confessed.

She nodded slowly, drawing herself up in the water. "I'll come quietly," she said. "Where are you taking me?"

"It's not for you to ask the questions," the guard said tersely.

"Merletta!" Andre hissed, as Merletta shifted forward. "Aren't you even going to try? You know they won't fight fair."

Merletta met his gaze, her own emotions amazingly calm. "This isn't something I can flee from, Andre." She glanced behind her, at the row of open-mouthed first years bobbing beside a resigned-looking Agner, and the collection of guards spread across the training area. "Speak to Indigo," she told Andre urgently. "And find Emil and Sage. Ask Indigo to tell you all what she just told me. I'll try to find news of Tish, but someone might need to warn the others that—"

There was no time for more, confused though Andre clearly was. The silver-tailed guard had moved forward, seizing Merletta's arm in a painfully tight grip, and she broke off.

"Where are you taking her?" Andre demanded combatively.

Merletta gave him the slightest shake of her head, silently imploring him not to land himself in hot water as well. The guard began to drag Merletta away, but Andre latched on to her other arm, whispering frantically to her.

"Don't lose your head, Merletta! They have no proof against you but your own word!"

Merletta had no chance to answer. The guard's grip was tighter than ever as he tugged her through the water, out of the training yard. Merletta relaxed slightly when she realized they were heading for the central spire. That was where she'd been hoping to go anyway.

It was amazing how little fear she felt. Such an open approach wasn't nearly as unsettling as the Center's usual tactics. Maybe they'd lock her up wherever they were holding Tish—that would be a relief.

The journey to the central spire attracted an absurd amount

of attention considering how short the distance was. In spite of the circumstances, Merletta felt faintly flattered by how newsworthy she seemed to be—word spread so rapidly that by the time she was led through the central spire's main doorway, the area was lined with onlookers.

Of course, it was nothing like the eager Tilssted mob who had preserved her from the Center's sly intentions more than once. This crowd was exclusively made up of merpeople from the Center, more likely than most to follow the line they'd been fed. But still, at least she wasn't being disposed of out of sight down some dark back alley.

The guards swam her across the large open lobby of the central spire, and as they reached the far side, Merletta caught sight of a simple holding cell, the entrance covered with crisscrossing whale bones.

To her dismay, there was no sign of Tish, or any other prisoner.

"Wait!" she said, starting to struggle for the first time. "Wait, you can't just throw me in there with no explanation!"

"You're under arrest," one of the guards said impassively. "What more explanation do you expect?"

"On what evidence are you accusing me?" Merletta asked, stalling for time as she searched the water on all sides. There was no way they'd held Tish here at any stage. It was too open and visible. There must be other holding cells, tucked away somewhere.

"On the basis of your own confession."

The voice drifted down from above Merletta's head, and she swiveled to see the Record Master's lithe, silver-haired form descending from the gloom at the top of the spire's inner chamber. He came to rest a short distance above her, so that she still had to crane her neck to look at him.

"Or had you forgotten?" he asked, his voice calm and quiet.

Merletta tugged fruitlessly at the guard's grip, her natural defiance flaring to life once again.

"My memory is unusually good, actually," she retorted. "It's how I've succeeded in the program."

"Succeeded, have you?" The Record Master raised an eyebrow.

"If that's all the evidence you're relying on, it's my word against yours," Merletta commented.

The other eyebrow went up to join the first. "And whose word do you think the populace will believe?"

"Many will believe yours," Merletta said. "Maybe most. But enough will believe me to cast your credibility into question for a long time to come. And I don't think that kind of attention is what you want."

There was no humor to the smile that curved the Record Master's lips.

"Once you would have been correct, Trainee. But things have changed, thanks to your own activities. The opinions of the masses are no longer of great interest to me."

Merletta glared back at him. He could say what he liked, but the fact that he'd bothered to formally arrest her—and in a public place—demonstrated that he wasn't done with manipulating public opinion just yet. Even now, the lobby had been cleared, and Center guards—no doubt acting on his orders— were keeping the crowd from entering the central spire and witnessing the petty confrontation.

"What are you doing about the threat of the dragons?" she blurted out. When he didn't answer, she added, "I may as well tell you that I crossed out of the barrier two days ago."

He knew that already, of course, due to Indigo's doctored report, but Merletta didn't want him to know she was aware of that.

"I saw a group of Center employees leaving," Merletta

persisted. "What are they up to? Have you found a safe secondary location? Will evacuation begin soon?"

The Record Master's eyes were narrowed, but he gave no confirmation of her guesses. "I don't think you need to concern yourself with matters of governance."

He jerked his head to his guards, who began to haul Merletta toward the cell.

"Wait!" she called, her eyes still on the Record Master. "Where's Letitia? I know you have her! What have you done to her?"

The Record Master had already turned away, but he stopped, his back to Merletta. Turning only his head, he looked at her with his usual unnerving lack of emotion.

"As always, Merletta of Tilssted, you know more than you should, and yet less than you think."

Merletta frowned. What did that mean?

He was leaving again, and it was clear that he didn't intend to tell her anything about Tish.

"What are you going to do with me?" she demanded. Panic once again threatened to rise—how would she find Tish if she was locked up, maybe even executed?

"It is hard to determine a fitting punishment for bringing about the end of our species," mused the Record Master conversationally. "You said the dragons attempted to kill you on sight —perhaps it is only you they find so offensive. Perhaps you did something reprehensible in their presence. I thought we could offer you to the dragons as a sacrifice, in exchange for sparing the rest of our civilization."

Merletta met his eyes unflinchingly. "I can understand the appeal of that idea. Given what's at stake—and my part in it all —I don't even blame you for wanting to try it. But don't pin your hopes on that, because it won't work. My death won't satisfy the dragons."

The Record Master exchanged a glance with his guards. It almost looked pitying.

"Thank you for educating me," he said blandly. "I am aware that offering your life to the dragons will not resolve the problems you have caused. But it may yet resolve other matters."

Merletta pressed her lips together grimly. She understood. The Record Master had no intention of actually doing what he'd described. But it would be a convenient explanation for her death to the masses, one which gave the impression he'd tried to bargain with the dragons, even though he evidently had no intention of doing so. Apparently satisfied that she had taken his grim meaning, the Record Master once again turned away.

"But what *are* you doing to prepare?" Merletta cried. "Tell me you're at least going to open the barrier! I saw that the guards are still keeping everyone inside. Surely you're not going to prevent the population from fleeing when the time comes?"

He sent her an amused look. "So they can scatter through the ocean, and encourage the dragons to search under every rock? I don't think so."

Merletta's mind raced, trying to make sense of what he wasn't saying. "You don't want the dragons to search and find your new safe haven," she realized. It made sense. "But why haven't you started the evacuation?" she demanded. "They could come any day. What if there isn't time to get everyone out?"

"Everyone?" the Record Master repeated, sounding amused. "I will miss your quaint perspectives, Tilssted trainee." Although he still spoke without excessive emotion, he pronounced the last phrase with a strange emphasis, as if it was a contradiction.

He glanced carelessly at the guards. "Her sentence will be pronounced in one hour."

CHAPTER SEVENTEEN

Merletta

"One hour?" Merletta barely had time to protest before she was shoved into the holding cell and the door was latched behind her.

She supposed she shouldn't be surprised. The Record Master had openly told her that he didn't care as much for public opinion as he did for whatever scheme he was building to respond to the threat of the dragons. Having decided to be rid of her, there was no reason for him to delay.

But what was his scheme? The thought troubled her, worrying at her mind as the minutes ticked by. He hadn't contradicted her guess about a safe haven outside the triple kingdoms. But he'd scorned her suggestion that everyone would be evacuated to this place. Was it only a backup, then? Did they have some better plan, something to give hope of holding off the dragons altogether?

"Heath," she murmured into the empty water. "If you're listening, or watching, or whatever it is you do...I think it's very possible I'm going to be executed in an hour." She winced. "I know that's...awful for you. I wish..." She paused, struggling with a sudden rush of emotion. "I wish we at least had the chance to say goodbye. Or that there was a way to protect you from it. But I think I'm out of options. I've reached the end of the line."

Strangely enough, the thought brought her mind around to her recently discovered family of origin. Her mother's line really had reached its end, all but dying out. Her father's line was still strong, but it wouldn't continue through her. And likely wouldn't continue at all, once the dragons wreaked havoc on them all.

Merletta thought of the account she and Sage had read, of the dragon attack on the fledgling mermaid colony near Valoria, and a shudder ran over her. It was a horrible image. The record described the dragons spearing merpeople through with a single talon.

But then, Merletta reminded herself bitterly, merpeople didn't need outside help for that. The Center was plenty adept at killing off their own kind. Her own parents had been speared through the heart by Center guards just for exploring the idea of outward settlement. The Center would prefer merpeople to die than to let them go outside the barrier.

Merletta stilled in the water as the truth crept over her. That was the simple reality. The Center had held that position for years—for generations—and there was no reason to think it had changed. Nothing in the Record Master's demeanor suggested that the imminent dragon attack had rattled him out of his usual priorities.

They weren't going to help everyone get to a different, safer, location. Of course they weren't. Because in spite of their claims, none of their rules or secrets had ever really been about keeping everyone safe. They'd been about control. The Record Master wasn't even going to let anyone flee, because that would encourage the dragons to search the ocean, and possibly find the favored few holed up somewhere secure.

No, he was going to keep the inhabitants of the triple king-doms—or at least the vast majority of them—trapped inside the barrier for as long as possible, in the hope that their slaughter would be a distraction for the escaping few.

Fury welled up inside Merletta, powerful and scorching. It was for this that she'd put her own life on the line to tell the Record Master what was coming? For this that she'd come quietly with the arresting guards, not resisting the conse-quences for her mistakes? She'd told him what was coming in the belief that he was best placed to give everyone a chance at survival. But instead he'd taken that knowledge and used it for his own benefit, even to the point of costing the lives of most of those under his influence.

That wasn't leadership. That was tyranny—a worse sort of tyranny than even the disillusioned Merletta had believed the Center capable of.

She threw herself forward, letting out a shout of wordless rage as she rattled the bars of her cage uselessly. Andre had been right. She should never have come tamely, not when she knew the kind of tactics the Center employed. And she should *never* have been so foolish as to give any trust to the Record Master in averting the coming disaster. Telling him had seemed the honorable course, but all it had achieved was to create yet another barrier to everyone's survival.

And now it might be too late for her to warn anyone else.

The guards had let others back into the lobby, but no one was coming near Merletta's holding cell. The various Center employees went about their business, casting her the odd wary look, with no idea of the doom hanging over them all. Two guards floated to attention not far away, and Merletta had no doubt they would prevent anyone from approaching too close, or her from speaking to the passers-by.

Her best hope, she decided, was to use the trial, or sentencing, or whatever it was, to shout the truth to as many as she could, and hope that the news would spread. Surely if enough merpeople stormed the barrier, they could break through the restrictive presence of the guards. And the Record Master clearly still wanted her disposal to have the veneer of legitimacy. With any luck the hearing would be a dramatic, public affair.

But as she should have realized, Merletta's luck had run out. At the end of what was possibly the longest hour of her life, Merletta's hands were bound with twisted kelp rope, and she was led not to some large central square, but back to the training yard where she'd been arrested. It had been cleared of training guards, and only about three dozen merpeople were gathered to watch the drama, all three of her instructors included.

Ibsen's eyes were narrowed, but he didn't look gleeful as Merletta might have expected. He looked tense—she supposed he'd seen her dodge disaster too many times to feel really secure in her removal until she was actually done for. Wivell didn't look at her at all, his expression neutral, and his posture formal. Agner, on the other hand, followed her progress so closely he seemed to be trying to catch her eye.

Merletta glanced at him, but she had no interest in the apology she saw on his face. There might be sorrow there for her fate, but there was at least as much resignation. Agner had always liked her, but although he claimed to enjoy seeing her shake up the system, he wasn't actually willing to fight the status quo.

How absurd, Merletta thought in a detached way. Absurd for all these intelligent, well-connected merpeople to be sacrificing so much to preserve a status quo which was about to be wiped from the ocean by a colony of vengeful dragons. How many of those present knew about that, she couldn't say, of course.

Her eyes sought friendlier faces, and she was relieved to see

Sage and Andre hovering anxiously near the instructors. As painful as the coming scene might be for them, she couldn't have borne to face this reckoning without anyone she trusted by her side. It wasn't as though she was actually to be killed on the spot. The Record Master would need her to die out of sight if he wanted to claim he'd offered her life as forfeit to the dragons.

Emil didn't seem to be with them, and Merletta frowned as she searched the crowd for him in vain. It wasn't like him to be absent for such a crucial moment.

"Merletta of Tilssted."

It was the Record Master himself who spoke, to Merletta's surprise. He floated in the middle of the training yard, his fins at about the level of her face. Everyone looked up at him as he opened the proceedings, and Merletta felt another flash of anger. It was as though she'd never truly seen him until this moment. He'd been a master at staying in the background, not drawing unnecessary attention to himself. But that had all been a disguise for the truth, which was revealed in this moment— this merman's pride was strong enough to sacrifice a civilization for himself. He had set himself up as a king, woven the whole civilization around himself as if he should be revered, never questioned, always obeyed. And from the very beginning, she'd upset the balance he'd created. He'd shown himself restrained so far, but no more. He was finally going to correct the mistake in his calculations.

"You have been found guilty of treasonous communication with dragons," he said simply. "Your betrayal has put us all at risk. There is no greater crime."

"On what evidence is she found guilty?" Emil swam suddenly into Merletta's view, his voice clear and carrying.

Surprise shot through Merletta at the sight of his companion. It was Elfin, looking tense and horrified as his eyes darted rapidly between Merletta and the Record Master floating above her.

"Record Holder Emil Waveracer of Skulssted," the Record Master said calmly. "You have not been invited to speak at these proceedings." His eyes passed coldly to Elfin. "And you are?"

Elfin bowed his head slightly. "I am Elfin of Hemssted, head of the El family line."

"Is that so?" The Record Master gave no sign of recognition, but something in his eyes as they slid smoothly to Merletta convinced her that he knew exactly who the El family was to her. He'd probably always known. His gaze returned unhurriedly to Elfin. "Why have you interrupted these proceedings, Elfin of the El family line?"

Elfin hesitated, his eyes on Merletta and his face strained. She stared straight back at him, neither entreaty nor apology in her own eyes.

"It was not my intention to interrupt, sir," Elfin said, dropping his gaze. "I am merely here as a witness."

Merletta could sense Emil's disappointment that the other merman hadn't spoken in Merletta's defense, and she couldn't help the rush of pain that shot through her. She told herself it was foolish to be hurt. This merman barely knew her, and when he'd offered to recognize her, she'd refused. Could she really expect him to override that refusal now, when she'd just publicly been declared guilty of the worst crime against their kind?

She realized Emil was trying to catch her eye, and she threw him a reassuring smile. Elfin might not have done what Emil hoped, but that didn't lessen her appreciation for her friend's actions. Even here, at the end of her tumultuous current, she didn't float alone. That meant everything to her.

"As I was saying." The Record Master returned his attention

to Merletta. "In light of the egregious nature of your crime, your sentence can only be—"

"You didn't answer Emil's question," Andre interrupted loudly.

"That's right," Sage agreed, swimming forward. "Where's the evidence against Merletta?"

"Sage!" The frantic murmur came from Rowena, Sage's mother, who was swimming through the crowd toward her daughter.

Sage ignored her completely. "You can't sentence her without evidence. Are there any witnesses to this so-called crime?"

"Of course such an accusation is backed by a credible witness account," said the Record Master coolly.

Merletta felt a surge of satisfaction. If nothing else, her friends were going to make the Record Master implicate himself in the whole process. He would have to acknowledge that the accusation came from him personally, and that information would surely filter back to those inclined to take her side. Would it be enough to make them rebel in time to save themselves?

But the Record Master had outmaneuvered her once again.

"Witness, come forward," he said curtly.

A familiar form emerged from the small crowd, a form Merletta had been hoping to spot for days.

"Tish!" she cried, both relieved and confused to see her friend moving freely rather than bound like she was. Tish didn't respond, stealing only the briefest look in Merletta's direction.

Merletta knew Tish—had known her all her life. She had no difficultly reading her friend's face. There was enough sorrow and shame and desperate entreaty in Tish's one glance to tell Merletta everything, even without the words that followed.

Waves of grief washed over Merletta, this betrayal so much more painful than Elfin's silence. She barely heard it as the

Record Master interrogated Tish, who confirmed to the crowd that she had heard Merletta speak of her interactions with dragons, even seen them from a distance. Tish's voice was so halting, so miserable, Merletta felt sorry for her in spite of everything. Tish had bought her way back into the triple kingdoms, but she had paid a heavy price for it. And how could she think it would be worth it, knowing what was coming for them all?

"In light of the severity of the offense, I am left with no option but to sentence Merletta of Tilssted to execution. I do so with a heavy heart, as it is a sentence almost never applied in our history," the Record Master said gravely.

Merletta didn't even try to hold in her snort. "Tell that to the members of August's patrol who you murdered," she said boldly. "Like you've murdered so many others. You've tried to knock me off more than once." She gestured. "You even tried to murder Tish!"

"You have forfeited your life with your conduct," the Record Master told her blandly. "There is no need to forfeit your dignity as well. These feeble accusations will not deflect the blame you've brought on yourself."

A glance around showed Merletta that he was reading the crowd correctly. With the exception of her friends, everyone looked more embarrassed by her claims than actually suspicious.

"Do you think I care about dignity in the face of what's coming?" she demanded, her voice raised. "I could even forgive this farce—what does it really matter whether you murder me through the law or spear me outright like your guards did to my parents?" In her peripheral vision, she could see Elfin clenching and unclenching his hands, but she didn't turn to look at him.

"The only thing that matters is that the dragons are coming! And if you don't let everyone out through the barrier, they're all going to be killed!"

The crowd responded this time, an uneasy shifting passing around the training yard.

"That is nonsense," said the Record Master, and Merletta had to admit that his total calm made him seem credible. "The barrier that keeps us safe was designed to keep dragons out—they will not be able to penetrate it. But due to the accused's actions, all those required to leave the barrier for legitimate purposes, such as harvesting and patrols, will now be in danger."

"That's a lie!" cried Merletta. "I don't deny that I brought this danger on us—although I didn't mean to do it, I still take the blame. But we can at least try to survive! Open the borders and let them out, or they'll be slaughtered!"

"I will not allow this fear-mongering," the Record Master said imperiously. "Guards, you know where to take her."

The guards grabbed Merletta's elbows, but a moment later one of them spun, weapon raised. Andre had barreled into him from the side, his spear still tucked into its sling across his back, but his fists raised. Sage and Emil were right behind him.

"And take these three into custody," the Record Master said with a touch of impatience. "They are clearly her accomplices."

"No!" Rowena's cry rang out as guards seized all three of Merletta's friends.

But the word had barely left her lips when she and everyone else in the training yard froze, each head snapping up toward the distant surface as the water was suddenly filled with a rock-shattering, reverberating roar.

Merletta's heart leaped into her throat, horror momentarily freezing her in place. It was all too late. They were out of time.

CHAPTER EIGHTEEN

Heath. Merletta's familiar voice, although quiet in his ear, saturated every layer of Heath's awareness. The breakfast table at Bexley Manor disappeared from his sight, his vision filled by the image of Merletta's face, defeated and weary.

If you're listening, or watching, or whatever it is you do...I think it's very possible I'm going to be executed in an hour.

Heath heard a faint crash, some part of his mind noting in a detached way that it didn't seem like an underwater sound. It took him a moment to realize it came from his world. He pushed impatiently at the awareness of his true surroundings as it tried to intrude on his extra sight. He was dimly conscious of servants bustling around to his side of the table, but it meant nothing to him. He didn't care if he'd smashed a hundred pitchers of milk. Not after what Merletta had just said to him.

I know that's...awful for you, Merletta went on. *I wish...* Her voice thickened. *I wish we at least had the chance to say goodbye. Or that there was a way to protect you from it. But I think I'm out of options. I've reached the end of the line.*

Even Heath's farsight spun, and he reached out a hand,

expecting to grip the pale bars of Merletta's cell. But it was a solid wooden table that he grasped to steady himself. Had she said an hour? But that wasn't long enough for him to reach her!

"Reka!" he cried, surging to his feet and upending his chair in the process.

A servant let out a cry as the sugar bowl joined the milk pitcher, its contents strewn across the rug. Heath ignored it all, striding out of the manor as he called once again for his friend.

He'd been feeling guilty for the last three days about hiding away at the manor instead of facing up to the difficult decision before him back in Bryford. He knew his family hadn't approved of him leaving, with Percival still in the dungeons.

But now, he was fervently grateful that he'd gotten Reka to bring him home to Bexley Manor after their conversation in the garden. Not only was Heath closer to Vazula, but Reka was on hand as well. Presumably down by the cliffs, in his favorite spot.

Not that there was any point going to Vazula. That wasn't where Merletta floated in a cell, awaiting imminent execution.

Without his permission, Heath's farsight flickered to Percival, whose posture was unnervingly similar to the mermaid's. A groan escaped Heath's lips as Reka's familiar form descended into the courtyard.

"What's wrong, Heath?"

"Merletta," Heath gasped. "We have to get to her. Right now."

"We have discussed this," Reka reminded him. "If I go to Vazula, the elders may well see where—"

"She's not on Vazula," Heath interrupted. "She's underwater. She's been arrested, and she thinks she's going to be executed in an hour. Can you find the triple kingdoms, do you think? Can you get there quickly enough?"

Reka considered the matter, his demeanor maddeningly unhurried. "I do not anticipate that it will be difficult to find the cities. I may be able to fly there in an hour, particularly if I am not carrying a burden."

Heath groaned again. He could hardly bear the idea of staying behind, but Reka was right. He would only be a burden, in more ways than one.

"All right," he said. "She's in some kind of holding cell, inside a building, I think."

"I can find her," Reka told him evenly. "I have become gradually more aware of her. My farsight locates her with relative ease now. But do you truly wish to risk the elders discovering the location of the hidden underwater cities this very day?"

Heath ran a hand over his hair, thinking rapidly. The frantic part of him wanted to throw caution to the winds. What did he care if the dragons attacked, so long as Reka got Merletta out safely?

But, quite apart from the fact that Merletta would probably hate him for the decision, it was an unforgivably selfish way to think. He wasn't willing to just leave her to her fate. But for the sake of his own conscience as well as what she would feel, he had to at least try to protect the rest of the triple kingdoms.

"What can we do to hide your flight from the elders?" Heath demanded.

Reka did a rippling shrug. "I do not think I can hide from them. Their farsight is far superior to mine. Perhaps if I had the heart magic of concealment...but I do not believe there has been anyone with that ability in our colony for many human generations. It was for that reason I was so struck by the concealment magic displayed by your sister's child."

"Never mind that right now," Heath said in agitation. "There isn't time to go get little Jacqueline, even if her magic was strong enough. If we can't hide you, can we distract them somehow?"

Rekavidur considered the idea. "Perhaps," he said. "It would not be free of risk, however. If my position is being watched, they will notice me leaving Valoria, whatever you do to distract them."

"No course is free of risk now," said Heath. "Head for the underwater kingdoms. I'll go to Wyvern Islands to attempt to distract the elders."

"What's your plan?" Reka demanded.

"I have an idea," said Heath. "But I don't think I'll tell you the details."

"Why not?" asked Reka.

"Because I don't think you'll like it, and there's no time to argue," Heath said bluntly. "The main question is how I'll get there quickly enough. You can't afford to delay in order to take me."

"My father is sympathetic to our cause," said Reka. "I will request his assistance."

He threw his head back abruptly, letting out a shrieking cry that caused Heath to cover his ears with his hands. When Reka lowered his vast head again, he looked satisfied.

"Fortune is with us. He was already flying over the mainland, not on Wyvern Islands, and he is willing to assist us."

"How do you know?" Heath asked.

Reka gave him a superior look. "Dragons do not always need words to communicate via farsight."

Had the situation been less tense, Heath would have rolled his eyes at Reka's lofty tone. But all other thoughts were driven away as Rekavidur seized his shoulders unceremoniously, launching into the air.

"What are you doing?" Heath shouted above the wind, as his legs dangled below him, far above the ground. "There's no time for you to take me to Wyvern Islands! You need to go to Merletta!"

"I have a better idea," Reka called back calmly. "We'll meet my father halfway."

The dragon was moving at such speed that speech quickly became impossible. Within only a few minutes, he began to slow, just as Heath caught sight of another scaled form speeding through the air toward them. Heath expected Reka to land, but instead he merely wheeled eastward, heading toward the coast as he continued to fly at a decreased speed.

The other dragon matched the movement, and soon they were flying side by side, the ocean visible ahead.

"Greetings, my sire," Rekavidur said in an unhurried way. "I thank you for your swift response."

"Greetings, Rekavidur," said Elddreki. The larger dragon's scales reflected the early morning light, glints of green, purple, and blue dancing out. "What is the nature of your need?"

"In point of fact, it is more Heath's need," said Rekavidur. "He has seen that the mermaid Merletta, with whom his life is entangled, is under threat of imminent death. He wishes me to fly to the underwater city where she is being held, and liberate her."

Elddreki said nothing, waiting patiently for his son to explain further.

"I wish to assist him," Reka went on. Even though they were flying slowly, Heath had to strain to hear the words. "But I believe that if I leave this kingdom, my flight will be followed, and the location of the merpeople's home will be revealed to the elders, leading to the slaughter of its inhabitants."

"I concur," said Elddreki.

"Heath intends to distract the elders," Rekavidur continued. "However, I suspect that if he were to approach them, my absence would be suspicious enough that my location would be sought."

"Again, I agree," Elddreki replied.

"Are you willing to go in my place?" Rekavidur asked his father. "To retrieve Merletta from the danger in which she finds herself, for the sake of my friendship with Heath? I know I ask a great deal."

Elddreki didn't reply immediately, and Heath found himself holding his breath.

"Although I wish no harm to the descendant of my dragon-friend, I do not feel any obligation to undertake such a task for Lord Heath," the dragon responded at last. "It is for your sake, Rekavidur, that I will undertake this journey."

"Thank you, my sire, for the unearned favor," said Reka, dipping his head in a gesture of submission.

Hope flared to life inside Heath. Elddreki was older and more powerful than Reka. If anything, he would get there more quickly. Provided he could find the place.

As if reading his thoughts, Reka spoke again, describing the location to his father according to his best guess based on Vazula's location and Merletta's various comments.

"I will not follow your journey with my farsight," Reka told the other dragon. "Due to the risk that the elders would recognize the use of my magic, and follow its trajectory."

"Very wise," said Elddreki unemotionally. "I do not anticipate the need for further instructions."

And without another word, he wheeled away, picking up speed as he raced out over the ocean, heading southeast.

"How is that dragons are so slow, but so abrupt?" Heath muttered.

"What was that?" Reka asked him placidly.

"Never mind," shouted Heath. Reka had also begun to increase his speed, traveling northeast along the coastline. "So you're coming with me to Wyvern Islands?"

"That is my intention," Reka confirmed. "My welcome is very thin after my last visit. I must hope that they do not react with violence to this second breach of my exile."

Heath felt a moment of guilt at the position he'd placed his friend in, but it was eclipsed by his terror for Merletta. His thoughts flew to her, and with them, his farsight. She remained in her cell, her expression a distressing blend of anger and despair.

The rocky cliffs raced away beneath them as they sped toward Wyvern Islands. They didn't speak again, and Heath's thoughts vacillated constantly between Merletta's current state and the challenge ahead of him. It seemed unlikely Elddreki was being followed by the elders as closely as his son was, but Heath didn't want to take any chances. What would be the good of saving Merletta from execution by the merpeople only to transport her straight into the dragons' jaws? He had to distract the elders.

When Reka veered eastward over the water, Heath cut off his image of Merletta. He couldn't erase their connection, however —not that he would ever want to—so he was still nervous about Reka's speculation that the dragons would sense the use of the magic.

Reka made for the largest island, the one where Heath had pushed Merletta from the cliffs only a few short months before. The memory was vivid in his mind. He could feel again the falling, the bruising crush of the water, the feel of Merletta's cool scales as her tail wrapped around him.

Heath banished the image, trying to gather his thoughts. Rekavidur didn't make for the center of the island's inner ring, instead alighting on a section of grass near the outside. Heath barely heard it as Reka responded to the dragon who protested his arrival, notifying his challenger that a power-wielder of the line of Dragonfriend wished to address the elders. Heath was sneaking the opportunity to check in on Merletta.

Nothing had changed yet in her situation. How long had it been since she'd told him she had an hour? Impossible to tell— time felt suspended, unreal. Heath tried vainly to see Elddreki's flight, but he had no connection with the older dragon which would make his farsight latch on.

Looking around, he realized he and Rekavidur were alone. The other dragon must be carrying their message.

"Will the elders see me?" Heath asked.

"I doubt they will convene just on your request," Reka told him. "But I imagine they will send a representative or two. And the others will certainly hear of your request. I would be amazed if they did not all watch from wherever they are in such unusual circumstances. Hopefully it will be enough."

They were kept waiting long enough that Heath began to get nervous. Reka seemed unruffled, but Heath was gripped by the fear that the dragons had already seen what Elddreki was doing, and weren't going to fall for the ploy. Again, he wished he could see Elddreki, but his attempts were met with blank nothingness. And all the while, Merletta still floated in her cell, while Percival was stretched motionless across his pallet, and King Matlock went about his day, evidently speaking of matters other than the condemned prisoner below his feet, given that Heath's farsight wasn't activated in that direction.

Heath remembered his grandmother's prediction that he'd be torn in two if he tried to keep up with it all for much longer. That had been generous. Right now, his mind felt like it was being ripped into about half a dozen pieces. But he couldn't let himself lose sight of the most urgent thing.

Merletta.

He continued to watch her, and he and Reka were idle for long enough that he saw when she left the cell, flanked by guards. Where was Elddreki? Was he going to make it in time?

Heath strained his vision, his body as tense as his mind.

"They approach." The calm quiet warning from Reka brought Heath's mind snapping back to Wyvern Islands.

Just as Rekavidur had predicted, two dark-scaled dragons

had accompanied the messenger back, each so large, they made Reka look like a dragonling in comparison.

Heath waited in tense silence as the dragons exchanged long and formal greetings with one another. The occasional snatches he allowed his farsight showed that Merletta was before some kind of assembly, although Heath wasn't willing to use his magic powerfully enough to follow what was being said.

He could hardly bear the slow pace of the dragons' conversation, but a moment's reflection reminded him it was for the best. After the frantic haste he'd felt a short time before, it was hard to remember that he actually wanted to draw it out now. The aim was to keep the elders distracted for as long as it took Elddreki to extract Merletta.

"Are we to understand by your return that you are now ready to reveal to your elders those matters which you have chosen in your youthful folly to conceal from your colony?" one of the elders was asking Reka, his voice so cold Heath actually shivered.

"That is not my purpose in returning to the colony," acknowledged Reka calmly.

"Then you are here in contravention of our ruling," growled the other elder. "If we are to remove you by force, your human companion may suffer harm."

"I do not wish that," said Reka gravely. "If you say I must leave immediately, so be it. But I respectfully request that you allow him to remain for long enough to speak. It is for his sake that I have come here, as he had no other way to reach you."

The elders turned their yellow, orb-like eyes on Heath, and it was all he could do not to gulp like a guilty child.

"Son of the House of Dragonfriend," one of them intoned solemnly. "For what purpose do you seek us out? We are not accustomed to being summoned by your kind, however noble the line from which you come."

Heath dipped his head deeply. "It is not my intention to offer you disrespect, Mighty Beasts," he said formally. "But I would be grateful if you would hear my testimony regarding the plight of my fellow power-wielders in Valoria."

He phrased the words carefully, aware that if he told the elders that his purpose in coming was to speak to them of the power-wielders—even that he *wished* to speak to them on that matter—they would sense his deception and dig deeper.

"We are aware of their plight," said one of the elders. "We have made our feelings on the matter clear to your sovereign. We have no further interest in involving ourselves."

Heath could see he was losing them. Already the silent elder was looking to the sky, as if ready to be done with the unsought conversation.

"Even when the power-wielders harbor dragon magic?" Heath pressed. "Your own essence, in effect?"

One of the elders flicked his tail in what might have been irritation.

"Although your magic has its origin in one of our kind, it is your line which wields it," the dragon said. "It is not dragon magic in the way you suggest."

Heath paused before answering, not because he didn't have his words ready, but because of the intensity of the vision that flashed before his eyes. He hadn't intended to activate his farsight, but Merletta's situation was so dire, the connection between them tugged at his mind without his permission.

He could see the crowd surrounding Merletta, but not whoever was addressing her. The merman's words were clear, however, as he pronounced a death sentence on the unflinching young trainee.

No!

It was all Heath could do not to shout the word aloud. Where was Elddreki? If he took much longer, he'd be too late.

But there was nothing Heath could do to speed the dragon up. With a supreme effort, he cut off his farsight, blinking back at the elders who were watching him suspiciously. Undoubtedly, they'd noticed his use of magic.

"You say our magic isn't dragon magic?" Heath said, struggling to regain the thread of the conversation. "But I thought farsight was a dragon ability."

Rekavidur remained silent and motionless beside him, but Heath could nevertheless *see* the sudden tension that filled his friend. The elders stared unblinkingly at Heath, and he was suddenly absolutely confident that he had their full attention.

Which was a very good thing, because his extra vision suddenly flared back to life, to show a sight he most definitely didn't want them to witness through their own farsight: Elddreki's multi-colored form plummeting through the water, sending the gathered merpeople scattering.

"What is the truth hidden behind those words?" one of the elders demanded, drawing Heath back to Wyvern Islands.

"I am a power-wielder, as I believe you know," Heath answered simply. "My magic was slow to develop in human terms. But it has now done so, and one form it takes is an extra vision which, from all I can tell, is essentially farsight."

The elders were silent, undoubtedly able to assess the truth of his words. Heath's connection with Merletta tugged at his mind, and although he tried to ignore it, the sheer quantity of magic in the air made it near impossible to subdue the farsight. Elddreki had her in his talons, but there was confusion all around.

"You're using it now, aren't you?" said one of the elders, his tone making it an accusation.

With a snap, Heath shut off the connection as best he could. He gave no answer—it was unnecessary, since they knew the truth. He could only hope their interest was in the revelation about his farsight, not its current focus.

"If you truly thought this information would change our approach toward the discord in the human community, you have substantially misjudged our attitude," one of the elders told him. "We do, however, accept this revelation with interest. It will be the subject of further discussion." He directed his stony gaze to Rekavidur. "As will your role in the situation, Rekavidur. It seems there is no end to the matters you have concealed from your elders. You know our ruling as to your presence here. You will not receive another warning."

With those words, the elders took to the sky, along with the dragon who had carried the message. For a moment, Heath and Reka stood in silence. Then, in a fluid motion, Reka seized Heath in his talons and took off as well.

"I'm sorry if I got you into further trouble," Heath called over the rushing air as they flew swiftly back toward the mainland.

"It is no matter," Reka responded calmly. "I believe your distraction was sufficient. I see that my sire has left the water. Merletta is with him, and the rest of her kind are not subject to violent death."

A shudder of relief went over Heath, but his thoughts remained grim.

"At least not today."

CHAPTER NINETEEN

Merletta stared at the dragon swimming swiftly toward her. It wasn't Rekavidur, that much was certain. But it was familiar, nevertheless. One she'd seen on Wyvern Islands, perhaps. The full memory hit her a moment before the shocked silence erupted into screams. This was Rekavidur's father! He'd defended her when the others tried to kill her—was it possible he was actually here to help?

It was clear that such a thought hadn't occurred to anyone else, and understandably so. Panicked forms fled around her, some of the guards even abandoning their positions to race out of the training yard. As terrified cries spread out from the site, Merletta's eyes darted to the Record Master. He was frozen in place, his shock and displeasure clear. If it wasn't for...well, everything, Merletta would have felt a hint of satisfaction at seeing his chagrin. His lie about the protection of the barrier had just been exposed. He would have a harder time keeping his disposable decoys inside the triple kingdoms now.

Even as she watched, the Record Master flipped in the water, diving down from his elevated position and sliding through a gap into a storage area, like a sea snake disappearing into a crevice. It was no surprise to Merletta—she didn't doubt for a moment that he'd find a way not only to survive the incident, but to turn it to his purposes.

And there was no reason he wouldn't get away with it, because the dragon wasn't focused on him. As soon as the enormous beast reached the seabed, he drew up, his eyes scanning the water.

"You are Merletta," he announced, when his gaze found her. "I've come for you at Rekavidur's request."

Merletta just gaped back at him, hardly able to process his words. Reka had sent him? It was Heath's doing, no question. She remembered the goodbye she'd sent out into the water back in the holding cell, trusting that Heath would hear. He certainly hadn't been idle in the short time since then.

"Do not let her leave—or any of them!" The Record Master's words issued from his hiding place.

One of the guards holding Merletta released her, raising his spear as he turned to the dragon. The other shoved Merletta behind him, and she found herself colliding with Sage. Several guards formed a ring around the two friends.

"Do you have your weapon?" Merletta demanded, although a quick scan of her friend provided an answer.

Sage grimaced. "They grabbed me before I even got a good defense up. I was never strong with combat."

"You're hardly to be blamed for being distracted by a dragon penetrating into the Center," Merletta reassured her.

Looking over her friend's shoulder, she saw that other guards were attempting to apprehend Emil and Andre, both of whom were giving a very good account of themselves.

"Really?" Merletta said, exasperated. "Even in the midst of a dragon attack they're focused on arresting you all for daring to support me?"

But she wasn't really surprised that the guards were still

blindly following the Record Master's instructions. They had been well trained. And it was becoming increasingly clear that this one dragon's presence didn't constitute a true attack.

Sage gave a small cry, and Merletta followed her gaze to see Emil being swarmed by half a dozen guards. One of their spears caught his arm, and blood trickled into the water. Andre was hanging on amazingly well, but he also was outnumbered, and would surely soon be overwhelmed.

Merletta saw at a glance that most of those who'd been watching her sham trial had fled the training yard. Many of the guards had stayed, however, and more were beginning to pour in, presumably summoned from the barracks nearby. And one figure was fighting against the tide, trying to reach the two mermaids who were being hemmed in by guards.

"Sage, your mother," Merletta said.

Sage's expression was hard to read as she spotted the older mermaid. But there was no time to focus on Rowena. A scream brought their attention back to the scene before them, as the dragon swept three guards out of his way with a single swish of his tail. He lowered his enormous head so that it was at eye level with Merletta's.

"Do you wish to come with me, or not?"

"Of course she does!" Sage said, her voice strong even as she trembled at bringing the dragon's attention on herself.

Merletta inclined her head, dimly aware of the guards raining spears upon the dragon. The weapons glanced off, the hardened tips making a musical tinkling sound against the dragon's scales. The creature didn't seem to be noticing the assault.

"Greetings, Mighty Beast," Merletta said, as Heath had taught her. "I thank you for your kind offer. I would be glad to accept if not for the danger in which I would leave my friends."

"Don't be absurd, Merletta, you were about to be executed!" Sage cried. She shoved her friend toward the dragon. "Go!"

As she said the word, Emil came hurtling through the water, thrown by a vicious stroke of someone's spear. His form broke through the still partially intact ring of guards, thudding into Merletta's side.

"Isn't the beast here to rescue you?" he grunted, his eyes flying between Merletta and the dragon. "What are you waiting for?"

"She doesn't want to leave us," Sage said in evident exasperation.

"I could carry a second," the dragon said, taking in the ongoing fight with clinical interest. Andre was flagging. "But not all four of you."

"Take Sage as well." Emil's answer was instant and predictable. "Andre and I will manage."

"Wha—?" Sage's protest turned into a cry of surprise as the dragon's talons closed around her middle. He seized Merletta in a similar fashion, and with a single beat of his mighty wings, sent them all propelling up toward the distant surface.

"NO! SAGE!" The agonized cry from Rowena cut Merletta to the heart. She could only hope Emil and Andre would succeed in convincing the record holder that her daughter wasn't going to be killed by the dragon.

A glance down revealed total pandemonium below. Merletta could almost see the news of the dragon's appearance spreading like ink from the training yard outward. But soon the Center was nothing more than a pearlescent glow beneath them as the light of the sun grew steadily brighter above.

"What about Emil and Andre?" Sage cried, as they broke the surface and shed their tails for legs—for only the second time for Sage. "What if they execute them in your place?"

Fear choked Merletta, making it hard to speak.

"Heath!" she cried haltingly. "Heath, please, I have to know what happens to them! Can you see Emil and Andre? Can you —" But what? What could Heath do, from all the way in Valoria? Nothing. Nothing at all. "Just please watch them," she begged. She had no idea if Heath's magic was strong enough for that, but she had to at least try.

"Where are you taking us?" she called to the dragon carrying them. "Back to Valoria?"

"Yes," he replied calmly, speeding over the water. "To Heath."

To Heath. The words filled Merletta with a jittery energy, a measure of excitement thrown into her panic and fear. The weeks since she'd seen him had felt impossibly long.

It was hard for Merletta to judge time, everything passing in a blur of rushing wind around her, rippling water below her, and a growing ache in her torso, where the dragon held her in an unyielding grip. It was unnerving, the way her legs dangled freely between her and the ocean far below. She could only imagine it was more terrifying for Sage, unused to being out of the water in the first place.

After what felt like an eternity, land came into sight ahead of them. She'd expected the dragon to make for Bexley Manor, so was surprised when he wheeled further west. When they finally alighted not far inland, in a dell which she hadn't been able to see until they were almost upon it, Merletta's breath caught at the sight of both Heath and Rekavidur waiting for them.

Heath's face was upturned toward them, his eyes locked on Merletta as they descended. The sight of him, after so many tension-filled weeks, almost overwhelmed her. The moment the dragon released her, she found herself in Heath's arms, and something deep within her relaxed. It might be a stretch to say she was safe, given her proximity to the dragon colony, but the release of tension was undeniable.

"Merletta," Heath murmured. "I thought I was going to lose you."

"I thought my luck had run out as well," Merletta acknowledged, the words muffled from where her face was pressed into his tunic. She pulled back, beaming up at him, and hoping the smile hid the moisture building inconveniently at the corners of her eyes. "I should have known you'd come to my rescue."

His answering smile was so intimate, Merletta became acutely conscious of Sage shifting beside her.

"I wish I'd been able to," Heath told her, stepping back a little as though also reminded of their company. "But it's Elddreki we have to thank for that."

Merletta turned to the dragon, bowing as deeply as she could manage with one of Heath's arms still around her waist. "Thank you, Elddreki," she said solemnly. "I am more grateful than I can say."

"You had best thank Rekavidur, for whose sake I acted," Elddreki said, although there was the hint of a smile about his thin reptilian lips.

"Thank you, Reka," Merletta said obediently, turning her fervent gaze on him. Again she felt Sage shift, and hurried to repair her omission. "This is my friend, Sage. She was being seized by the guards for sticking up for me, and Elddreki kindly brought her as well."

"You're very welcome, Sage," Heath told her, with his easy smile. "Merletta has spoken of you often. I'm glad you're here, and I'm sorry not to be able to give you a better welcome. I would have preferred to receive you at my family's home, but I was concerned the dragons might keep an eye on the place."

"Do they know we're here?" Merletta asked sharply.

"I hope not," Rekavidur responded. "Given the lengths Heath went to in order to distract them from my sire's journey to retrieve you."

Merletta frowned at Heath. "What lengths?"

"Never mind that," he said, apparently unconcerned. Merletta shivered a little, and he ran a hand up and down her arm to warm her. "Reka and I did stop at Bexley Manor, to get some of the clothes you left last time, Merletta. Hopefully one of the gowns can fit Sage."

"Gowns?" Sage repeated curiously.

"They'll fit," Merletta said, detaching herself from Heath to enable him to retrieve the garments. "Wait until you try them on, Sage. It's hilarious how much covering humans wear. You can hardly move in them, at least until you get used to it."

"I would have said that sounds awful, but I'll admit I've never felt this cold before," said Sage, shivering as she received a dress and watched Merletta don one by way of example.

"It's your human form," Merletta told her wisely. "It's not built for the cold of the depths like our mermaid forms are. It's fine on Vazula, where it's always warm, but here it can be brutal. We'll have to accustom ourselves if we're going to be hiding in the open."

"Of course you won't have to stay in the open," said Heath quickly. "I have to return to the capital—I've already been away longer than I should have—and you can come with me. The dragons don't tend to come there, and if Rekavidur keeps his distance, I don't think they'll try to watch me."

"I seem to remember them coming to the city last time I was here," Merletta said skeptically.

Heath shook his head. "We won't stick around long enough for the Winter Solstice Festival. I learned my lesson last year." Sage and Merletta had both struggled into gowns and boots by now, and Heath looked them over. "If you're ready, Reka and Elddreki will carry us to within walking distance of the city. It will be best for us to arrive inconspicuously, I think."

Sage bit her lip, but said nothing. With no better ideas to

offer, Merletta gave Heath a curt nod, and soon they were back in the air. It wasn't long before the city of Bryford came into view. As Heath had instructed, the dragons set them down again in a grove of trees within sight of the walls.

"We will leave you now," said Elddreki.

Heath nodded. "I know you didn't do it for me, but I must thank you again," he told the older dragon seriously. "It hasn't escaped my notice that you're now as implicated in all this as Reka is."

"More so," Elddreki agreed placidly. "Unlike Rekavidur, I have now actually visited the underwater civilization, and know its precise location."

He glanced at the two mermaids, perhaps sensing their sudden tension. His lips again stretched in that slightly unnerving dragon smile.

"But I will not betray your secrets. I will stand with Rekavidur's decision." He glanced at his son. "I mean the dragons of Wyvern Islands no harm, but I was not born of that colony. If there is to be conflict, my loyalty is first to Rekavidur, who carries within him my own lifeblood. If you knew the cost paid for his life—not only by me, but even by Heath's own house—you would understand."

With those words, the two dragons took to the sky.

"They're...inscrutable creatures, aren't they?" Sage said blankly.

Heath chuckled. "What do you mean? That was a dragon being incredibly expansive. I don't think any dragon apart from Reka and his father would openly share that much about their thoughts with a group of humans."

Sage looked a little taken aback at being referred to as a human, but she didn't comment.

"What was all that about your house paying a price for Reka's life?" Merletta asked curiously.

Heath waved a hand. "Ancient history. I'm more concerned with getting you two into Bryford without attracting unfriendly attention."

"It might be difficult to get all the way there," Sage said awkwardly.

Heath looked at her in surprise. "It's not as far as it looks," he said kindly. "We can walk there in half an hour, I'd say."

She gave a dry laugh. "*You* might be able to."

Merletta slapped a hand to her face in sudden understanding. "Oh, Sage, I'm so sorry! I forgot you can't walk." She looked at Heath. "This is only Sage's second time with legs. She hasn't even learned the basics yet."

"Oh." She could see Heath recalculating. "No matter," he said, amicable as always. "We can go as slowly as we need. It will give us time to catch up."

"There's plenty to catch up on," said Merletta, as they began to make their slow and labored way out of the grove, Sage leaning heavily on her arm for support. "Even before what happened today." She cast an anxious glance at Sage, whose face looked more strained than Merletta had ever seen it. "Did you watch what happened to our friends? I asked, but...I don't know if you could hear."

"I heard," Heath told her quickly. "I didn't think I'd be able to, to be honest. I can usually only follow people whom I have some personal investment in," he added, presumably for Sage's benefit. "But it was clear how important it was to you, so I tried."

His voice took on an eager edge, as if, in spite of everything, he was excited to be sharing his discoveries about his magic with Merletta. "It was amazing. I don't know if it was the presence of Reka's magic, or just the strength of my connection with you, but when I focused on how important Andre and Emil are to you, I could see them. It was almost like—like your priorities became mine."

She could hear his self-consciousness in the last words, and knew he was as aware of Sage's presence as she was. But still, the words sent something warm shooting through her. No matter how often they were parted, no matter for how long, the connection between them was always instant and potent.

Their eyes held for a moment, all the things there was never opportunity to speak passing between them. Then Sage cleared her throat.

"So what did you see?" The fear in her voice brought Merletta's thoughts back to the friends they'd left behind. "What happened to Emil and Andre?"

"They were all right last I saw," Heath reassured Sage quickly.

"Didn't they get captured?" Merletta demanded.

He nodded. "They did. They were locked up in some kind of cell. But they've escaped. They had some help."

"Who from?" asked Sage, her face taking on slightly more color.

"I didn't recognize either of the mermaids, but they were about our age," Heath explained. "One of them had a pale blue tail and blond hair. She seemed to be providing some kind of distraction while the other one—also pale, but with a green tail—broke them out."

Sage frowned at Merletta, still shuffling her feet awkwardly forward as she mused. "The blue-tailed mermaid must be Indigo, don't you think? But who's the other?"

"Ileana," said Merletta, amazed. "It must be." She shook her head. "She wasn't joking that she wanted to change sides. Even with me out of the way, she's still siding against the Center."

"But where did they go?" Sage pressed.

Heath looked troubled. "I'm not exactly sure. It didn't look like they left the cities, but they must have, because the place they ended up was nothing like the area Elddreki found you in. It looked like…well, like a war zone."

Merletta let out a long breath. "So they're hiding in Tilssted."

Sage nodded, clearly having reached the same conclusion. "It's probably the best they can find within the triple kingdoms."

"And they won't leave now," Merletta said with confidence. "Not with everyone in danger, and no one else to warn them."

Sage's lips were pressed into a thin line, and she stopped walking for a minute. "No, of course not," she said, an edge to her voice. "They're much too brave and clever to swim away like frightened minnows."

Merletta paused as well, looking at her friend in concern. "Are you all right, Sage?"

"If we all survive this, I'm going to kill him myself!" Sage burst out.

Merletta stared at her blankly. "Who?"

"Emil!" Sage cried. She was trembling now, although apparently more from anger than cold. "*Take Sage,*" she repeated bitterly. "*Andre and I will manage.*" She glowered. "No doubt getting himself killed in the process."

"He was just trying to protect you," Merletta sighed. "I know you think he doesn't recognize how strong you are, but—"

"No," Sage cut her off, suddenly deflating. "He recognizes exactly how strong I am, which is why it stings. He's right—I am the least capable one in our group, and the most in need of—"

"I don't mean to get in the middle of something I know nothing about." It was Heath's turn to interrupt. "But I doubt that's what he thinks."

Sage stared at him, her cheeks heating as if just remembering their audience. "What do you mean?" she asked cautiously.

"Emil is the one with the long fair hair and the green tail, right?" Heath asked. "I watched him from the time you left the water, like Merletta asked. He had some kind of argument with an older mermaid. From what she said, I'm guessing she was your mother."

Sage had gone still, her eyes riveted on him.

"She was beside herself over you being carried off by a dragon. Emil tried to tell her that the dragon wasn't going to kill you like she seemed to think, and that you'd clearly gone willingly. She didn't seem reassured. She was full of accusations about what he and the others had gotten you mixed up in and how it had gotten you killed."

"What did he say?" Merletta pressed. Sage seemed to be struggling to master herself enough to speak.

"I don't remember word for word," Heath admitted. He shot Merletta a warm smile. "I don't claim to have your superior memory." He returned his gaze to Sage. "But the gist of it was that given she raised you, she should know better than anyone that you're too smart to be taken in by some hoax, too strong to let yourself be so easily killed, and have too much integrity to side with liars and murderers." He frowned slightly. "I didn't really understand the next part, but he said something about how you've clearly outdone your mother in that area. He was dragged away by guards at that point, and I didn't see what happened to the older mermaid."

"Sage's mother is a record holder," Merletta explained quietly. "He was calling her out on being part of something sinister." She looked at her friend. "Something Sage was smart enough to see through, and brave enough to fight against."

"It had nothing to do with being smart or brave," Sage said faintly. "It was just because I happened to become friends with you. Otherwise I would never have seen through the lies."

"Maybe," said Merletta. "Although we can never know that. And you didn't *happen* to become friends with me, you know.

You were the only one to befriend me in my first year, which shows that you have a kind heart. Something I have no doubt Emil values as much as he does your intelligence and courage."

"I need a minute," Sage said, lowering herself onto a nearby boulder. "This is all a bit much for my...legs."

"Of course," Merletta said quickly, giving Heath a look. "Take as long as you need. We'll...scout ahead."

She tugged on Heath's arm, pulling him alongside her until the dip of the land hid Sage from their sight.

"We don't really need to scout," he informed her. "It's just open fields between here and the city, and I'm not anticipating any danger."

"I know," Merletta laughed. "She just clearly needed a minute." She sobered. "There's history there you don't know about."

"Fair enough," said Heath readily. He stepped closer. "I'm definitely not complaining about a moment alone with you."

Merletta met his eyes, holding his gaze steadily as he raised a hand and brushed hair from her face. His own face looked drawn, as if he hadn't slept much in the weeks since they'd been together. He'd always been clean-shaven before, but now he had a definite shadow. Merletta touched the dark bristles tentatively, noting how they changed the whole look of his face.

She found she liked it.

With her fingers lingering so close to his lips, it was impossible not to think of the last time they'd met, when he'd held her on Vazula, and they'd kissed as though the world was ending— which was true, at least of Merletta's world. And now, against expectations, they were together again.

"I've missed you," Heath whispered, the same memory reflected in his eyes.

She swallowed, leaning toward him. "Believe me, I know."

Then his arm was around her, and he'd pulled her flush

against him. He didn't immediately press his lips to hers, however. The fingers of his free hand brushed her chin invitingly, and she readily tilted her head up toward him. For a long moment his eyes searched hers, as if drinking in her presence, memorizing every line of her face.

A reckless impatience raced suddenly over Merletta. How many times now had she thought she'd reached the end of her good fortune, only to be given one more stolen moment with Heath? It couldn't last—it never did. She didn't want to waste a second of it.

She surged up, flinging her arms around his neck as their lips met. Heath's grip on her tightened, and his lips moved urgently against hers. Merletta responded in kind, hardly aware of it as the strength of his embrace lifted her almost from her feet, her weight pressed into him. They were clasped as close as they'd ever been, but it was never close enough. No number of stolen moments would ever be enough. The undeniable reality blazed through Merletta, its impossibility making it as searing as dragon fire. She wanted forever with him. An unbroken, unconditional future, not just these erratic snatches of a beautiful but tantalizing present.

"What's wrong?" Heath had pulled back, his voice husky and his words coming in pants after the intensity of their kiss. "Merletta?"

His thumb traced her cheek, following the track left by a single tear that had escaped her control.

"Nothing," she gasped, trying to pull herself together.

Heath searched her eyes for a moment, then leaned his forehead against hers. Closing her eyes, she allowed herself a few seconds of just breathing him in, accepting the gift of being together for what it was, without letting herself feel the bitterness of the inevitable parting that would come.

"Let's go," she said once she'd collected herself.

She pulled away and saw his confusion as he studied her face. Giving him a small smile, Merletta tipped forward again, pressing a light kiss to his lips. He made no move to draw her back against him. He must feel it too—their stolen moment had passed, and all the impossible obstacles once again stood between them.

"Let's get Sage, and get to the city," she said briskly. "There's work to be done."

CHAPTER TWENTY

"**B**ut they have no things except my old dresses. How did they *get* here?" Laura leaned forward across the breakfast table, her eyes fixed shrewdly on Heath's face.

Only the two of them were present at the table—no one else had yet emerged for the meal. Probably because it was two hours earlier than the normal breakfast hour. At least Laura had twin infants to blame for her sleepless night. Heath, meanwhile, had lain awake thinking about Merletta asleep a mere few rooms away.

"I told you," Heath insisted, "a dragon carried them. As a favor."

"You may as well say Rekavidur," his sister responded skeptically. "It's not like your friendship is a secret."

"It wasn't him, actually," said Heath. "It was Elddreki. Not that it really matters."

She frowned at him. "But did he bring them across the land, or across the sea?"

"Across the sea," Heath said shortly.

She narrowed her eyes. "Are you telling me the truth, Heath?

I know all those rumors that circulated last year were nonsense —about Merletta and her guardian being from some little-known Thoranian island." She named one of the kingdoms that formed the South Lands continent.

Goaded, Heath put down his spoon with a flourish. "You want the full truth?"

"Obviously," said Laura shortly.

Heath glanced surreptitiously to the side, waiting as a maid-servant who'd just carried in a steaming bowl of porridge edged back out of the room. Once they were alone, he turned to face his sister.

"Fine. The truth is that Merletta—and her friend Sage, whom I hadn't met before yesterday—come from a kingdom hidden in the middle of the ocean. She's gotten on the wrong side of those in power there, because she's made it her mission to expose their lies and corruption. She had just been sentenced to execution when she was rescued yesterday by Elddreki."

Laura just blinked at him, her mouth hanging open well before the end of his matter-of-fact speech.

"How can there be a kingdom that close by which I don't know about?" she demanded at last.

Heath sighed. "You know the East Seas are impassable—no one can sail further than three days in that direction. Well, there's a reason for that. There's actually a magical barrier there —dragon-made, from what we can tell. It's like how human ships can't sail through the waters surrounding Wyvern Islands. But as in that case, dragons can fly straight through with no problems. Reka and I discovered the kingdom by accident a few years ago, and we were the only ones who knew about it, up until last Winter Solstice Festival."

"What happened then?" Laura asked warily.

"The dragons saw Merletta and her guardian, and they realized her civilization is out there. Now they're determined to kill them."

"Kill who?" Laura asked, aghast. "Merletta and her friend?"

Heath shook his head. "No. Well, yes. But not just them. All of them. The whole population of her kingdom."

"But why?" Laura demanded.

Heath ran a hand through his hair, the release of letting this information out almost overwhelming. Laura had always been adept at weaseling confidences out of both her brothers, and she somehow managed to do it in such a way that they never resented telling her afterward.

Probably her mood-altering magic at work, if the truth were told.

"Because they have power...sort of," Heath hedged, not quite ready to reveal all Merletta's mysteries without even discussing it with her. "Not like ours—they can't work magic. But there's a magic about them, passed through the bloodline of every single one of her people. There's a complicated history with the dragons, but the long and short of it is that the dragons resent their magic, and want to wipe it out."

"Why are you telling me all this?" Laura asked blankly. "You've been so secretive about this girl for so long."

Heath let out a long sigh. "Too secretive, probably," he acknowledged. He scowled. "Although the reaction of the dragons probably justifies my reluctance to betray Merletta's secrets to anyone. But I think we're past that point. Especially given what the dragons know about her, and about me, I think I have to tell the king everything." He grimaced. "I just hope Merletta can forgive me."

"What do the dragons know about you?" Laura asked.

"About my farsight magic," Heath clarified. "I told them yesterday—it was a distraction to hopefully stop them using *their* farsight on Elddreki while he went to Merletta's rescue. You see, they don't know exactly where Merletta's kingdom is." His voice turned gloomy. "Not yet, anyway."

Laura massaged her temple. "Let me get this straight," she said. "As of yesterday, you had your brother locked up in one kingdom, pending execution for rebellion against the crown, and your sweetheart in the identical situation in a different kingdom? With some murderous dragons thrown in, and then you...somehow in the middle of it all?"

Heath actually laughed. When she put it like that, it was all so absurd, he couldn't help himself. "Well, the circumstances of their arrests were pretty different, but yes, that's basically it," he acknowledged.

"I don't mean to accuse you, but you are the one and only common element," Laura said, joining in with his humor.

This time Heath's laugh was half groan. "Believe me, I'm aware. And I've had way too much of a hand in all of it. Especially in the disaster with the dragons—that's pretty much entirely my fault."

"I dispute that." The soft voice made the siblings turn, to see Merletta framed in the doorway.

"Merletta!" Heath shot to his feet, glad it had been her and not a servant who'd been listening unseen. "I didn't realize you were up."

"I was drawn by the unmistakable and familiar sounds of you blaming yourself for the problems of the world," Merletta said cheerfully, stepping through the doorway to reveal Sage behind her. The other mermaid still looked a little overwhelmed, but she wasn't visibly wobbling now, at least.

"I like her." Laura, also rising to her feet, grinned at Merletta.

Merletta flushed, although she returned the grin. "I'm guessing you're Laura," she said. "Heath speaks very highly of you."

"And if he didn't, I'm sure you wouldn't tell me," laughed

Laura. She looked Merletta up and down unashamedly. "I'm very glad to finally meet you," she said. "And I must say, my dress is an excellent fit for you."

Merletta flushed again, this time thrown off balance. "I hope you don't mind—" she started, but Laura waved her off.

"Of course I don't." She gestured the two girls into seats, and lowered herself again. "Although I am very curious about what you're wearing underneath."

"Laura!" Heath had been making to sit as well, but at his sister's words he froze halfway down, the horrified protest slipping from him.

Laura just laughed again. "I'm not trying to scandalize you, Heath. I was asking about the clothing native to Merletta's kingdom. Bianca gave me a very intriguing account of Merletta's attire, and I'm a little disappointed to see her looking so Valorian."

Merletta laughed as well, falling for Laura's charm as readily as everyone always did. "Yes, Bianca helped me get ready for the Winter Solstice Ball when I was here last. She was very kind not to make fun of my confusion...conventions around attire couldn't be more different between my kingdom and yours."

She shot Sage a knowing grin—the other mermaid was fidgeting uncomfortably in her heavy gown.

"Rekavidur claims that the humans have to compensate with excessive coverings because they don't have scales."

"Well, I don't see any scales on you, so what's your excuse?" Laura protested, still smiling.

Merletta froze slightly as she realized her slip, and Sage let out a quickly stifled gurgle.

"Enough with the interrogation," Heath cut in smoothly. "And you're surprised I didn't invite you to come meet Merletta last time!"

Laura raised her hands in mock surrender. "All right, all

right." She narrowed her eyes at her brother. "Don't think I've forgotten what we were talking about. If it's true that the dragons have decided to start eliminating unfamiliar sources of magic, don't you think you endangered yourself by telling them about your farsight?"

Merletta's head turned sharply, and Heath scowled at his sister.

"Why would you tell the dragons that?" Merletta demanded.

Heath sighed, shifting in his chair to face her. "It was a calculated risk, Merletta. They might not like knowing a human has farsight, but I really don't think they'll kill me for it."

"Because they're so peaceable," she said sarcastically.

Seeing that she was genuinely distressed, Heath laid a hand surreptitiously over hers. "Like I said, it was a calculated risk," he assured her. "And it was worth it."

She searched his eyes for a moment, then understanding hit. He felt her hand tighten under his. "That was your distraction," she said softly.

He didn't confirm it, but he didn't need to.

"Heath," Merletta started, but he cut her off with a tiny shake of his head.

"I told you, Merletta," he said, his voice calm and quiet. "Nothing could get me to abandon you now."

She remained frozen for a moment, then her hand flipped under his, so their palms were flush. She clasped his hand in a quick and tight squeeze, then slipped hers out again.

Heath looked up to see Laura watching with great interest, her expression telling him that she was seeing everything— more than he wanted her to, probably. He met her look squarely, and her slight smirk turned slowly serious again as she remembered all that was at stake.

"What in the oceans is this?" Sage muttered, holding up a hard-boiled egg.

"Oh, you have to shell it!" Merletta informed her.

"This thing is a shell?" Sage asked, sounding fascinated as she tapped a fingernail on the eggshell. "Was the thing inside alive once, then?"

Merletta shook her head, not showing any hint of amusement at what she clearly considered very reasonable questions. "Not exactly. It tastes good, though, once you add salt to it."

"Their food comes without salt and they *add* it on purpose?" Sage demanded.

Heath took a bite of porridge to hide his grin. He could feel Laura's eyes on him—clearly she wasn't going to let the peculiar conversation sidetrack her from getting answers from her brother.

"Telling the dragons your secrets in order to distract them is all well and good," she said bluntly. "But why did you say you think you have to tell the king everything? That seems incredibly foolhardy."

Heath put down his spoon, turning his gaze on Merletta, who'd once again looked up quickly.

"Everything?" she asked faintly.

"I was going to talk to you first," he assured her. "I don't want to betray your confidence, but..." He ran a hand through his hair. "I don't know what else to do. I've been wrestling for days, and it's time for me to stop running from it. Even if we spirited Percival out of the kingdom, I don't think I could keep Reka's and my suspicions about the attacks secret." He paused, seeing Merletta's confusion. "But of course, you don't even know about that yet."

"She's not the only one!" Laura protested. "What are you talking about, Heath? What does any of this have to do with Percival's situation?"

Heath swallowed. "The matching situations you described earlier might be more entwined than you think," he told her. His gaze flicked to Merletta, then back to his sister. "You remember I told you Merletta's people have a kind of latent magic?"

Laura nodded mutely.

"Well..." Heath winced slightly in anticipation. "I think I sensed it at the attack on Percival. And the one on me. And although I didn't sense it at the fire which almost killed King Matlock, I have to assume whoever set the blaze and then fled must be the same as the other attacks."

He felt Merletta go still beside him. She said nothing, but her eyes widened in horror. Clearly she understood what he was saying.

Sage was slower to put the pieces together, frowning between Heath and Merletta as she visibly tried to catch up. After several long moments of silence, Heath saw comprehension fill her eyes, as she actually slapped a hand to her mouth. It seemed Merletta had told her friend about the attacks on Heath and Percival.

"You mean, it was some of...of us who..." She trailed off, her eyes meeting Merletta's. "But how is that possible?"

Merletta was trembling slightly. "It goes deeper even than we knew," she whispered. "And I thought I was the first to ever come here. How long has this been happening?" Her face darkened. "Always another layer of deception. Will we never reach the bottom of it?"

She turned abruptly to her friend. "We have to go back," she said. "The ones behind all the lies might have somewhere to flee, but everyone else is stuck. They'll all die if we don't find a way to intervene. They should at least be given the chance to escape!"

Sage nodded gravely. "Of course. I never thought we were going to stay here. My family are all back there, not to mention...our friends." She stumbled over the amendment, apparently still not ready to openly name whatever was happening between her and Emil. "Surely we're here to regroup and make a strategy."

Merletta nodded, her eyes apprehensive as she looked at Heath. Clearly she expected him to object.

He raised a hand hopelessly. "I know better than to try to convince you to hide," he said. He gave her a sad smile. "I've been pretty thick about it, but I am capable of learning."

"I can't think of any way to change what's happening in the triple kingdoms without help from those dragons," mused Sage, clearly not as caught up in their moment as they were. "And if they go back to the triple kingdoms, the rest of the dragons find out where it is, right?"

Merletta pulled her eyes from Heath, looking over at Sage. "Maybe it's worth that risk at this point. We'll have to think carefully through all the possibilities."

"Let me know if you come up with anything revolutionary," Heath said, pushing to his feet.

"Where are you going?" Merletta asked, just as the door opened, and the duke and duchess entered the room together.

"Good morning Merletta, Sage," the duchess said politely. "I trust you slept well?"

Heath looked his parents over as Merletta gave the expected polite response. Their faces looked drawn—as was normal since Percival's arrest. He squared his shoulders. Surely the king would release Percival if Heath could prove that someone from the triple kingdoms had been setting them all up.

Of course, that may not be a great comfort to his parents if the king simply executed Heath instead, for conspiring with enemies of the kingdom, or whatever warped way King Matlock took Heath's revelations.

"Merletta," Heath said, as the duke and duchess settled into seats. Edmund, Laura's husband, was just arriving, looking around for his early-rising wife.

Merletta looked up, and without needing further explanation, she slid from her seat and followed Heath out of the room.

"I feel I need to come clean to the king," Heath told her. "But that involves breaking the promise I made you, that I wouldn't tell anyone about the triple kingdoms. And I never wanted to do that."

Merletta shook her head quickly. "Heath, that was so long ago, before either of us knew...well, anything. I asked you not to tell anyone based on the belief that we were the only point of contact between our worlds. If someone from the triple kingdoms has been coming here and stirring up trouble, that changes everything." Her voice grew grim. "Besides which, there's not much point trying to protect our cities from exposure to humans if they're about to be annihilated by dragons."

Heath slipped an arm around her waist, squeezing reassuringly. "We're not done fighting that future, remember."

Merletta leaned her head against his shoulder for a moment, and he felt her relax slightly. He would have loved nothing more than to put his other arm around her and hold her properly, in the hope that she'd release her burdens at least for a moment. But the sound of someone's approach made him pull back.

"I'm going to the castle now," he said, trying to speak normally as a servant bustled past. "You and Sage should be safe enough here."

Merletta shook her head. "I'm coming with you."

Heath frowned. "You need to keep a low profile, Merletta. Don't forget that we can't let the rest of the dragons find out you're here."

"I haven't forgotten," Merletta told him dryly. "But your story will be much more credible if I'm there." Her eyes softened as she studied his face. "I have recent experience of making confessions to those with the power to kill me. I've wished you could be at my side to give me strength every time. Don't deny me this unexpected opportunity to do it for you."

Heath had nothing that could stand against such an argument. A pair of servants were once again passing, but he ignored them. He slipped his hand into Merletta's, entwining their fingers as he stepped close. He brought his other hand up to her cheek, searching her eyes for an endless moment. As she gazed back at him unwaveringly, he could almost *see* her soul. Her core was all steel and determination and incorruptibility, but it was encased in the softest, kindest frame. He'd never met anyone like her, and he had no doubt he never would again.

"The more I see you, the more beautiful you are," he said softly. "Almost unbearably so."

Merletta stilled, clearly surprised by the compliment. Heath could feel her cheek heat under his fingers. She was still searching for a reply when Heath gave her hand another squeeze.

"Come on," he said, dropping his touch from her face and tugging her toward the manor's main entrance. "Let's go to the castle."

CHAPTER TWENTY-ONE

In spite of having chosen his course, Heath was in no
hurry to get to the castle. He set a slow pace on the much
too short walk, his hand still interlinked with Merletta's as
he pointed out anything he thought might interest her. They'd
spent so little time in the capital during her last visit, and he'd
tried to hide her from anyone of prominence.

Not this time. The pride he felt at walking down the street
with Merletta by his side was indescribable. He knew that their
two worlds were set for a collision course that might bring both
crashing down around them, but he couldn't help but feel at
peace. Everything always felt right when he and Merletta were
together, and all wrong when they were at opposite ends of the
ocean.

Far too soon, the castle loomed up before them. Heath
spared a glance for the large stone basin suspended above the
entranceway. It was empty—the Flame of Friendship had not
been re-lit at the previous Winter Solstice Festival, and it had
gone out. Someone had hung a pennant in Valoria's royal colors
of purple and silver from the basin, but it did little to soften the

stark reminder of the tension that had taken the place of the friendship they'd once shared with the dragon colony.

Heath lowered his gaze, sobered. He remembered being awed at his grandmother's explanations about the value of marking the friendship, given how easily the dragons could wipe the humans out if they turned on them. He'd hoped fervently that nothing would ever ignite their wrath.

And now it looked like he had personally brought the full force of their destruction down, not on his people, but on Merletta's.

"It's going to be all right, Heath." Merletta's quiet voice pulled him from these grim reflections. He hadn't even realized how tightly he was gripping her hand until she spoke.

"Sorry," he said, loosening his hold a little. They'd reached the castle's entranceway, and he stopped to speak to one of the guards on duty. He knew the man by sight, although they'd never spoken. He would certainly know Heath's identity, however.

"I need to seek an audience with the king," Heath said confidently.

"You'll have to come back next week," the guard informed him.

Heath shook his head. "This is important. I need to speak with him immediately."

"You can't, I'm afraid." Heath turned at the new voice, to see Lachlan striding across the entranceway. "But maybe I can help."

"Lachlan." Heath stepped forward to meet the prince. He was uncomfortably aware that he'd been avoiding his cousin since Reka had backed up his suspicions about the involvement of Merletta's people in the attacks.

The prince's eyes slid to Merletta. His expression remained aloof and princely, but Heath's magic curled out from him, testing and revealing. Lachlan was very curious about Merletta's identity. He would have seen her during her visit the year before, but Heath had taken care that they never met.

"Lachlan, this is Merletta," Heath said. "She's a guest of my family, and she brings greetings from her kingdom. Merletta, this is Crown Prince Lachlan."

Merletta inclined her head deeply to the prince. It wasn't the appropriate response, but Heath supposed you didn't learn to curtsy when you had a scaled tail instead of legs and voluminous skirts.

The prince seemed unsure whether or not to take Merletta's lackluster response as an insult, so Heath barreled on before he had too much time to think about it.

"You know I'd prefer to talk to you, Lachlan, but I really do think I should speak with King Matlock."

Lachlan gestured for them to walk with him, and the three of them put some distance between themselves and the guards. Plenty of people were milling about the lobby, but all kept a respectful distance, with the exception of Lachlan's personal guards, who trailed close behind.

"The guard wasn't baiting you, Heath," Lachlan explained, as they walked the corridors. "You really can't speak with my father now. He's not here."

"Where is he?" Heath demanded, startled.

"He's in Arinton," said Lachlan. "Or perhaps still on his way there. He left late last night and traveled through the night hours."

"I had no idea he was going on a journey," Heath said.

The prince raised an eyebrow. "Well, you wouldn't, would you? Haven't you been away from the capital?"

Heath squirmed a little at the hint of reproach.

"He didn't advertise the trip, in any event," Lachlan continued. "In case you've forgotten, someone recently attempted to assassinate him."

"That's what I want to talk to him about," Heath said.

Lachlan shot him a sharp look. He'd come to a stop outside a closed door. Heath had assumed they were heading for the prince's study, but he realized now they'd gone in the wrong direction.

"You've discovered something." Lachlan's words weren't a question. He glanced at the door, clearly frustrated. "I was expected ten minutes ago. My father's journey was last minute, and there are things I need to see to in his place. But I want to hear whatever it is."

His eyes flicked to Merletta.

"This concerns Merletta as well," Heath told him. "I'd be grateful if she could join our discussion." He frowned. "What precipitated such a sudden journey by your father?"

The prince hesitated, and Heath had the sense he was debating whether to answer.

"I believe he received some urgent correspondence." Lachlan's eyes bored into Heath's, almost as if he was trying to communicate something more than the simple words.

Heath stared back blankly. "From whom?"

Lachlan sighed. "I don't know." He set his hand on the door. "I'll speak to you as soon as I'm free, Heath." With a slight nod of his head to Merletta, he disappeared into the room.

"What is it?" Merletta had clearly picked up on Heath's unease.

He shook his head slowly. "I don't know. But it's surely not normal for the king to drop everything and travel *through the night*. What could have been so urgent?"

Merletta, of course, had no answer. On a whim, Heath directed them not out of the castle, but toward Brody's room.

"Fair warning, I know my cousin's morning habits, and he'll

probably be a bear at being woken before noon," he told Merletta.

She looked at him blankly. "What's a bear?"

Heath was still chuckling when he knocked on a broad wooden door, fully expecting to be met by a ruffled, groggy Brody. His suspicions were instantly raised when Brody appeared, fully dressed and sharp-eyed.

"Heath." Brody's eyes flicked between them. "What are you doing here? Did Bianca tell you?"

"Tell me what?" Heath pushed the door all the way open to reveal several of his cousins huddled in conversation on the far side of the sitting room. "Brody, what are you up to?"

"Nothing new," Brody said calmly. Apparently accepting their presence, he closed the door behind Heath and Merletta. "You know our plans."

"Bianca thinks there's a storm coming tonight," Max piped up excitedly. "And we've just found out the king's away. It's the perfect opportunity."

Bianca had stepped forward to greet Merletta—at least one of Heath's cousins had some semblance of manners—but she turned at Max's words.

"I do think there's a storm coming," she told Heath. "I can sort of...feel it on the wind. We would have told you we were meeting, but we thought you were still away from the capital."

"Did you?" Heath glanced at Brody's expression, unconvinced. He frowned at his cousin. "I thought we decided not to do anything drastic until we'd tried every avenue for clearing Percival's name honestly."

"*You* decided," corrected Brody. "We're not going to pass up an opportunity like this. If no one's managed to talk the king out of his idiocy in weeks, why would he listen to you?"

Heath took a breath. "Because I have new information for him. About who really attacked him."

All other conversation in the room ceased, and every eye flew to Heath.

"You've found evidence?" Bianca demanded, sounding excited. "What is it?"

Lord Percival? That's what you requested so urgently to speak about?

King Matlock's voice in Heath's head ripped his attention immediately away from his cousins. His vision of the room around him became fuzzy as he was transported in thought to Arinton. He could see the king's face as clearly as if he was standing next to him, but not any of his surroundings. Judging by the late morning sun on his face, he was outside, but that was all Heath could tell.

Not just him, Your Majesty, responded a smooth, cool voice. *I primarily wished to warn you about a new imminent threat. But I would be remiss if I didn't take the opportunity to urge you to deal with the traitor while you have him in your power. I am amazed that you have let him live this long, given the nature of his crime.*

King Matlock didn't look impressed. *I have no need to explain my decisions to you,* he reminded his companion. His eyes narrowed. *How can I be sure that you are truly the author of the letters I have been receiving? And why, after restricting yourself to correspondence until now, was it so urgent that you meet with me in person?*

I have no proof to offer you beyond my information. There was a placating edge to the other man's words. Heath wished desperately that he could see his face. *But who else would know the contents of my warnings? As for the urgency, I have reason to suspect that there is a new plot against your life. Is there someone among the power-wielders by the name of Heath?*

Heath's heart lurched, dread filling him. He didn't know the identity or agenda of the king's companion, but being mentioned by name couldn't be a good thing.

Heath? repeated King Matlock, a slightly defensive edge to his voice. *Lord Percival's brother is named Heath. But he's the only one of the power-wielders I trust. In point of fact, he's not a true power-wielder. His magic is so weak it achieves nothing but giving him a place in the family, which he has used faithfully in his role as liaison. It was he who thwarted his brother's attempt on my life.*

Indeed. The other man didn't skip a beat. *According to my information, he has had a change of heart.*

And what information is that? King Matlock's voice and face gave nothing away—without being actually present to read the king with his magic, it was impossible for Heath to tell whether King Matlock was buying the stranger's story.

That Heath has brought a member of the Dragonfriend line we spoke of into Valoria itself, with the intention of turning her considerable magic against you.

Her? repeated King Matlock.

She is a young woman, the other man confirmed. *From the island we've spoken of, off the coast of Thorania. The strongest of the exiled line of Dragonfriends. She has recently arrived in Valoria, with the aid of a renegade dragon. Her magic is fearsome and strong, bent toward destruction. I came to you in haste the moment I became aware—my sources say that she is to use her magic to free the prisoner, then combine her powers with his and Heath's to finish the task of vacating the throne of Valoria. If you want to stop them, you must eliminate the girl before she can join forces with Lord Percival. And of course you would be wise not to delay carrying out his sentence.*

The king was silent for a moment, and Heath could hardly breathe. There could be absolutely no question who this man's lies referred to. The only question was whether King Matlock already knew of Merletta's arrival. If he'd learned of it before leaving Bryford, it would go a long way to making the stranger's story sound credible.

You claim these power-wielders are determined to seize the throne,

King Matlock said unemotionally. *That they believe their magic gives them the right. Well, I think* you *have magic. I think perhaps you are one of them, with grand expectations of your own.*

Heath heard the other man's self-deprecating laugh. *It is understandable that you would make such a speculation, Your Majesty. But there is no magic about me. As I have told you, my family has served the Dragonfriends on the island for a generation now. I assure you, they are not satisfied with the place of their exile—they are determined to rule a kingdom, as their Kyonan brethren do. I believe there is a scheme to join the Valorian and exiled lines, to rule Valoria together.*

Heath's blood was boiling by now. They were such clever lies—just enough brush with the truth to make King Matlock pause. It wouldn't be hard for any inquirer to discover how Heath felt about Merletta. If she really was some distant cousin with powerful magic in her veins, and if his family really did have visions of seizing the crown, it would make sense for the two of them to have more reasons than love to come together.

There was a moment of silence between the king and his companion, during which Heath became vaguely aware of his cousins trying in increasing anxiety to get his attention. He must seem like he was in some kind of a trance. He ignored them.

I will consider these matters, said King Matlock at last. *I expect I will wish to discuss them with you further.*

Of course, Your Majesty, said the smooth voice. *There is some urgency to my own travels, but I am willing to stay in Arinton for two days to make myself available to you.*

The king nodded what was clearly a dismissal, and panic started to rise in Heath. He had to know who the king was speaking to!

"Help me!" he yelled aloud, keeping one eye on the king as he pulled his awareness back to Brody's room. "I need to see more—everyone, pool your magic!"

"What...what are you talking about?" demanded someone. It sounded like Jasmine. "Heath, what's going on?"

"I'm watching King Matlock with my farsight, but I'm not strong enough to see his surroundings on my own," said Heath impatiently.

"You're doing what?!" Several voices spoke in chorus now, and Heath actually growled in frustration. The man would surely be out of the king's vicinity soon.

"Your magic!" he yelled. "Right now!"

There was a moment's pause, then he felt a tendril of Bianca's familiar power reaching toward him. He latched on to it eagerly, feeling the way it swelled around his own magic. Soon more strands followed, and he reeled from the rush to his head as his extra sight received a sudden boost. His view zoomed backward, and he saw that King Matlock was standing on a grassy mound, his guards watching closely from just out of hearing range. Heath cast his sight around the area, searching for the other man. The king stood close to a large body of water, its hilly bank covered with yellow flowers. On a nearby slope, a town of gray stone rose up, the buildings starting right at the water's edge, and continuing up a central street which was so straight it was visible even from a distance.

There! A lithe, silver-haired man was walking toward the town. Heath pressed forward mentally, his sight following the lone figure. The man glanced back, and Heath received a shock.

He knew that face.

Send a courier to my steward immediately. King Matlock's words alerted Heath to the fact that one of his guards had approached him. *I want Lord Heath and his foreign visitor watched at all times. And I have been more than gracious with the depth of the formal investigation. Lord Percival's execution will take place in one week.* The guard gave a smart nod and jogged briskly away. King Matlock's next words were murmured to himself, with no expectation that anyone could hear—certainly not the subject of his mutterings.

And I had better not find that Lord Heath has been playing me for a fool.

Heath broke the connection with a gasp, his hands groping blindly around him as he tried to regain a sense of his true surroundings. A warm hand gripped one of his, squeezing reassuringly. His sight came into focus to see Merletta watching him grimly.

"What did you see?" she asked.

"It's him," Heath panted, feeling like he'd run a great distance. Merletta's brow creased in confusion, but before Heath could explain further, he was swamped by his cousins.

"Heath, what was that?"

"Do you have magic after all?"

"Did you say you have *farsight*? Like the dragons?"

"You can actually watch King Matlock? This is brilliant! We can anticipate his every move, and he'll never know why he can't outsmart us!"

This last enthusiastic comment came from the well-meaning but young Max, and it snapped Heath out of his stupor.

"Yes, I have magic." He frowned around at his cousins. "It's been emerging over the last few years. According to Reka, it's the strongest of our generation."

"This is excellent, Heath!" Leonora cried. "You're one of us! What exactly can you do?"

"But why didn't you tell us?" Brody demanded over the top of her.

Heath turned slowly toward Leonora, his heart suddenly so heavy he could hardly bear to have the conversation.

"I thought I was always one of you," he said quietly. "I thought we were blood."

The room fell instantly silent, and Heath met Brody's eyes before he continued.

"But that wasn't true, was it? Maybe daring to be loyal to our own kingdom could have been overlooked if I'd had overt magic like the rest of you. But combine the two, and I was no longer allowed inside, was I?"

Brody shifted uncomfortably, and Bianca looked close to tears. Merletta's hand was still in Heath's, and the steady warmth of the pressure helped ground him. He was still feeling too bruised to want his cousins' conditional acceptance, but that didn't mean he was alone.

"As for what I can do," he told Leonora, "I can watch people from afar, like the dragons do, within certain limits. I can also see other things that no one else can see." He cast his eyes around the group. "For example, I can tell that Bianca feels guilty, and that Brody is deeply convicted because he knows I'm right, but will probably wrestle for days before he acknowledges it." His eyes traveled along the group, smiling slightly. "Max is a clear brook—constantly in motion, nothing hidden far beneath the surface." He cocked his head to the side. "Leonora, you're keeping some secret from Jasmine. Nothing serious, I think," he mused, reading her chagrin with his magic. "Some petty affair between sisters. But it's weighing on you, always on your mind. Maybe that's why I can see it so painfully clearly."

"Heath!" Leonora protested, her face flushed and horrified.

He raised an eyebrow. "What's the matter? Don't you like the feeling that someone is using magic on you, when you have no way to predict or control it, or even to know it's happening? Does it make you feel powerless, maybe even afraid? Does it maybe even make your reactions less rational than normal?"

The room was so silent, it seemed no one was breathing.

Heath turned to Max. "I know you mean well, Max, but I hope I don't need to explain to you why I *won't* be using my magic to spy on King Matlock and report back to you every order he gives so that you can all outwit him and try to make him look a fool."

Max looked ashamed, and still no one spoke.

"I only watch him in a very limited way," Heath continued. "Only when he mentions Percival." A shudder went over him. "Which he just did. The execution is to be set for a week away."

There was a collective gasp. "Tonight is going ahead, then," said Brody determinedly.

Heath shook his head wildly. "No. If he runs now, he'll look more guilty than ever." He glanced at Merletta. "And so will others, if it comes to it. I know for a fact now that someone is working against us from outside. I just have to convince the king of that."

"We're not waiting on your diplomacy, Heath," Brody burst out. "You said yourself that if the king set a date—"

"A lot has changed since then," said Heath. "But I know it's not just up to me. Why don't you go ask Percival? Let him decide. I have to go to Arinton immediately. If you'll take my advice, you'll all come. It's time to have this out once and for all." He shrugged. "But I don't pretend to have any authority. Suit yourselves."

And without another word, he pulled Merletta from the room. She hurried behind him down two corridors, before he dragged her into an alcove behind a suit of armor.

"What is it?" she demanded. "What did you see?"

"I saw the man who's been in the king's ear," said Heath grimly. "Or merman, I should say, because I have no doubt he's from your world. He's setting a trap specifically for you." He quickly recounted the lies that had been told about Merletta.

She snorted. "If only I did have some kind of fabulous magic," she muttered.

"There's more," said Heath urgently. "I saw his face, and I recognize him."

She looked up sharply. "How is that possible? Surely it wasn't August or one of the other guards? They're the only mermen you've met, aren't they?"

"I didn't meet him recently," said Heath. "I saw him when I was a small child, in the markets in Bryford. It's one of my earliest memories. I sensed power on him, and I asked about it loudly. It made a bit of a scene, and my mother was very embarrassed. My father hoped it might be the first sign of my magic coming out, but when he realized the man wasn't one of the power-wielders, he figured it was just a misunderstanding."

Merletta stared at him. "You mean this merman has been coming to Valoria for almost two decades?"

Heath nodded. "At least. And he's come more recently than that. I saw him at the Winter Solstice Festival the year before last. He was there with two others, although I didn't recognize them. I sensed the same power I've been feeling at the attacks, so I know I wasn't wrong about his face."

Merletta's expression had hardened, and her face was set in familiar lines of determination.

"It's him," she murmured. "Him and his guards. I have no idea how they got here so quickly, but it must be them." She clenched her jaw. "But that means he's been behind all of it, from the beginning of our relationship...from well before that." She gave her head a little shake. "I have to see this correspondent to be sure—he probably didn't come in person, but I know what the guards look like. We need to get to this town."

Heath seized her hand, tugging her back out into the corridor. "We'll leave within the hour."

CHAPTER TWENTY-TWO

Merletta

Merletta clasped her hands together around Heath's waist, clinging on tightly and trying not to let her nerves show.

Of course, Heath had that irritating ability to see things others couldn't, so...

"Are you sure you wouldn't rather go in a carriage?" Heath swiveled slightly from his position in front of her on the horse. "It's going to be a long ride, and I'm going to be pushing us as fast as I can."

"Exactly," said Merletta firmly. "You said horseback is faster, so this is what we're doing. I'll manage." She sent him a cheeky grin. "I'll just have to trust you not to let me fall off."

Heath chuckled. "I promise." His expression sobered as he glanced at their companions. "Everyone ready?"

Bianca nodded from the closest horse, the rest of Heath's cousins copying. There was quite an array of them, and Heath's father and sister were planning to follow afterward in a carriage, as soon as they could get everything in order. The duchess was going to stay behind so as not to fully abandon her imprisoned oldest son.

"I see Brody has positioned himself as far from me as possible," Heath commented lightly to Bianca.

The friendly girl sent a long-suffering look toward her twin. "He thinks he's still sore over what he calls Percival's ingratitude, but in actual fact he's becoming more convinced by the minute that you're right about everything," Bianca informed Heath.

Heath shook his head, but he was smiling a little. Merletta squeezed his waist. Knowing everything that had passed between Heath and his brother, she'd shared Heath's satisfaction at hearing Percival's reaction to the plan. Apparently the prisoner had no sooner grasped the basics than he'd unequivocally insisted they abandon any break-out attempt and follow Heath's plan. He hadn't even wanted to hear the details—he'd just told them to stop wasting time and go do whatever Heath had instructed them to do.

Merletta didn't have magic that allowed her to see inside people, but she knew Heath well enough to read the pride in his bearing when he'd learned of his brother's support.

They were just trotting across the courtyard when a group of royal guards appeared in Merletta's peripheral vision. She glanced uncertainly at Heath, who had pulled up and was watching them warily. His tension turned to surprise when a lean figure on a large chestnut emerged from the center of the group.

"Lachlan," Heath said blankly. "Where are you going?"

"Same place as you," said the prince calmly. "Which I'm assuming is Arinton. We had an appointment to speak about important matters, didn't we?"

Heath bit his lip. "I'm sorry to run out on you, Lachlan," he told his cousin. "I did intend to speak to you about...everything. But something urgent came up."

"So I apprehend," said the prince, still unruffled. "So I will accompany you."

"But surely you can't just leave," Heath protested.

The prince gave him a look which bordered on exasperated —it made him seem younger, and much more approachable. "I'm not a fool, Heath. Clearly something big is about to go down, and I intend to be present for it."

Merletta could feel Heath wavering, but he made one more attempt to fight it. "It's a long journey. We'll have to stop overnight, and—"

"Thank you, Heath, I am fairly familiar with the geography of my own kingdom." The prince's tone made it clear the matter was closed, and Heath gave up. No doubt he was as impatient to be on the way as Merletta was.

The group left the city swiftly, taking few provisions. Heath explained to Merletta that the prince would no doubt have carriages following with servants and supplies, similar to the group currently being organized by the duke. Once she would have been rattled by the reminder of the dramatic difference in station between her and Heath, but all that seemed foolish now. It was the least of their obstacles, and yet—in spite of all barriers—they were together now. At least for the moment.

Merletta spared a thought for Sage, who had no such comfort. Everyone she loved, everything she'd ever known, was still in great peril back in the triple kingdoms. At least she wasn't being left behind in Bryford. She was going to follow in the carriage with Heath's sister—who had kindly taken Sage under her fins. So to speak.

The first day was long and tedious, and every muscle in Merletta's body was sore long before they stopped for the night. Her arms were weary from clinging on, and one of her legs kept bumping painfully against Heath's bow, which was attached to the horse's saddle.

They'd traveled as quickly as the horses could manage. It had been necessary for Merletta to take turns riding double with others throughout the day, to give Heath's horse a break. When they made camp for the night—the prince's retinue having sidetracked to spend the night at the manor of an accommodating noble—Merletta stumbled gratefully from Max's horse toward Heath.

"Maybe we should have considered Lachlan's offer more seriously, about asking the earl to let us stay as well," Heath said, casting a concerned look over her.

She shook her head. "I'm fine. Just in need of sleep." She groaned as she plopped down onto the grass, her back against a boulder. "Shame we're so far from the coast," she muttered. "I'd be tempted to slip into the water to sleep otherwise. So much more comfortable."

"Is it?" Heath asked, sounding intrigued. "What's it like?" He settled beside her and placed his hand next to hers.

She shifted slightly so their fingers were entwined. "The current rocks you to sleep. It's amazing."

For a moment they sat in companionable silence, watching one of the guards who'd accompanied the group building a fire.

"You should ride with me the whole time tomorrow," Heath said suddenly.

Merletta looked at him in surprise. "I'd prefer that, of course, but what about your horse?"

"Never mind my horse," said Heath curtly. "I'm more worried about Max."

"Why?" Merletta asked. "He seemed happy enough to me."

"Exactly," nodded Heath. "He was much *too* happy to have a pretty girl clinging on to him and sharing his horse."

Merletta laughed. "Surely you're not jealous, Lord Heath."

He smiled disarmingly at her. "My time with you has always been so contested, I'm jealous of anyone who manages to claim a moment that could have been mine."

"Your cousin Max is nice enough," Merletta said. "But he's not exactly a threat. A little young for me, don't you think?"

Heath grinned. "Actually, he's the same age as you."

"Oh." Merletta considered this. "I suppose you make him seem young. You've always been old for your age, at least since I've known you." She searched his face thoughtfully. "You have changed, you know, since we met. You've grown. You're more... solid now." She gave him a rueful smile. "Or maybe I just think that because I've come to depend on you more."

That surprised a laugh out of Heath. "If only that were true," he protested. "If anything, you seem to do better without my interference in your world."

Merletta shifted again, leaning her head against his shoulder. "Never," she declared.

Her eyelids drifted down, unbearably heavy after the exhausting day. The boulder was uncomfortable at her back, but Heath's arm around her was warm and reassuring. He must be tired, too, but he showed no sign of flagging, his presence strong and steady. Someone out of Merletta's range of vision asked him a question. She didn't even try to hear the words of his reply, just sinking into the comforting rumble of his voice. Her head had slipped from his shoulder to his chest, and she could feel the vibrations as he spoke.

It was soothing, almost like the current's gentle flow.

Merletta came to suddenly as her head slipped forward. She seemed to have shifted—she was now curled up more or less on Heath's lap, his arms around her keeping the chill of the night at bay. She looked up groggily to find his eyes on her, a smile in their depths.

"How long have I been asleep?" she asked.

"Probably two hours," he told her. "I saved you some food."

A glance around showed that the fire was burning low, and the area was mostly deserted. She could see Bianca picking her way toward them, past guards who were laying out simple pallets near the fire.

"What are those?" she asked, taking note of several shelters which hadn't been there before.

"The carriages caught up an hour ago, and they've set up simple tents," Heath explained. "I think you're sharing with Bianca."

Merletta pushed herself off Heath's lap. He let her go, but he seemed reluctant.

"Why did you let me sleep so long?" she asked. "You must be uncomfortable."

"A little," he admitted. "And I let you sleep because holding you in my arms for two hours was one of the best experiences of my life."

Merletta's breath caught in her throat. He had said the words simply, almost unemotionally, but that did nothing to hide the intensity behind them. All the unsaid words, the impossible hopes were spilling out of his eyes as he watched her in the firelight.

Longing rose up in Merletta, so sharp it was almost painful, so deeply intimate she could find no words for it.

"Can you imagine if it was this easy?" she whispered, reaching up to lay her fingers on his chest. She felt bold in the flickering light of the flames. "If we could just...be together?"

There was a definite edge of sadness to Heath's smile. "I don't dare to. That's the sort of imagination that has the power to make reality unendurable."

Merletta swallowed, her mind full of everything and nothing at once. The intensity of Heath's full attention was a weighty thing, not to be taken lightly. His eyes roamed over her face, as if he was memorizing her, and she saw his gaze linger on her lips.

Almost unconsciously, she leaned forward.

"Merletta, you're awake."

Bianca's cheerful voice reminded Merletta of her surroundings, and she shifted quickly away from Heath.

"I have some food for you, and a pallet where you can sleep properly. Come on."

Merletta didn't even look back at Heath as she rose. Their moment was broken, their time stolen away just as it began. It had always been that way for them, and Heath was right. Dreaming of a different future was too dangerous a distraction from the reality they had to deal with right here and now.

The next day passed more quickly. Merletta rode with Heath, and she could feel his tension mount as they drew closer to Arinton. The carriages had left very early, but the riders still overtook them before noon. Sage waved wearily to Merletta as they passed, looking like she hadn't slept much on the hard ground either. The prince's group, who'd stayed in the nearby manor, reconnected with them at about the same time.

Heath and Merletta shared no more charged moments. Mostly they whiled away the time with catching each other up on everything they'd missed in recent months.

"So tell me everything about this power you sensed at the attacks," Merletta said, halfway through the afternoon. "You really think there were merpeople there?"

"I know it seems absurd," said Heath, "but it's the only explanation that makes sense." He patiently repeated every detail of the relevant encounters.

"And you and the prince investigated, but you could find no trace of the attackers in Valoria?" Merletta pressed.

"Lachlan did find something," Heath corrected.

Merletta listened as he explained about the missing guard uniforms, and their conclusion that someone had paid mercenaries to impersonate royal guards during the attack on Percival.

"We think we may have even identified some of the mercenaries," Heath told her grimly. "Not that it did us much good. They were all dead."

"What? How?" Merletta demanded.

Heath sighed. "Various circumstances, no clear evidence of foul play. But we're pretty convinced they were all poisoned."

"Poisoned?" repeated Merletta, aghast. She shook her head, her voice dropping to a mutter. "It's him. It has to be. Poisoning is his preferred method underwater. Why change a winning approach, when it can just be adapted to work on land?"

"You're talking about the Record Master?" Heath asked sharply. "You think he's behind the times you were poisoned?"

"I think he's behind everything," Merletta said darkly. "I once thought it might have been a conspiracy somewhere in the middle ranks, but..." She shook her head. "You should have seen him at my trial, Heath. He hides it well, because he keeps out of sight. But he's at the center—the center of the world, as far as he's concerned. It's always been all about him."

Heath's voice was grim, and he held himself tightly in the saddle. "He might have the power to lead the triple kingdoms to total destruction," he said. "But in my world, he's not at the center. If it is him with the king in Arinton, we won't let him get away with this."

The horse was topping a small rise, and Merletta drew in a breath at the sight before them.

"Looks like we'll know one way or the other soon enough," Heath said. "We're almost there. That's Loch Arine."

"It's like a mini ocean," Merletta breathed, her eyes drinking in the view of the long body of water stretching between them and a small town which rose up a hill on the far side. "The town is still a couple of hours away, isn't it? Will we make it in time?"

"The king's mysterious correspondent said he would stay for two days," Heath said, uttering the title with a touch of sarcasm. "I think we'll make it."

There were still a few hours before sunset when the group approached the town. The prince and his guards pulled up alongside them as Heath urged his horse up the start of the gentle slope.

"I think it will be best if I speak with my father first," the prince told Heath. There hadn't been much opportunity for speech with the closely guarded Prince Lachlan, but Merletta knew that Heath had filled his cousin in on the basic reason for their hasty journey.

"All right," said Heath. "But I'm not going to risk letting the correspondent get away. If I have to barge in where I'm not wanted in order to stop that, I will."

The prince frowned at his cousin, keeping his horse abreast of Heath's with a steady hand.

"I think it's time you told me why we're here." Prince Lachlan's gaze flicked to Merletta, but he seemed to decide her presence was unavoidable, since he pushed on. "I've been frank with you, so you know that I haven't been able to discover anything concrete about my suspicion that someone unknown to me has been in my father's ear. Why exactly are you so convinced that my father is in Arinton specifically to meet with this person?"

Merletta could almost feel Heath's wince from her position behind him. She certainly felt the deep breath he took before speaking.

"I haven't been as frank with you as you've been with me," he admitted. "Not even close. I know the king is meeting with his correspondent because I saw it happen."

"You saw my father meet with him in Bryford and didn't tell me?" Prince Lachlan demanded. "When?"

Heath shook his head. "Not in Bryford. In Arinton. Yesterday morning."

"But..." The prince trailed off. He was clearly confused, but perhaps it was part of his royal training not to admit he didn't understand.

"I saw it with my magic," Heath said bluntly. "I can see things I shouldn't be able to." His words tumbled over each other, the dramatic revelation clearly not well rehearsed. "I know you must be wondering why my family always claimed I had no magic to speak of, but they didn't know. *I* didn't know. It only started a couple years ago. It was Merletta that triggered it, actually."

"Me?" Merletta asked, startled.

Heath nodded. "When I thought you were dead, I used to see you. It took a long time for me to realize it wasn't just my imagination."

"You're saying..." The prince's voice sounded hollow. "You're saying you can watch whoever you want, like the dragons can watch us if they choose? And you've been using that to spy on my father?"

"It's not quite like that," Heath said quickly. "I—"

"Your Highness." One of the guards cut Heath off. "Perhaps we should ride separately from Lord Heath."

The other guard grunted. "I agree, Your Highness. Our orders are to protect you from exposure to magic. And Lord Heath has just admitted to wielding fully untested magic."

Heath looked quickly at his cousin—Merletta had the impression he expected the prince to disagree. But Prince Lachlan merely gave a curt nod, turning his horse's head away.

"We will speak more of this," he told Heath, his words icy.

Merletta felt Heath deflate slightly as the prince rode away from him. "And my cousins have been asking why I kept my magic hidden so long," he muttered.

"All things considered, I think he took it well. It's possible he's more upset about you hiding it than he is about the magic," Merletta pointed out fairly. "Not that I mean to criticize," she added. "It's just that I have a world of experience with keeping far more than I should from my friends."

Heath didn't respond, and she said no more. Within minutes they were riding up the town's main street, heading toward a central square visible up ahead.

The prince's retinue had gone before them, and was now out of sight. While Merletta could sense that Heath was as impatient as she was, they both endured the necessary delay as the group secured rooms at the town's largest inn, both for themselves and the occupants of the carriages which arrived a bit more than an hour later, having made good time.

"Merletta!" Sage literally fell from the carriage, only prevented from tumbling face first onto the cobblestones by Merletta, who darted forward to catch her. "These legs are impossible," Sage muttered, quietly enough that no one else could hear.

Or at least, that's what Merletta thought, until she heard Heath's low chuckle.

"You poor thing, you must be exhausted," Merletta said, feeling repentant at how she'd abandoned her friend.

Sage shook her head in determination. "Not too exhausted to find out which of our kind has known about this kingdom for decades." Her face was grim, and Merletta understood. The deceptions had become personal for Sage as much as for Merletta by now.

"I agree," said Merletta. "But I'm guessing it will be a while before—"

"Lachlan was sent to the edge of town to speak with the king," Heath interrupted.

"How do you know?" Merletta demanded.

Heath nodded toward his own father, who was listening intently to a guard who'd ridden from the capital with their group. "Father's receiving a report right now."

Sage raised her eyebrows as she looked between Heath and the distant pair. "Is your hearing enhanced as well as your sight? Or do humans just hear better than we do?"

Heath grinned. "Not most humans. But I wasn't listening with my ears. I was listening with my magic." He must have seen Merletta's surprise, because he shrugged. "It doesn't only work from across kingdoms. Closer distances are just as good. And my father is easy for me to follow."

"That's very handy," Merletta said, feeling like she was only just grasping the full possibilities of Heath's magic.

"Blast," Heath muttered.

Merletta followed his gaze to see the duke watching them with narrowed eyes. The older man gave a curt nod to the guard, then strode toward them.

"I forgot how good he is at sensing it when I use my magic," Heath said sheepishly. "No slipping off, I guess."

CHAPTER TWENTY-THREE

Merletta

To Merletta's relief, the duke made no attempt to stop them. When he heard that his son was determined to seek the king out immediately, he instructed the group at large to fall in line.

"If you're right that someone is using lies to turn the king against us, the more witnesses to the coming confrontation, the better," he told Heath. "Lies and half-truths thrive best in secrecy. They tend to fall apart quickly in the light."

"Your father is very wise, I think," Merletta told Heath, as the group set out in the direction indicated by the guard.

Heath smiled, slinging his bow and quiver over his shoulder as he walked. "He is. He also has a lifetime of experience dealing with deception, thanks to the form of his magic."

"Shame he can't come sort out the Center," Merletta said grimly. She sighed. "Maybe that's why their lies are so successful—not enough light penetrates to the depth of the ocean."

Heath and Sage both chuckled at the joke, but Merletta's mind was already on the coming confrontation. Would it truly be one of the Record Master's personal guards meeting with

King Matlock? What would they do when they saw her? From Heath's account, it seemed clear that one purpose in coming to Valoria was to see her killed. Whether out of fear of her exposing the triple kingdoms to the Valorians or just out of spite she wasn't sure.

Spite, probably.

Heath slipped his hand into hers as they walked, the pressure reassuring. His thoughts were likely following a similar course to hers, and she was grateful that he hadn't tried to talk her into staying back from this crucial encounter. They'd come a long way.

Their path took them around the edge of the town, back toward the water. The road into Arinton had led them from the water's edge up a gentle slope, but at this point of the shore the ground fell away in a cliff, the water some fifteen feet directly below.

On top of the cliff there was a paved courtyard, its edge lined with a waist-high balustrade. Half a dozen guards stood some distance back from the barrier, next to which there were three figures.

Recognizing Prince Lachlan, Merletta realized that some of the guards must be his. The others were undoubtedly there for King Matlock, who was in conversation with the third figure, a lithe silver-haired man with his back to the approaching group.

The king saw them over his companion's shoulder, and his face visibly hardened. His eyes flicked to Heath and Merletta's joined hands, and his own hand actually strayed to the hilt of his sword. Merletta swallowed. Clearly he believed his informant's lies about Merletta having some powerful destructive magic.

Issuing a curt command they were still too far away to hear, the king shifted to face them fully, his son maneuvering beside him. The guards converged, not quite forming a barrier between the trio and the oncoming group, but certainly making their presence felt.

"Your Majesty," the duke greeted the king calmly. "There's no need for your guards to be alarmed."

"I'll be the judge of that, Norik," said the king, his voice curt.

His next words were lost to Merletta as the silver-haired man turned. Merletta and Sage let out audible gasps, drawing instinctively together.

"It's him," Sage whispered. Her eyes flicked down the Record Master's form. "He has his legs—he's wearing human coverings and everything!"

Merletta nodded grimly. "He looks very comfortable in this world, doesn't he?" She shook her head. "I can hardly believe he's actually here. I thought for sure he would have sent someone else to do his dirty work."

The Record Master's gray eyes met hers, and Merletta drew back slightly. His expression might be calm, but he couldn't hide the murder in his eyes. He wanted her dead. Perhaps more than he wanted anything else in this moment.

Heath seemed to sense it, too—perhaps reading the Record Master with his extra sight—because he tightened his hold on Merletta's hand, shifting slightly so she was partially behind him.

"Stay away from her," he said, his voice as cold as the depths.

The Record Master's eyes flew to Heath, seeming taken aback. He hadn't moved, or given any visible sign of wanting to hurt Merletta. Perhaps he was surprised to have the young human respond to his thoughts rather than his actions.

The duke followed his son's gaze, and Merletta actually heard him catch his breath.

"Who is this man, Your Majesty?" he asked.

"It is no affair of yours whom I speak to, Norik," the king reminded him.

"I imagine that means you don't know yourself," said Heath's father dispassionately. "And I'm not surprised. I've never encountered anyone to equal him. His every breath radiates deception. I doubt any detail of whatever he's told you is the truth."

"What a convenient assessment by your magic, cousin," the king said, with a humorless laugh. He stepped forward, his eyes glinting. "Is this what it comes to? I thought the dangerous aspirations were limited to your sons, but have you coveted my crown as well? For how many years have you played your part, preparing for the day when you would use your magic to overthrow me?"

"How dare you, Your Majesty?" The impassioned protest came, most unexpectedly, from Laura. Heath's sister stepped forward from the group, her eyes blazing. "My father has given you nothing but faithful service all his life, and you have repaid him with hateful suspicion."

"Laura." The duke's quiet admonishment came as no surprise to Merletta. Her exposure to him was enough to tell her he wouldn't want his children putting themselves on dangerous ground for his sake. No wonder Heath had such honor, and such a strong instinct of protection for those he loved.

"Nothing but faithful service?" repeated Prince Lachlan, weighing in. His eyes flicked to Heath and away again, one hand balled into a fist. "Is that what you call concealing the fact that his own son was spying on his sovereign with dangerous magic?"

"That's right," said the king in a hard voice. "I know all about Lord Heath's illicit magic."

"I assumed you would," Heath said calmly. "I would never

expect Prince Lachlan would keep it a secret from you—I know I didn't enjoy keeping it a secret from him. But you can't blame my father for any of that. If my magic had showed up when I was a child, like most of my family's magic did, I would never have dreamed of keeping it to myself. But it only became evident after you had introduced restrictions which were—forgive my bluntness, Your Majesty—utterly impossible for us to keep. For that reason, and because I was concerned that my developing magic would make me *less* effective in my role as liaison, I chose not to tell even my own family."

"Oh, Heath." The quiet words came from Heath's cousin Bianca, who'd sidled up to the front of the group. "I wish we hadn't made you feel that way."

Heath acknowledged her words with a nod, but his eyes were on Prince Lachlan, who looked ever so slightly less rigid.

"It wasn't because I had any nefarious intentions," Heath said quietly, his words clearly directed to the prince.

"Do not be distracted by these tactics, Your Majesty." The Record Master's smooth voice—its tones hatefully familiar—carried across the courtyard. His eyes flicked to Merletta. "That is the young woman I spoke to you about. Remove her—do not underestimate her!" His eyes narrowed as he seemed to notice Sage for the first time. "And she's brought another of her line! You cannot allow them the opportunity to use their magic against you!"

"The potency of your deception is almost suffocating," the duke said, in the tone one might use on an erring child. "Who are you, and what is your true intention here?"

Heath was a little less restrained in his reaction. He released Merletta's hand, stepping forward furiously. "You're a despicable liar!" he spat at the Record Master. "Do you think I'll let you kill Merletta to cover your crimes? I know everything—I know you've been trying to kill her for years, only because she dared to expose your corruption."

"She has bewitched the boy with her magic," the Record Master told the king, ignoring Heath completely. "Do not let yourself be similarly taken in."

"You hypocrite!" Heath cried. "She has no magic you don't have."

"Enough!" the king said sternly, as the Record Master gave a pitying shake of the head. "You are hardly one to make accusations about hidden magic, Lord Heath."

"If only we could show them the truth," Sage muttered from beside Merletta. She sent a considering glance toward the lake. "There is water right there..."

Merletta shook her head. "Fresh water doesn't work. I've tried it in the streams on Vazula. That lake wouldn't reveal anything—it has to be the ocean."

"I have no idea what you're talking about, but it sounds important." The quiet words came from Heath's cousin Brody, who was standing not far behind Sage. "So it seems like I should tell you—that's not a lake. It's a loch. It's actually connected to the ocean by an underground inlet."

"That's seawater down there?" Merletta demanded sharply.

Brody nodded, and Merletta turned to Sage with determination. "That's all the opportunity we need."

Sage gave a curt nod. "You're too visible. He'll notice if you try anything. I'm going to see if I can get around. The guards only care about the king and the prince, right?"

Merletta shifted so she was blocking Sage from view, putting on a look of great concentration, as if she was listening to the argument still raging between the king and the power-wielders. She felt Sage move away from her, and a short time later, caught sight of her friend in her peripheral vision, inching around the edge of the courtyard.

"One of them is trying to escape, Your Majesty!" The Record Master's pointing finger drew everyone's attention to Sage's progress, and two of the guards stepped toward her meaningfully.

"So much for stealth," muttered Merletta.

Shoving past Heath and his father, who stood shoulder to shoulder in front of her, Merletta sprinted across the courtyard. One of the guards lunged forward with a shout, positioning himself in front of the king. Merletta dodged nimbly, giving him a wide berth as she streaked straight past King Matlock and his son.

She saw the moment the Record Master realized her intent. His hand shot out, reaching for his belt, but he was too late. Before he could withdraw whatever was hidden, Merletta collided bodily with him, sending him staggering back against the balustrade. For an instant it seemed he would regain his balance, but Merletta pushed her feet against the paving stones with all her might as she threw herself against him once more. He reached out instinctively, seizing her arms in a bruising grip, but all it achieved was to bring her with him as he toppled backward over the edge of the cliff.

There was a moment of suspension as they fell, limbs flailing. Air rushed past Merletta's ears, and more than one startled scream sounded from above them. Then Merletta hit the water with a splash that felt as if Heath's magically strong brother had slapped her back with all his might. She felt her legs turn smoothly into tail, and sucked in a reassuring mouthful of water. Brody hadn't been wrong—it had worked.

Flicking her tail as best she could around her impractical gown, she dove deeper, then looped back upward, shifting instantly into a defensive position. Her eyes darted around, and she spotted the Record Master, still righting himself. Her skirts hid most of her tail, but he hadn't fared so well. His human trousers had been torn apart by the formation of his tail, and his scales glinted in the dying light of the day.

The Record Master's eyes found Merletta, narrowing in fury. He pulled a short, sharpened staff from the belt still tied around his waist, above his tattered pants. Of course he'd carry that instead of a sword, like the humans used. Merfolk always trained with spears.

Not giving him a chance to plan his attack, Merletta sped toward him. He raised his weapon, but at the last minute she flicked up and then plummeted downward, in a move Agner had perfected with her over many painful training sessions.

Her tail lashed out as she flipped, catching her opponent with full force right in the face. He let out an oath as his head jerked back.

"Your guards aren't here to do your dirty work for you now, are they?" Merletta growled. "Where are they? Trapping innocent merpeople inside the barrier, or framing power-wielders up on land?"

The Record Master's gray eyes showed nothing but hatred. "Putting the pieces together so cleverly," he sneered. "But I don't need guards to fight for me. You forget—I once passed the program myself. Which is more than anyone will ever be able to say of you."

Merletta gave a hollow laugh. Could he possibly think she still cared about passing the program? Seeing that the Record Master was tensing for an attack, Merletta put on a spurt of speed, moving in a straight line as far from him as she could while she struggled to rip open the laces down the front of her gown. The fabric weighed her down dangerously, and she felt the Record Master's hand close around the tip of her fin just as the laces finally came loose.

With a mighty flick, she dislodged his grip—leaving a tiny bit of fin behind, judging by the searing pain—and shot downward, straight out of the garment. Before the Record Master could process her change in direction, Merletta streaked up toward the air above.

Her head and shoulders—now bare—broke the surface with hardly a splash, her eyes already searching the courtyard far above.

"Merletta!" Heath's cry held equal parts fear and relief at her appearance. She could see that he was itching to dive after her, but thankfully he had enough sense to realize that he'd be more hindrance than help to her in the water.

"Seize them both!" The order came from the king, but his guards hesitated, clearly unsure how best to obey.

A flurry of movement drew Merletta's eye to Prince Lachlan, who was running toward a set of steps which led steeply down to the water, shedding his jacket as he went. Two of his guards sprinted after him, but the rest of the group were leaning half over the rail, staring in open astonishment at Merletta's golden-tipped fins where they protruded from the water.

All this she noted in a moment, aware that the Record Master would be right behind her. Sure enough, Heath's warning cry made her turn, and she surged out of the way just in time.

"She needs a spear!" The frantic cry came from Sage, whom Merletta saw now was being held between two guards.

Heath turned his head sharply at the words. Unsurprisingly, none of the guards were carrying spears, but a moment later something came hurtling into the water. Merletta dove down after it, catching it before it disappeared into the loch's depths. It was some kind of decorative pole, but it was better than nothing. Ripping off the pennant that adorned it, Merletta turned in time to clumsily parry a slash from the Record Master.

He let out a growl as he renewed his attack, but Merletta fended him off ferociously. She felt much more secure with a spear in her hand, however makeshift. She wasn't a gritty untrained orphan from the slums anymore. Not for nothing had she spent countless hours over the last few years training to fight like a guard. She rained blows upon the Record Master, moving fluidly through the water as she advanced, constantly on the edge of breaking through his guard.

Wherever possible she forced him up toward the surface, and further toward the edge of the loch. At last, when he was almost against the rocky side of the cliff, she managed to land a thrust, not far below the point where his skin turned to scales. It didn't skewer him, as a proper spear likely would have, but it was still enough to send his blood pouring into the water.

He gave a harsh cry, his hand flying to the wound, and Merletta couldn't resist a taunt.

"Guess you shouldn't have let them train me for so long before trying to do me in."

The Record Master's face twisted in rage, but he had no chance to respond. Seeing what was just behind him, Merletta swung her blunt spear around, pressing the flat of its length against his midriff and forcing him back against the cliff.

Arms shot out from behind him, seizing him in an iron grip. Merletta saw him freeze as the tip of a blade was pressed to his back. Merletta still held him in place with her weapon, but before she knew what was happening, one of the guards had seized her arm as well, and was hauling her bodily from the water.

"Watch out!" she screamed, as she felt her scales ripple in preparation for the change.

But the warning was too late. The Record Master had taken full advantage of the sudden reprieve, twisting around toward the man who held him. In the same moment, he snatched a small blade from his still-intact belt. With a cry of horror,

Merletta watched as he stabbed it upward, catching Prince Lachlan in the arm.

The prince let out a grunt of agony, releasing his captive to clutch the wound. The Record Master drew his arm back, clearly ready to attack again. Merletta flailed uselessly against the guard who held her, while the other guard lunged toward the merman. It was clear he wouldn't make it in time.

Suddenly, the Record Master let out a shrill scream. Merletta blinked stupidly at him, her mind taking a moment too long to comprehend what she was seeing. An arrow was sticking straight out from his arm like an urchin's needle. It had been shot with such force she could actually see the arrowhead protruding out the other side of the arm.

Her stomach roiling, she followed the trajectory of the arrow to see Heath, one foot braced against the balustrade, a fresh arrow in the bow as he calmly surveyed the scene below.

With a gasp, the Record Master fell backward from the pale-faced Prince Lachlan, disappearing silently beneath the water. Merletta struggled harder against her captor, who issued a curt command to stay put.

"Are you going to retrieve him from the bottom of the loch?" Merletta demanded. "He's not dead! He can swim out to sea if we leave him!"

The guard wavered, and Merletta took the opening. Wrenching away, she dove back into the water, racing after the Record Master. To her relief, he wasn't making any attempt to escape. The arrow still stood out of his arm, and he seemed to be on the edge of consciousness. She wrapped an arm around his torso, flicking with her tail to bring him back to the surface.

As soon as they reached the bank, guards converged upon them. More had raced down the steps, and Merletta and the Record Master were both hauled back up to the courtyard. Merletta realized she was limping a little, her toes cut and bleeding from when the Record Master injured her fin. When they reached the platform, she realized that almost everyone was either staring at her in astonishment or carefully averting their eyes. A surreptitious glance down reassured her that her shells were still in position, as was her short, scaled skirt. Must be a human privacy thing.

"Merletta!" Heath rushed forward, his eyes scanning her, although clearly not out of interest in her attire. "Are you hurt?"

She shook her head. "I'm fine." Following his gaze, she got a good look at the Record Master. He still seemed barely conscious, blood pouring from the wound Merletta had inflicted to his thigh, and from the arm pierced by the arrow. "Did you miss?" she asked Heath. "Or weren't you trying to kill him?"

"I didn't miss." Heath's eyes had moved to Prince Lachlan, who was walking up the stairs between two guards, grasping his injured arm. "It seemed appropriate to go for the arm," Heath said. Concern creased his brow as he watched the prince. "Lachlan's wound is bad, Merletta. It's...worse than it looks."

"How do you know?" she demanded.

Heath shook his head. "I just do. When I look at the wound, I can just...see it."

King Matlock's face was pale as he strode forward to greet his son. After a brief conversation, he turned to Heath.

"Lord Heath," he said, his voice a little stiff. "I must thank you. It seems that once again your intervention was timely." His tone darkened. "Although do not think it will make me forget how much you have concealed from me."

Heath dipped his head. "I understand, Your Majesty," he said.

King Matlock had already moved on to the Record Master, however. Fury made his form tremble. "You carry no magic, you said? How many more lies have you fed me, with the veneer of truth?"

"Don't blame yourself, Your Majesty," said Merletta wearily. "He's made a life's work out of deception. He's very good at it, and he knows how to be convincing."

The duke nodded in agreement. "The complexity and scope of the deception that hangs around him is truly beyond anything I've ever encountered." He strode forward, his eyes narrowed as they rested on the Record Master. "Are you behind the attacks on my sons? Did you frame Percival for attempting to kill the king?"

"Of course not," the Record Master managed to grind out.

The duke drew in a sharp breath, his face twisted, as if the bald-faced lie was physically painful to him. "The deception is so potent, I could almost reach out a hand and grab it," he muttered. Determination set across his features. "All the better." He closed his eyes, taking on a look of great concentration.

Heath made a noise of jubilation, and Merletta looked at him questioningly.

"He's using his magic," Heath murmured. "Powerfully—it's the most I've ever felt from him." He saw she was still confused, and added, "My father mainly uses his magic to detect deception, but it's capable of going further. He can actually...break it. I don't know how else to explain it."

As if to confirm Heath's words, the king suddenly gasped. His look of horror changed quickly to anger. "You lied to me," he said, his eyes a little unfocused as he turned toward the Record Master. "Every word from your mouth is a poisonous lie." He straightened. "You will never have the chance to deceive me again—or anyone, for that matter. Guards, secure all three of the..." The king trailed off, clearly struggling for the word.

"Merpeople," Heath supplied helpfully. "But surely you don't intend to arrest Merletta and Sage?"

"All three of the prisoners will be transported back to Bryford immediately," the king went on, not looking at Heath. "And I want Lord Percival brought out of the dungeons for further questioning the moment we arrive." His eyes hardened as they rested again on the Record Master. "The investigation has uncovered new information."

CHAPTER TWENTY-FOUR

Heath strode toward the audience hall, his steps agitated. Laura hurried by his side, accompanied by her husband Edmund. He hadn't joined the group traveling to Arinton, but he'd heard about it in excruciating detail by now, if Heath knew Laura.

Heath had also heard enough opinions from his family during the several days since the incident to make him long for the solitude of Vazula.

"I'm just...struggling to get my head around it," Edmund said, for probably the fifth time. "Are you sure she—"

"Yes, I'm sure, Edmund," Laura said, exasperated. "I didn't imagine her sprouting a massive scaly tail. And neither did the other two dozen people who saw it."

Edmund looked uncertainly at Heath. "And you knew?"

Heath sighed, impatient with these unimportant details. "Of course I knew. I knew her for a year before I even realized she could get legs. She didn't even know."

The couple gaped at him, but he ignored them.

"Was it really necessary for the king to throw Merletta and Sage into the dungeons, too?"

Laura rolled her eyes. "They arrived an hour ago, Heath. I don't think that's long enough for the dysentery to set in."

"When you see the state Percival's in, you might not find that joke so funny," Edmund said mildly. "I went to see him yesterday."

Heath and Laura both fell silent, chastened. Heath was ashamed to realize he almost had forgotten his brother being in the dungeons, too. The idea of Merletta down there was just so awful, especially after she helped capture the Record Master who'd plotted so unconscionably against the king and kingdom.

"Try to see it from the king's perspective, Heath," Laura said softly. "You can't expect him to just believe you all at once."

Heath said nothing, knowing she was right.

When they reached the audience hall, it was to discover a large crowd already gathered. Lachlan stood at the front of the room, next to the raised dais where his father stood. The prince's arm was in a sling, and although he looked calm, Heath could see at a glance that something was very wrong. There was no physical sign—it must be Heath's magic at work identifying a problem.

Heath had expected a long and tedious address, so he almost cried with relief at the king's simple announcement.

"The investigation into the attack that threatened my life and that of my guards has brought to light a conspiracy against the crown, undertaken with the intent of implicating the power-wielders. The true culprit has been apprehended, and is being held in the dungeons. Lord Percival has accordingly been released, with a full pardon for his words against the crown, of which he now repents."

"That's a bit rich!" muttered Laura, but Heath hardly heard her. He was too busy soaking in the sight of his brother, who was being led in through an antechamber.

Edmund had been right. In spite of the fact that he'd clearly been given the opportunity to wash and put on fresh clothes, Percival looked awful. He was much skinnier than before his captivity, and his hair was shaggy in a way the proud young man would never have allowed had he been given the choice. None of this was news to Heath, who'd regularly watched Percival with his farsight—barely a day had gone by without him checking in with his brother from afar. But somehow it was much worse seeing it in person. Although, to Heath's relief, Percival seemed in good spirits in spite of it all.

Percival bowed to the king. "Your words are gracious, Your Majesty," he said, and to Heath's amazement he could detect no sarcasm. "I am relieved to be exonerated of a crime I never dreamed of committing. But I acknowledge that I was hasty in the expression of my anger, and in that way, I contributed to the misunderstanding."

Laura made a small noise of surprise, her mouth hanging open as she stared in amazement at her brother. "Who is that, and where's Percival?"

Heath couldn't quite suppress a smile.

"No, seriously," said Laura, turning to him with wide eyes. "We should have locked him up in the dungeon years ago."

Heath let out a noise halfway between a laugh and a choke, but the sound died as he realized that the audience was over.

"What about Merletta and Sage?" he demanded, as people began to file out of the audience hall, discussing the development excitedly. A number of young people converged on Percival, but he shook them off, making a beeline for his family.

Heath shoved his way through the crowd toward his brother, but he was only halfway there when a familiar voice hailed him.

"Heath."

He turned to see Lachlan standing nearby, flanked by guards.

"Lord Edmund, Lady Laura." The prince inclined his head.

"Lord Percival." Percival had reached them. "My father has requested that I speak with you all."

Glancing curiously at each other, they all followed Lachlan into an antechamber.

"Where's Mer—" The demand was half out of Heath's mouth when he spotted Merletta and Sage waiting in the room, and he cut himself off. "What's going on?"

Merletta met his eyes, her expression mutinous, but it was Lachlan who spoke.

"The party with the prisoners took longer to arrive partly because the injured captive required medical attention, and partly because my father wished him to be questioned immediately."

"In case he didn't make it," Merletta cut in. "But irritatingly, he's recovering quickly."

Lachlan waited with an expression of great patience until satisfied she was done interrupting.

"Based on the results of that interrogation, and on his inquiries into the information you provided, Heath, my father has accepted that the prisoner was indeed behind all of the attacks, and meant to frame Lord Percival."

"Although I still don't really understand why," Merletta interjected again, frowning.

"Maybe it was because of you and Heath," Sage suggested hesitantly.

"Maybe." Merletta didn't look convinced, and Heath agreed with her.

"That might explain why he tried to do away with me," he said. "I'd already suspected that. But why would he have attacked Percival so long before that? And why frame Percival for King Matlock's death? Both of those attacks seemed designed to inflame tensions between the crown and the power-wielders, and I don't see how that benefited the Record Master."

"There are many questions still to be answered," agreed Lachlan, his piercing gaze reminding Heath that a great deal of those answers would be expected from him. "Which is why my father is unable to grant your guest's request."

Heath frowned at Merletta. "What request?"

"I want to take the Record Master back to the triple kingdoms to face justice," Merletta said, stepping toward him eagerly. "He's finally been exposed for what he is, and none of the rest of my people even know it!"

"His crimes were committed here," Lachlan told her. "And it is here that he must face whatever sanction my father deems—"

"No offense, Your Highness," Merletta interrupted, "but the crimes he committed here are a drop of water compared to the ocean of wrongs he's caused in my home. He's been murdering with impunity for decades, and he's currently midway through a plot to see most of the triple kingdoms die as a diversion to allow him to escape the dragons."

"He won't need to worry about dragons," said Lachlan grimly. "He won't be making it out of Bryford alive, of that you can be confident."

"But that doesn't give me any confidence," Merletta protested. "I don't want him to die here, with his true nature still concealed from everyone back home. They need to know the truth of what he's done!"

Sage cleared her throat, looking a little conscious as every eye turned to her. "This seems like a good moment to remind everyone that while the Record Master might not need to worry about the dragons, we do. We were trying to conceal our presence, right? Don't you think word of the display at the loch will reach them?"

Heath let out a long breath. "Yes," he said heavily. "I do. I've already spoken with Reka about it. He's not actually with the colony right now, but he's doing his best to keep an eye on their progress."

"Sorry." Percival's voice, a little husky from limited use, cut across the conversation. "Are we really talking about dragons and sentencing and practical details?"

Heath frowned at him, concerned. "What would you prefer we talk about?"

"I don't know," said Percival sarcastically. "Maybe the fact that the girl you're clearly head over heels for is an *actual mermaid*? Am I the only one still struggling to comprehend that?"

"Thank you," said Edmund. "That's what I said."

"I'm not sure what more there is to be said about that," Heath shrugged.

"Not sure—Heath!" Percival exploded. "She's a MERMAID!"

"I am standing right here, you know," Merletta said mildly.

Percival eyed her. "I'm aware of that. He gestured at her gown. Do you have...scales under there?"

"Not at present," Merletta informed him, her lips twitching. Heath grinned at her.

"Percival!" Laura scolded her brother. "What a rude question. You can't ask a lady what's beneath her gown!" She cast an appraising look between Heath and Merletta. "It is all very strange at first," she agreed. "But once you adjust to it, it's not as big a matter as I would have thought. It certainly explains some of Heath's weirdness around it all."

She sent him a dark look. "Although I thought you said you were telling me the whole truth."

"Yes, well..." He smiled sheepishly at her. "I may have left some things out. But I did say her kingdom is in the middle of the ocean."

"It's not, though, is it?" Merletta pointed out vaguely. "It's, you know...at the bottom."

Sage nodded wisely from beside her, and Merletta hastened to turn to more important topics.

"Speaking of our kingdom, surely your king won't deny us the right to hold the Record Master to account for his crimes."

"You don't have any rights here," Lachlan informed her brutally. "My father is the king, and the prisoner is in his custody. Besides, the only crime that's been proved is his plotting against Valoria. Whatever he has or hasn't done in your kingdom hasn't really been exposed, has it?"

"All the more reason we need to take him back to face justice," Merletta argued.

"At least let us speak with him, Lachlan," Heath pleaded. "Ask questions of our own."

The prince shook his head. "He's been moved to a secure location. No one is allowed to approach him." He cleared his throat. "That's not what I wished to speak with you about, however."

Heath raised a questioning eyebrow, and his cousin let out a sigh.

"My father is grateful for the assistance offered by Merletta during the attack in Arinton. However, there can be no denying that she and her companion entered Valoria under false pretenses. As their kingdom is not recognized by our crown, their visit here must be considered to have occurred without royal sanction."

"What are you saying, Lachlan?" Heath demanded. "Drop the formality and get to the point. Is your father trying to put Merletta back in the dungeons? Because I'm telling you now, I won't let it happen."

"He is not," said Lachlan gravely. "But he has requested that she and her companion leave Valoria immediately."

"Which is no problem whatsoever," Merletta cut in. "Provided we can take *our* prisoner with us."

"That will not be possible," Lachlan said. "My father is not going to change his mind on that matter. You'd do best to drop it."

"I'm extremely bad at dropping things," Merletta said dryly. "Especially when those in power particularly want me to."

"It's true," Sage confirmed.

"So he's kicking them out, is he?" Heath barely had the energy to be angry. He met Merletta's eye, communicating silently. "We'll talk more amongst ourselves, decide what's best to be done."

She nodded curtly, accepting the request to stand down for now.

The family started filing out of the room, Heath at the rear. He'd almost reached the door when Lachlan held him back.

"I've been wanting the chance to speak with you, Heath," he said. "But in all honesty, I hardly know what to say. So much has changed."

Heath met his eyes. "I can understand why you feel that way," he said. "But for what it's worth, as far as I'm concerned, nothing has changed."

The prince considered him in silence for a moment, then gave a slow nod. His eyes didn't hold the openness they once had, but Heath could hardly blame him for needing more time given everything that had just been revealed. As Merletta had said, he'd taken it all remarkably well.

"How's your arm?" Heath blurted out.

A shadow crossed Lachlan's face. "Still healing."

"You can be honest with me, Lachlan," Heath said. He winced. "As ironic as I realize it is for me to say that."

Lachlan gave a faint smile. "The physician is concerned," he said. "And to be frank, so am I. I can tell something isn't right. I don't think it will heal fully."

"What, ever?" Heath asked, dismayed.

Lachlan looked troubled. "At first I thought it was just an ordinary sword injury, albeit a particularly painful one. But after a couple of hours, the pain settled enough that I noticed my arm was growing increasingly more numb, further down from the wound." He pointed to the bandage on the inside of his upper arm. "Even my hand..." He hesitated, then said in a rush. "I haven't been able to move my hand properly since the injury."

"But that was days ago!" said Heath, alarmed. "And it's your sword arm!"

"I'm aware," said Lachlan heavily. Silence fell between them as Heath thought through all the possible ramifications for Lachlan's life. For the kingdom, even. No wonder King Matlock wanted to exact punishment on the Record Master himself.

"I'd best let you go and make preparations," Lachlan said at last.

His eyes flicked to the doorway, and Heath realized Merletta was hovering on the other side, out of hearing, but within sight.

"I'm sorry about my father's decision regarding Merletta, Heath," Lachlan said.

Heath shrugged. "Honestly, it's the least of my problems at present."

Lachlan nodded. "I'm reasonable enough to understand your reluctance to tell my father about your magic, given everything going on," he said quietly. "But I confess, I wish you'd been honest with me."

"Maybe I should have been," Heath acknowledged. He smiled wearily at his cousin. "For what it's worth, I have no more secrets now."

"None whatsoever?" Lachlan's eyes darted again to Merletta.

"If you're talking about the fact that I'm desperately in love with Merletta, the answer is still the same," Heath said evenly. "That's not a secret, as Percival has already pointed out."

Lachlan was clearly taken aback by the candid reply. "What

will you do?" he asked, after a moment of silence. "She's been exiled from the kingdom, and my father isn't likely to bend on that anytime soon."

"I don't know," said Heath. "That's a problem for tomorrow, and today has plenty of its own."

Lachlan nodded, and Heath hurried to join the others.

"Heath, I'm not just leaving the Record Master here," said Merletta, the moment he reached her. "I understand that your king is angry with him, but his real crimes are against my people."

"I agree," Heath said. "But I don't want him going anywhere until I understand why he was trying to cause trouble between the power-wielders and the crown. I think the first step is speaking to him ourselves."

"How are we going to do that?" Percival chimed in. "He's been moved somewhere secure, remember? We have no idea where that is."

"No idea?" Heath scoffed. "You underestimate how invested I've become in the Record Master. With Laura's and your magic, it shouldn't be a problem." He closed his eyes, drawing on his siblings' power and focusing all his attention on the hated face of the man who'd tried to kill Merletta some half a dozen times by now.

"Huh," he said, emerging again. "I had no idea there was a smaller dungeon hidden under the far side of the public garden. "He looks uncomfortable in there, so that's something, at least."

"You can really see that?" Percival demanded. "Just...right now, from where you're standing?"

Heath nodded.

"Did you...did you watch *me* in the dungeons?"

"All the time," Heath responded promptly.

Percival made a face. "Well, that's a bit—"

"Unnerving?" Heath grinned unashamedly, almost giddy with the relief of having his brother back. "Good."

Merletta rolled her eyes, although she was smiling, too. "Let's go," she said.

The group made their way out of the castle, moving across the gardens with purpose. When they reached a set of semi-overgrown stairs leading underground, Percival shot Heath a look of respect. Apparently he hadn't been entirely convinced of his brother's skill until it had been proven.

There was a guard visible at the bottom of the stairs, and Heath paused. No doubt the man had orders not to let anyone past.

"What should we do?" Percival asked doubtfully. "I could knock him out, of course. But it seems like a bad idea."

"A very bad idea," agreed Laura. "And entirely unnecessary."

She traipsed past Heath, a cheerful smile on her face. After only a minute's conversation with the guard, she waved for the others to join her. Uncertainly, they all moved forward, but the guard just smiled them through.

"I thought you could change people's emotions, not their minds," Percival muttered to his sister as they entered the small dungeon.

"The two are very interconnected," she informed him cheerfully. "Grandmother and I have chatted about it many times."

"It could be dangerous in the wrong hands, couldn't it?" Percival commented.

Heath and Laura exchanged a long-suffering look at this shocking revelation.

"Heath isn't the only one who's held back on his powers to avoid causing tension, or even doing wrong to those around him, Percival," Laura said shortly. "In fact, you're probably the only one who *hasn't*. Uncle Aaron had to move his family halfway across the kingdom to avoid people like Lord Niel finding out he can create fear, and turning on him."

Percival said nothing, looking uncharacteristically chastened. It seemed many long weeks in a dungeon would do that to a person.

"You." Merletta's icy voice brought everyone's attention to the man laid out in a tiny cell. "Finally getting what you deserve."

The Record Master sat up, the motion slow and apparently painful. His gray eyes were dark with hatred as they rested on Merletta.

"Your turn will come," he told her. "Do you think the dragons will overlook the most flagrant example of our kind?"

"Maybe so," Merletta told him. "But rest assured I'll live long enough to see you exposed first."

"What you think you can do to me now, I can't imagine," he said simply.

Heath stepped up beside Merletta. "We have some questions for you," he said confidently.

The silver-haired man raised his eyebrows. "Why would I tell you anything at all?"

"Because," Heath told him evenly, "as much as it pains me to say it, we might be willing to spring you out of here."

"You expect me to believe that?" laughed the merman.

"If you think you can escape the wrath of the entire civilization you've wronged, think again," Merletta told him. "I'm taking you back to the triple kingdoms to face the justice you deserve."

This time the Record Master actually threw his head back in laughter. "Good luck with that, Trainee. Your optimism has never failed to entertain me." But there was a gleam of eagerness in his eyes as he turned back to Heath. "Very well, ask your questions."

"Did you personally carry out the attacks against Percival, me, and the king?" Heath asked.

The Record Master shook his head. "My associates took care of those matters for me."

"He means his two personal guards," Merletta said. "They follow him around like seal pups."

"But you orchestrated them," Heath pressed.

The Record Master nodded.

"Why? Was the aim to stir up tension between the king and the power-wielders?"

"With the exception of my apparently poorly planned attempt to kill you," the Record Master said casually. "I just wanted to get rid of you, after my informant in the palace told one of my associates that you were putting the pieces together about our role in the first attack." He paused. "Not that she knew that's what her information meant, of course."

"The maid!" Heath realized. "One of the castle maids heard me telling Grandmother that I sensed power at the attack on Percival." He frowned. "So you were worried I'd figure out it was a merperson?"

"If you want to know the true culprit behind the attacks, find a looking glass," the Record Master said, by way of answer. "You are entirely responsible."

"Me?" Heath demanded.

"Don't try your mind games on Heath," Merletta growled. "No one's falling for your tricks anymore."

"No trick," he said placidly. His eyes narrowed in thought as he looked back at Heath. "I don't know that I would have recognized you without assistance. You've grown more than I have in the intervening years, after all."

Heath drew in a sharp breath. "So you do remember our first encounter? When I saw you at the Winter Solstice Festival over a year ago, I recognized you immediately as the man I saw in the markets when I was a child. I sensed the strange power of your kind then, and I sensed it at the attacks."

"An excellent memory," said the Record Master lazily. "You would have made a good record holder. If you were advanced enough to have a tail, that is. And if our civilization weren't nearing total destruction."

Heath ignored the comment. "I don't see how me sensing your power in the markets as a small child makes me responsible for your plots against..." He trailed off, suddenly comprehending. "Are you saying that you've been planning this whole vendetta ever since then? Because I identified your magic?"

"That's right." In spite of his earlier show of reticence, the Record Master was clearly enjoying dropping these revelations. "We've known for much of our recorded history that dragons are a threat to us. But we've lived for generations without any fear of humans. Your ships can't cross our waters, and you can't descend into our world. But the entrance of magic into your bloodline had the potential to expose us—as I discovered in the markets that day. It would be...restrictive for me to be prevented from roaming the land when need arises. I was determined then to rid this place of your kind, but it took many years of careful prodding to ignite the right tensions."

He glanced dispassionately at Percival. "You were a boon, for certain. Easily visible magic, a natural arrogance, and a hot temper. Perfect. And you took my bait so wholeheartedly with the attack by the king's guards." His sneer as he said the last two words made Percival wince.

The newly released young man was pale, his horrified expression showing that he grasped the role he'd unwittingly played in the plot more soberly than Heath had ever dared to hope he would.

"So you've been pursuing a vendetta against us for more

than fifteen years," Heath said quietly. "All because of a chance meeting with a child in the markets."

"Your blame goes beyond that encounter," the merman told him. "Your friendship with the dragon certainly added urgency to my aim." His eyes shifted to Merletta, their expression nasty. "Given that dragons discovering our existence would be the worst kind of disaster, as any loyal merperson would know."

"You're hardly one to speak about loyalty," Heath said harshly, seeing the strained look on Merletta's face. "We know what you've done to your own people, so don't look for sympathy here."

"But I still don't understand," Laura chimed in. "How would it help you to provoke conflict between the crown and us? Did you hope it would distract everyone from searching for you?"

Merletta gave a hollow laugh. "You underestimate his depravity," she told Laura. "Didn't you hear him before? He wanted to rid the kingdom of you. He hoped to ignite enough conflict that the crown killed you all off."

"Presumably before we had any more generations to expand the bloodline of power-wielders," Heath agreed grimly.

Laura's eyes widened, and Heath had no doubt she was thinking of her children—the first power-wielders of the fourth generation.

"Just how much of the tension and unrest have you been behind?" Laura accused. "How long have you been whispering poisonous lies, and sowing division?"

The Record Master didn't speak, although the slight smirk on his face was answer enough.

Heath shook his head. "Far too long. I knew someone was in the king's ear, leading him astray. But I never dreamed it was someone from the triple kingdoms. It was you who convinced the king that Kyona couldn't be behind the attack on Percival, wasn't it? If you were worried about the truth being exposed, why didn't you take the offered decoy? If we all believed a Kyonan power-wielder had done it, no one would suspect you."

"But he didn't want everyone to blame Kyona," Merletta said slowly. "He wanted the power-wielders to blame the crown, and vice versa. Pursuing Kyona would have been a distraction from the focus on wiping you all out." She looked the Record Master in the eye. "Because that's what you do, isn't it? You skillfully provoke conflict, but you give the appearance of preventing it, because you only allow the *right* conflict, at the right time, between the right parties. All according to your own plan."

"You are finally catching up," he said in cold amusement.

Anger grew in Merletta's eyes. "That's always been your approach. Us and them, like Ileana said. I've seen you do it for years. I don't know why I didn't recognize it when Heath first brought me here."

She took a step forward, her hands balling into fists. "You've been doing it in the triple kingdoms all my life. Tilssted against everyone else. Were you willing to go as far there? Did you hope to get the other cities to wipe us out? Because last I saw, you were well on the way to achieving your goal."

"On the contrary," the Record Master said coldly. "Thanks to your foolish intervention, my goals have been considerably disrupted."

"How devastating for you," Merletta said, her icy rage rising. "You're supposed to be the leader! Why would you wish to provoke war among your own people? What kind of a monster would use the trust and authority of your elevated position that way?"

She took a final step forward, and the Record Master's hand shot out unexpectedly, seizing the hair that cascaded over her shoulder.

Heath let out a cry of anger, darting forward. But the Record Master made no attempt to physically harm Merletta. He just yanked on her hair until their faces were inches apart, only the iron bars separating them.

"You have ruined everything," he hissed. "And if it is my last act, I will see you die for it."

"That's enough." Heath grabbed the Record Master's hand, ripping it off Merletta's. Vindictively, he wished for Percival's strength so that he could crush the offending body part that had dared to touch Merletta.

"Come on," Heath said to the rest of the group, his eyes on Merletta. "We need to discuss our next move."

"Do not forget your promise!" the Record Master called after them as they mounted the steps. "My information came at a price!"

CHAPTER TWENTY-FIVE

Merletta

"Why are we doing this again?" Bianca stifled a yawn behind her hand. "Isn't this guy the one behind all our problems?"

"I don't think we can pass off all the blame," Heath said dryly from where he crouched beside Merletta. "But he's been a key player, yes."

"And we want to break him out of the dungeon because..."

"We've been over this, Bianca," Brody cut in. "It's because Heath can't say no to his girlfriend."

Merletta glared at Heath's cousin, but she couldn't help but be mollified when he softened the barb by sending Heath a cheeky grin. Not that it stopped Heath from rolling his eyes.

"Believe me," she said earnestly, "the things this man has done here are nothing to what he's done in my world. And if I don't get him back there and expose his lies, the rest of the Center will keep enforcing his instructions, most of them not even knowing that they're dooming everyone they know to slaughter by keeping them trapped inside the barrier."

"Most of that went over my head," Bianca said. "But I trust Heath. If he says we need to do this, I'll help you."

She narrowed her eyes, and Merletta felt a wind whip up around her. It grew steadily, and soon it was loud enough to make it hard to hear Heath right next to her.

"Thank you," he was whispering to his cousin, as he peered out from their hiding place in the garden. "It's quite helpful that you have a plan for this, actually."

"The plan relied on a storm," Bianca pointed out in a mutter. "Not to mention it was based around a different dungeon."

"What's a plan without a little improvisation?" Percival said cheerfully from Bianca's other side. "Besides, you have my strength now, which is more than you had last time."

"All right," Jasmine's voice whispered from out of the bushes nearby. "It's an hour until dawn. It's time."

Merletta felt nothing, but she could tell from the avid way Heath was looking from his cousin's position to the guard that Jasmine was using her magic somehow. She had the ability to move things with her mind, if Merletta recalled correctly. Just small things, Heath had told her.

As Merletta watched, the guard's cloak crept up into the air behind him, apparently unaided. He hadn't even noticed the strange phenomenon when the fabric suddenly dropped over his head, blinding him. He gave a yell, clutching at it, but it wouldn't budge. Percival darted forward silently with a rough sack in his hands. Unseen, he slipped it over the confused guard's head and shoulders, securing it with a rope.

"Quick, Brody!" Heath hissed. "His shouts will rouse other guards."

Brody nodded, his look of concentration suggesting he was already undertaking his role. Taking her cue, Merletta dashed past Percival and the struggling guard, down the steps into the dungeon, Heath on her heels.

She pulled up at the sight of the tunnel yawning in the ground at her feet, massive roots rotating in a constant motion that dug the edges out. The Record Master had already crawled into the hole on his side of the iron bars, clearly grasping what was expected of him instantly.

Merletta gritted her teeth, hating that he was getting what he wanted out of it all, even for a moment. At least his movements were labored, showing he was still weakened by his injuries.

The moment his head came up from the tunnel, Heath had a blade at his throat. The Record Master raised his hands in submission, and Merletta hastened to secure the chains Heath had given her around the merman's wrists. They would do his feet once they were clear of the castle.

As they half pushed, half dragged him up the steps, Merletta glanced back. The roots were already retreating back into the earth, leaving the tunnel behind, but no sign of their role in its creation. She shook her head, amazed by the power of Brody's magic.

The whole exercise had taken only a couple of minutes, and they emerged to find Percival still holding the shouting guard. The sound of running feet could be heard from across the garden, and the cousins scattered as previously discussed. All had gone to plan. No one had been injured, and nothing had been done that couldn't be explained without recourse to magic. Theoretically, at least.

Two figures appeared from the darkness. Sage fell into position beside Merletta as Percival picked up the Record Master and threw him over a shoulder as easily as if he was a small child. The four of them ran swiftly through the garden, Heath muttering directions as they wended their way through the manicured rows. His eyes were a little unfocused, and Merletta had to steer him away from running into a bush more than once —he was too busy watching the garden around them with his farsight, directing how to evade the guards now fanning out in search. Their calls split the night, but the fugitives had already reached the outer gate.

Percival took off at a brisk jog, setting the pace in spite of his burden. In only a few minutes they reached a small door leading through the city wall. The guard on duty nodded to Percival, then swung the door wide.

"Thank you," the young lord muttered to his friend as they edged through. They traveled in silence across a field, up a small rise, and down the other side into a small copse of trees.

"This is where Reka will meet us," Heath reminded his brother. "You need to get back before you're missed."

"Maybe I should stay with you after all," Percival said, clearly anxious.

Heath shook his head vehemently. "You just got out of the dungeons. I'm not landing you straight back in there."

Percival hesitated, then lowered the Record Master to the grass. The merman had remained silent the whole trip, and his face was ashen. Red was starting to seep through one of his bandages—the flight must have reopened a wound.

"Let me secure him properly first at least," Percival said gruffly, producing another chain which he clasped around the Record Master's feet. He glared at the unresisting merman then looked up at Heath, his expression still concerned.

"How is Merletta going to get him back to her kingdom? I thought Reka couldn't take her without tipping off the other dragons."

"We're still working on that," said Heath. "But we won't do anything that would risk him getting away. Don't worry. You need to get going, Perce. Are you sure you can make it back in without rousing suspicion?"

"Of course I can." Percival searched his brother's face. "Take care, little brother. I expect to see you again soon, and in one piece."

Heath gripped Percival's offered arm, a slight smile on his face. "Don't worry about me," he said. "I'll be all right. Just don't get yourself into any trouble while I'm gone."

"I'll try," Percival said ruefully.

He smiled at Merletta in farewell, and she returned the gesture. He was a far cry from the cocky young man she'd met the year before, and although she'd warmed to him even then, she found she liked this more sober version better.

Once Percival was out of sight, they made much slower progress through the trees. None of them were strong enough to carry the Record Master, and he could barely shuffle with his legs in chains.

"It makes me nervous that he's not resisting more." Sage muttered to Merletta.

Merletta shrugged. "He's pretty injured. And I suppose he has nothing to lose at this point."

"You underestimate me." The Record Master's quiet voice made her jump. She hadn't thought he could hear. "You think you have the upper hand, but when we get back to our home, whom do you think the guards—and in fact the whole populace of the triple kingdoms—will rush to aid? The upstart slum-dweller, or the leader she's kidnapped and chained up? There's no path forward where you win over me, Merletta."

"We'll see about that," she snapped, turning her shoulder on him. She wished she felt as confident as she was trying to sound. Her plan of showing everyone in the triple kingdoms the letters Heath had stolen was flimsier than she wanted to admit. It was possible they'd accept this evidence and believe that the Record Master had known the truth about drying out all along, and had been plotting against both Valoria and the triple kingdoms. But it was equally possible she'd never be given the chance to fully explain herself.

Her back up plan was a little more solid—surely if

Rekavidur testified to the Record Master's crimes, he would be believed. Who would doubt a dragon? But she was hoping it wouldn't come to that, partly because she wasn't entirely sure Reka would agree to do it, and partly because bringing another dragon into the triple kingdoms might just reignite the fear that Elddreki's arrival had surely created.

The clanking of the Record Master's chains seemed deafening in the chill quiet of the dark trees, but as yet they heard no shout of pursuing guards.

"So do you have a plan for how we will return to the triple kingdoms?" the Record Master asked Merletta after a minute's silence. "Or do you imagine I can swim there like this?"

Merletta remained silent, refusing to engage with him.

"If you let me send word to Arinton, we could travel on my ship," he said conversationally.

Merletta and Sage both stopped walking, exchanging a stunned look before staring at their captive.

"*Your* ship?" Sage demanded.

"Well, ship is perhaps generous," acknowledged the Record Master, wincing a little as the chains dangling from his hands bumped against the wound on his thigh. "It is a small vessel, able to be manned by only two if necessary. But it covers the distance ten times as quickly as swimming."

"That's how you got here so quickly!" Merletta said. "You must have left straight after we did."

"Did you expect me to do nothing when you were carried off by a dragon when I had you at the point of execution?" he asked dryly. "It didn't take great intelligence to guess where you'd gone."

"So you thought you'd pursue her here and murder her before she could mess up your despicable plans any further, did you?" Sage said bitterly. "And to think so many look to you as a wise and trusted leader."

"No need to bring your mother into this," the Record Master said in an oily voice that made Merletta want to slap him. He watched Sage vindictively, clearly pleased by the sudden flush that rose up her cheeks. It was no surprise he'd identified her main point of personal bitterness, and was ready for the faintest opportunity to prod at it.

"But where do you moor the ship?" Merletta asked, steering the conversation away from personal matters back to the practical. "And how do you pay for the supplies, and all the other costs you must incur on land?"

"I have my sources of wealth," the Record Master said, sounding smug.

Unimpressed, Merletta raised an eyebrow. "You scavenge in shipwrecks, don't you?" she guessed. "Or more likely others do it on your behalf. I know for a fact your guards were in the area of all those sunken ships near the maelstrom when I had my second year test, because they hung about to try to murder me when I emerged." She shook her head. "I suppose if you've had your underlings hunting for years, you could have amassed quite a store of human wealth."

Frowning, she added, "But that still doesn't explain where you moor your vessel."

"I don't think you need quite so many details," he said maddeningly. "But your island is not the only bit of rock in the ocean to which a vessel can be tied." Merletta could barely see his face in the darkness, but there was a definite sneer accompanying the word *island*.

"What do you have against Vazula?" she demanded. "Why try to keep it such a secret?"

"You think you deserve to dictate the future of our kind just because you stumbled on one relic of our past," he said, his tone dark. "But it is not you who has spent generations building toward a future for our civilization. A future which is stable and secure. Or would have been."

"Stable and secure?" Sage repeated, outraged. "You mean completely within your control. How can you dare to talk about the future of our civilization when your whole plan is to escape the dragons' attack on the triple kingdoms by using the rest of the population as a decoy?"

"It is almost impossible to believe that either of you could reach the rank you hold while still remaining so naive," snapped the Record Master. "Individual lives do not matter in the scheme of history. A record holder should understand that. Our civilization will continue—the loss of some of its members is hardly enough to forever cease its progress."

"Some of its members?" repeated Merletta incredulously. "You mean most!"

"It is not my actions which have made the scale of the cull so drastic," the Record Master told her angrily. "It is yours."

Merletta glared at him out of narrowed eyes, hoping he couldn't see the pang that went through her at the truth in his words. Because he didn't deserve any exoneration.

"What do you mean *the scale of the cull*?" she asked. "I've seen that word before, in an account in the restricted records about silencing dissenters. Just what were you planning before you found out about the threat of the dragons?"

The Record Master looked bored. "Nothing you need concern yourself with. Now, shall I send word to my associate to bring the vessel down the coast to our location?" the Record Master pressed.

"One of your guards is still in Valoria?" Merletta asked sharply. She glanced at Heath, who'd been listening silently to the whole conversation. "We should warn...someone."

"How would you send him word?" Sage demanded. "And how did you correspond with the king? Surely you didn't come all the way to Bryford every time you wanted to drop him a letter."

"Hardly," laughed the Record Master. "I have my ways."

"He's exaggerating for effect," Heath interjected. "I've seen those letters now, remember? There weren't as many as I was expecting. Just a few well-timed ones, I'd say. He probably did have one of his guards bring some of them to Valoria. Others were marked by the steward as coming via carrier bird. It's not often used, but the castle does have a dovecote for the purpose."

A glance at the Record Master showed him scowling at this prosaic demystifying of his methods. Merletta couldn't help a little smirk.

"Nice try," she told him, "but you're not sending anything to anyone. We don't need your assistance to get home."

They were halfway into the copse now, and they stopped, shoving the Record Master down so he sat in a small dell. Sage stayed near, keeping a wary eye on him, and Merletta hurried over to Heath, who'd continued on several paces away and was looking upward through the branches.

"I hope Reka is here soon, or we'll risk the guards finding us," Merletta said by way of greeting.

Heath squinted, his eyes unfocused. "He's on his way, I think. He's certainly flying." He glanced over at her. "I hesitate to add my voice to his, and I'm certainly not suggesting you trust him with the task, but how *are* you going to get the Record Master back to the triple kingdoms, Merletta?"

She bit her lip. "As much as I hate to agree with him, the only solution I can think of is for us to hire a vessel. Sage and I can take turns propelling it, I suppose. When we get there, we'll have to drag him down to the seabed."

"That journey will take days," Heath protested. "And it won't be easy to find your way above the waterline like you can below it. So many things could go wrong in that time."

"I know," Merletta sighed. "But I don't have any better ideas. If it was possible for Rekavidur to take us, of course I'd prefer it. But it's more imperative than ever that we delay the dragons finding out where our cities are—now there's actually a chance we can evacuate everyone." She sighed. "Of course, Reka's presence would also have been helpful when it came to convincing everyone of the Record Master's crimes."

"Speaking of which, don't forget this," Heath said, pulling a bundle of rolled up parchments from a pocket of his cloak. "You'll have to figure out how to protect it from the water."

Merletta nodded her thanks as she took it. "Will the king notice that someone has stolen some of the letters he received from the Record Master?"

Heath shrugged. "It's safe to say he's going to notice that someone's stolen the Record Master himself, so I'm not sure what difference it makes."

Merletta laid a hand on his arm. "How much trouble am I leaving you in, Heath?" she asked softly. "I know this was an outrageous thing to ask you to do. You shouldn't have helped me, probably."

"Probably not, but apparently I can't say no to you." Heath flashed her a grin as cheeky as Brody's had been when he'd said the words.

Merletta didn't laugh, a flush rising up her face instead. "He's not wrong that I'm taking advantage. This brings you a lot of risk and no benefit."

"I was joking, Merletta," Heath said easily. He put a hand on her shoulder, his fingers kneading some of the tension out of the base of her neck. The pressure was warm and reassuring in the cold pre-dawn air. "Any benefit to you *is* benefit to me. And I had as much of a hand as you did in exposing the triple kingdoms to the dragons. If there's a chance we can help them escape, we *have* to try. It's not a matter of taking advantage."

Merletta was about to respond, but Heath suddenly stiffened, his eyes glazing over again as his magic clearly came into effect. She waited anxiously, but it was only a matter of seconds before he returned to her.

"It's Reka," he said grimly. "He's almost here, and he has news. Very bad news."

CHAPTER TWENTY-SIX

Merletta

The words had barely left Heath's mouth when Merletta heard the rush of wind that always heralded the dragon's arrival. Reka landed soundlessly amidst the trees, although Merletta couldn't figure out how he'd navigated the trunks on his descent.

"Greetings, Heath, Merletta," the dragon said. He glanced behind them, his eyes landing first on Sage, then the Record Master. "Friend of Merletta, Deceiver," he continued the greetings.

"Reka, what do you mean the dragons know?" Heath pressed, clearly impatient of the formalities. "Has word reached them about the incident at Loch Arine?"

"So my sire has just informed me," Rekavidur confirmed. "They are aware that merfolk walk among you and have now been exposed to your king."

"Does that mean they're going to seek retribution against Valoria?" Heath asked, anxiety clear in his voice.

"I believe the more immediate effect is to reinforce the urgency of their original mission," Rekavidur said. "I am told they had already sent out the first scouts, but others are joining them even as we speak. I have no doubt they will find the under-water stronghold before the day is out."

Merletta turned to Heath, feeling the color drain from her face. "We're out of time," she whispered, reeling from the truth of it. Neither her method of taking the Record Master back to Vazula nor her plans for how to expose his crimes were viable anymore. They had to change direction, and they had to do it fast. The first hints of dawn were lightening the air—it was unendurable to think that the sun might be rising on the triple kingdoms' final day.

"There's certainly no time for the journey you described," Heath agreed grimly. "It doesn't seem like there's anything to lose from Rekavidur carrying you back there. Not if they're going to find it within the day either way." He turned to the dragon. "Are you willing, Reka?"

He nodded his vast head gravely. "I am willing. But I can carry only two."

"Sage, maybe you can stay here," Merletta suggested desperately. "No one actually saw you transform. If you keep a low profile, you might slip through the notice of..." She trailed off at the look on Sage's face, raising her hands in surrender. "All right, all right. I know."

"There's also no way in the world I'm staying behind," Heath said flatly. "Not a chance."

"But Heath!" Merletta turned to him, aghast. "You coming was never part of the plan."

"That was before we knew the reckoning was today," Heath told her simply. "I'm not staying here while you go flying toward likely death."

"But what's the point in you dying as well?" Merletta cried, reaching out and grabbing his arm. Her eyes pleaded with him to see reason. "Please, Heath. Don't come just so you can die with us. It's not as though you can do anything to help once we're underwater."

"I wasn't suggesting I go underwater," said Heath. "But ever since we found out about the dragons' threat, I've been itching to get back to Vazula, to properly hunt for answers about the inhabitants, like I intended to do when I first went there. I never tried very hard before, because the island quickly became about you, not about the power-wielders who may or may not have lived there once."

"This is madness," cut in the Record Master, his voice harsh. "My predecessors have combed that island, and removed anything of significant value. There is nothing there which will convince the dragons not to attack. Surely you cannot seriously be intending for us all to return to the triple kingdoms if the dragons are truly on their way."

"If you think you're staying here, safely far away from the carnage, you can think again," Merletta told him viciously. "If we get there too late to let everyone out, then you'll suffer for your lies along with the rest of your victims. Perhaps you'll have the chance to explain to them just why you assured everyone the barrier would keep dragons out." She bit her lip. "Although they know that's a lie already, since Elddreki came through. Maybe that's been enough to spur everyone to flee."

"Elddreki!" Heath cried. He looked hopefully at Rekavidur. "Do you think he'd be willing to help us again? If he can take two as well, that's all of us."

"I will ask him," said Rekavidur. He lifted his head to the sky, and although he uttered no sound and made no movement, when he lowered his face again, he gave Heath a nod. "He is coming."

"So it's decided, then," said Heath firmly. "I'll go to the island while Merletta and the others go to warn the triple kingdoms.

We should get moving now, though, put some distance between us and the castle while we wait for Elddreki."

He turned his face purposefully toward the coast, but Merletta wasn't ready to give in. She still gripped his arm, and she let her fingers slide down until she clasped his hand, pulling him back to face her.

"Heath, please. I want you far away from this. I know you want to help, but August and the others have been searching the island for weeks. Last I heard, they'd found nothing."

"But Heath can see things others can't see," Rekavidur said simply.

Merletta blinked up at him. The dragon spoke calmly, with no trace of emotion, as was his usual way. The comment was so matter-of-fact it seemed out of place in this highly charged debate over life and death, but at the same time it was irrefutable. What if Heath really could find something no one had yet found?

"It shouldn't be necessary for you to put your life at risk," Merletta said, a snap in her voice as she turned back to the Record Master. "If your predecessors stripped the island of any relevant records, surely you have them still, or copies of them. Don't you have any accounts that would convince the dragons?"

"I do not, but feel free to spend the few remaining hours left to your life searching through every record in the Center," the Record Master said, anger burning in his eyes as his options for escaping the coming massacre receded rapidly.

Merletta looked at Heath. "Is he lying?"

Heath shrugged helplessly. "I don't think so, but I can't be sure. There are so many layers to him, it's hard to even know what I'm seeing let alone be sure I haven't missed something. If my father was here, he could tell us with certainty, but..."

Merletta nodded as he trailed off. If the Record Master

wasn't going to direct them, it hardly even mattered if there were relevant records. There was no time to trawl through everything.

With Reka carrying the Record Master, the other three were able to move much more quickly as they headed southeast, toward the distant coast. By the time the dragon Elddreki reached them, the sun had come up over the eastern farmland, Merletta's anxiety rising with it.

The larger dragon wasted no time in seizing Sage in one taloned front foot and the still-chained Record Master in the other. Rekavidur copied his father, grasping Heath and Merletta in one fluid motion as he took to the sky.

The flight over the ocean felt twice as long as the trip to Valoria had done. Merletta kept searching the skies, expecting at any moment to see dragons swarming around them. No such vision appeared, but halfway to their destination, Elddreki swooped close above them, calling aloud for the humans' benefit.

"They have seen us. They follow our journey with their sight, and are gathering a large enough party to pursue their purpose. They will not be far behind."

Merletta met Heath's eyes, seeing her own fear reflected there. She reached for him instinctively, and he mirrored the gesture, their hands meeting in the air, nothing between their clasped fingers and the surface of the ocean far, far below.

"Merletta," Heath whispered.

She shook her head, too full of emotions to name any. There was no need to say any of it. They both knew...they both understood. Heath's hand shifted, entwining their fingers in an intimate clasp that only succeeded in reminding Merletta of the distance between them. They'd fought fate for an impressively long time, but they'd reached the end of the current.

"Heath," she said earnestly. "Just promise me that if you

don't find anything, you'll stay on Vazula until it's over. Don't get caught up in something impossible to change."

He met her eyes, but remained stubbornly silent, refusing to give the promise she sought. Her fear spiked, but she knew there was nothing she could do to convince him. As much as she'd always loved the gentleness of his spirit compared to hers, she'd learned long ago that he had plenty of his own stubbornness.

There were no more words between them. Merletta wished desperately that they'd made time for a better farewell, but zooming through the air in a dragon's talons was not that time.

They crossed the maelstrom far below, the deadly tumult looking small and unthreatening from their height. When Merletta caught sight of Vazula way off to her left, she knew they were almost at the triple kingdoms. She hadn't even needed to direct—of course Elddreki had been there before.

"Do you want to go to the island first?" Rekavidur called out over the rushing air.

Merletta shook her head. "No time! Drop us right over the Center. It should be that way." She pointed, and Reka adjusted his trajectory slightly.

"Yes, I can feel the concentration of your strange type of latent magic," he commented, sounding clinically fascinated, as if they weren't racing toward mass slaughter. "I'll drop you in the middle of the patch, as best I can judge."

Barely a minute later, he began to descend, lowering himself to a safer height for releasing his burden. Elddreki followed, wheeling down alongside him.

"Merletta!" Heath cried, as she pulled her hand from his and ripped at the laces on her gown in preparation for entering the water.

She looked over at him, again wishing she had the words, or the time, or anything more to give him. But she didn't, and the next moment Rekavidur had released her without a warning.

She plummeted toward the surface, entering the water with a splash. She could hear two more bodies hit the water beside her, and she twisted, shedding her gown as efficiently as she could. Sage was doing the same, and the Record Master—still chained at the hands and around the base of his tail where his ankles had been—was sinking rapidly down below them.

"Unbind me!" he shouted furiously.

"No, I don't think we will," Merletta said coolly, as she dove down to match his descent. "In fact..."

She paused to snag her discarded gown, which was slowly drifting down through the water. It had a decorative sash tied around it, which she detached fairly easily and affixed to the Record Master as a gag. She could see that the chain from his feet was cutting uncomfortably into his tail. Hopefully it would be enough to hamper him from swimming properly. She also saw that the impact with the water had caused one of his injuries to start bleeding again, and she glanced around nervously. They weren't inside the barrier yet, which meant they were still vulnerable to sharks and other predators. That was the last thing they needed right now.

"Come on," she said to Sage. The two of them seized the Record Master by either arm, flipping downward and streaming toward the distant ocean floor.

It soon became evident that Rekavidur had judged the location well as the Center came into view below them. They weren't right over the central spire, but Merletta could see it not far away. They appeared to be north of it, descending toward the inner edge of the drop off.

Merletta had expected trouble at the barrier, assuming they would hit the web formation she and Sage had witnessed guarding the barrier in an upward direction. But they met no such resistance. Merletta felt the moment they passed through the magical shield, and she and Sage exchanged uneasy glances.

Scanning the water below and around her, Merletta heard the faint sound of conflict. She shifted direction toward the noise, fear clutching at her as she realized where it was coming from.

"There's still fighting in Tilssted," she cried to Sage. "We have to stop them! If they're too busy fighting each other, they won't even know about the threat from the dragons until it's far too late."

Sage nodded fervently. "Emil and Andre are in Tilssted, too!" she reminded Merletta. "Indigo and Ileana took them there."

Merletta's eyes widened. She'd momentarily forgotten. A brief selfish hope crossed her mind, that her friends were hiding safe somewhere far from the fighting. Andre's eager, incorruptible face flashed before her sight, and she smiled grimly. Not a chance of that.

They swam over the top of the Center, far enough up to make it unlikely anyone would see them. Merletta made for the poorest city's central square, and it quickly became clear that her instinct hadn't failed her. The clash of stone spears filled the water, and there seemed to be a large concentration of merpeople in the open space. As they neared it, a familiar voice rose above the babble.

"Do not give in! Fight your way through! If you stay inside the barrier, you'll die!"

"Emil!"

Sage's gasp told Merletta she'd spotted their friend as well. Emil was floating at the top of the stone sculpture which sat in the middle of the square, his spear out as he repeated the same simple instructions over and over, interspersed with directions on how to find temporary haven in Vazula's shallows.

Below him battle raged, dozens of what looked like Tilssted residents clashing with armed guards. Gathered more closely around Emil was a small group, fighting off any guards who made it through and attempted to silence him. In addition to Andre, Indigo, and Ileana, Merletta saw Freja and most of her old patrol, Felix included. She even caught sight of Paul and Griffin—clearly they'd made it back into the triple kingdoms as planned. Her heart swelled painfully as she increased the speed of her strokes.

"Emil!" Sage called, more loudly this time.

The young record holder's head jerked upward, a rare display of strong emotion crossing his face as he caught sight of them.

"Sage!" He propelled himself upward, meeting her halfway.

For a moment Merletta was distracted by their reunion. To her astonishment, Sage looked to be berating him, rather than falling on him in relief as Merletta had expected. Emil looked stunned for a moment, then—even more astonishingly—he pulled Sage into his arms and kissed her with a recklessness that was entirely out of character for the cautious merman.

Feeling a little dazed, but knowing it wasn't the moment to get distracted, Merletta shifted her attention to the fighters below.

"We're out of time!" she roared as loudly as she could over the seething mass of limbs and scales below. "The dragons are coming, and we need to flee the triple kingdoms NOW!"

There was a lull in the fighting, many faces turning up to them in confusion.

"Flee!" Merletta cried again. "The dragons are on their way!"

Panicked cries rang out, and the crowd devolved into utter chaos. Some eyes stayed fixed on the new arrivals, however, and Merletta saw many widening as they caught sight of her captive.

"But that's the Record Master!" cried a guard, scandalized.

"He doesn't deserve the title!" Sage's voice rang out, surprising Merletta with its ferocity. She'd extricated herself from Emil, but he hovered close behind her. "He's the one who revealed himself near the dragon colony, and he's the reason they're coming this very day. He even has a plan to flee to a safe location, but he only intends to take a select few with him. The rest of us are expendable."

It was unclear how many had heard her—probably not many given the pandemonium—but Merletta didn't try to reason with the crowd. She flicked her fins, still dragging the wounded Record Master with her. When she dropped into the center of the ring which had until a moment before been protecting Emil, she passed the chained and injured prisoner to Freja.

"Don't let him get away," she told the demoted squad leader. "The things binding him are metal chains—they should be too strong for him to break, so it shouldn't be too hard to keep him subdued. But he'll escape if he's given any opportunity, and won't hesitate to murder anyone who gets in his way."

The letters Heath had given her were getting ruined by the water as they spoke, but she couldn't think about that now. If they survived this, she'd have to find another way to expose the Record Master to the populace he'd betrayed.

Putting that problem aside for later, she met the older mermaid's eyes. "I wasn't exaggerating. The dragons are coming right now. They'll slaughter anyone they can get their talons on. We have to scatter to have any hope."

"I'm not scattering any more than you are," said Freja grimly. "But we'll keep trying to tell the others."

Felix floated up beside her, nodding. "We'll fight beside you until the end, Merletta," he said. "None of us would be guards if our lives meant more to us than our duty."

Merletta gripped his offered arm, too overcome to speak. After everything, she could hardly comprehend that at the very end of her mostly futile defiance, she had so many good merpeople willing to float beside her. It was undoubtedly more than she deserved.

"Merletta!" Andre swam out of the clump to embrace her in a crushing hug, the tension clear in his lean frame. "I'm so glad you and Sage are alive." He grinned. "But I won't follow Emil's lead and kiss you in greeting, if it's all the same to you."

Merletta gave a choking laugh. Clearly her friend had witnessed the astonishing event as well.

"I'm glad you're all right," she told him. "What happened to you all?"

Andre shrugged. "Nothing much worth telling. Ileana and Indigo helped break us out of the holding cell." He sent his cousin a warm look. "We've been hiding out here ever since. Some shellsmith apprentices took us in, if you'd believe it."

Merletta smiled grimly, not doubting for a moment that Tish's loud-mouthed but good-hearted colleague had been behind it. "I do believe it."

"Well, we didn't waste the time," Andre said. "We've been spreading the word as widely as we could, about the coming dragons, and the fact that the Center knows about it but is doing nothing to protect us and is still actively keeping us trapped inside."

"So there's been no lifting of that since the Record Master left?" Merletta asked.

Andre shook his head. "I didn't even know he *had* left. The only change to the orders seems to have been to stop bothering with a guard on the upward barrier—given everyone now knows dragons can get through it—and instead intensifying the fortification of the borders around Tilssted. From what I hear, the other cities are still swallowing the Center's line. But in Tilssted—maybe thanks to our efforts—no one's buying it. As soon as the guard was doubled, they got the message, and the attempts to escape were tripled."

"Good," said Merletta grimly. "At least someone's listening."

A guard formation sped past on the far side of the square, and Merletta caught sight of a familiar form.

"Agner," she muttered. Without a word to Andre, she flicked her tail, ducking her way through the swirling mass of panic toward the instructor. He had a full complement of guards behind him, and they were heading for the barrier with purpose.

"Agner!" she called, when she was within hailing distance.

He checked, turning to find the source of the shout, and even from across the square she saw his eyebrows go up at sight of her.

Merletta closed the gap, pulling up in relief when she reached him. "Agner, I'm glad I found you. The guards will listen to you. We have to stop this! All these people will die if—"

"Oh, Merletta," Agner cut her off, sounding exasperated. "This is so typical of you. You manage another absurdly unlikely escape, and within a week you've thrown yourself right back in it! You should have stayed away until this was all over. I was really hoping you would. Then there might have been a chance to patch things up for you."

Merletta stared at him. "Patch things up? How would you do that if every last one of us is dead?"

Agner shifted his spear from one hand to the other, getting impatient. "Let's not exaggerate. I know you don't want this to happen. I don't blame you—truth be told, I don't really want it to happen, either. I like the grit of Tilssted folk. I always have. But sacrifices need to be made for the gain of everyone."

"The gain of everyone?" Merletta could hardly believe her ears. "You're not talking about the dragon attack, are you?" she said slowly. "You're talking about the Record Master's plan to provoke war by turning the other cities against Tilssted."

Agner gave his usual chuckle—a sound that was singularly

out of place in the midst of the battle zone. "I don't know if the current Record Master should get quite that much credit," he said dryly. "This type of conflict is how the triple kingdoms have handled population control for generations." He shook his head, a stern look coming over his face. "You know I liked to see you shake things up a bit, but you never understood what you were interfering with. Stirring up trouble in all the cities will lead to no good—what if you'd triggered a larger scale cull, generations before it was necessary?"

Merletta's blood pounded in her ears, horror washing over her. Agner was supposed to be the one instructor she could actually see eye to eye with, and here he was, openly admitting to knowledge of the mass murder that stained the Center's history.

"That's why the records don't go back far enough to make sense," she whispered, at long, long last realizing the full extent of the deception. "Like Andre's family record, and the census accounts...whatever came before was wiped clean...they started fresh, and claimed that the written language hadn't existed before then."

The realization rocked her, as she finally grasped the true lengths to which the Center had gone, not just once, but probably many times. And the ocean had always been on their side, wiping away all record of their ancestors' existence, like so much sand before the tide.

"You're a fourth year trainee, Merletta, and much smarter than most," Agner said firmly. "It's time for you to stop fighting every little battle you come across, and start learning how to operate within the system."

Merletta shook off the familiar crushing feeling of disillusionment, pulling herself back to her present reality with an effort. However abhorrent the practices of the past were, the current crisis was even more disastrous.

"None of that matters now," she said. "There won't be any system to operate in by the end of the day. Didn't you hear what I said? The dragons are coming right now! They'll kill every merperson they find."

Agner gave her a long-suffering look. "Merletta, I don't know how or why you got mixed up with the dragon who saved you from your trial. But I'm amazed you've let whatever tale you've been told sink in so deeply. The stories of dragon aggression are just part of the necessary narrative. They're a scary tale to keep naughty children in line. There's no way a colony of dragons is going to seek us out all the way down here just to—"

He cut off abruptly, and Merletta didn't have to ask why. She heard it, too—the unmistakable escalation of the hysteria around them. Screams filled the water, and Merletta's eyes darted upward. For the briefest of moments she allowed herself to hope that the enormous shapes streaking through the water were Rekavidur and his father, bringing good news from Vazula.

But the unfamiliarity of the dragons—not to mention their sheer number—quickly dashed that vain hope.

No more false alarms, no more last-minute escapes. They were out of options, and out of time.

The dragons had come to kill them all.

CHAPTER TWENTY-SEVEN

Heath's heart was in his throat as he watched Merletta splash into the water. He had to twist around to see the others join her, as Reka was already wheeling northward, toward Vazula. Having dropped his own burdens, Elddreki followed his son.

It was hard to fight the feeling of panic, but Heath tried to keep it at bay. He needed a clear head. He called on his magic, expending no great effort to draw Merletta's image to mind. She'd never been more central than this moment. He watched her and Sage dragging the chained Record Master through the water. Although he'd watched her in the triple kingdoms many times, he'd never before caught such an aerial view of the underwater world.

It was incredible, an otherworldly vista, the spires of the Center glowing slightly in the dim light. Whether it was from mollusk shells, luminescent plankton, or some latent magic, he couldn't tell from the distance. But it was breathtaking. The Center was ringed by a beautiful reef, the bright array of sea creatures inhabiting it visible even from far above. And as

Merletta and Sage moved across the drop off, he caught sight of many structures up ahead, where two cities merged into one mass of life.

His wonder faded, fear once again taking its place when Merletta and her companions entered the war zone Tilssted had become.

Heath started with surprise as his feet hit sand. He hadn't realized they'd approached Vazula—he'd been fully engrossed in Merletta's underwater experiences, marveling in the beautiful unfamiliarity of her world.

He was going to miss that when she was gone.

No! he shouted at himself, angry that he'd allowed his thoughts to take that direction, even for a moment. Merletta may not expect to emerge from the coming confrontation alive, but that didn't mean there was no hope. He and Reka would find the proof they needed on Vazula—they *had* to.

And if they didn't, and the worst came to it...well, Heath had no more desire to die than he had the day he'd been speared on this very beach. But he was just as willing to give his life to save Merletta's, if such an exchange were possible.

More willing, in fact, because while he'd admired Merletta then, he was desperately and irrevocably in love with her now. As impossible as a future together had always seemed, his own future without her still seemed bleak and featureless.

"Heath!" The cry came from the tree line, as August emerged from the jungle, his wife close behind him. "What's going on?" His eyes flicked to Rekavidur and Elddreki. "We saw the dragons flying past minutes ago. What's happening?"

"We're out of time," Heath said grimly. "Rekavidur and his father, Elddreki, are here to help. But the rest of the dragons are on their way, and their only purpose is to empty the triple kingdoms."

The couple exchanged a silent look, and August held out his hand. Eloise placed hers in it, and Heath saw the merman's knuckles whiten as he squeezed. The gesture was matter-of-fact, and yet somehow so deeply personal and profound that Heath looked away, feeling like an intruder on an intimate moment.

"Thank you for bringing us the news," August said. He set off toward the water at a jog, his wife's hand still clasped in his as she kept pace.

"Wait!" Heath called.

They turned, both holding themselves with tense impatience as they waited for him to speak.

"We didn't just come to tell you," Heath said. "We're here to search the island, to try to find some evidence of where the merpeople came from, something that will convince the dragons they're not abominations. Would your efforts maybe be better spent helping us?"

August shook his head curtly. "We wish you all success, of course," he said. "But we've scoured every inch of this island. There's nothing here. At least, nothing we can find."

Eloise nodded her agreement. "Our entire civilization is under attack right now. There is no better use of our effort than to float beside them as they face their final threat."

Without another word, the couple resumed their sprint to the water, releasing hands only as they dove into the shallows in a synchronized motion.

"They race so willingly to their certain deaths," commented Elddreki dispassionately. "Not blindly, or in foolish optimism, but out of loyalty and love. Surely those are not the actions of abominations. I can see no evidence that their kind is of lesser nobility than humans."

"They *are* humans," Heath said fiercely. "I know it in my bones." He groaned. If only the elders were as willing to be convinced as Rekavidur and his father. But they were so much older, so much more set in their ways.

There was no time to dwell on such frustrations.

"Where do we start looking?" he demanded, turning toward the jungle. "Reka, you used to hunt over the island for evidence of dragons, didn't you?"

Reka nodded gravely. "I did. I spent many hours doing so, while you lost your heart and head over Merletta."

The dragon spoke without malice, simply stating facts. But regret knifed through Heath as he remembered again all the wasted opportunities to find the answers he knew Vazula must hide.

"And?" he prompted, when Rekavidur didn't elaborate.

Reka gave a rippling shrug, the movement maddeningly slow and measured for such a crisis situation.

"I found very little. It surprised me, as I had been led to believe that in the rare event that dragons leave a place forever, they usually leave behind some mark of their presence." He swiveled his head to face his father.

Elddreki nodded. "I would expect as much. Jocelyn and I certainly discovered such markings when we examined the site the humans call Dragoncave. There was no true, detailed record, only runes that still breathed of the dragons' longing for the sea, even after many human generations. And of course, the lingering presence of the magic. That much is here, at least."

Rekavidur inclined his head. "I sense it, too. And I did find a few instances of runes. But nothing revealing. Only sensations, as you described. Conflict, and frustration...perhaps even regret."

"Regret?" Elddreki seemed surprised. "That is a rare mark for a dragon to leave. Perhaps the merpeople really were abominations, created by dragons of this colony forfeiting their magic. They would certainly regret that."

"Merletta and her kind are *not* abominations," Heath said

firmly. "There are lots of reasons we're convinced of that. Let's not waste time covering ground we've already been over."

Elddreki regarded him with what seemed maddeningly like amusement.

"Always in such a hurry, never a moment to waste." He cocked his head to the side, considering the matter. "Although, I suppose in this instance you do have some reason."

Heath balled his hands into fists, trying desperately to rein in his frustration at the dragons' glacial pace.

"I don't understand what you mean by the dragons leaving markers, but would those locations be a good place to start?"

Elddreki nodded serenely. "As good a place as any. But while dragons leave traces of their presence—generally detectable only to other dragons, although the full potential of power-wielders to sense them is as yet untested—I am surprised Rekavidur didn't find more if he conducted a thorough search. The location I mentioned—Dragoncave—was visited by dragons only briefly on their journey from Vasilisa in Kyona's mountains to their eventual new home on Wyvern Islands. If your speculations are correct, a colony of dragons actually lived here for some time."

"So...what are you saying?" Heath asked, too impatient to be properly polite. "There should be more markers?"

"There should be more *than* markers," Elddreki corrected. "We value our history highly, Heath of the Dragonfriends. Our uncountable past is as precious to us as the fast-disappearing years of your future are to you mortals. And history is tied to places. Dragons sometimes leave a colony to seek a home elsewhere, as I did many years ago. But that was done in the knowledge that many dragons stayed behind to continue to steward Vasilisa and the history that dwells there. In this instance, it seems the dragons all left. We do not abandon a location and its associated history lightly."

"But the dragons who left could carry that history with them, couldn't they?" Heath said. "They could remember it, tell it to others, maybe even write it down?"

"They could," Elddreki acknowledged. "But it is not the same. History will never be as complete when it is separated from the place of its birth."

Heath ran a hand over his face, too tense and frantic to take any great interest in this fascinating insight into dragon lore. He took a moment to check in with Merletta, the massive amount of magic in the air from Reka and his father boosting his sight so that he had no trouble viewing her whole surroundings. Conflict raged around her, but she seemed to be enveloped by friends for the moment. Heath thought he recognized the merman with her—Andre. He didn't even feel the tiniest pang of emotion when the dark-haired young trainee embraced Merletta.

It was funny how the threat of imminent death put foolish little things like jealousy into perspective.

"No offense, but why are we talking about what you expected to find instead of searching for what we might actually find?" Heath asked Elddreki.

The older dragon regarded him indulgently. "I hope it will guide our search," he explained. "I would anticipate that the dragons who departed here would have left a more substantial record of their presence than just runes and markings."

"Truly?" Rekavidur sounded intrigued. "You mean they might have intentionally left memories? I would not have thought it likely—I certainly never came across any that I recognized."

"How do you leave memories?" Heath demanded.

Elddreki turned to face him, looking bewildered. "I thought you were in a hurry, Heath of the Dragonfriends. I am happy to oblige your request, but I confess it surprises me that you wish to select this moment for an explanation of the mechanics of memory imprinting, which is a complex and intricate process."

"I don't!" Heath said, exasperated. "I just meant...never mind." He shook his head. "If there *are* memories left here, would they be reliable enough to convince the elders they were accurate?"

"Of course," said Rekavidur simply. "You cannot tamper with a sealed memory. No dragon would doubt their authenticity. But do not get your hopes up," he cautioned, clearly seeing Heath's rising excitement. "I explored this island on many occasions. If memories were left for future discovery, I would expect to have found them."

"Yes, that would be my expectation also," said Elddreki, nodding. "Humans would not be able to sense it." He turned to Heath. "Although, as I said, the ability of power-wielders to detect memories is untested. But to any dragon, it should shine like a beacon. The purpose of preserving history is for it to be freely known, after all."

"Tell that to Merletta's world," said Heath grimly. At the words, his extra sight activated and his mind involuntarily dove back underwater. Merletta was speaking with an older merman now, her expression horrified.

"The skies."

Reka's sharp words brought Heath's head snapping up. His eyes widened in dismay at the sight of dragons—dozens of dragons—streaking past some distance away. Horribly, they were right on target, heading unerringly for the location where they'd just left Merletta and the others.

"They're here!" Heath gasped. "We're out of time!"

One of the dragons turned its head, and even from the

distance, Heath caught the glow of yellow as its orb-like eyes found the trio on the beach. No doubt there would be repercussions for Rekavidur and his father later, but none of the dragons diverted toward them now.

"The sealed memories!" Heath cried, turning in desperation to his companions. "Where would they be if they were anywhere?"

"As I said," Elddreki's voice was grave, but still unhurried, "the location of the runes Rekavidur observed would be as sensible a place to search as any."

"Take us there, Reka," Heath begged. "And please hurry."

Rekavidur scooped Heath up, as he'd done so many times before. Elddreki followed, the three of them streaking toward a spot on the far side of the island. They covered the distance so quickly, Heath's eyes were streaming and his face stung from the lash of the wind.

When Reka set him down, he stumbled forward, looking wildly around at a small clearing he'd never visited before.

"Here?" he said, looking up at Reka. "Is this the place? What's special about it?"

Reka folded his wings against his sides. "Do you sense nothing different?"

"Reka, there's no time for—"

"There is no time for you to delay the process Rekavidur is attempting to take you through," interrupted Elddreki sternly. "He is a dragon. He does not act without purpose."

Heath shut his mouth, chastised but still incredibly frustrated. His mind tried to pull him back underwater, to show him what was happening in Merletta's vicinity, but he refused to let it. He knew that if he watched the dragons wreaking death and destruction on the merpeople, he'd never be able to focus on the task before him.

"My sire is correct," Reka said. "There is an intention behind my question. If you cannot sense the signature of dragon magic here, there is no point in you continuing to search for anything the dragons may have left behind."

Heath made no more attempt to argue, knowing it would only waste time. Instead, he closed his eyes and drew in a deep breath. He wanted to still his mind, but that was an impossible task. Instead, he pushed his fear and urgency to one side, minimizing rather than banishing them as he let his senses roam the area.

"I do feel it," he said, his voice a little surprised as he opened his eyes. "There's magic here other than yours and mine. It's... deeper. Older."

"Good," said Reka calmly. "Where?"

Heath didn't close his eyes this time, letting his sight join the inexplicable extra sense of power-wielders as he searched the area.

"There," he said, pointing across the clearing to a large, mossy boulder.

Heath covered the distance quickly, squinting down at the stone. There might have been markings there—it was difficult to tell under the moss. He put out one hand, intending to scratch away the green, and a gasp escaped him as his fingers made contact.

The message of the runes flared in his awareness, not words so much as sensations. It was imprecise, but incredibly vivid. He pulled his hand away, a little unnerved as he turned to Reka.

"I don't know that I'd call it regret," he said softly. "It's more complex than that. Sorrow might be closer to the mark."

"Yes, you might be right," Reka agreed, seeming pleased at Heath's understanding.

Heath shook his head, trying to clear the intensity of the experience. "I thought dragons didn't tend to really feel emotions like humans do."

"They do not generally experience emotions like humans do," Elddreki said. "If anything, they experience them more deeply. Further below the surface, I mean. In their core. Not in the way of intense but fleeting human feelings. Dragons' emotions affect the actions of the moment much less, but affect their inner selves much more."

That was debatable in Heath's mind, but he wasn't about to argue the point with the dragon right now.

"Is this the kind of record you meant?" he said instead, gesturing at the rock.

Reka shook his head. "There are dragon runes under there. They are mere markers, not sealed history. But it is possible that such markers might appear near the location of a more substantial record."

Heath cast his eyes around, his impatience once again rising. His vision flashed to Merletta, and fear clenched at his heart. All he allowed himself to take in was the flash of scales, the screams cutting through the water, the sleek bodies of dragons moving as smoothly as if they were in air. Then he ruthlessly pulled his attention back to the jungle clearing, where the air hummed with the buzz of insects, and the moisture made Heath's hair curl against the back of his neck.

"I can't sense any magical beacon," he said shortly. "Can either of you?"

Reka shook his head. "I cannot. And I did not on any of my previous explorations."

Heath ran a hand through his hair. "Were there any other locations you thought might be promising?"

"I can take you to another place where I found dragon runes," Reka offered. "Although I do not expect a different outcome."

"We have to try," Heath said desperately. "We have to try them all."

"Very well." Rekavidur once again grasped hold of Heath as he shot up through the branches. This time he glided smoothly through the thick air, making for a spot on the other side of the lagoon where Heath had first met Merletta.

The memory sent a pang through him. She'd fascinated him from that first moment—dark, tangled hair, beautiful features, scandalously bare shoulders...eyes wild with the familiar frustration of being caged.

"*Focus*," he told himself, the word coming out in an audible grunt as Reka once again descended.

"There are many runes here," Elddreki commented once they'd landed on the rocky ground.

They were still surrounded by trees, but some of the taller species were giving way to mangroves just behind them, indicating the proximity of the lagoon.

The older dragon lowered his head to sniff at a nearby rock, his expression keen. "There is a certain theme to the sensation of these. They seem like parting markers. I think they may have departed from this spot."

"Really?" Rekavidur sounded intrigued. "How can you tell?"

His father launched into what promised to be a detailed and technical explanation of the indicators, but Heath cut across him.

"Perhaps you could discuss that later," he suggested. "Given you have potentially forever, and the merpeople have minutes to live."

"A reasonable point," Elddreki said, nodding sagely.

Heath made an ushering motion with his hands, prodding Reka. "If this is where they left from, they might have left memories here, right? Can't you look?"

"I have looked," said Reka simply. "As I told you, I've been here before, and I found nothing of the kind."

"Certainly nothing is immediately obvious," his father agreed.

Heath let out a groan.

"We didn't come here for me to look, Heath," Reka told him. "If it was something I would easily find, I would have found it long ago. We came here for you to look."

"But if you can't find it, how would I have any hope of—"

"Because your heart magic is the ability to see things others do not," said Rekavidur simply. "So use it, and see."

Heath stared at him, taken aback by the blunt command. Just like that? Reka made it sound so simple, but Heath didn't know how to do what he was asking, or even if he could.

He pulled on his magic, but his vision went instantly to Merletta. She was streaking through the water, not attempting to fight the dragons, but trying to usher others toward hiding places. She must know it was a futile attempt, but Heath wasn't surprised to see her trying. At least she was so far still alive.

Heath wrenched his sight from her, trying to command it to go somewhere else. His brother sprang into his range of vision, deep in what seemed to be a heated but controlled argument with Lachlan, whose arm was still in a sling.

No, not Percival, Heath told his magic in frustration. *Focus on right here, right now*. But that hadn't been his strong point for some time. He'd so often been lost in his extra sight, letting his mind be pulled in at least one additional direction rather than being present in his true surroundings, and he was paying for it now.

I can do this, Heath tried to convince himself.

He reached inward and teased out his magic, as Reka had taught him to do. The dragon had said he just needed practice, and Heath had found Reka was right. The more he'd exercised the newfound ability in recent months, the more confident he'd become in directing his magic. He would just have to hope it would be enough.

The presence of the two powerful dragons didn't hurt. He could feel the magic emanating from them in constant waves, and his power responded to it. The magic still clinging to the various dragon runes in the area flared across his awareness, like so many small flames. They weren't exactly the shining beacons Elddreki had described—they were only runes, after all, not some hidden treasure trove of magically preserved memories.

Heath drew desperately on the dragons' magic, even as doubt wavered inside him. What was the point of him using their magic? If there was anything their magic could find, they would have found it immediately. He couldn't wield their magic more effectively than they could. It had taken him until adult-hood to even wield his own, unlike the rest of his family, whose powers showed up when they were children.

The thought made him pause. A memory flashed through his mind, of himself telling Reka that his power didn't feel like his own. And following close behind, his grandmother's thoughtful gaze as she speculated that something in him had been resisting his own magic, perhaps even rejecting it, since the moment it appeared.

Even now, in the most crucial of moments, he was thinking of his magic like it didn't belong to him. Like it was just some kind of bridge, allowing him to access the magic of Rekavidur and his father. A mentality that left him feeling like an imposter, pilfering their power without any true ability to use it.

But it's not their power, he reminded himself. *They've used their magic, and if there are any sealed memories here, they can't find them with their usual dragon abilities. It's* my *magic that gives me the capacity to see things others can't.*

The thought felt arrogant. Seeing things other humans couldn't was one thing, but out-performing dragons?

But this wasn't the moment to worry about pride and humility. Merpeople were dying at this very moment—Merletta could be moments from death. If ever he'd wanted his magic to be strong, it was now.

And his magic was strong. Rekavidur had told him as much —Heath had even felt it, when he'd allowed himself to truly draw on the potential inside him.

The dragons' magic might be swelling the potency of his own, but the ability still came from *his* magic, not theirs. And he wanted his magic—he wanted every last bit of magic available inside him. Nothing less was going to save Merletta.

He reached inside again, and gasped aloud at the torrent of magic that welled up. He embraced it, feeling something within him taking ownership of it with a confidence he'd never exercised before. He didn't close his eyes, trying to avoid letting his natural senses distract from the use of his magic. Nor did he try to push Merletta's situation to the corner of his mind. He could see her clearly, ascending toward the surface with purposeful strokes while chaos reigned around her, her familiar face overcome with intense emotion. No part of Heath shied away from her reality. But it didn't detract from what he was seeing on the island.

With a clear gaze, he looked around the area, the runes visible to him as much by the flare of magic that somehow seared across his sight when he looked at them as by the markings themselves.

At first he saw nothing further, but the longer he scanned the area, the more some dim awareness began to grow. It certainly wasn't a beacon. It was more like a glowing ember, buried deep beneath the earth.

But in spite of the many muffling layers that seemed

metaphorically piled on top of it, the ember was still aglow. Whatever it was, it still emitted something that Heath could *see*, although not with his normal eyes.

"There," he said, pointing to an otherwise unremarkable boulder.

CHAPTER TWENTY-EIGHT

Rekavidur

Rekavidur tilted his head with interest, sensing the confidence of Heath's declaration on the air. It seemed his human friend really had found something.

"Something is there," Heath repeated. "I don't know if it's inside, or under, or...I don't know, smeared across it. But there's something. Something which is meant to be found, but which has been hidden."

Rekavidur moved closer, his sire joining him as the two of them examined the point in question. After a moment's consideration, however, Rekavidur felt a definite sense of disappointment.

"I don't think so." He pulled back. "I sense no magic there whatsoever."

"It's there," Heath said, still sounding entirely confident. "I don't know what it is, but some kind of magic is definitely there."

"I don't sense magic either," said Rekavidur's sire, but he remained crouched, sniffing the boulder. "In fact, the absence of magic is conspicuous, now I consider it. This area is permeated with power. Why would this spot be bare of it?"

Rekavidur leaned forward again, struck by the older dragon's words. "I hadn't considered that," he acknowledged. "It is curious."

Elddreki didn't immediately respond, still inspecting the area Heath had indicated. Rekavidur felt a flare of impatience from Heath's direction, but the human wisely refrained from commenting. He must realize that trying to hurry the dragons would only distract them from their task, thereby prolonging the process.

"I wonder..." Elddreki mused. "It would make no sense, given preserved memories are intended to be accessed, not hidden. But it could be that concealment magic has been used to render them indiscernible."

"Concealment magic?" Heath looked at Rekavidur. "Like little Jacqueline was born with? Didn't you say that's a dragon ability?"

"I did," Rekavidur confirmed, contemplating his sire's suggestion. "Although this would be a strange use of it. No such measures are necessary to conceal something like this from humans—they do not have the capacity to locate or unlock it. Only dragons do, and I have never heard of a dragon using concealment magic on other dragons."

"Just because you have not heard of it does not mean it has not occurred," intoned Elddreki solemnly. "If there is conceal-ment magic at work, a direct assault should identify it, and hopefully remove it if it is not too strong." He cocked his head to the side, his eyes fixed on his son. "Do you feel capable of assisting me, Rekavidur?"

"Of course," said Rekavidur, a surge of pride racing through him at the request. He would not fail in this test.

He shifted so that his shoulder touched his father's flank,

connecting on a much lower point than the older dragon's shoulder, given his sire was almost twice his size. Rekavidur felt the rush of magic that flowed between them and combined, connecting both their minds and their power into one force, much more competent than either of them would be alone.

The two of them leaned forward, pooling their magic, and sending it toward the boulder in a wave that started gentle and increased steadily in force. Elddreki's magic was certainly stronger, but Rekavidur sensed with satisfaction that his contribution was nothing to be ashamed of.

The magic wrapped around the identified point, probing and testing, breaking into the boulder itself. With no need to comment aloud, Rekavidur sent his surprise straight into his father's mind when he felt his magic connect with a barrier which was most definitely not natural. Whatever the magic was, it hadn't been obvious prior to their targeted examination.

He felt his sire's grim acknowledgment of their find, and focused his attention even more strongly on dismantling what was becoming increasingly recognizable as a dragon enchantment. His father's voice sounded in his mind, confirming that it was indeed concealment magic, undoubtedly worked by a dragon. The more Rekavidur explored it, the more he realized that while the enchantment was complex by its very nature, it did not contain an excessive amount of power.

With Elddreki doing the same as Rekavidur, his efforts both more powerful and more precise than his son's, they had more than enough magic for the task.

Rekavidur felt the moment they succeeded in breaking apart the enchantment. The hold of the concealment magic yielded quite suddenly, and another stream of magic burst potently forth.

Heath drew in an audible breath. "It really is like a beacon," he muttered.

Rekavidur gave a satisfied nod. Clearly the human could sense the sealed memories as well. Rekavidur closed his eyes, immersing himself in the memories for a single moment that lasted many generations of thought. He could feel his father doing the same.

"Well," Rekavidur said mildly, emerging from the magic. "That answers many questions."

He sat back on his haunches, his thoughts tracing their gradual way through the information he'd just received. The answers provided interested him less than the questions still left unaddressed. Heath would be glad to know what had passed during the dragons' residence on this island. But that had never been Rekavidur's main concern. What he wanted to know was where had the dragons gone? They'd been intending to go somewhere when they left these memories, that much was certain. So which destination had they eventually reached? On what far shore did he have distant kin, and what discoveries might they have made—about magic, about themselves, perhaps even about humans—which were still unknown to the dragons of Rekavidur's colony? He felt the taste for adventure stirring within him, the desire for more knowledge, more experience. It had only grown more keen over recent years. It began to feel...insatiable.

Although no one had ever described the matter to him in such terms, Rekavidur suspected he knew what that burning desire meant. He felt his decision creeping toward him, not quite certain yet, but almost there. He no longer had much doubt of the final outcome. But now was not the moment. There were other tasks to be done first.

"It does?" Heath, of course, knew nothing of Rekavidur's thoughts. He responded only to the dragon's declaration that questions had been answered. His voice was eager as he raced forward, pushing his way between the dragons to get a closer look at the boulder. "It looks much the same as before," he said. He frowned. "Except for those faint markings."

Following his gaze, Rekavidur noticed the dragon runes now visible on the boulder. A physical marker of the memories stored there.

"But it *feels* so different," Heath went on. "It's not sight exactly, but to...whatever this other sense is, the difference is indescribable."

The young human reached out a confident hand, placing it on the rock. His whole body jerked back violently, and Rekavidur had no doubt the same barrage of images and impressions he had just experienced now overtook Heath's mind. For a moment he feared his friend's inferior mind being overwhelmed by it, but then he felt Heath's magic at work, deciphering the communication. Rekavidur felt a surge of vicarious pride. His young friend's power was potent indeed to grapple so successfully with dragon magic of this scale, and it was clear that Rekavidur's training had helped to hone it far beyond what it had been a few short years before.

After a matter of seconds, which Rekavidur knew would have contained decades worth of information, Heath pulled his hand back with a gasp.

"This is it," he said blankly, turning his eyes on Rekavidur. "This is what we've been looking for. This is enough to save them."

"It is indeed," Rekavidur responded, his voice grave.

"But will they believe us?" Heath demanded. He looked like he was hardly able to grasp that they'd really found evidence so powerful, his human mind struggling to change direction so quickly. "Will the elders accept it?"

"They will have no choice but to accept it," said Elddreki, entering the conversation. "They will know I am not lying."

"Then what are we waiting for?" Heath cried. "We need to go now! Every moment we delay, more people die!"

"I am ready when you are," said Rekavidur amicably.

Heath gestured frantically, and Rekavidur started fluidly into motion. A moment later, he had Heath in his clutches and had pushed his way up through the trees.

"Wait!" Heath called, as they neared the island's shore.

Looking down, Rekavidur caught sight of figures in the shallows below.

"Who are they?" Heath cried. "None of them look familiar."

Rekavidur noted that the figures were not emerging onto the beach. Perhaps these merpeople didn't know about their legs.

"I heard Merletta talking to her friends in the water just before," Heath said. "They were sending people toward the island. It's heartening to know that some at least are escaping the dragons' attack, and making it through the barrier that was never intended to be a prison."

Rekavidur shook his head slowly. "It is an immeasurable difference, is it not? Between what the original merpeople intended the barrier to be, and what it has become, I mean."

"It's heartbreaking," Heath said heavily.

Rekavidur restrained a smile. How easily humans invested their whole hearts into matters outside of themselves. How easily those hearts broke, and were reformed, and broke again. It was both endearing and absurd.

"So much makes sense since seeing those memories," Heath added. "And yet, so much else is incomprehensible."

"Indeed," Rekavidur agreed gravely. "Human motivations are so often incomprehensible."

A few heads had poked tentatively above the surface on reaching the island, but Rekavidur saw that they disappeared back under quickly as the dragons flew overhead.

"I hope they'll realize that you're leaving," Heath said

anxiously. "I hope they don't lose their heads and flee into the open ocean alone."

Rekavidur gave no response either to Heath's words or to his anxiety. He felt not the smallest interest in the fate of the unknown individuals below him.

He felt magic stretching out from Heath, and cocked his head to the side as he flew.

"You are using your farsight. What do you see?"

"Merletta is still alive," Heath said, unutterable relief in his voice. "She's not even fighting at present. She's talking to someone. It doesn't look like she's injured, although she looks tense." There was a pause. "Wait!" Heath cried, fear creeping into his voice.

"What has she done now?" Rekavidur asked indulgently. "Likely put herself into more danger, as is her habit."

Heath's groan seemed to contain confirmation. "Out of nowhere, she's abandoned her conversation and thrown herself in front of a clump of merpeople. They don't seem to be fleeing like everyone else. They're...I don't know, hypnotized. They're staring at something I can't see."

Heath's magic intensified as he presumably attempted to extend his farsight further out to cover a greater area. Wearying of relying on Heath's descriptions, Rekavidur sent out his own farsight, letting it follow the path left flagrantly by Heath's. Merletta's form and surroundings came quickly into his view, and he had no difficulty identifying the reason for Heath's strangled cry.

A dragon was swimming rapidly toward the mermaid, jaws open.

"We have to get to Merletta NOW!" Heath screamed.

By Rekavidur's estimation, they were moments away—a glance at the water ahead showing churning, as though battle was happening just below the surface.

But he could feel Heath's terror, and he understood the cause of it. Moments away meant they were moments too late. Both of them could only watch through farsight—Heath's horror a potent taste on the air—as the dragon's jaws closed around Merletta's torso.

CHAPTER TWENTY-NINE

Merletta

Merletta didn't pause to listen to Agner's horrified oath. She took no pleasure in being right at his expense. Not in these circumstances.

Everywhere she looked, the water was full of fleeing, panicking bodies. Merletta could see unwary merpeople being buffeted mercilessly by the crowd, some of them clearly not even having seen the approaching dragons.

Merletta streaked back toward her friends, her mind oddly clear in light of everything. This was the moment they'd dreaded and waited for all this time. In a strange way, there was some twisted relief in its arrival—whatever happened, there would be no more waiting.

"Merletta!"

Sage's scream helped Merletta locate the others, and she closed the last distance, even as the first dragon reached the central square. Merletta spun in the water, colliding with Sage and Emil as her attention darted behind her, to the horrible sight of a dragon snatching a fleeing merman in its jaws, then streaming toward the surface with his burden. The victim's terrified screams faded away, and Merletta turned to look at Sage.

Her friend's face was as ashen as hers felt, and she knew they were both thinking of the account they'd read in the restricted records room. It was like seeing it acted out in front of them, just as they'd feared.

"What can we do?" Andre cried, his face tormented. "We hardly got anyone out. They're all still here. How can we save them?"

"The dragons are going for precision over speed," Emil said briskly, his matter-of-fact tone pulling Merletta from her horror back into a functional frame of mind. "It will take them a long time to individually pick off the entire triple kingdoms. Clearly they have a lot of time, so I doubt it bothers them. But it means there's still every reason for everyone to flee. Many might survive if they can get far enough away."

Merletta nodded approvingly. The idea of having something to do amidst the chaos made her feel centered again, more herself.

"You're right," she agreed. "We need to keep people moving, make it as hard for the dragons as we can. Don't let them get a whole group at once—distract them, and keep telling people about the island. Heath is there, with Reka and his father. Maybe they can help protect anyone who makes it that far."

The group split up, not pausing for any emotional farewells. There simply wasn't time. Merletta sped toward a young mermaid who was cowering behind a stone sculpture.

"You can't hide here!" Merletta told her. "It's too open! Make for the barrier, get out into the open sea. Try to stay in a group." She saw that a few others were listening, and she repeated the directions to the island that Emil had been shouting earlier. Then she moved on to another group, and another.

The dragons continued their attack, but it was no frenzied bloodbath. As Emil had observed, they were methodical and precise, not to mention utterly unemotional. There seemed to be more than two dozen of them, but that was nothing to the sheer number of merpeople packed into Tilssted. At least the merpeople had stopped fighting each other. Not a single guard was grappling with their own kind, and she could only assume the barrier was no longer being held. At least, she hoped so.

Merletta let out a cry of warning as she saw a Center guard some distance ahead of her, raising his spear against an oncoming dragon. There was no point trying to fight the beasts off like that. She reached out a hand, as if she could span the distance and stop the attack, but of course she could do nothing of the kind.

The dragon extended a clawed front foot, spearing the guard through the heart with a talon. Merletta's shout turned to a gurgling sob at the waste of life. It had been quick, at least, but she took little comfort from that. The dragon turned away, seeking another victim and apparently not seeing Merletta.

She sped toward the guard, but she knew before she reached him that it was too late for her to do him any good. She didn't recognize him, but a lump still rose in her throat. It could so easily have been Felix, or Griffin, or any of her friends.

"I'm so sorry," she whispered to the still form, as she took his spear. He wouldn't be needing it any longer. She crossed his arms in a traditional position of burial, then pushed upward from the seabed.

There was no longer any sign of the dragon in question, but distant screams told her the attack was ongoing. She looked up, seeing how the water above her was churning. The dragons had descended right into the deeps, and clearly some of the merpeople had taken it as their cue to abandon the habits of a lifetime and speed toward the surface.

Merletta followed them, making her way upward with the spear gripped in her hand. She dodged around many fleeing forms, and more than one who had no more opportunity to flee.

When she reached the surface, she saw a dragon lifting its victim from the water, seeming to prefer to attack in the more familiar environment of the air.

The mermaid screamed in shock as her orange tail turned to legs, and Merletta saw her staring in abject astonishment at her own wriggling toes. Then the dragon tossed her in the air, preparing to spear her.

With a cry of challenge, Merletta hefted her newly acquired spear, aiming for the dragon's open mouth. She knew it wouldn't injure the beast, but she hoped to distract it from its own target.

She wasn't disappointed. The spear lodged itself into the dragon's mouth, and the beast abandoned the flailing mermaid —who dropped into the water with a splash—looking instead for the source of the attack.

Merletta ducked under the water line again, swimming swiftly to the dragon's would-be victim.

"Get as far away as quickly as you can!" she shouted.

"But..." The mermaid looked dazed as she ran a hand down her scales. "My tail...I had...legs."

"Yes, that's what you're supposed to have above water, but there's no time to talk about that now!" Merletta cried. "Get out of here!"

The mermaid came to with a shake of the head, taking off before Merletta could say another word. Merletta also fled, moving in a different direction and hoping the dragon would follow her if it was to follow either.

She moved through the water without much purpose, panic clouding her mind. When someone seized her from behind, she gave a yell, her logic abandoning her as she spun around expecting to see a dragon.

But of course dragons didn't have hands, and the face glaring at her was decidedly not reptilian.

"You!" shouted the Center guard, whom she vaguely recognized but whose name she didn't know. "You brought this on us —you're the one they want! We should give you to them, then they'll stop attacking the rest of us!"

"No!" A green-tailed form came shooting out of nowhere, barreling into the guard and sending him jolting backward.

"Tish!" Merletta gasped, staring at the last mermaid she'd expected to see championing her. "Tish, get out of here!"

"It's not her fault!" Tish shouted at the guard, seeming close to tears. "The Center knew—they had time, so much time! And they did nothing to stop this!"

"Tish, it's all right," Merletta told her, gripping her friend's arm.

"No, it's not all right." Tish turned to her, definitely crying now. "Merletta, I'm so sorry. I just wanted to come back, so desperately. And I really thought if they knew, they could stop it. At least," she lowered her eyes in shame, "that's the excuse I told myself."

"Tish, I forgive you," Merletta said, tightening her grip. "I'm a hundred times more at fault than you in all this. But this isn't the time."

As if to emphasize her point, a dragon sped over the top of them. Tish flinched, and the accusing guard took off, clearly not willing to lose his life in attempting to bring Merletta to justice.

"Why aren't they eating anyone?" Tish demanded, her face fearful. "I thought they wanted to eat us."

Merletta shook her head. "They don't want to eat us. They don't really want to kill us. But—" Her words cut off as she caught sight of a whole group of merpeople, floating as if stunned in the path of the dragon.

"Get out of here, Tish!" Merletta shouted over her shoulder as she fled. "Go back to the island if you can!"

Putting on a burst of speed, she set herself on a collision path for the motionless group.

With a shout at them to swim for it, she threw herself in front of them, spinning just in time to face the dragon now streaking straight for her.

She no longer had the spear she'd pilfered, so she just braced herself, hoping the others had enough time to get away. The dragon swam with open jaws, and Merletta barely had time to gasp before its teeth closed around her.

She flailed and flapped, slapping the creature with her tail as it rose through the water. She could feel its teeth cutting into her skin, but it was far from the impaling she'd been expecting. It was being surprisingly gentle, showing no sign of wanting to rip her to pieces as the Center had described. She remembered her words to Tish, that the dragons didn't really want to kill them all, and she could have wept for the tragedy of it. This dragon wasn't savage. As far as it was concerned, it was carrying out an unpleasant but necessary task.

"You have it all wrong!" she shouted, knowing it was useless. "We're not abominations! We're—"

They cleared the water, and her words broke off as her tail changed seamlessly to legs. She'd barely processed the change when the dragon tossed her upward, making the world spin so that for a moment sea was above and sky was below. Then she started to fall, and saw the dragon's mouth open again, flame growing.

"MERLETTA!"

The familiar voice roared in her ears as Merletta fell, making her wonder if she'd lost her mind. Then Heath's arms closed around her, and the breath was knocked from her body as they flew sideways.

It took her several terrified seconds to grasp what had happened, then she realized she was clutched against Heath as they sped through the air, the human held in Rekavidur's talons. The timing of their intervention was unbelievable, and a glance back showed the thwarted dragon hovering right where it had been, looking stunned.

Swiveling around, Merletta saw Elddreki performing a similar rescue for a merman who'd been about to suffer the same fate by the flame of a different dragon.

"Heath, what are you doing here?" Merletta cried, her words near a sob. "You promised you'd stay at the island if you didn't find anything."

"Firstly, I certainly did not promise," Heath said into her ear, his voice warm against her neck as he continued to clutch her in his arms. "And secondly, we did find something."

Merletta went still, hardly daring to believe it. "You mean... you can stop this?"

Heath's voice was grim, and he squeezed her even more tightly as he spoke. "We're about to find out."

Heath's heart was racing so frantically, he thought it might burst from his chest. He'd really thought they'd been too late—they'd come so close to being too late.

His arms were as unyielding as iron as he held Merletta against him. Not that it was necessary. She was clinging so tightly, he could probably let go altogether without losing her to the water below. Her form was warm again, back in its human shape. She trembled slightly against him, but he didn't think it was from cold. He slid a hand up her mostly bare back just in case, and was horrified to feel something other than water coming with him.

"You're hurt!" he cried, lifting his hand to view the smear of blood.

She shook her head. "Barely. It was the dragon's teeth, but they hardly broke the skin. I have no idea how that's even possible."

Heath's breath almost failed him at the fresh reminder of how close it had been, but he knew it wasn't the time to obsess over such things.

"How do we get the message to them, Reka?" he shouted to his carrier.

"It is already underway," Reka responded.

Heath followed the dragon's gaze to see Elddreki enter the water at a steep angle. "Let's follow!" he called. He needed to see this, and he had no doubt Merletta would feel the same.

"It's safer to enter the water separately," Reka said, and with no other warning, he suddenly released them.

Heath and Merletta plummeted downward, still entangled. Heath barely had time to draw in a breath before he hit the water hard. His limbs flailed as he tried to find the surface, but before he could panic, he felt Merletta tighten one arm around him, tugging him up to the surface.

His face emerged into air, and he took a deep breath.

"Did Reka forget you need to breathe?" Merletta asked dryly.

"Quite possibly," said Heath, humor in his voice in spite of the situation.

He was just so relieved to have Merletta with him, still in one piece against all the odds. He knew that chaos was still raging somewhere in the water beneath them, but there was no one else above the surface, and for a heartbeat, it felt like they were truly alone, just the two of them in the middle of a vast ocean.

Merletta's tail moved steadily, keeping both of them afloat with ease, meaning Heath's hand was free to reach for her face. Her hair looked like it had started in a braid, although now it bore little resemblance to one. It was almost impossible to believe that it had been only that very dawn they were fleeing Bryford. He laid his palm flat against her cheek, his fingers tangling in the hair streaming over one shoulder.

"We should follow if we want to see what's happening," Merletta said, her voice not quite even.

Heath nodded. "We should."

But neither of them made any move to leave, and his hand

stayed where it was. Unbelievably, impossibly, here they were yet again, and he was suddenly overcome by the desire to kiss her like it was the end of the world.

So he did. Sliding his hand around to the back of her head and snaking the other around her back, he crushed her against him, the cool of her mermaid skin searing him almost as powerfully as heat through his sopping clothes.

She responded in kind, her arms closing around his neck and the strokes of her tail faltering as she threw herself into the embrace. When they bobbed so low in the water that Heath got a faceful and came up spluttering, they pulled apart.

"What are we doing?" Merletta gasped, half laughing, half groaning. She gripped his arm, keeping him afloat with no evident effort. "The dragons are still slaughtering everyone, and we're..."

She trailed off, and Heath squeezed her shoulder. "Elddreki is doing a better job of convincing the dragons than anything we could do."

"Did you really find something?" she asked breathlessly.

He nodded. "We found *everything*."

Merletta's hand tightened on his arm, both hope and tension radiating from her. She cast a glance around the still-empty ocean, and Heath could understand her unease. It was too still after the chaos of a short time before. The dragon who'd been about to roast her was gone, but all that meant was that it was probably attacking someone else below.

"I need to see what's going on," Merletta said tightly.

Heath nodded, filling his lungs with air and following as Merletta dove beneath the surface. The salt stung his eyes, but he could see a long way through the murky water. He knew his vision was better than any other human's would be in the circumstances. Understanding the role of his magic in his enhanced eyesight better than he once had, he encouraged his power to focus on his physical eyes. The clump of hovering dragons some distance below him came into focus.

Merpeople still fled in all directions, but he couldn't actually see any dragons attacking. It seemed they were at least going to hear Elddreki out.

However superior his eyesight might be, Heath had no superhuman ability to survive without air. Merletta was swimming straight downward as sleekly as a fish, and he soon had to pull up to return to the surface. He'd traveled further than he realized, and his lungs burned as he propelled himself frantically upward.

Before he could reach the air, a familiar arm slid around his torso, pulling him the remaining distance at twice the speed.

"Sorry," Merletta said, as he gasped in air. "I forgot for a moment."

"Don't worry about me," Heath told her. "Go find out what's happening. Just be careful!"

She shook her head. "I want to stay together," she said simply. "If we lose sight of one another—"

"Who knows if we'll be able to find each other again," Heath finished for her. He understood, and he made no more attempt to convince her.

Merletta slipped her hand into his. "Come on," she said. "Tell me when you need to come up for air."

He barely had time to once again take a breath before she dove back under, taking him with her. He kicked half-heartedly, but soon realized it would be faster to let her pull him along. It was incredible to watch her move, here in her home environment. She'd never been so graceful, or so formidable. Heath could barely take his eyes off her. They made it halfway to the dragons, close enough to see that the beasts were gathering from the surrounding area, before Heath reluctantly squeezed Merletta's hand.

She responded at once, turning upward with just a single glance behind. They'd gone only a few strokes, however, when a merman came darting out of nowhere, almost upon them before Heath even saw him.

He carried a spear, and it was raised in obvious aggression. Merletta let out a cry, changing direction so rapidly, Heath almost missed the nimble way she flicked her tail up and around, using it to deliver a solid blow to the merman's outstretched arm.

He retained his grip on the spear, unfortunately, but he checked his advance, watching her warily. Heath's heart hammered in fear—Merletta carried no weapon, and he knew he was worse than useless in their current environment.

Even as he watched, he could feel his body begin to panic at the lack of air. He glanced up. The surface was still several body lengths away. He'd waited too long to turn around.

"Your luck ends here," the merman hissed, his blue eyes blazing as they rested on Merletta. "I know what you did to him up there on the land, and I will personally make you pay."

Merletta ignored the threat, her eyes darting to Heath. "Go," she told him desperately. "Swim for the surface."

Heath's limbs ached to obey, but he hesitated, looking from her to the merman. He was thickset, his blue tail thicker than Heath's torso, and he clearly meant what he said. Whoever he was, he knew Merletta's identity, and he was here to kill her. The merman's eyes took in Heath as well, lingering on his underwater legs. It was clear from his gaze that he'd instantly dismissed Heath as any possible threat.

"And when you're food for the sharks, I'll be sure to deal with your pet human as well," he added for good measure.

Merletta let out a growl. She'd taken up a defensive stance, but unarmed, she surely stood little chance. Heath's body convulsed, his mind screaming at him to get air, and get it now.

But he ruthlessly forced the instinct to submit to his will. He struck out through the water, moving upward. But as soon as he was satisfied that neither Merletta nor her attacker were focused on him, he changed direction, striking downward toward the merman's unguarded back.

Pulling his knife from his belt, Heath slashed out. His aim wasn't very good—already his vision was going black. But he felt the blade connect with something, and heard the merman cry out in pain and shock.

Unable to resist the compulsion any longer, Heath attempted blindly to take a breath. Instead, his mouth filled with water, of course, and his body began to truly spasm. He forced his eyes open, gratified to see that the merman had dropped his spear. That should help even the odds a bit.

Merletta's cry of horror reached him only in a detached way, and he didn't immediately realize what was happening as her arms closed around him.

No, he wanted to tell her, *we're too far from the surface anyway. You need to defend yourself!* But of course he couldn't speak the words, and it seemed they weren't true after all. Because a moment later he felt a sharp pressure around his middle, and the water began to rush past him at an impossible speed, even for a mermaid.

Within an instant, he emerged into the sweet, life-giving air. He coughed violently, the motion entirely instinctive, and felt water gush out of his mouth.

"Heath! What were you thinking?" Merletta's voice came from impossibly close, and Heath belatedly realized that she was still crushed against him, both of them held in the talons of one of Reka's front feet.

"I leave you alone for a matter of minutes," the dragon rumbled from above them. "It really seems absurd how prone you humans are to sudden death."

"Thanks, Reka," Heath said sincerely. "That was closer than I care to admit."

Merletta said nothing, but Heath could feel her trembling against him as her mind caught up with their narrow escape.

The dragon just shook his head indulgently. "Who was that aggressive merman I just rescued you from?"

"He was one of the Record Master's personal guards," said Merletta grimly. "And he's obviously found out what happened in Valoria."

"Should I have speared him for you?" Reka asked. "He was attempting to stab you in the back with some kind of small blade, but I was more focused on getting Heath to the air."

"That was the right focus," Merletta assured him. She shook her head. "He must have had a paua knife in addition to his spear." She wriggled against Heath. "Is there any way you can shift us, Reka? This is highly uncomfortable."

Heath nodded his agreement, but the dragon was unconcerned.

"It's not far to Vazula," Reka told them. "You can manage until then—it will teach you not to be so careless with your fragile human lives."

"We're going to Vazula?" Merletta demanded. "And are the other dragons—"

"Look," Heath cut her off, gesturing with his head.

She craned her neck as best she could in their cramped position, and her face visibly lightened at the sight of many dragons winging through the air around them.

"They listened to Elddreki," Heath said, relieved. "They must be coming to the island to see the memories for themselves."

"That's right," Rekavidur agreed placidly. "They will not be fully convinced until they have personally examined the evidence, but they are at the very least suspending the extermination."

As he spoke, Vazula came into view, a glittering emerald in the middle of the sapphire sea. As beautiful as the day Heath first saw it, but now so much more than a site to be explored. It held his dearest memories, and—more to the point—other memories, which just might be the salvation of Merletta's people.

Rekavidur alighted near the lagoon, and Heath and Merletta fell awkwardly to the ground.

"Why have we come here?" Merletta asked, as dragons touched down all around them.

"Because the memories left by the dragon colony are just over there," Heath said, pointing through the trees. "Come on."

"Why have you brought a human and an abomination?" rumbled one of the nearby dragons, disapproval clear in his tone.

"As you will soon see, she is not an abomination," Elddreki said patiently, from where he'd landed next to his son. "And Lord Heath of the Dragonfriends has earned the right to his presence. It was his magic that discovered the whereabouts of the memories, and he was able to experience them as a dragon would."

"What?" another dragon protested. "That ought not to be possible."

"He carries a powerful magic," Rekavidur chimed in.

"We are aware of his farsight," the dragon said in a deep, reverberating voice. "But farsight should not allow him to access sealed memories."

Reka shook his vast head. "His magic isn't farsight. His magic is the ability to see things others cannot. One of the multiple ways that manifests is in farsight. The truth is that the full potential of his magic could be virtually limitless. If he develops it as it deserves."

A dozen pairs of yellow eyes were suddenly trained on Heath, and he swallowed nervously. "Should we show you the memories, then?"

Elddreki led the way through the trees to the area with the various runes, although there wasn't any real need. Since Reka and his father had deconstructed whatever magic had been keeping them hidden, the memories truly did emit power as conspicuous as a beacon. Heath had no doubt that everyone present—with the exception of Merletta—must sense it.

Keeping that in mind, he explained the discovery to Merletta quietly as they made their way through the trees, him leading her by the hand this time. Her eyes were wide, and she seemed tense at being surrounded by such a large group of the creatures who had, until minutes before, been intent on eliminating her entire species. But she followed him readily, clearly as eager for answers as he had been.

"Why did you not tell us of these memories from the outset?" complained a large dragon when they reached the boulder. "They are clearly present, marked without ambiguity." The creature inclined its head toward the markings that had appeared on the rock when Elddreki and Reka did their work. "Memories recorded by Tanin." He frowned. "It is a familiar name, although I do not believe it has been known in my lifetime. It is possible one of the elders may remember this Tanin."

"Recorded by Tanin, sealed by Idric," Elddreki amended. "And the only conclusion I can draw is that one of them carried powerful heart magic of concealment. These memories were most definitely concealed, and only brought into the light by the exercise of Lord Heath's magic."

Again, many heads swiveled in Heath's direction, and none of the dragons looked very happy. "Why would a dragon place memories only to conceal them from their own kind?" demanded one of them.

"That I cannot answer," Elddreki said. "But if you choose to enter the memories, you will see that they were not damaged in any way, merely concealed."

One by one, the dragons raised their heads so they pointed upward, and Heath felt a tendril—or rather, more like a powerful shoot—of magic snake out from each one. Power saturated the space, and by the time each strand had connected with the beam of magic shooting up from the boulder, the humid air seemed to hum with power, making it even thicker and heavier than usual.

"What are they all doing?" Merletta whispered.

"They're accessing the memories," Heath told her in a murmur. "I have to touch the boulder to do it, but that's not necessary for them. Come on." Still gripping her hand, he moved toward the rock, placing his palm flat against it.

Instantly, he was once more assailed by memories not his own. The mind that had formed them was unlike his, and much of the draconic impressions were beyond his ability to decipher. He let those details go, focusing instead on the physical realities recorded.

"It's not what I thought," he murmured to Merletta, as months and years and decades seemed to flash before his eyes. "When I first came to Vazula, I hoped to find encouragement that it was possible for power-wielders and other humans to live in harmony. When it was abandoned, Reka and I feared that it demonstrated the opposite—that the type of conflict growing in Valoria had happened here as well, and they'd wiped each other out. But it was nothing like that."

"What was it like?" Merletta pressed, fascinated. "What do you see?"

"I see...life," said Heath simply. "In all its complexity. A whole culture grew, flourished, lived, and eventually passed away here. There was conflict, but that's inevitable in any community. There was love and cooperation and fulfillment as well."

"Were merpeople here?" Merletta asked. "Is this where we came from?"

Heath nodded. "It was just the dragons first. They'd fled... something on the mainland. The details aren't recorded...whatever it was falls outside the scope of these memories. I don't think they intended to stay so long—I don't know how to explain it, but the flavor of the memory is one of movement, of a journey. They were seeking a new home, I think. But then humans arrived, a motley collection from both the North and South Lands who trickled in for various reasons. This place isn't big enough for the dragons to sequester themselves away like they do in Valoria and Kyona. So they interacted with the humans...formed a bond, I think."

"And the merpeople?" Merletta was clearly nervous, afraid the memory wouldn't contain enough detail to satisfy the dragons.

"There were no merpeople then," Heath said simply. "Only people. They formed their own kingdom—the kingdom of Vazula. There was a line of kings and everything. It was a small colony of dragons, but they respected the royals, as dragons seem to do."

His eyes flicked to Reka, thinking of his frequent disparaging remarks about King Matlock. The younger dragon was something of an anomaly in that area, although Heath agreed with his friend that the Valorian king had brought the censure on himself.

"There was one king who had two sons, and his heart was torn because he wanted to leave his kingdom to both. The humans had been on Vazula for many generations now, and both princes loved it fiercely. One knew every inch of the island, the other every inch of the surrounding waters. The humans had begun to absorb dragon magic by this time, as happened to my grandmother and her twin. One of the princes showed such signs—the one who loved the water. The other did not."

Heath paused, and he could feel Merletta's impatience beside him.

"The dragons made the king an offer," Heath went on. "They believed that if they poured their own power into channeling the magic some of the humans were absorbing, they could shape it, could actually determine in what form it would be received. They offered the king to give his magic-susceptible son the ability to transform, so that he could survive underwater and create a kingdom for himself there. The same gift would be given to all the humans who showed signs of taking on the magic, to create a second populace. There would be no other lingering effects of the magic he was absorbing, but that capacity would belong to them and their bloodlines forever."

"Did they accept?" Merletta whispered, clearly spellbound.

Heath nodded. "The king was concerned at first about the safety of his underwater son. But the dragons offered to construct a magical barrier around the location of his choice, to keep out predators and other dangerous creatures. With that understanding, the king accepted."

"So that's it," Merletta breathed. "That's where my kind came from."

Heath nodded again. "It's just as we thought. Forfeited magic had nothing to do with it. The dragons didn't relinquish their magic and die. They just used it to help give form to the magic already being carried by the humans."

"I didn't know that was possible," Merletta said.

"Neither did I." Heath glanced around at the dragons, all of whom were still considering the memories. "And by their reactions, I don't think they did either."

"Will it satisfy them?" Merletta asked anxiously. "Will it be enough to convince them they don't need to destroy us?"

"Oh, yes." Elddreki's voice rumbled from closer beside them than Heath had expected. "The account is conclusive. There is no longer any doubt."

Merletta's whole form slumped, her relief palpable. Looking over, Heath saw that there were actually tears brimming over from her eyes. He drew her against him, his arms wrapped reassuringly around the warm skin of her back.

"It's over," he murmured into her hair. "You're safe. They're all safe."

"Yes," she whispered, leaning her head for a moment into the crook of his neck. Then she straightened, her tone a little grim. "From the dragons, at any rate." She frowned over at the stone, as if willing it to speak to her as well. "But where did they all go?" she demanded. "If they lived here so harmoniously?"

"They were primarily harmonious," Heath corrected. "Tension did grow between the two kingdoms. Mainly because the one on land dwindled as the undersea one grew."

"Why?" Merletta asked.

Heath gave her a wry smile. "Because of troublemakers like you and me, that's why."

She cocked her head to the side in confusion, and he let out a throaty laugh.

"They continued to intermingle freely, and many fell in love across the divide," he explained. "Even if only one parent had the ability to transform, it invariably passed to their children."

Merletta stilled slightly as her eyes searched his face. Heath met her gaze evenly, knowing her thoughts were going the same direction as his. If they ever found a way to be together—impossible as it still seemed—that would be the future of their family.

The thought of having children with Merletta, of raising a family of dark-haired, stubborn-willed little people who were human on land and merkind in water, was almost too poignant to bear.

Longing rose up in Heath, so powerful it scared him. For a moment everything else melted away, and he was hit with the urge to once again pull her into his arms and kiss her, not like the world was ending, but like it had been reborn, and they could write whatever future they wanted.

But they weren't alone this time, and their futures were still dictated by too many forces outside their control. He mastered the impulse, taking a deep breath.

"The tension between the two crowns—not the actual brothers, but their descendants—grew to the point that the dragons began to wonder if they'd made a mistake. It was then they formed the intention of continuing the journey that had been interrupted by a stop on Vazula spanning many human generations."

"So when they left these memories, they didn't know what happened to the two kingdoms?" Merletta asked, sounding disappointed.

"They had a pretty good idea," Heath said with a smile. "The time between deciding to leave and actually leaving was significant. The situation had progressed by then. There were some hold outs, some humans whose lines had never mixed with the merfolk, most notably the royal line. But they were few...the two groups had ultimately become one, and the center of power had shifted to the underwater world. I imagine the few humans eventually died off, leaving the island vacant."

Merletta had looked up sharply at the phrase *center of power*, no doubt thinking of the hierarchy of control in the triple kingdoms. "Why did the merpeople stop coming here if they used to move so freely between?" she mused. "Why don't we know any of this history?"

"That the dragons' memories don't answer," Heath told her. "I suspect the truth of that lies in the records of your own kind. It seems it was only after the dragons left that your ancestors fully submerged themselves and were deceived as to their origins." His voice turned dry. "Believe it or not, the role of record holders existed even in the time of the dragons. They were guardians who were supposed to live between both worlds, charged with the duty to ensure neither forgot the history of the other, and the common origins. As with the rest of the culture, it seems that role shifted to be fully underwater in time."

"Where they did the opposite of their intended duty," Merletta growled. "Instead of protecting our origins from being forgotten, they went out of their way to ensure they *were*. Somewhere along the way they became so obsessed with keeping control that they even began culling the population in order to keep the triple kingdoms contained and within their power." Her hands clenched into fists at her sides. "If this history had been freely taught, as it was intended to be, merpeople would never have been mistaken for abominations, and no one would have had to die."

There was an unnatural hush at the end of her words, and Heath looked up abruptly to see that all the dragons had their eyes on Merletta. She flushed, clearly also not having realized they were listening.

"Is that an accurate account of the situation in your world?" one of the dragons asked her. "Has this history been purposefully hidden by those in power?"

Merletta nodded. "That's exactly what's happened."

"That is an offense which has impacted more than just the civilization over which these leaders have responsibility," said another dragon, his tone dark. "Through their deception, our kind have been implicated in a slaughter which has now become repugnant to us."

"We did try to warn you," Merletta muttered.

Heath gave her hand a warning squeeze. She was absolutely right, of course, but these dragons weren't like Reka and his father. They were much less likely to listen to humans, and much less predictable in their responses.

"The crime should not go unpunished," a large, deep green dragon agreed. "So it is these record holders who are accountable?"

"What?" Merletta's face went ashen, and Heath knew she was thinking of her friends. "No, of course not! Most of them don't know about all this. The initial crime occurred centuries ago."

"That may seem a long time to you, but it does not exonerate in our eyes," the dragon said dismissively.

"The record holders aren't to blame," Merletta said fiercely. "It's the Record Masters, both those of the past and the one in power today, who have orchestrated this deception. The current Record Master even carried his attacks all the way to Valoria."

"Very well," the dragon said, in a voice like rock scraping against rock. "We will hold this Record Master to account."

Without another word, the dragons all took to the sky, with the exception of Rekavidur and his father.

"Are they going back underwater?" Merletta asked frantically.

Reka nodded.

"I need to be there," said Merletta. "Will you take me?"

"I will do so, if you wish," Elddreki offered amicably. The dragon spread his wings in readiness, and Heath grabbed Merletta's arm.

"Wait!"

She turned to him apologetically. "I think we'll have to go deeper than you can follow this time."

"I know," he said. "But when will I see you? I don't know what's going to happen."

"Neither do I." She gave him a sad smile. "Isn't that more or less the basis of our relationship?"

Heath groaned, and Merletta let out a chuckle that didn't contain much real humor. Disregarding their dragon audience, she stepped close to him.

"We've been here before, Heath," she murmured, her sweet salty smell enveloping him. "We just need to both stay alive, and we'll find our way to each other."

She gripped his dripping tunic with one hand, tugging him against her before he could respond. She pushed up onto her toes to press her lips to his in a quick, fierce kiss.

"We always do," she added, the words somehow a promise.

And then, with a swish of dragon wings, she was gone.

CHAPTER THIRTY-ONE

Merletta

The delay with Heath had set them behind, but Elddreki moved quickly, and by the time the main group of dragons entered the water, they'd come within sight. Elddreki's talons—considerably larger than his son's—closed tightly around Merletta as he dove below the surface, his pace barely checking.

Merletta's legs disappeared, her fins flicking with eagerness to be swimming freely. But she knew that even in her natural environment, the dragon could move much more quickly than she could, so she didn't attempt to wriggle free.

Elddreki streaked downward, hard on the trail of the others. Merletta expected the dragons to make for Tilssted, where the fighting had seemed to be focused before her hasty departure. But they'd shot straight past it, entering the water high above the drop off that surrounded the Center.

Of course, they all passed smoothly through the barrier without the slightest check, causing Merletta's thoughts to dwell darkly on the Record Master's lies about the non-existent protection. How many had died that day, believing until the last moment that they would be safe if they just cowered inside the barrier as instructed?

As Elddreki moved down into the familiar streets of the Center, Merletta choked on a cry. Clearly the attack hadn't been limited to Tilssted, as she'd originally thought. There could be no doubt dragons had been active here as well. A number of buildings had been affected, entire walls demolished by what looked like the sweep of a dragon's tail. Rubble littered the seabed, and luminescent jellyfish floated aimlessly, freed from their lanterns. Plenty of merpeople were milling around, although they began to scatter as the dragons reappeared, screams once again lancing through the water.

"It's all right!" Merletta called desperately, her heart wrenched by the fear in their eyes. "They won't attack this time!"

If anyone heard her, they took no notice. At this rate, there'd be no one left in the area to hear the dragons' reassurances.

"We do not come to destroy." One of the larger dragons spoke in a voice that vibrated through the water with such strength that everyone stopped mid-stroke.

Many pairs of wary eyes turned toward the arrivals, and Merletta saw recognition on more than one face as they caught sight of her. She shifted at last, pushing at Elddreki's talons until he released her into the water. She swam away from the dragons, ranging herself alongside the other merpeople.

"Merletta!"

Searching for the source of the hiss, Merletta's eyes landed on Ileana. She hurried toward the young guard.

"You're alive!" Ileana said. She shook her head. "I suppose I shouldn't be surprised. You have as many lives as a catfish. Why didn't the dragons kill you?"

"A couple tried," Merletta assured her. "I got lucky. But they're not trying to kill us now, I promise." She looked Ileana over. "I'm glad you survived." It was genuinely true, even if her words carried no great warmth. "What about the others?"

"They were all in one piece last I saw," Ileana said curtly. "It was absolute chaos, I know, but the dragons were picking everyone off one by one. Not as many were killed before they withdrew as you might think. Why *did* they withdraw?"

Merletta was about to answer, but the same older dragon spoke.

"We have been released from the obligation we believed ourselves under to destroy your kind," he said grandly, addressing the merpeople at large.

Merletta gritted her teeth. There was that dragon willingness to take responsibility, she reflected sarcastically.

"We acknowledge that we acted under a misapprehension," the dragon went on. "Based in part on deceptions perpetrated by your own leaders." He examined the crowd. "Where is the one you call the Record Master?"

There was a deathly hush, no one coming forward. Merletta scanned the area as well, unable to catch any sight of him or the one of his personal guards who'd already tried to kill her. The other must still be in Valoria, she realized with relief.

"He was in Tilssted last I saw," she muttered to Ileana. "Still bound. Do you think he's there?"

She shook her head. "I don't think so. August took charge of him when he and his wife arrived, and I thought they were going to move to a different location."

The words had barely left Ileana's mouth when Merletta caught sight of Eloise wending her way through the crowd, her head swiveling as she apparently searched for something. Merletta darted forward to intercept the older mermaid.

"Merletta!" Eloise cried gladly, gripping Merletta's arm. "I'm so glad you've made it through this. Is it true what the dragons are saying? They're not going to attack us again?"

"It's true," Merletta assured her. "Eloise, where's August? Is the Record Master with him?"

A look of distress crossed Eloise's face. "I'm so sorry, Merletta, but he got away from us. One of his guards took us by surprise—the blue-tailed one. He skewered August with his spear, and while I was distracted he got the Record Master away from us."

Merletta's eyes widened in horror. "Is August—?"

"He'll be all right," Eloise said briskly. "It's not a life-threatening injury, although it certainly seemed that way at first. He got lucky."

Merletta ran a hand over her face, shaking with relief. After Eloise had believed herself to have lost her husband once through the Center's lies, it would be too crushing for her to lose him in earnest so soon before the removal of all danger.

"We need to find the Record Master," Merletta said grimly. "He'll get away if he possibly can."

"Where do you suggest we look?" Elddreki's voice startled Merletta. She hadn't realized he'd approached close enough to hear the conversation.

"Well, he definitely had an escape plan," Merletta mused. "But he didn't have time to properly activate it. He may have left the triple kingdoms already, of course."

Eloise shook her head. "Unlikely. It was mere minutes ago that he got away from us."

"In that case," said Merletta, "the only place I can think he'd go is his home. He talked some nonsense about how even though most would die, the civilization would still be preserved. I wouldn't be surprised if he had some stash he intended to take with him on his final flight. Presumably he expected more warning."

"Where is his home?" Elddreki asked.

Merletta pointed to the central spire. "Up there, I think. That's the only place I've ever seen him come out of."

Elddreki folded his wings to his side, weaving through the water like a sea snake. When he reached the other dragons, he spoke in a carrying voice.

"The mermaid Merletta believes the Record Master may be hiding in that building." He indicated the central spire, and the dragons all turned to examine it.

"Let us investigate," one said evenly.

To the shocked cries of many gathered onlookers, the dragons set upon the building, tails, talons, and teeth ripping at the smooth stone.

If the Record Master was sheltering in there, he wasn't the only one. Many figures streamed in terror from the building's main entrance, dodging falling chunks of rock. The dragons made no attempt to hinder them, too focused on the building.

"There!"

Ileana's sharp cry brought Merletta's head whipping around. The guard was pointing at the fleeing mass, her eyes fixed on one silver-haired figure who was trying to blend in with the rest.

"He's trying to get away!" Merletta called.

The dragons looked around, but Ileana had already streaked away. Unlike Merletta, she was armed with her Center-issued spear, and she had the Record Master in her sights.

Seeing the cold fury in Ileana's form, Merletta remembered the other mermaid's declaration that she wanted to help bring the Center down as retribution for the way they'd cast her aside. The memory made Merletta shudder for some reason.

Ileana reached the Record Master, spear extended, and everyone around scattered like minnows. His loyal guards were nowhere to be seen, and it seemed that the events of the day had eroded anyone else's willingness to float by him in the face of the dragons' ire.

Before Ileana could do anything, and before the Record Master had the chance to do more than reach for the satchel around his back, one of the dragons reached out his talons and plucked the older merman from the seabed.

"Are you the Record Master?" he asked gravely, as if admonishing a child.

"I am not responsible for the events of this day!" the Record Master cried. His face was pale, and the bandage around his injured arm was frayed and tattered in the water. "The responsibility rests solely on the shoulders of that traitorous trainee."

He pointed an accusing finger at Merletta, but none of the dragons even followed its trajectory. Collectively, they drew back, their faces twisting as if they'd smelled something foul.

"Do you not know that dragons can detect deception?" Elddreki asked coldly. "If we needed further proof that your origins are human, the shamelessness of your lies provides it."

A slight stirring went through the crowd, like kelp fronds waving in the current. But no one spoke, no one put themselves forward.

"We have seen the true history of your kind, and we know the solemn duty entrusted to you," said the dragon still holding the Record Master. "You are the keeper of your civilization's history, and had you stewarded it well, it would have become known by the humans as soon as there was contact between your kinds. In such a situation, it is most unlikely that we would have come to believe your people to be abominations. Your deceptions have involved more races than your own in shameful deeds this day. We do not forgive such a crime lightly."

The Record Master was trembling, apparently unable to find words. Merletta would have expected to feel triumph at this end to his reign of surreptitious fear and violence, but instead she felt sick at the display. She turned her face away, to see Ileana watching avidly, a hungry gleam in her eyes.

"And who will pass judgment on me for these so-called crimes?" the Record Master said, attempting to sound lofty and not achieving it. "There is no authority in the triple kingdoms higher than mine."

"We are not interested in the politics of your kingdoms," said the dragon simply. "Or in how you may have wronged your people. We take offense at your crimes against us, and we will deal with you accordingly."

With that, the dragon streaked toward the surface far above. With a cry, Merletta followed, and she wasn't the only one. Many of the merpeople seemed intent on witnessing what was going to happen, in spite of the potential danger.

None of them could keep up with the dragon, however, so it was from beneath the water that they watched as the beast cleared the surface and tossed the Record Master in the air. Something fell into the water with a soft splash, and Merletta moved to the side, not wanting her view to be obstructed.

A moment later, blazing orange flame lit the sky, and Merletta half wished she hadn't seen it. The Record Master's cry was cut off abruptly, and his form fell heavily into the water. One quick glance was enough to make Merletta look away. No one would be rushing to his aid. It was very clear that there was no longer any point.

The first item that had fallen drifted down past Merletta and Ileana, and Merletta reached out instinctively to grab it. Her mind could hardly process the abrupt end to the Record Master's schemes, and she was relieved to have something else to focus on, even if only for a moment.

She realized as soon as she touched it that it was the satchel the Record Master had been wearing. Flipping it open, she revealed a long tube, sealed with what looked like wax. It was a method of waterproofing Heath had told her about, and her curiosity was instantly raised.

She propelled herself up to the surface, popping open the tube as soon as it was in air rather than water. Handling the parchments within carefully in light of her wet hands, she scanned the words, her brow growing steadily darker.

"What is it?" Ileana asked, emerging beside her.

"Records—real records—about the first king of the triple kingdoms, among other things." She clenched her teeth as she slid them back into the tube. "It's entirely possible these could have saved the people who died today." She sighed. "Well, if the dragons accepted them, which they may well have refused to do."

Securing the tube again, she dove back under, propelling herself downward as quickly as she could, afraid of missing something else crucial.

She reached the seabed to find all the dragons watching her descent, as though they'd been waiting for her. When she pulled up warily, one of the larger ones inclined its head to her.

"We acknowledge the role you have played in exposing the deceptions that led to this day's events, Merletta of the Sea People. We trust that under your auspices, the full truth will be known by future generations."

Merletta floated, stunned at being personally addressed, and unsure how to answer. But they didn't wait for an answer. As one, the whole group shot upward, ascending through the water and presumably taking to the air far above Merletta's head.

"Is that it?" Ileana demanded, outraged. "They're just leaving? Is there no accountability for the fact that they slaughtered some of us for no valid reason whatsoever?"

"It seems not," Merletta said heavily. She felt too weary for anger, although she was sure it would come again as she looked back on the work of this day. "They're just too powerful. No one can exercise control over them, so they act with impunity. I suppose we should be grateful they're not prone to violence more often."

Ileana's mutinous face didn't show any such gratitude, and Merletta didn't blame her. She was far from feeling as calm as she sounded. But there was nothing to be gained from raging against the dragons in that moment.

Merletta turned, her eyes falling on the central spire. Dozens of forms were weaving in and out through the damaged building. A clump of waxy green caught her eye, and she looked down to see writing leaves strewn across the seabed. The outer wall of the restricted records room had been smashed open, and the records were spilling out. Merletta saw many merpeople picking through them, only some of them wearing the markers of Center employees.

"Someone should really collect those records before they're lost," Merletta said dully. "Not that we want to stop anyone from reading them, of course. Just to make sure they don't get destroyed in the chaos."

Ileana nodded. "I see a senior record holder over there. I'll speak to her about it."

She took off, and Merletta found herself swimming slowly toward the central spire. She was aching to see Sage and the others, to assure herself they were all right. But for all she knew they were still in Tilssted, not yet even aware of the dramatic happenings in the Center.

They would know soon enough. News like this always traveled through the water with astonishing speed. Merletta drifted into the lobby, although she had no desire to browse the restricted records room. She'd seen enough of it to last her a lifetime in the two days before her third year test.

Was that really only a matter of weeks ago? It was hard to wrap her head around.

She continued upward through the ruined building, driven

forward by a vague idea of finding where the airtight record had come from, in case there were more. She ascended all the way up through the lobby unhindered. The upper part of the building was even more damaged than the base, and she had to dodge the occasional sinking stone. It was so unstable, she wondered if the whole thing would have to be torn down and rebuilt.

Near the top, a strange looking room caught her eye. It was clearly not intended to be exposed to view—part of the surrounding wall had been destroyed. Merletta swum through a long corridor to reach it, entering the space cautiously in case the whole thing collapsed.

The room looked like a private living area, larger than any Merletta had seen before. From the way items were strewn around, it looked like someone had rifled through them in haste. And Merletta had a pretty good idea who. Surely these were the most luxurious living quarters in the Center. And they could only belong to one individual.

None of this was what had caught her eye, however. The central spire was all polished stone, gleaming and perfect and well-maintained. It had been a surprise, therefore, to see what looked like the wall of a rough stone grotto rising up in the middle of what must have been the Record Master's home.

She ran a hand along it, realizing as she moved around the edge that it was a large column.

A large column with a mermaid-sized hole near the base. Frowning, Merletta ducked down, swimming into the confined space before she could talk herself out of it.

When she emerged on the other side, she gave a gasp. She didn't know if it was a natural phenomenon, or another instance of the magic used to establish this place, like the barrier. But her head came up into air, not water. She was in a small circular room, and with a push, she clambered up onto the rocky floor, her human form settling instantly into place.

The walls were lined with shelves, and many records sat on them. Not records on writing leaves, either. They were on paper, and they had clearly never been copied out by any Center scribe.

Again, Merletta's exhaustion was too great to allow for much anger. It was impossible by now for any new layer of the Record Master's deceptions to surprise her. But she was glad to have found this place, all the same. She would need to speak to Heath about relocating these records to land, perhaps reproducing them for dissemination, if they could find a way to mark the copies as authentic.

Merletta didn't linger, her skin crawling a little at the thought of standing where the Record Master had carried out his scheming. Plus, she was cold in her human form, here in the depths of the ocean.

She dropped back into the water legs first, her tail reappearing as her torso slid in. But before she could make it through the small tunnel, something grabbed her fins, yanking mercilessly.

CHAPTER THIRTY-TWO

Merletta

Merletta gave a cry that started above water and ended below it, as she was dragged out into the Record Master's personal room. The moment her captor came into sight, she began to struggle wildly, desperate to be free.

She'd almost forgotten that the Record Master's personal guard remained at large. A hysterical sound bubbled up inside her, the relentlessness of it all too absurd even for fear. It would be too ridiculous if she survived everything—even managed to help drive off the dragons from destroying merkind—only to be murdered after the fact by this disgruntled stranger.

And, worst of all, she *still* didn't have a spear. If she got out of this alive, she was never going anywhere without a weapon again.

Unable to free her tail, she twisted around in the water, bringing her fist to bear against the merman's exposed stomach. He let out a grunt, but his hold on her didn't loosen. With a swift motion, he brought his spear down, pinning her fins to the stony ground.

Merletta let out a cry of pain as blood trickled into the water.

The guard gave no reaction as slowly, purposefully, he raised a knife—not a paua knife, but a real, metal blade which had obviously come from the human world—his eyes locked on Merletta's.

"Why, though?" she demanded. "What do you have to gain from killing me now?"

"A foolish question," the guard growled, "when directed at someone who has lost *everything* due to your intervention."

"There, Agner!"

The new voice caused both Merletta and her attacker to turn, but neither had more than a second's warning before a spear sliced through the water, taking the guard full in the chest. His eyes widened for the briefest moment, then he fell backward, his motionless form drifting to the smooth stone floor.

"No stabbing my favorite trainee," Agner said cheerfully, swimming into sight. He tutted as he removed the guard's spear from Merletta's fins. "What's this, Merletta? I thought I trained you better—never let yourself be pinned!"

Merletta winced as she wiggled her fins. She hated to think how mangled her toes might be when she next assumed human form. Maybe better to let the injury heal underwater first.

"What are you doing here?" she asked Agner blankly. He was still grinning at her, but she could no longer take pleasure in his approval. Not since he'd revealed his true attitude to the death the Center planned to mete out on Tilssted.

"Well, it was actually Instructor Wivell who alerted me to the fact that you'd been followed in here," Agner said. "We had a bad feeling about it, and as neither of us wanted to see you dead, we thought we'd just paddle in and make sure you weren't in any kind of trouble."

"Thank you," Merletta said mechanically, her eyes passing between them. "Both of you." She met Wivell's eyes stonily. "It's something of a surprise to learn that you don't want to see me dead, Instructor."

"I never had any especial desire to see you dead," Wivell said with dignity. "I even disapproved of it when I learned, early in your studies, that orders were being given above my head to remove you in whatever way was practical. That's not how things ought to be run within the program, in my opinion."

"How generous," Merletta said dryly. "But your disapproval didn't extend so far as to actually protect me, did it? So I'm sure you'll understand if I'm still surprised you did so just now."

"I won't pretend to have acted altruistically," said Wivell calmly. "I see no benefit in dishonesty. I can read the current, and I realize you constitute one of the most likely avenues for the program's future success."

"The program?" Merletta demanded. "How can you care about the program when our civilization just came to the brink of destruction?"

"The program is one of the foundational pillars of our civilization," Wivell said with familiar cold disapproval. "Its preservation is as important as the preservation of the lives of our kind."

"There we'll have to disagree," Merletta said tartly. Weary, she closed her eyes for a moment, leaning her head back against the rough stone wall of the grotto. When she opened them again, it was to see disappointment clear on Wivell's face. "Did you really think I would champion the program for you, after everything I experienced there? After the rot at its very core?"

"There may have been rot at the core of the Center," Wivell said quickly. "But not within the program. It remains pure, and it serves a crucial function."

Merletta made a noise in the back of her throat. "It was *designed* to serve a crucial function," she corrected. "But if you can't see how far from that purpose it strayed, you're more blinded even than I realized. The program was in tatters long before I entered it, Instructor. It began to fall apart the moment trainees were openly taught lies, and the process was completed when they were taught to *tell* lies to the rest of the populace."

Wivell's lips were pressed in a thin line, and he didn't immediately respond.

"She's right, Wivell," Agner said jovially. "The importance of the classroom teaching has always been exaggerated. Unless I'm mistaken, it's my training that's helped Merletta survive all this."

Merletta turned her face away from him, unable to bear his cheerfulness in light of everything. "I want to get out of here," she said, trying not to look at the unmoving body of the guard.

"Of course," Agner said, ushering her out of the room.

He and Wivell swam beside her, and for a moment none of them spoke. Then suddenly it occurred to Merletta that she may not have such a clear opportunity to ask Wivell her questions again—whatever he seemed to think, she certainly had no intention of turning up for class the following morning.

"Did you know who my parents were?" she asked abruptly. "Did you know my story when I first arrived at the program?"

Agner's look of surprise told her that he still didn't know it, but Wivell was silent for a long moment before replying.

"Not the moment you arrived, but soon after," he said. "I was made aware through official channels that you were the daughter of known dissenters who had been silenced, and that through an oversight, you had been relocated to a Tilssted charity home rather than joining your parents. I believe it was some years before the Center's investigators learned of your existence, and by that time it was not considered necessary to eliminate you."

"How nice," Merletta said hollowly. It was gut-wrenching to hear him speak so calmly of the cold-blooded murder of her parents. Perhaps the worst part of it was that she no longer felt surprise, or even great disgust. It was all so familiar by now.

Wivell gave no reaction to her words. "Had they guessed you would succeed in winning a place in the program, I suspect a different decision would have been made. Given your parents' history, there was some apprehension when you became a trainee, on top of the concern already felt at the admission of an applicant from Tilssted. But by then it was too late to prevent you from arriving. You had to be dealt with under different conditions."

"And my parents really are dead?" Merletta asked, not much caring about the anxiety she'd apparently caused through her arrival.

"They are," Wivell confirmed gravely. His lips were once again pressed together tightly. "Although I'm afraid you won't find their fate in any record." He shook his head, his tone suggesting they were discussing a poor harvest report. "A bad business. I never approved of such tactics."

"But you never pushed back against them," Merletta said swiftly. "Just like you didn't actively obstruct my learning, but neither did you help me, or stop Ibsen from blocking me at every turn."

Wivell gave no response, for the first time looking a little uncomfortable.

Merletta narrowed her eyes. "Speaking of Ibsen, did he know as well? About my parents, I mean? Was that why he was so determined to be rid of me?"

"No," said Wivell unemotionally. "I hold the position of primary instructor. As a regular instructor, Instructor Ibsen was not senior enough to be notified either of your origins or of the order to be rid of you. He just hated you for your own sake."

Merletta let out a strangled laugh, a hysterical edge to the sound. "At least he's consistent," she said.

They'd descended most of the way through the lobby by this time, and Merletta could hear some kind of hubbub outside. She drew in a weary pull of water, too overwhelmed to deal with any fresh drama.

"Your point is sound," Wivell said unexpectedly, sounding like the words were difficult to say. "I did choose to be passive in the face of decisions I disapproved of. I thought in so doing, I was protecting the program—protecting our history. But it seems that the opposite was achieved. I did not anticipate the scale of disaster that would arise from the many layers of secrets kept locked within the Center. And I have the honesty to acknowledge that you did recognize that danger. You saw it with a swiftness that is truly impressive."

Before Merletta could respond to this astonishingly positive comment, Wivell tempered it.

"Of course, it all arose because you were unwilling to leave matters alone. Had you kept your head down as a trainee is expected to do—"

"Then the Center's cycle of murder and control would have continued indefinitely," Merletta interrupted harshly. She piled enough guilt on herself—she refused to take it from the equally culpable merman beside her. "They killed my parents, and so many others, just for dreaming of going outside the barrier. And there's no valid reason whatsoever that we can't live outside the barrier—outside the water, even! Half of August's patrol were killed just for seeing land. And silencing dissenters is the least of the Center's violence."

She turned her furious gaze on Agner. "Not two hours ago, you openly acknowledged that the plan was always to provoke war, to kill off most of Tilssted in boundary disputes so as to keep the population of the triple kingdoms under control."

She shook her head, lengthening her strokes in her agitation. "Although I know it will be little comfort to their families, I have no doubt that those who died today are far fewer than those who would have died had the dragon attack not interrupted the Center's scheduled *cull*."

The last word came out laden with emotion, and there was a long moment of uncomfortable silence.

"Perhaps you have a point," Wivell said softly. A wry smile curved his lips. "Perhaps they are even right with what they're chanting outside."

Merletta glanced at him in confusion, but she wasn't in the mood to ask him for explanations. She put on another spurt of speed as she finally left the building, emerging into open water.

"Merletta!" a voice hailed her from some distance away.

"Sage!" The sound of her friend's voice was so welcome, it almost brought tears to Merletta's eyes. She watched eagerly as Sage streaked toward her, Emil by her side and Andre and Indigo following close behind.

But before they could reach her, another figure came into view, drawing to a stop just in front of Merletta.

"Elfin," she said blankly. She'd seen no sign of the older merman during the fighting—in fact, the last she'd seen of him was when he declined to speak for her at her trial—but she was glad in a detached sort of way that he'd survived the melee.

"Merletta," he said softly. His eyes searched her face. "I'm glad you survived this nightmare." He bit his lip. "I know you have reason to resent me, but I won't pretend to think I acted unwisely. Sharing your blood wasn't enough to win me to your cause when I knew nothing of it. But..." He hesitated. "But I am glad you weren't executed. And sharing your blood is certainly enough to make me wish to build a relationship with you. Me and my family."

"Thank you," said Merletta, her voice quiet as well. "And I don't blame you for not leaping to my side. I never expected that of you. I would like to know more of you and your family, but I can make no promises to anyone about my future right now—too much is still uncertain."

And with a polite nod, she glided past him, heading straight for her friends, who shared no blood with her, but had shared everything else—her victories, her fears, her dangers.

"Merletta." Sage rammed into her so forcefully, Merletta flew backward through the water.

She made no complaint, half laughing and half crying as she returned her friend's embrace.

"I'm so glad you're alive," Sage said, gripping Merletta like she'd never let go.

"Likewise," said Merletta fervently, reaching out a hand to grasp first Andre's arm, then Emil's.

"Is it really over?" Sage demanded. "Are we really safe?"

"Yes," Merletta told her. "The dragons aren't coming back, and the Record Master is gone forever. I don't think any of us are in immediate danger."

"Well." Andre flashed her a grin. "That will make life seem pretty dull, won't it?"

Emil made a long-suffering noise in his throat, then his arm snaked out to tug gently on Sage's shoulder. Responsive to the pressure, Sage released Merletta at last, settling her back against Emil's chest with apparent contentment as he pulled her close.

Merletta raised an eyebrow, and Sage beamed back at her. Merletta felt her heart lighten—it was wonderful to think there were happy spots ahead in the debrief of all this chaos, along-side the inevitable grief and pain.

"Well," Andre said brightly, giving no visible reaction to the display. "I'll admit I didn't think it was likely we'd have anything like this much success with our desperate attempts to avert disaster."

"Those attempts aren't done yet," Emil cautioned him gravely. "I'm glad the Record Master is gone, but it isn't as simple as just removing him. Someone has to take his place. And if we're not careful, we might end up with someone just as bad as he was."

"You're a shaft of sunlight in cold waters, aren't you?" Andre said.

Merletta shook her head. "No, Emil is right. This is the end of a very dark era for the triple kingdoms, but it's only the beginning of whatever comes next. And we can't know yet whether it will be any brighter than what's come before. It all depends on whether anything actually changes."

"Well, they seem to want it to change pretty drastically," Sage pointed out.

"They?" Merletta asked, bemused.

Andre gave an incredulous laugh. "Are you really not hearing what they're chanting?"

Merletta blinked, turning to look around her properly for the first time since exiting the spire. She'd tuned out the hubbub of the crowd, but she realized now that it wasn't jumbled noise. It was a repeated chant, gaining momentum, and it seemed to be directed at her.

"I don't understand," she said stupidly. "Why are they saying *Record Master*?"

"It's not so surprising," Emil said. "You've been a public figure for some time now, seen by many as the opposite force pushing against the established system. A system which has just been dramatically dismantled beyond repair. And if the rumors swirling around here are accurate, a dragon publicly credited you with a hand in stopping the attack and unravelling the lies that led to it. You're far too young and inexperienced for it, really, but no one is thinking very clearly."

"So complimentary, Emil," Sage said dryly, rising to Merletta's defense.

"Too young for what?" Merletta demanded. Emil gave her

his long-suffering look, and she suddenly caught up. "They want *me* to be the new Record Master?"

"To train for it, at least," he corrected.

"But that's...absurd," Merletta said blankly.

"Is it?" Andre demanded, ever loyal. "You undoubtedly have the makings of a leader, Merletta. There's something about you that makes people want to follow you, and you're unerringly honest and trustworthy. I don't think the position would corrupt you. And you understand the importance of history better than anyone."

Merletta stared at him, still feeling it must all be some strange joke.

"It *has* always been your life's ambition to become a record holder," Sage pointed out tentatively. "Isn't Record Master the epitome of that goal? I mean...we've stopped the coming disaster, like Andre said. We've even exposed the Center's lies, which seemed too impossible to contemplate a short time ago. I know you, Merletta, you can't just settle into a simple, repetitive life. You need a project, a passion. What better than the very state of the Center, and through it, the triple kingdoms? If not that, then what *do* you want to do with yourself now?"

The challenge hung in the water, no ready answer rising to Merletta's lips. It was too sudden, too abrupt a change from the large scale life and death struggle to the simple but all-encompassing question she hadn't allowed herself to genuinely ask for so long.

What did she want?

CHAPTER THIRTY-THREE

Heath slumped onto the sand, tension draining from him.

"It's over," he told Reka, his sight still idly following Merletta's reunion with her friends. "She's safe."

The dragon's lips stretched in a thin smile. "I am glad," he told Heath, sincerity clear in the words. "Perhaps now you can relax. You have not been a restful person to be around for the last few years."

The comment surprised a laugh out of Heath. "I apologize," he said humorously.

"I accept the apology," Rekavidur responded, in full seriousness.

"Will you return now with me to Wyvern Islands?" Elddreki asked his son. When the rest of the dragons had flown past, he had diverted to the island to join them. "Your exile has been lifted."

"I will first accompany Heath to the destination of his choice," Rekavidur said.

"Thank you," Heath told him.

He pushed himself up from his knees, realizing for the first time just how exhausted he was. Had it only been the early hours of that morning that he and his cousins had crouched in the gardens of the castle, waiting to bust the Record Master out of prison? It felt a week ago, at least.

Fleetingly, he wondered just how much of a mess that decision had left behind in Bryford. His farsight instantly reached out, ready to find an answer, but he suppressed it. He didn't actually want to know yet. One disaster at a time was plenty.

"I need to go back to Bryford," he said. "I don't think Merletta will be leaving the triple kingdoms anytime soon. It looks like she has plenty of responsibilities to keep her there."

His heart grew heavier as he contemplated the words of her friends. From what he could tell, if the rest of the merpeople got their way, Merletta would be positively drowning in responsibility from now on. It was unlikely she would have much leisure to meet him above the surface, and more impossible than ever that she could relocate permanently to Valoria to pursue a future with him.

"Besides," he added quickly, realizing the two dragons were still watching him, "if the king has figured out who helped the Record Master escape, it should be me taking the punishment. I'm the one who talked them all into helping."

Rekavidur made a noise of impatience. "Is that king of yours really going to make a fuss over every little thing you do? Does he have no better way in which to spend his time?"

Heath chuckled. "On this occasion, it's not so unreasonable for him to have a strong reaction, Reka," he said fairly.

"I will accompany you, if you would welcome it," Elddreki said. "I would be glad of speech with Jocelyn, in light of all that has passed." He pinned Heath with a thoughtful stare. "I wish to hear her reaction to the incredible capacity you have shown, young Dragonfriend. Your magic has astounded more dragons than myself this day."

Heath fidgeted, self-conscious under the scrutiny. "I'm sure my grandmother would be delighted to receive a visit from you," he said politely.

"Naturally," Elddreki agreed, inclining his head in a stately manner.

Heath hid a smile as he turned to Reka. "I suppose there's no reason to delay."

In spite of his words, he couldn't help a wistful glance back at the island sanctuary as they sped through the air away from it. The merpeople who'd made it there were in the shallows no longer—Heath and the dragons had sent them back as soon as they ascertained that the threat to the triple kingdoms was over. But there was no keeping the island a secret anymore. All the merpeople would soon know of it.

And that was how it ought to be, Heath reminded himself as the island faded from view. Still, he couldn't help a pang at the knowledge that it would never again be the secluded haven where he and Merletta had stolen a connection that was never supposed to be formed.

Heath was so weary, he almost dozed off a few times during the flight. On each occasion, the wind whipping against his face recalled him to reality. There were plenty more confrontations to come before he could let himself rest.

It was astonishing given all that had passed, but it wasn't much after noon when the trio set down in the courtyard outside the castle in Bryford. Heath had at last allowed his farsight to reach for his family, so he had some warning of what to expect.

Thanking Reka, he mounted the steps immediately, taking them two at a time. In light of Elddreki's desire, Heath sent a servant to inform the elderly Princess Jocelyn of her visitor. He asked for no directions himself, his farsight telling him exactly where he'd find the action.

When he reached the long dining hall which the king sometimes used as a meeting room, the guards at the door made no attempt to bar his entry. It seemed his presence was desired, if not exactly expected.

Heath hurried into the room, casting a glance down the long table. Most of his immediate family were present, in addition to several of his cousins. The king and crown prince were also there, postures tense. They all had chairs pulled out behind them, as though they'd started the meeting seated, but every one of them was now on their feet. Heath was struck with a sudden memory, of a meeting in this very room where the king announced to the young power-wielders that they were to be required to swear their loyalty to the crown at a public ceremony on reaching twenty-one years of age.

It was surreal to remember it. At the time, Heath had thought his loyalty was unerringly and forever to Valoria. Now... he felt differently. Not that he was disloyal to his kingdom, of course, or that he would ever intentionally bring harm to Valoria. But there were other priorities which ruled him equally now. The matter was more complex.

From the hall, he'd been able to hear raised voices, but a temporary hush fell over the group as he strode along the table toward them. For a moment no one moved, every eye on him. Then he reached his sister, and she threw one arm around him.

"Heath! You're all right. We were worried when no one could find you this morning."

He pulled back, smiling at her. "Yes, I'm fine. And the dragons have relinquished their vendetta against the mermaids."

"So Merletta is all right?" Laura demanded. She glanced behind him. "Where is she?"

"She's safe," Heath assured her. He kept his voice carefully even as he added, "She's gone home, of course. To her own city."

"Lord Heath." The king's voice was at its iciest, and Heath turned to face him. "Perhaps you can explain what the rest of your family are apparently unwilling to—how a prisoner escaped from my dungeon this morning with no trace whatsoever."

"Yes, I can explain that," Heath said evenly. "I helped Merletta break him out."

The king made a noise of outrage, although it didn't quite cover Lachlan's groan.

"I realize there will be a consequence for my actions," Heath said. "But I didn't make the decision lightly, and I'm willing to face whatever you think reasonable."

"That man was in the dungeons for a reason!" King Matlock exploded, taking Heath aback with the strength of his anger. "He needs to face justice!"

"Well, he's faced as much justice as anyone can impose," Heath assured him. "He's dead."

The king paused, and Lachlan's eyes flew to Heath's. "Are you sure?"

Heath nodded grimly. "Very sure." The murky view he'd gotten while watching Merletta's progress had been quite enough detail. "The dragons took offense at the crimes he'd committed in the underwater world, for reasons I won't go into, and one of them killed him with its flame."

Everyone looked a little stunned, but after a moment King Matlock's eyes narrowed in suspicion. "So you claim."

"He's telling the truth," Heath's father cut in, looking irritated at the implication.

Before the king could express any skepticism about his

father's honesty and therefore inflame the already tense situation, Heath spoke again.

"Elddreki and Rekavidur are currently in the courtyard. They can tell you about it if it would make it more credible. Plus," he added, suddenly remembering, "one of the Record Master's accomplices is still in Arinton. You can, and really should, make sure he faces the consequences of his crimes. I can help you identify him—the signature of merpeople's magic is quite distinctive."

The king considered him. "Even if the prisoner is now dead, it does not excuse your actions in breaking him out of my dungeon—attacking my guard in the process, I might add."

"Was someone injured?" Heath asked, concerned. "I tried to be very careful."

King Matlock paused, looking a little resentful. "No one was injured," he admitted. "But that does not change the fact that you committed a serious crime."

"I know," said Heath, tapping his fist on the table. "As I said, I will take whatever consequence you deem—"

"Oh, this is ridiculous," Brody interjected. "We only kept quiet because we weren't sure if they were clear. I was involved in the breakout as well, so if you're going to punish Heath, you'd better make it two."

"Three," Bianca said firmly. "I helped."

"As did I," chorused several other voices.

"Father."

Lachlan spoke quietly, but Heath didn't underestimate the weight of the word. He wasn't the only one who'd come a long way since the last time they all sat in this room. It was encouraging to see the crown prince challenging his father. Encouraging both for Lachlan and for the future of Valoria.

"Locking up or otherwise publicly sanctioning every power-wielder of my generation is exactly the type of inflammatory display I feel we should avoid right now."

The king turned his furious gaze upon his son. "They snatched the prisoner out of my keeping, Lachlan."

"He's dead now, Father," Lachlan said quietly.

"That makes it all the worse!" the king growled. "He is now permanently beyond our reach to bring him to justice. You suggest I just forgive the betrayal that led my own relatives to bring that about?"

"I don't see it as a betrayal," said the prince simply. He met his father's eyes. "And if I can forgive it, surely you can."

The king held his son's gaze for a pregnant moment, then his face hardened. "No," he said curtly. "I'm not sure I can." He turned abruptly on his heel. "I will speak with these dragons."

With that he strode from the room, the rest of the group exchanging uncertain looks before hastening to follow.

Heath lingered back, wanting to catch Lachlan. The prince gave him a wan smile as he caught up to him, looking as weary as Heath felt.

"Heath. I am glad you're back in one piece. I was a little concerned when your family clearly didn't know where you were."

"I was never intending to leave with Merletta," Heath acknowledged. "But Reka brought us word that the dragons had decided to move on Merletta's kingdom, and I couldn't let her go without me, not into that kind of crisis."

His cousin considered him. "You care very deeply about her, don't you?"

"She means more to me than my own life," Heath said simply. He flashed the prince a grin. "Although I won't deny I'm pleased it didn't come down to that in the end." Running a hand over his face, he added, "As impossible as this seemed a short time ago, it looks as though we now both have every chance of living a long life."

Lachlan studied his face. "And she has returned to her own kind? To stay?"

Heath dropped his hand with a sigh, understanding the words Lachlan wasn't saying. *Every chance of living a long life, but not together.*

"Yes," he said aloud. "She has." His eyes drifted to the doorway, and the two of them began to walk, following more slowly in the king's footsteps. "I expected your father to be angry about the prisoner's escape," he said. "I don't blame him. But the anger hides something, and I'm not clear on what that is. It seemed like grief, but surely he doesn't feel any regret over the prisoner's death?"

"Far from it," Lachlan said heavily. He cast his cousin a glance. "Your extra sight is astute. Father is grieved. And although you may think him unreasonable, you judge him too harshly, I think. If the offense was against him, I truly believe he would find it easier to forgive."

Heath frowned. "What do you mean?"

Lachlan lifted his arm, still secured in a sling. "I mean that the prisoner is the one who inflicted this injury. The physician is now quite confident that I will never be able to move my hand properly again. Apparently it was a most unlucky strike—the blade pierced a nerve just here." Using his other hand, he tapped the inside of his upper arm, above the sling. "And it seems the damage that passed all the way to my hand will long outlive the wound itself. The restrictions will be...considerable. And Father is finding it harder to accept than I am, I think."

Heath stared at his cousin in horror. "Lachlan," he said. "I'm so sorry."

"As am I," Lachlan said calmly. He gave Heath a rueful smile.

"It will teach me not to throw myself into a fight where I ought to let my guards do their job, I suppose."

Heath was silent. It seemed a heavy price to pay for what had been a well-intentioned mistake. And not only would the injury be a constant frustration to Lachlan on a personal level, but it would be under endless scrutiny, the reactions of his subjects reminding him daily of how visible his limitations were.

"I don't blame my father for being angry," Lachlan said abruptly. "But I do believe I can talk him down from pursuing any serious consequence regarding the prisoner's...escape."

"That would be gracious of you both," Heath acknowledged.

Lachlan let out a weary sigh that made him seem far older than twenty-one. "If there's a time to be gracious, this is it. We're all sick of conflict and tension, Heath. We want to move forward, hopefully along a very different path from the one that man was helping lead us down."

"I wish we could just blame him," Heath said. "But I think we all played our part."

"Very true," Lachlan agreed.

They'd reached the entranceway by this time, and Heath could see the dragons through the open front doors. His grandmother had arrived, and seemed to be in conversation with both Elddreki and King Matlock.

"I will of course take any reprieve your father gives gratefully," Heath said to his cousin. "But I do understand the gravity of what I've done, both in terms of the escape and the secrets that came before it. I'm as relieved to have it all behind us as you are. I don't like keeping secrets, and I don't want to do it anymore."

Lachlan met his eyes seriously, his gaze more forgiving than Heath deserved.

"I'm glad to hear you say that," he said. "I hope we haven't lost the trust we once had between us."

"You've certainly done nothing to lose mine," Heath said emphatically. "If you feel the same, it'll be more than I deserve." His eyes strayed toward the figure of the king. "And I don't blame your father if he doesn't fully trust me. He has reason to argue that I showed my loyalty to Merletta to outweigh my loyalty to the crown of Valoria. I don't expect him to ever forget that, and I accept that it will likely always stand between us."

As will the time when he publicly flogged me, he added silently. He knew Lachlan was deeply grieved over that decision of his father's. There was no need to further distress him when he'd had no hand in the event.

Lachlan looked a little troubled.

"Heath," he started. "My father..."

"You don't need to apologize for him," Heath reassured his cousin.

Lachlan shook his head. "I know," he said. "In fact, it's not in my power to do so."

The unspoken implication hung in the air. Only the king could do that, and he was most likely still too stiff-necked.

"But," Lachlan continued, "I don't want you to think he has no regrets." Lachlan hesitated, and Heath was sure he was weighing up how much of his private conversations with his father he could repeat without disrespecting the king beyond what his own rigid sense of duty and loyalty would allow.

"My father and I have spoken about what passed with the man you call the Record Master, and I have no doubt we will discuss it much more in the days and weeks to come. He is still learning to what extent he was deceived, and I believe he is humbled by the realization that he gave trust where he should not have, and the actions that led him to take."

"That's encouraging to hear," Heath said gravely, recognizing the faith Lachlan was showing in telling him as much.

Lachlan paused for a moment, then seemed to decide to say

no more. He offered his good arm, and Heath gripped it, before the two men jogged down the steps to join the others.

"I believe the elders are willing to consider the elimination of this Record Master to close the matter," Elddreki was saying to King Matlock. "And they now recognize the legitimacy of the group of humans in question, the ones in whom magic has taken a different form from that of the House of Dragonfriend."

"You mean the...mermaids?" The king stumbled over the word, as if he felt ridiculous even saying it.

"Call them what you will." Elddreki gave a rippling shrug. "They are ultimately human."

The king seemed unable to find a response to this, and after a moment, he bowed. "Please convey my greetings and respect to the elders of your colony," he said formally. "And remind them that they are, as always, most welcome at the Winter Solstice Festival."

Heath started slightly. He'd forgotten how soon that event was. It was a mere month away—the snow was late this year, not yet having shown up, so it was easy to forget how advanced the winter was.

"I will pass on your message," Elddreki said regally. With a springing crouch, he took to the sky.

Rekavidur lingered for a moment, his gaze catching Heath.

"Is all well?" he asked.

Heath nodded. "It will be."

Reka considered him for a moment, then his eyes passed to King Matlock. "I cannot speak for the elders," he said. "But I believe my father will do his best to convince them to come to your festival. They may be more inclined to bend than you expect, especially if you reconsider your ill-advised restrictions on the exercise of the power-wielders' magic."

King Matlock stiffened, clearly trying to hide his displeasure at being lectured by such a junior dragon. But Rekavidur's next words softened the rebuke.

"I believe none of us should underestimate the impact of my colony learning that even dragons can be gravely wrong."

The king was silent for a moment, then he bent in what was almost a bow. "I am not too proud to acknowledge the same capacity in humans," he said stiffly. "Even those who wear crowns. I will hope for a more peaceful and amicable future between our kinds."

"Let us all hope for that," Reka agreed.

His eyes again found Heath, and Heath moved forward to say a more private farewell. He was glad that Reka was allowed to go back to Wyvern Islands, but also conscious that he wasn't sure how long it might be until they next met.

"Do not lose hope, Heath," Reka said softly.

Heath looked up, startled. Lose hope about what? They'd achieved their ends, against all the odds. Percival was free of the dungeons, and the triple kingdoms were safe from the dragons. What was left to fear?

Reka's knowing smile said that he saw straight through Heath's apparent nonchalance.

"Your bond with her is strong," the dragon said evenly. "With a strength that almost tastes of magic." He shook his head. "There is a reason you recognized the power on the attackers when I did not. You are more intimately familiar with that signature of magic than probably anyone else in existence, outside of the merpeople themselves. Your connection to Merletta has given you a link to her kind that no other human can boast. The strength of your ability to follow her in farsight is remarkable for one so early in learning the craft. I have even suspected from some of your words that you may have been able to see her memories in your dreams, as dragons can construct their own."

Stunned, Heath said nothing.

"My point is," Reka went on, "I do not believe that simple realities such as distance and form will be powerful enough to break that connection, or permanently separate you."

"Thanks, Reka," Heath said softly. From where he was standing, distance and form seemed fairly substantial barriers, but he appreciated the sentiment behind his friend's words.

With a nod, Reka took to the air in pursuit of his father, leaving the group of humans standing in the wintry courtyard.

CHAPTER THIRTY-FOUR

The first snow fell only days later, and Heath greeted it without any great enthusiasm. He used to be able to see the magic in winter, but now his body longed for the humid warmth of a very different climate.

He kept a regular eye on Merletta as he went about life over the following couple of weeks. She was very much occupied with the affairs of the triple kingdoms, and Heath was reassured to see that she was no longer vulnerable and exposed. Her friends were usually with her, and she seemed to have guards shadowing her most of the time.

All a natural lead up to commencing her training to one day take on the role of Record Master.

His breakthrough on the island didn't fade—Heath felt much more in control of his magic than he ever had before, and it presented no challenge for him to follow Merletta while still focusing on his true surroundings. The Record Master's surviving guard had been arrested in Arinton, and had since faced sentence for his part in the plot against Valoria. Not that it had done much to mollify the king regarding the prisoner's escape, from what Heath had seen.

But life went on. Preparations for the Winter Solstice Festival were in full swing, and although Heath could muster no excitement, he undertook any task asked of him without complaint.

When he was called to the castle to meet with the king a week before the festival, however, he found himself reluctant to perform the requested feat.

"Be honest," Lachlan said calmly. "I only agreed to this on the basis that you would be entirely free to speak your mind, without consequences."

Heath looked from the prince to the king, wondering how to phrase it. His father shifted beside him—the duke had been with him when he'd received the king's summons, and had casually announced his intention to accompany his son.

"Firstly, I don't actually know whether Rekavidur has the ability to heal your hand," Heath said. "He probably doesn't know himself. He's still a young dragon, and much of his power hasn't yet been tested."

The king waited, clearly grasping that there was more to come.

"My other concern is..." Heath hesitated, then sighed. There was no point beating about the bush. "He doesn't have an overly high opinion of you, Your Majesty," he said frankly. "I'm sure you'll conclude that I've disparaged you to him, but in actual fact, he's drawn his own conclusions." He glanced at Lachlan. "Perhaps as you took the attack against your son more to heart than Lachlan did himself, as my friend, Rekavidur had a stronger reaction to the restrictions against me as a power-wielder—not to mention the public penalty I received—even than I did."

The king still said nothing, his expression grave but not angry as Heath had half-expected. He almost looked regretful. Heath didn't know what had passed between Lachlan and his father in the weeks since the Record Master's death—he had most fastidiously resisted using his farsight to find out—but the changes in the king, although subtle, were noticeable. It seemed Lachlan had spoken the truth when he hinted at his father having learned something from his own errors. Much as he would have liked a true apology from the king, he realized it was unlikely. It was a comfort to think that in his new confidence, Lachlan had most likely spoken to his father about the events much more frankly in private than he ever would in public.

The door to the small receiving room opened, and Heath looked up to see his grandmother entering, little Jacqueline perched on her hip.

He blinked in surprise at the sight of his infant niece, even more confused when Laura came into the room behind her grandmother, Germain in her arms.

"I apologize for my delay in responding to your invitation, Matlock," said the elderly princess pleasantly. "I had Laura and her children visiting with me."

"And I rudely invited myself along," Laura said brightly. In spite of her cheerful words, she cast Heath a look of concern, and he could feel her magic probing the mood of the group.

He understood—she must have heard that he had been summoned as well as their grandmother, and come to make sure belated punishment wasn't being meted out for his actions. Unless he was mistaken, it was the same reason his father had tagged along.

He gave her a reassuring smile, and she came to stand beside him. The king repeated his request to his aunt, the plea making him sound more vulnerable than Heath had ever heard him. He had no doubt that had the injury been to himself, King Matlock would not have been willing to go to these lengths. But for his son, it seemed he was.

The elderly princess considered for a long moment before responding.

"I have wondered if you would make this request," she said softly. She let out a sigh. "But I don't have an encouraging answer for you."

The king frowned. "But surely your dragon friend, Elddreki, is capable. Didn't he heal your mother of a potentially fatal wound?"

"Yes, he did," the princess said. "And from all we can tell, that act was the main factor in planting the seed of magic inside her that would eventually lead her to give birth to the first power-wielders, thereby causing magic to enter human bloodlines."

She looked from the king to Lachlan, her expression softening. "My point being, I have no doubt the incident is cited among the dragons as one of the greatest examples of how magical interference with humans is likely to have unintended —and far-reaching—consequences. I don't think Elddreki would be willing to perform such a function, and I admit I would be loath to ask him. I suspect any dragon would be concerned about the precedent, and I wouldn't blame them— imagine a future where humans pester dragons to heal every hurt, fix every problem."

The king visibly deflated, and even Lachlan looked disappointed. Whatever he'd said, he must have gotten his hopes up.

"It's not worth asking if there's any chance it would cause offense," the prince said stoically. "Not when they've just informed us they intend to come to the festival."

Heath looked up sharply, but the king spoke before he could ask.

"I suppose there is nothing to be done."

"Actually, Your Majesty..." Heath trailed off, his eyes shifting to Laura's. "Maybe you underestimate the treasures your own kingdom boasts."

The king looked confused, and Heath went on, although his eyes were still on Laura.

"We don't necessarily need to look to the dragons for magical solutions. After all, we have magic in our population, don't we?"

Laura held his gaze, a spark of defiance in her eyes. Heath knew she had so far continued to keep the form of her children's magic secret from anyone outside the family.

"It's up to you," Heath murmured to her. "I won't force your hand."

Laura let out a long sigh that was halfway to a groan. Her gaze traveled across the king, landing on Lachlan. After a tight moment, her expression softened.

"He's right," she said in resignation. "There may be another way. Although I can't promise anything. He's not old enough to properly control it, of course, but he does seem to have some level of impact. If he doesn't like you, or doesn't want to be held by you, it probably won't work." A hint of pride entered her voice. "But if he's amenable, I don't doubt his magic is strong enough, even at this age."

The king and prince both looked utterly bewildered, but Laura didn't explain. She just hoisted Germain up her hip, striding across the room toward her second cousin. With a tilt of her head, she held the child out, inviting Lachlan to hold him.

"What do you—"

Lachlan cut himself off as she jiggled her son impatiently. Moving like he thought the robust one-year-old might break, he held out his good arm, and Laura placed her son into its crook. For a moment Lachlan stared uncertainly at the boy, then his expression softened. He settled Germain more naturally against himself, smiling a little.

"He's a jolly little chap, isn't he? You know, I don't think I've actually held him before."

Germain gave a gurgling chuckle, waving a fat fist so vigorously he narrowly avoided whacking the crown prince's face.

"Oh good," Laura said, pleased. "He's taken with you. Offer him your injured hand."

"My—?" Lachlan looked from her to Heath, confused. "I can't really move it, actually," he reminded her.

"Oh yes," she said. Stepping forward, she carefully maneuvered Lachlan's immobile arm so that his hand connected with little Germain. "Here, Ger," she said. "What do you think of this, hey?"

The baby grabbed the hand with such clumsy force Heath actually saw King Matlock wince. Lachlan, however, went totally still, a look of wonder dawning on his face. Although he wouldn't be able to sense the unsteady torrent of magic that poured from Germain's little form, he could clearly feel something happening.

Everyone seemed to hold their breath, then Germain gave another squealing giggle, releasing Lachlan's hand and launching himself back toward his mother in a death-defying dive.

"Whoops!" Laura lunged forward to catch him before he could plummet to the polished floor below. "He does that sometimes," she explained sagely, as she pulled him more securely against herself. "It's quite terrifying."

"I...I can move it," Lachlan said, his voice hushed. He ripped the sling from his shoulder, holding out his hand to show his father. "It's like it was before."

The king's face was pale and stunned as his gaze passed from his son's hand to the gurgling one-year-old. "His magic... did that?"

Laura nodded. "Amazing, isn't it?" Her face grew suddenly

stern, as if she was scolding a child rather than addressing her king. "But I absolutely will not have him exploited, Your Majesty. I'll leave Valoria first—taking all my family's magic with me—and never look back."

The king regarded her gravely, his eyes thoughtful as they again passed between Laura's son and his own. "I understand, Lady Laura," he said mildly. "It is in the nature of a parent to wish to protect their child."

"Well, that's worked out nicely," Heath's grandmother said brightly. "But what did you say before about the dragons coming to the festival, Lachlan? That's excellent news!"

Lachlan nodded, still looking dazed. "Yes, Father informed them that he will be announcing at the festival that the restrictions on the use of magic are to be dropped."

"Truly?" Laura cried.

The king nodded gravely. "The restrictions did not serve their purpose as intended. They are no longer necessary. Naturally," his tone was dignified, "that does not affect the requirement that all magic be registered, for the benefit and protection of everyone." He glanced down at Germain. "The appropriate records will be updated to reflect your son's remarkable gift."

"Hm." Laura's lips were pressed in a thin line, but the duke cleared his throat meaningfully, and after a glance at her father, Laura stepped back, Germain in her arms. Heath reached out to touch her arm gently. It was progress—huge progress—and everyone was going to have to give a little if they were going to keep moving forward.

With a sigh, she nodded, letting it go for the moment.

"I had not intended to raise the matter of the Winter Solstice Festival today," King Matlock said, his eyes on the duke. "But since you are present, Norik, perhaps this is as good an opportunity as any."

Heath's father nodded, and the king's attention moved to

Heath. "A great deal has passed between us, Lord Heath. Although I will never approve of your decision to take the prisoner's fate into your own hands, I have certainly not forgotten your actions in saving my life from that same enemy's attack. And I accept the testimony of the dragons that the capacity of your magic exceeds that of any others in your own generation or the generation above you."

Heath waited, with no idea whatsoever where the speech was going.

"Your ability to see hidden things, both literally and more subtly, has particular promise," the king went on. "Your father and I have discussed it, and I would like to make another announcement at the Winter Solstice Festival, if you are willing. I think it is time for you to join the tradition of service established by your father, and by Lord Leo."

Heath frowned at this mention of his uncle, who, thanks to his ability to detect danger, had overseen the king's royal guard for as long as Heath had been alive. It was similar to the way in which Heath's father used his magic for the kingdom, certainly, but Heath wasn't sure what that had to do with him.

"Tradition of service?" he repeated, looking between his father and the king in confusion. "What announcement do you mean?"

"I would like you to train to take over your father's position in my court," King Matlock said. "Not as Duke of Bexley, of course," he clarified. "I'm not suggesting you become your father's heir. Merely that you take on his advisory role when the time is right."

"But..." Heath struggled for words, stunned. He looked at his father. "I can't do what you can do."

"On the contrary," his father said calmly. "You have already surpassed me, and you are only beginning to exercise your magic. I would fully support you taking on such a role." His eyes bored into Heath's. "But only if that's what you want."

What he wanted. Heath opened his mouth, then closed it again.

"Take some time to think about it," said the king. "You needn't give an answer right away. If the festival is too soon, we can make the decision at a later time."

Heath nodded gratefully, eager to be away from the royals and with his own thoughts. He hurried from the room, Laura and his father close behind him.

"What do you think, Heath?" Laura asked. She screwed her face up a little as she tested him with her magic. "You don't exactly feel excited. Do you want the role?"

Heath gave a helpless shrug, too thrown by the unexpected offer to immediately know what he thought. His father's position in the court was an incredibly influential one, far above the liaison role Heath had so reluctantly filled.

"I believe you'd do a good job of helping us all work through the tensions we've endured," the duke said. A frown creased his forehead. "But only if you wanted the role."

Heath said nothing, his thoughts still too jumbled.

The king's offer played constantly on his mind in the week that followed. When the day of the Winter Solstice Festival arrived, his thoughts were still in a mess. He'd given the king no answer, so could only assume the matter wasn't to be formally raised. Part of him didn't know why he was hesitating—wasn't it the best way for him to serve both his kingdom and his family? Wasn't it as good an opportunity as he'd ever receive to use his magic well, and to good purpose?

Merletta had been offered a new purpose, a new way to effect the change she so desperately wanted to see in her world. Shouldn't he be glad to receive the same chance?

His mind was so full of the dilemma, he struggled to share

the excitement of everyone around him when the dragons showed up as promised. It was good, of course, that they were once again willing to publicly claim friendship with Valoria. Heath smiled in response to Reka's silent greeting, glad to see his friend. Friendship between humans and dragons was what he wanted, after all. Everything was back as it should be.

What he wanted...his father's words rang through his mind. *Only if that's what you want*, he'd said. *You'd do a good job...but only if you wanted the role.*

Some realization danced on the edge of Heath's awareness, not quite bursting into full view. Elddreki was lighting the Flame of Friendship this year, Rekavidur watching with the other dragons. Heath saw it all in a detached way, his mind not really on the scene before him.

Suddenly, his ever-present awareness of Merletta took central place, and he realized with a start that she was leaving the triple kingdoms. She was already outside the barrier, a sizable group accompanying her as she started on the familiar journey to Vazula.

Quite suddenly, everything fell together in Heath's mind, and he let out an amazed laugh that caused his neighbors to glance curiously at him. He'd been struggling to even know what he wanted, because that hadn't truly been the question he'd been asking himself.

He'd asked every other question—what was best, what was responsible, what was *possible*?

But none of those were the question he was supposed to be answering. And *that* question was the easiest one in the world.

What did he want? The same thing he'd wanted for years. Since the moment those dark eyes had claimed him, never to let him go.

He also saw with blinding clarity what he *didn't* want. He didn't want to spend his life pulled between two camps, trying to bring them together while never feeling like he truly belonged in either. The king had valued him because he was perceived to be without magic, and had readily turned on him when he showed himself to have allegiances elsewhere. Even his cousins, his own flesh and blood, had frozen him out when they decided he was in the "other" camp in their constant, exhausting conflict.

He didn't harbor any bitterness—he understood all the factors that had brought them to where they were. But it wasn't how he wanted to spend his life. For someone who was supposed to have magically enhanced sight, he'd certainly taken a long time to see the beautiful simplicity of it.

"Reka," he said, stepping out of the line of extended royals, and ignoring the ongoing formalities. "Got some time?" He shed his outer layers, a delicious shiver going over him in the frigid air.

"I have all the time you could comprehend," Reka said in his gravelly voice, swiveling to face Heath. He glanced over Heath's form. "Will you not be cold without your coverings?"

Heath grinned. "Not where we're going. Up for a flight?"

A smile stretched across Reka's thin reptilian lips.

"For you, my dragonfriend, always."

CHAPTER THIRTY-FIVE

Merletta

Merletta strode confidently up the beach, exaggerating her steps to make the movements easier to follow.

"Like this, you see?" She turned to the half dozen faces bobbing in the shallows, staring at her in astonishment.

Sage flicked her tail clumsily up around her, pushing herself up as soon as her feet took shape.

"You'll get used to it," she said blithely, her smile a little cheeky as she met Emil's eyes.

With a deep breath, the young merman copied her gesture, his expression mildly alarmed as the transformation took place.

"Wow," Merletta said. "That's an impressive reaction for your first time drying out."

"He is pretty remarkable," Sage said, sounding a trifle smug.

Merletta was prevented from mocking her friend's lovesickness by Andre's shout of excitement as he threw himself onto the sand beside Emil, flopping around like a fish thrown onto a rock. A moment later he rose on shaky legs, his eyes wide with enthusiasm.

"This is amazing!" he cried, trying to take a step and promptly falling over.

"Slow and steady, Andre." Eloise's calm voice cut through the friends' laughter as she rose gracefully from the water. "It will take time to master this new skill."

Merletta left others to help Indigo and the rest, turning a calculating look toward the tree line.

"There's a clearing not far through there," she said, to no one in particular. "The ruins are probably too far gone to salvage, but I don't think it will be that hard to clear them, and it's a good site for a sort of receiving hall, I think."

Excitement swelled in her as she thought about the future. She'd been waiting for this day ever since the dragon attack was turned back, but there had been so much else requiring her attention—and everyone else's. Now, after the somber but very important memorial the day before, honoring the memory of those killed by the dragons, it felt like others than just her were finally ready to look ahead.

She received no response to her words, the whole group freezing at the sudden sound of rushing wind. Merletta saw fear flash across many faces, but her heart soared up into her throat. Surely not! She hadn't even dared to hope!

But sure enough, when her eyes searched the sky eagerly, she was met with her very favorite sight. The reptilian shape descending, sunlight glinting off his yellow scales, with a lithe, tousle-haired burden in his talons.

"Heath!" Merletta cried, sprinting across the sand and throwing herself against him before he'd had a chance to get his footing. The two of them tumbled into the sand, rolling into the shallows before Merletta righted herself, laughing. "I thought it would be too much to hope for."

"Are you mad?" Heath demanded, sitting up as well and grinning as he lifted a dripping rope of hair from her face. "I've been keeping an eye on you since we parted. The moment I saw you heading here, there was nothing in all the world that could have kept me from following."

Merletta raised an eyebrow, her laugh dying a little. "Nothing?" she challenged.

But Heath didn't falter, his eyes warm as he continued to smile at her. "Nothing," he repeated, his voice changing somehow, softening.

All at once the moment felt intimate, and Merletta was suddenly acutely aware both that they were still tangled up in the sand, and that they weren't alone.

"We need to talk," she said, struggling to her feet and holding out her hand. Heath took it, and even after everything, her heart skipped a beat as he drew up beside her, standing close enough that she could feel his warmth, his eyes boring down into hers.

"I have all the time in the world," he told her, a simple intensity in the words that took her breath away.

She linked her fingers through his, pulling him toward the clump of merpeople who were still straggling their way out of the water. Over a dozen had come on this first exploratory trip.

"Everyone, this is Heath," she said brightly. "And this is Rekavidur. They found the memories here on the island, and convinced the other dragons to stop slaughtering us."

Appreciative murmurs passed around the group, and Heath made a noise of protest in his throat. Merletta didn't allow him the opportunity to disclaim, instead waving a hand vaguely over the assembled audience.

"Heath, this is everyone. I'll introduce you properly later."

Without waiting for him to respond, she turned away again, tugging him across the sand. Heath fell into step beside her, clearly recognizing their path. They walked in silence to the lagoon. Merletta could feel Heath's eyes on her, but she kept hers trained ahead, feeling unaccountably nervous.

They picked their way through the mangroves, their hands still linked. When they reached the rocky bank of the lagoon, Heath let go of her hand and stepped forward.

"That's where I first saw you," he reflected, pointing into the water. He turned to face her, that same smile in his eyes. "You were glorious, and I was captivated the moment I laid eyes on you."

Merletta swallowed, lost in his gaze. He'd said such things before, but something was different now. The tension was gone, the anxiety and uncertainty. He was at peace, seeming confident in himself and sure of his path. Her eyes passed over the lithe muscles of his arms, and the steady way he held himself.

She stepped forward silently, closing the distance between them and reaching up to run her fingers along the short beard still stretching darkly down his cheek. When had the earnest teenager who'd looked at her with such unexpected admiration become this confident, capable man?

He was utterly breathtaking.

"I was terrified by you," she said, and Heath laughed at this unromantic reply. She grinned. "Not anything about you, of course. Just the overturning of my world that you represented." She shook her head ruefully. "I had no idea. To think I was stunned to discover humans weren't mythical after all. That's nothing compared to learning that I *am* human."

Heath smiled again, his hand traveling up to trap hers where it still rested against his cheek. He turned his head suddenly, pressing his lips to her hand, and Merletta's heart began to race.

"What's been happening, Heath?" she asked, her voice a little breathless. "Did you arrive home to a world of trouble?"

"Not a world of it." He shook his head slightly, his eyes

drifting closed as he released her hand and instead pressed his forehead against hers. "Just a village worth."

Merletta chuckled, but the sound was a little unsteady. She thought she'd grown used to his nearness by now, but it seemed twice as potent as usual, intoxicating her.

"We have plenty of mess to sort out underwater, as well," she said. "Although you probably know that."

He nodded, pulling back enough to look at her properly, although he still stood very close. "I've been keeping one eye on it all," he acknowledged. His eyes searched hers. "It seems like you've got your hands full."

She acknowledged it with a grimace, and a hint of sadness crept into his smile.

"You couldn't be more different from the previous Record Master," he observed. "But I have no doubt you will be infinitely better. Provided you have the right support."

"What?" Merletta looked up at him, startled. "You obviously haven't been paying as close attention as you thought. I'm not going to be the next Record Master."

Heath stared at her. "You're not?"

She shook her head, a laugh bubbling up at the thought. "Of course not. Can you imagine? I mean, it's true that there's a bit of a mob pushing for me to do it, but that's only because I'm a sensation right now. I don't have the patience for that role." Her eyes met his, and she laid one hand against his chest. "And it's not what I want."

Again, his hand crept up to cover hers, entwining their fingers.

"No, one of the senior record holders is taking over the role for the time being. She doesn't want to commit for more than three years, and during that time she's going to train Emil to take over. Everyone agrees it might be best to have someone young, not as entrenched in the complex layers of deception the more experienced record holders have been indoctrinated with. I have no idea how it's going to play out...but to be honest, I don't seem to care nearly as much as I should."

"But...why not? I mean...I thought passing the program was your life's ambition," Heath said. "Isn't this the greatest success you could achieve?"

Heath was clearly struggling to understand her carefree mood. His forehead creased adorably in his confusion, and Merletta smiled as she ran a thumb over it to smooth it.

"I'm not interested in that kind of success," she told him. "Maybe I was once. Whatever I told myself about being independent and not needing anyone's approval, I can see now that when I got into the program I was desperate to achieve highly so I could be accepted. I wanted to earn a place in a world that had no room for me." She shook her head, a smile still on her lips. "But I don't need their approval to find success, or happiness. As strange as it sounds, the moment that really hit me was when I knew the dragons were coming, and I found myself desperate to get back in time to at least die alongside my kin, if I could do nothing more. The last time I'd been in the triple kingdoms, I'd been on the point of execution as a traitor. If I had the love and the loyalty inside me to actually be willing to die for the triple kingdoms even without their approval, surely I have what it takes to live a happy life without it."

Her fingers splayed over Heath's chest, taking in the warmth of him, feeling the grit of the sand that still clung to his clothes from when she'd bowled him over.

"And that's what I intend to do," she said simply. "Live a happy life. I don't need the triple kingdoms' acceptance to have a future."

"So...so what will you do?" Heath asked, and it was his turn to sound a little breathless.

Merletta tilted her head back toward the beach. "Well, for a start, we're going to rebuild Vazula. The triple kingdoms are in desperate need of space to expand, and while discussions are already underway for how to safely expand underwater outside the barrier, there's enough interest in the island, and the idea of living on land, to start construction straight away." She smiled ruefully. "Not that we have any idea what we're doing— we'll have a lot to learn." Meeting his eyes again, she added, "So I'd like to stick around to help at least get that process started."

"And then?" Heath prompted, his eyes more intense than ever.

Merletta removed her hand from his chest, instead sliding both arms around his neck. "And then I'm free to follow my heart. I've been doing a lot of thinking about what I actually want, and all I need for the future I want is you, Heath. I'm willing to live in Valoria if that's what it takes."

Heath's arms were suddenly around her, and he pulled her tightly against him. For a beautiful moment he just held her close, his face buried in her hair and his whole frame taut with some intense emotion. Then he drew back, his hands dropping to her sides and his heart in his eyes.

"Merletta," he whispered. "What I've done to deserve your love, I'll never know. But you can't live in Valoria. You're too much a creature of the sea. Not to mention the politics would drive you mad, and the clothes would suffocate you."

Merletta laughed. "There is that," she acknowledged. "But surely we can make it work. After all, we've faced worse together."

"True enough," Heath agreed with a smile. His fingers tightened against her bare skin, squeezing her sides. "But the place would dry you out, and that's the last thing I ever want to see. The thing is, I've been doing some thinking of my own. The king has requested me to take over my father's role as one of his key advisors, in light of how my magic can benefit the kingdom."

"Heath, that's amazing," said Merletta, her expression earnest. "You deserve no less honor, and it's a real mark of trust in—"

"I'm not going to do it," Heath interrupted her bluntly. "I don't want to. I care about Valoria—I always will. But I don't have to hold the two camps together. I can't. I'll do what I can along the way to help, of course. But everyone has to acknowledge that the tension won't go away overnight. It goes too deep for that, and the kingdom needs to face it and work through it, not avoid it."

The warmth was back in his eyes as he tugged her a little closer.

"Just like we've had to face our divided loyalties since the moment we met each other. We've both had to decide what's really important enough to prioritize. And Merletta, I choose you. Without reservation, without a shadow of doubt. I came here not knowing what solution to suggest, just knowing my heart, and for the first time in my life, giving it the right to rule my choices. But now I know that you're not tied irrevocably to the underwater world..."

Excitement grew in his eyes as he spoke, and Merletta could feel herself catching it. "Merletta, we should live on Vazula! Together. We could build a life here, if the others who wanted to live here would accept me. We know from the history of this place that it's perfectly possible to coexist peacefully. And it's not like there would be lasting tension. Our children will be able to transform like you, and I can handle being the only one stuck on land from time to time." He gestured around at the lush jungle, and the peaceful lagoon. "There are worse places to be stuck, after all."

Merletta was staring at him, hardly able to comprehend his

words. It was too implausibly perfect, too impossible to think they could actually live the dreams that had seemed so hopeless since they'd first lost their hearts to one another. To hear Heath talking so confidently of their children, their home, their *future*, quite literally took her breath away.

"Merletta?" Heath asked, a hint of uncertainty creeping back in at her prolonged silence. "I may be getting ahead of myself." His hands once again tightened on her sides, in nerves this time, she thought. "You said you were willing to come to Valoria, but I shouldn't have assumed that meant you wanted to make promises about forever, which I suppose is what—"

"Heath," Merletta cut off his rambling forcefully. She laid her hands on either side of his face, holding his gaze with hers. "There's nothing I want more than forever with you. And nowhere I'd rather spend it than here."

A broad grin split Heath's face for a moment, then he pulled her all the way against him, crushing his lips to hers. She reached up eagerly, drinking him in, his touch as life-giving as fresh water after a day in human form. He was everything, absolutely everything, and she was almost dizzy with the rush of realizing he was as willing as she was to leave everything behind to be together.

After a heavenly minute, she pulled back, panting slightly as their foreheads rested together.

"But your family," she said. "Your responsibilities. You're a nobleman, Heath."

"There are plenty of noblemen," he murmured, his lips tickling her skin as he spoke. "They can manage just fine without me." He pulled back a little further, his eyes aflame as they roamed her face. "Although we may have to go back there to get married, assuming you'll have me."

Merletta laughed, a delightful shiver running down her. "Didn't I just promise you forever? Of course I'll have you."

Heath seized her hand, squeezing it. "Well, the wedding will need to be in Valoria, given I can't go underwater. In fact, I imagine I'll need to go back and forth a fair bit for some time, if Reka's willing to help with that."

"Well, I am," said a gravelly voice, causing them both to jump.

"Reka!" Heath cried. Outrage crossed his face as he took in the dragon draped over the rocks a stone's throw away, his tail dangling lazily into the lagoon. "Dragon's flame! How long have you been there?"

"I followed you when you walked here," Reka said, sounding faintly surprised. "Why?"

For a moment Heath struggled for words, until Merletta broke the moment with a snorting laugh that she just couldn't hold in.

Heath met her eyes, shaking his head in disbelief at his dragon friend's tactlessness. He gave a groan, but there was humor in his eyes.

"Why can't you get married here?" Reka asked, apparently accepting that Heath wasn't going to explain himself. "If this is where you wish to live?"

"It's a bit challenging given the island's inaccessibility," Heath explained. "The power-wielding side of my family could get here through the magical barrier, I suppose, but no one else can, and bringing supplies will be complicated."

"It's a shame," Merletta agreed. "That kind of access would be enormously helpful for us if we want to build a new land settlement here. There's only so much we can acquire underwater."

The dragon uncoiled himself, rising to his feet and shaking himself off a bit like the dogs Merletta had seen in Valoria. "The obvious solution would be to unseal Vazula," he commented.

"Then it would be a mere three day voyage for a human ship to travel between Valoria and Vazula."

"Is that possible?" Heath demanded.

"Most things are possible," Reka said calmly. He loped up to them, settling back on his haunches with a tinkling of scales. "To speak truthfully, I have already made the request of my colony." He turned his orb-like eyes on Heath. "I sensed that you remained discouraged about the likelihood of a future with Merletta, and I wished to assist if I could."

"Thank you, Reka," Heath said, sounding moved. "That was...very kind of you."

Reka nodded in regal acknowledgment of the praise, then continued. "I confess I was disappointed that they refused."

Merletta deflated. "Why?"

Reka let out a sigh that smelled faintly of smoke. "Because the barrier which hides this place from the outside was put in place by dragons, who cannot now be consulted as to their full reasons. My kind is hesitant to undo the actions of our fore-bears, because without all the knowledge that led to those actions, it is impossible to see the full ramifications of reversing them."

"I can understand that," Heath said, although he sounded as disappointed as Merletta felt.

"I asked my father to try to persuade the others, but he said we must trust the decisions of our elders, unless we have compelling reasons to go against them, as in the case of the mermaid attack." Reka gave a thin lipped smile. "I think he fears I am growing too rebellious by nature, always wishing to defy my elders for the sake of defiance."

Again he sighed. "It is not so, however. It is simply that I am not satisfied to unquestioningly trust the elders because, as we've seen, the elders blindly follow decisions made long and long and long ago." He shook his head slowly from side to side. "The strongest argument against blindly following the past decisions of elders who've gone before is the possibility that I could one day live to an age befitting an elder. Would others of my kind one day look back and blindly trust my past decisions as a result of my future position? I would not desire that."

He raised his head, adding with an air of great concession, "I may be a dragon, but I am not infallible." His eyes sought Merletta. "I have made too many mistakes, especially as regards you, Merletta."

She just stared back at him, unsure how to respond to these disclosures.

"You might not ever have to worry about others blindly following your decisions, you know," Heath pointed out. "You haven't yet chosen between mortality and immortality, so it's very possible you won't live long enough to be an elder."

Reka's head swiveled slowly from Merletta to Heath, but he gave no answer.

Thinking through his words, Merletta said, "If you asked your colony to assist you, does that mean you can't unseal Vazula by yourself?"

Reka's yellow eyes returned to her. "To remove a barrier such as this one would take great power. As a young, mortal dragon, I do not possess the requisite power."

Merletta nodded slowly, but Heath was watching Reka shrewdly, clearly sensing something more.

"What aren't you saying, Reka?" he asked. "What do you mean *as a young, mortal dragon*? How does your status as to mortality or immortality affect the level of your power?"

Reka didn't immediately answer. "Is that definitely your wish?" he asked instead. "If it was in your power, would you unseal Vazula and open it to the rest of the world?"

"If it was in my power, of course I would," Heath said. "It

would bring my worlds together and allow me to live here with Merletta without losing my family. But—"

"Very good," Reka cut him off, crouching suddenly. With a crack like a whip, the dragon surged into the sky, his wings snapping out so that he hovered high above the island, directly over their heads.

Merletta turned to Heath. "What's he—?"

Heath's cry of shock rang over her words, as he put his hands over his head as if not sure whether to shield his ears or eyes.

"What is it?" Merletta demanded, grabbing his arm in concern. "Are you all right?"

"I'm fine," Heath said, sounding dazed. "That was just...overwhelming. I don't know where it came from, but that was an immeasurable amount of magic Reka just expended." He swallowed, shaking his head. "I thought it was going to burn my senses."

A shadow made Merletta look up, to see Reka descending once more. In another moment, he'd landed beside them. He looked exactly the same as before, his expression placid.

"What did you do, Reka?" Heath demanded.

The dragon looked bemused. "Was it not clear? I unsealed Vazula, as you desired."

"But..." Heath and Merletta exchanged incredulous looks. "But how? Where did all the magic come from?"

"It was mine to spend," Reka said cryptically.

"Rekavidur," Heath said, his voice stern. "What did you just give up for me?"

The dragon's expression was faintly amused as it rested on Heath. "Do not exaggerate your own role in my decision, Heath. The choice had been growing in me for some time. In fact, it hardened near to the point of certainty when we stood on this very island a short time ago and experienced the memories left by the dragons. I did not act rashly. I am not *human*."

"What choice?" Merletta demanded.

But it was Heath who answered, his eyes on the dragon. "You just solidified your decision," he said slowly. "You chose immortality. You'll never be able to have offspring, but you'll never die."

Reka dipped his head in a nod. "That is correct."

A lump rose in Merletta's throat, the rush of emotion surprising her. "But...you'll never have dragonlings. Doesn't that make you...sad?"

Rekavidur considered her. "All emotions have their place," he said gravely. "There is sadness, yes. But it sits comfortably alongside its fellows, such as excitement for the possibilities ahead."

"But...why now?" Heath asked, seeming to struggle to get his head around this development. "Where did that magic come from?"

Reka sighed. "I forget at times how little humans know of dragons' ways," he commented. "When a dragon chooses mortality, a reserve of great power burrows inward, lying dormant, ready for when it will be passed to that dragon's offspring. When a dragon chooses immortality, that same reserve bursts upon him or her, available for the dragon's purposes. It is an amount of power exponentially greater than what is generally available to a dragon as young as myself."

"I've never heard of that," Heath said suspiciously. "What's it usually used for?"

Reka considered him for a moment, then smiled. "You are shrewd, my dragonfriend. It is customary to use that burst of power to divine the dragon's heart magic. But it was mine to access. I was free to use it as I chose, and I chose to use it for this purpose."

"Does that mean you won't have a specific heart magic?" Heath demanded, aghast. "Or that you'll have less power for the rest of your endless life?"

Rekavidur gave a guttural chuckle. "Of course not. What an idea. It will just take additional time for me to identify my heart magic. That is no issue—now my decision is made, I have a century or two to spare to the task."

Merletta blinked, totally unable to comprehend such a view of time.

"I don't know what to say, Reka," Heath said, his voice a little choked.

Reka stretched his neck up, in a gesture Merletta could only describe as preening. "I believe thank you is conventional."

Heath's eyes slid to Merletta's, and they shared a moment of suppressed mirth.

"Thank you, Reka," Heath said meekly, and Merletta added her voice.

"Thank you, Rekavidur." She stepped up to him, throwing her arms around his scaled hide as best she could. "You've changed our short lives for the better."

"I am glad," Reka said regally. With a satisfied nod, he loped back to the water's edge, laying himself once again across the rocks.

Merletta turned to find Heath watching her with a look that made every nerve tingle.

"What now?" he asked softly.

"Now," she said, stepping in and fisting her hands in his tunic, "we start making our own history. One where our paths never have to diverge again."

He let out a low chuckle that sent a thrill down to her toes as he once again lowered his face to hers, the kiss setting a seal to their promise of forever.

EPILOGUE

Merletta

Six months later

"Merletta."

Sage's exasperated voice caused Merletta to look up, her arms wobbling under the strain of the cleanly cut stone she was hauling onto the unfinished wall before her.

"Merletta, *what* are you doing?"

Merletta stared blankly at her friend. "I'm helping build this wall," she said. "It's going to be a public records room."

"Yes, I'm aware of that," Sage said, unimpressed. "I helped you trawl through the plans, if you recall. What I meant was, why are you still here? You're supposed to be getting married in two hours!"

"Oh, that," Merletta said, a tingle of excitement passing over her. "Is the morning that far gone already?" She lowered the stone with a grunt. "I guess I should leave it for today. There's just so much to do here."

"Don't be absurd!" Freja spoke scoldingly from beside Merletta. "I had no idea the wedding was so early in the day. Get out of here—we've got it under control."

Smiling her thanks, Merletta followed Sage through the trees, swatting a particularly large insect with her hand.

"I don't know why I need so long to get ready," she complained to her friend. "Heath said he doesn't expect me to wear any big fancy Valorian gown. He said I can get married in the attire I'm comfortable in, and any fastidious human guests can take a swim in the lagoon if they complain."

Sage grinned. "As entertaining as that would be to see, I trust it won't be necessary."

She cast an appraising look over Merletta, taking in her friend's shells, and the simple, fitted skirt she'd now taken to wearing over her legs. It was more secure, and more covering, than the one made from Merletta's scales, but not long enough to hamper her in the water should she choose to transform for some reason.

"Do you have your heart set on wearing that?" Sage asked, an edge of uncertainty in her voice.

"Not really," Merletta said, surprised. "I just didn't want to be forced into a dozen layers in this heat. And I want to be able to actually move as I walk down the aisle."

Sage shook her head at this reference to the coming ceremony. "Amazing, isn't it, the similarities between our wedding rituals and the humans'?"

"Not so amazing, really," Merletta smiled. "Just further proof of the fact that our origins are theirs."

Their path took them not far from the beach where the ceremony was to take place, and Merletta could hear the sounds of preparation. Nerves swept over her as she peered through the trees, trying to catch a glimpse of the ship anchored just past Vazula's protective coral ring.

"I'm not sure whether to be glad or alarmed by how many Valorians apparently took up the invitation to attend," Merletta told Sage. "It's a good sign for future relations between Vazula and Valoria, of course, and we're going to need all the help we can get from them. But it's a bit alarming to think of them all coming to watch Heath marry a scandalous sea creature." She bit her lip. "I mean, apparently the crown prince is coming!"

"He's already here," Sage told her matter-of-factly. "With about ten guards following him around everywhere." She saw Merletta trying again to look through the trees, and tugged on her arm.

"Come on, stop dawdling! You won't see them there. All Heath's family members are getting ready with him, over in the finished dwellings." She waved a hand vaguely toward the jungle, in the direction of what they were fairly certain had once been Vazula's central clearing.

When they emerged from the trees, Merletta blinked at the dwelling taking shape some distance back from the lagoon's edge.

"It's really coming together, isn't it?" Sage said, sounding pleased as she looked at Merletta and Heath's future home.

Merletta nodded, hardly paying attention as Sage half-shoved her toward the water, insisting that she wash herself off.

"I still don't understand why Heath and I aren't allowed to help," Merletta complained, as she completed a rapid wash. "For some ridiculous reason, they're making it the biggest dwelling yet, so you'd think the more workers the better."

"People are grateful to you," said a new voice. "You exposed the lies we were living under, and brought us out into the open. If they want to do something to thank you, I don't know why you'd turn it down!"

Merletta turned to frown slightly at Indigo, who'd stepped out of the temporary canvas structure set up near the lagoon.

"Not everyone's grateful," Merletta said. Her thoughts strayed to the anger they'd all faced from those who didn't like the shift in power happening in the triple kingdoms. Elfin had been particularly good with using his influence to push back against the complainers.

"Yes, well those ones are staying underwater, and good riddance to them," Sage said brightly. "Indigo is right. Now come."

She chivvied her friend toward the tent, and Merletta followed, casting one last glance at the partially constructed home. It wasn't that she didn't appreciate it—she was thrilled at the thought of living in the beautiful dwelling with Heath, building a future there, one day a family. But it all seemed...too much.

"I don't remember there being a tower like that on the plans," she commented. "Is it just me, or is it starting to look a bit like a miniature castle?"

"Hopefully not too miniature," said Sage cheerfully. "We don't want to be completely outdone by the other land kingdoms."

"I don't know if you can really call Vazula a kingdom," Merletta said.

"Not yet," Sage agreed, giving Merletta a sideways look she couldn't interpret.

"Sage," Merletta said warily. "Why would Heath and I need to live in a castle?"

They'd entered the tent by this time, and Ileana strode forward, her spear in her hand, as always.

"Well, you're about to become a lady, aren't you?" she said.

"In Valoria," Merletta protested. "That doesn't count here."

"True," Ileana agreed. "Vazula doesn't have its own royal family...yet."

"You mean *anymore*, not yet," Merletta corrected. "There was one once, of course, before they all died out or were submerged."

"Yes," Ileana said expressionlessly. "That's what I meant."

The guard exchanged a look with Sage and Indigo that left Merletta frowning between them. "What in the tides are you all looking so shifty about?"

"Nothing you need to trouble your head about on your wedding day," Sage said, her voice turning businesslike. "On with the dress!"

Turning, Merletta felt her mouth fall open at the sight of the shimmering garment in her friend's arms. She reached out, glad now that Sage had made her wash her hands as she ran her fingers down the soft fabric. It moved so fluidly under her touch that it almost felt like water.

"It's called silk, apparently," Indigo chimed in. "One of Lord Heath's cousins organized it."

"You really should just call him Heath," Merletta told Indigo. "He's not expecting any great titles here."

The young mermaid looked scandalized. "I can't do that!" she insisted. "I can't be on a first name basis with our future—"

"Not now, Indigo," Sage cut her off firmly.

Merletta stared between them, but her attention was quickly recaptured by the dress Sage was slipping over her head. She shimmied out of the simple skirt she'd been wearing, leaving her scaled skirt on.

It wasn't visible once the dress was settled, however. The silk was white, although the tiny crystal beads threaded across it gave the appearance of a pale, clear blue shimmering throughout. Like looking through shallow water at white sand.

Some other kind of fabric was sewed on the bodice of the dress, blending seamlessly thanks to the beads which covered it. The neckline was scalloped across the two rounded edges, making it look much like Merletta's shells, over which it perfectly settled. And the skirts, while long at the back, weren't quite to Merletta's knees at the front, meaning it didn't hinder her mobility at all.

"It's perfect," Merletta breathed, admiring herself in the tall looking glass that had traveled all the way from Valoria. "I love it." She ran a hand over the fabric again. "I can hardly believe it was made in Heath's kingdom. I never saw anyone wear anything like this there."

Indigo nodded at Sage. "Sage helped Lady Bianca design it, actually."

Merletta turned her gaze to her friend. "I think you missed your calling," she said, awed.

Sage laughed. "No thanks. I don't want to design coverings. I think I'll have plenty to occupy me as a record holder."

"Not to mention the wife of the next Record Master!" Indigo pointed out, elbowing a blushing Sage in the ribs. "Everyone will be gathering again soon, for your turn!"

Sage laughed self-consciously, although she couldn't hide her grin. "Not everyone, thankfully. We'll have a much quieter ceremony, underwater. So no foreign princes will be capable of attending, even if they wanted to."

"Heath is sad he'll miss out," Merletta commented, still examining her reflection in the mirror. Indigo was twisting her hair up into a loose knot at the base of her neck, leaving several waving strands to flow out. "Although of course he understands."

She found Sage's hand, giving it a squeeze. "I'm sad you won't be living up here with us, but I understand, too. Emil's leadership—and yours, of course—will be the best thing that could happen to the triple kingdoms."

"We'll be up here so often you'll be sick of us," Sage said cheerfully. "Since most of our records will be stored up here, both our roles will require it. Speaking of which, do you know if

Heath had any suggestions for Emil about the development of a records authentication process?"

Merletta nodded. "I heard them talking about it just yesterday. Heath was explaining about this unique royal seal human monarchs often carry. They think something like that could be adapted to make sure any records produced by the Center will be verifiable. It will require a lot of tedious effort from Emil if he's the one carrying it, though, especially in the early days. Or months." She grimaced. "Or years."

"He won't mind," Sage said confidently. She smirked a little. "And it's a good thing he's so good at combat, given he'll need to keep this seal safe."

"No talk about work!" Indigo said firmly. "It's your wedding day!"

"Did I just hear someone say Emil is good at combat?" Andre's head poked through the entrance of the tent, a look of incredulity on his face. "Because that's a bit of an exagger—"

"ANDRE!" shrieked his cousin. "Get out of here! You can't interrupt the bride while she's getting dressed!"

Andre stared blankly between Indigo and Merletta. "What do you mean? She's about ten times as covered as normal. What's the problem?"

Merletta couldn't help laughing. "No problem, Andre," she said. "But it's a little crowded in here."

"Sorry," he said cheerfully. "I didn't mean to interrupt. I just heard you talking when I was going past on my hourly run."

He puffed out his chest a little, and Merletta bit back a grin. Predictably, Andre was absolutely loving his legs, and taking the challenge of not only learning but mastering a new skill very seriously. He was well on his way to being the best on-land fighter of all the merpeople.

Indigo rolled her eyes as her cousin ducked back out.

"Speaking of people who'll be here so often you'll be sick of them..."

Merletta laughed again. "Not a chance. I'm glad Andre is going to live on Vazula. We'll need his relentless optimism with all the challenges ahead." She smiled warmly at the younger mermaid. "And I'm glad you're staying, too, Indigo."

"You're missing something," Ileana said curtly, casting a critical eye over Merletta's hair.

She ducked out of the tent, leaving Merletta to send a bemused glance at Sage.

"You know, even though I'm marrying a human, and gaining a title, and living on *land*, I think the strangest part of all of this is that *Ileana* is helping me get ready for my wedding!"

Sage choked on her laugh as Ileana reappeared, a string of pearls in her hand.

"You need more of the ocean in the mix," she said matter-of-factly, draping the string through Merletta's dark hair with unexpected finesse.

"Thank you," Merletta said, touched and surprised.

Ileana gave a curt nod, hesitating. Then she spoke in a rush.

"Since we're talking about who's living up here and who's staying underwater...I've been wanting to discuss it."

Merletta swiveled to properly face the other mermaid, her eyebrows raised. "You want to live on Vazula? Even though Emil was willing to give you a position among his guards?"

Ileana nodded. "I know that's the highest position a guard can occupy down there, but I don't want to guard the Record Master, even if it is Emil." She looked incredibly uncomfortable, but she pushed on. "I was willing to give everything to the Center's cause when they were giving me access, and when they stopped, I was willing to give everything to destroy them. I wanted to bring the old Record Master down, make him pay."

"Well, you did have a hand in that," Merletta commented

quietly, remembering how Ileana had identified the Record Master to the dragons.

Ileana nodded again. "I've been wrestling with it ever since, and I have to acknowledge to myself that I took no pleasure in his death. It didn't fix anything—it didn't even take away the anger. I don't know if it's because my resentment was against a concept and never a person, or because the problem was in me all the time, not in the Center." She drew in a tight, angry breath. "In a way, his death was worse than all the rest. It didn't feel like justice, not when the dragons who did it had just murdered innocent merpeople for no good reason. Then they just flew away, without really even acknowledging their mistake."

She scowled, and Merletta reflected that the other girl clearly still had plenty of anger to work through.

"I don't like the idea that power puts you above all accountability," Ileana continued. "It doesn't seem right. There's nothing we can do about the dragons, but I think you're the best hope I've seen of building a world where that isn't the case. You know better than most what the true cost is when those in charge think they don't have to answer to anyone."

Merletta was silent for a moment, overwhelmed by the faith apparently being placed in her. "The dragons aren't all like that," she reminded Ileana. "Rekavidur isn't, and neither is his father. And that means dragons are capable of change." She smiled ruefully. "It's just maybe a bigger job than any of us can take on...we'll have to depend on those dragons who can see sense to bring about change in the others of their kind."

Ileana shrugged, clearly not placing much stock in the idea.

"It's not just that I think you can be trusted with power," she said abruptly.

Merletta frowned, ready to correct the apparent misconception about the level of authority she was likely to have on Vazula, but Ileana barreled on without giving her a chance.

"It's also that you've clearly got something right. Because you've suffered more from them than I have—you've been targeted so much worse—and not only did you never let it stop you from pursuing your goals, you seem to have managed not to be bitter about it. If I take you as an example, I have to conclude that vengeance isn't a path forward. It's a path that leads nowhere, changes nothing. So *you're* the one I want to guard, if you'll let me."

Merletta stared at the other mermaid, too stunned to find words. A memory raced across her mind, of Ileana's spear flashing as it sped through the water, piercing Heath with a near fatal strike. But Ileana's words about vengeance chastened Merletta. She was humbled to think someone had learned from her example without her even knowing it. She didn't want to betray that trust.

"I'd be glad," she said quietly.

Ileana let out a long breath. "Thank you," she said. She hovered for a moment, the silence in the small space absolute, and a little awkward. "I'll go check that everything's in hand," she said, striding out of the tent.

"Tides above," Sage said blankly, as soon as Ileana was gone.

Merletta gave a fervent nod. "Yes. Precisely."

Never, when she was a raw and combative new trainee, could she have predicted any of this. Ileana was certainly the last mermaid she would have expected to be assisting her on her wedding day.

She sighed. She would probably have expected it to be Tish. Her heart still ached at her first friend's absence. Merletta had hoped that once the threat of the dragons was gone—not to mention the prohibitions of the Center—Tish might have been willing to give her legs another chance. But the other girl had no interest in coming near land. She'd sent a message, wishing Merletta all the best for her wedding, but she clearly intended to stay inside the triple kingdoms. She was likely in her shell-smith tower right now, leaning over an intricate task, struggling to meet her quota. She'd chosen a path for her life well before the tumult of the last couple of years, and she had shown no desire to deviate from it since.

A part of Merletta wondered dully what the point was of opening the borders, exposing the Center's suppression, creating a world of new opportunities, if even her closest child-hood friend remained too wary to take advantage of any of it. But she recognized that it wasn't in her control—she couldn't force change on anyone. Sometimes change was just too fright-ening, even if from the outside it was unarguably change for the better.

"Merletta, are you in there?"

"Yes!" Merletta called, recognizing the voice.

Sure enough, Bianca stepped into the tent a moment later, beaming at the effect of Merletta in the gown she'd commissioned.

"Are you ready?"

"As ready as a mermaid dressed up like a human can be to marry into the nobility," Merletta quipped.

Bianca's face fell slightly. "You don't like it? Too human?"

"Oh, no, I didn't mean that!" Merletta hastened to assure her. "I love it! It's absolutely perfect." She cast another look at herself in the looking glass, struggling to comprehend that the polished, elegant figure was her. "It's just the nerves coming out."

"You have nothing to be nervous about," Bianca said with a smile. "Heath's practically bursting with eagerness to marry you, and nobody else's opinion matters all that much, surely."

"Well said." Indigo nodded approvingly. "Now let's go."

Merletta followed the others out of the tent, noting that work had now stopped on the nearby dwelling. Bianca kept step beside them, seeming very at ease in the light gown she'd adopted for the humid weather. She'd arrived with the first group of Valorians, and had been on Vazula for a couple of weeks, now. Merletta had been impressed with how uncomplainingly the young noblewoman had taken the very primitive conditions the island currently had to offer.

"You and Heath couldn't have picked a more beautiful spot to get married," Bianca said, as if in response to Merletta's thoughts. She flashed her soon-to-be cousin a grin. "The air can be a little stifling, though."

With a flick of her hand, she sent a cool breeze swirling around them, ruffling Merletta's silken skirts and lifting the tendrils of hair from her neck.

"Ooh, I could get used to that!" Merletta said.

"I was hoping you might say that," Bianca responded, with a hint of eagerness.

Merletta looked at her in surprise. "Are you considering staying?" Her heart lifted at the idea—Heath had expressed no hint of regret or hesitation about their plans, but she knew how much it would mean to him to have family by his side in his new life.

"Considering it," Bianca admitted. "If I'm welcome."

"Of course you are!"

The Valorian girl smiled. "I really do like it here," she said, casting her gaze around the lush jungle. Her brow creased. "And I'm not sure I'm satisfied with the changes to King Matlock's restrictive laws. I don't especially appreciate being required to register and catalogue my magic, and I know I'm not the only one."

Merletta considered her. "Well, I don't think you'd have to

worry about that here. In fact, you'd be quite unremarkable given your sadly limited form."

Bianca laughed at her teasing tone, the sound light and carefree.

When they neared the beach, a small escort stepped out of the tree line, forming an honor guard of sorts. Sage took Merletta's hand, giving it a final squeeze, then she and Indigo hurried forward to find their places.

"My Lady," Felix said politely, gesturing for Bianca to precede them. "Allow me to show you to your position."

"Thank you," Bianca said brightly, taking his offered arm.

A smile tugged at Merletta's lips as the pair stepped out of the trees. From the looks of it, Bianca was sending another wind whipping around, and Felix was watching in open admiration. Merletta couldn't help wondering how long it would take Bianca to realize that not all of the honored Valorian guests were being offered personal guard services.

From the way Brody watched the pair out of narrowed eyes, she had a feeling Bianca's twin had already realized it. Merletta's smile grew. Chances were if they got Bianca on Vazula, they'd get Brody, too. Perhaps there would be others, especially if Bianca was right that others in her family shared her dissatisfaction with Valoria's laws regarding magic. Vazula could become a haven for anyone wanting a fresh start, power-wielder or otherwise.

Peering through the trees at the gathered crowd, Merletta felt her nerves begin to rise again. It was all well and good for Bianca to say that no one else's opinion mattered, but there seemed to be a lot of someones gathered to watch the spectacle. It was hard not to feel vulnerable, all alone, waiting for her cue.

But then the group of guards parted, and August stepped forward. His normally stoic face was softened by a smile, and his approving nod caused Merletta to stand a little straighter.

"That was the signal," he said gravely.

At a gesture from him, the guards moved out onto the sand, assuming a formation of two lines, spears interlinked in an arch. August took his position at the top of the formation, and Merletta stepped through, feeling suddenly stronger. She wasn't a lonely unclaimed orphan with no home. She came from a proud people, and although she was forging a new path, she had the joy of knowing she'd left her first home better than she'd found it.

Merletta's bare feet touched sand, and she moved forward on the arranged route, straight toward the water. The onlookers were gathered on the sand, but Merletta tried not to look too closely at them all. She did catch sight of Elfin and his wife, and sent them a small smile. She was still early in the process of getting to know them, but it meant a great deal to her to have some of her birth family present on such an important day. Then her eyes darted ahead, and all other thoughts fled, her breath hitching when she finally caught sight of the man waiting for her.

She'd expected Heath to be on the sand, but he was so close to the waterline that the waves lapped over his feet and ankles. Merletta's heart swelled as she understood his silent message—her future with him didn't require her to leave the ocean behind. He would straddle the line of land and sea with her, embracing both.

His face was glowing, his dark hair cropped neatly, and his beard now permanently grown in. He wasn't dressed with any great formality—the light tunic he wore was plenty thick enough for the warm air. And his eyes were fixed on her with intoxicating intensity.

Merletta forgot about everyone else, needing no more reminder that today, there *was* only one opinion that really mattered. The love in Heath's eyes was a mirror of her own, drawing her across the sand to him as irresistibly as the tide.

The ceremony passed in a blur, even the unfamiliar part making Merletta's heart sing. She knew the words were the legal requirement to make the union binding in Valoria as well as the triple kingdoms.

Heath was hers, and she was his, and no one above or below water would be able to dispute that after today.

She hadn't expected the invitation at the end for Heath to kiss her, but she reflected as he pressed his lips triumphantly to hers that it was the very best kind of surprise.

"We did it," Heath whispered, pulling back to the sound of their audience's celebration. "I can hardly believe we've made it here."

"It was very much against the odds," Merletta agreed, smiling blissfully up at him.

"I don't know." Heath's eyes were deliciously warm as he lifted an errant strand of hair from Merletta's neck. "I'd never bet against you."

They turned to accept the congratulations of the crowd, Percival the first to grip his brother's arm, and sweep Merletta into a powerful hug.

"Well, there had to be one time in your life that you beat me at something, Heath," he said jovially. "And I certainly can't fault your choice."

Heath rolled his eyes, but returned his brother's smile. "I'll keep an eye out for a nice mermaid for you, so you don't feel too eclipsed by me."

Percival laughed. "I think I'd do best to look for a Valorian wife," he said good-naturedly. "But thanks for the offer."

Merletta smiled as Percival slapped his brother on the back. She'd half expected the young lord to declare a desire for escape or adventure, as Bianca had done. But from all Heath had told her, Percival's focus was very much elsewhere, as he took a real interest in his duties as his father's heir for the first time in his life. A quick glance at the duke showed pride in his eyes as he regarded both his sons. It was a happy sight.

Even Heath's grandparents, elderly as they were, had made the voyage to attend the wedding. And, to Merletta's relief, she no longer saw any trace of the concern that had lingered on the elderly princess's face when she'd first met Merletta. On the contrary, Heath's grandmother looked utterly delighted as her gaze rested on her grandson and his bride.

"Congratulations, my dragonfriend." Reka's gravelly voice caused half the guests to still as it rumbled over the now-milling crowd.

Heath and Merletta both looked up at the only dragon in attendance.

"Thank you, Reka," Heath said gravely. "And thank you for your part in our happiness. It would have been hard to find a way forward without your assistance." His expression grew more somber. "I hope you know how much I appreciate the sacrifice you made."

"Sacrifice is a weighty word for a decision that was most likely always part of my future," Reka said lightly. "I do not regret my decision." He lowered his head, his gaze passing thoughtfully over them both. "I suspect I will miss you when you are dust in the ground. That is, perhaps, one cost to my choice. But," his tone brightened, "I will most likely continue our friendship through your offspring."

"Thank you, Reka," Heath said, his tone dry this time. Merletta squeezed his hand, choking back a laugh.

"You are welcome," Rekavidur said serenely. "On that matter, I am curious to see what offspring you will produce. Presumably they will receive both the ability to transform from their mother and the seed of magic from their father. The future of Vazula will be unlike any past that has come before."

Merletta exchanged a look with Heath. The image was a little unnerving, but it was also exciting. Tantalizing, she would have said not long ago. Except now, for the first time, it was truly within reach.

Rekavidur raised his snout upward and sniffed at the wind. "I am glad you discovered what you first wished to know of this place, Heath—what became of its human inhabitants, and the magic they possessed. But I confess myself unsatisfied."

"Why?" Heath demanded.

Reka's head lowered slowly. "I wish to know what became of the dragons. A small colony lived here, and then they went elsewhere. I know from the history of my own colony that they did not return to Wyvern Islands."

"The sealed memories didn't say, did they?" mused Heath.

Reka snaked his long neck from side to side. "They did not. The only information they contained was the colony's intention to travel east. So east I shall go."

"You're leaving?" Heath demanded, his hand tightening in Merletta's. "What, now?"

Reka nodded serenely. "I catch the scent of discovery in my nostrils. There is more to learn, and although I have an endless amount of time in which to learn it, I find myself eager to begin."

"I'll miss you," Heath said frankly.

The dragon lowered his head further, bumping it against Heath's shoulder in a gesture Merletta had never seen before.

"I will return, my dragonfriend. And I will endeavor to do so within the short span of your lifetime."

And with only an inclination of the head to the newly married couple, he launched into the air and winged his way out of sight. As he'd said, he flew eastward, away from Valoria and Wyvern Islands.

Merletta blinked up at the empty sky, taken aback by the abruptness of the departure. Although she should really have learned by now.

"*I will endeavor to do so within the short span of your lifetime,*" Heath repeated, sounding irked. "He's been saying maddeningly lofty things like that constantly, ever since he chose immortality."

Merletta laid a hand on his cheek, not fooled by the exasperated words. "I know you'll miss him," she said. "But maybe you can follow him with your farsight."

"That's true," Heath said, perking up. "I hadn't thought of that."

"And," Merletta pressed, her thumb tracing a circle on his cheek, "there's plenty to occupy you here. I'm trusting you won't get too lonely."

Heath smiled down at her, his attention fully caught. "With you at my side, something tells me that's the last thing I'll be."

Done with waiting once and for all, Merletta stretched up on her toes to press a kiss to her husband's lips. No more living in fear that each stolen moment would be their last. Somehow, impossibly, she'd found her way to a future where she could have both the land and the sea. And, more importantly, Heath.

The future was as bright as the unfiltered sunshine that beat down on their shoulders. And it was theirs to write.

The End

NOTE FROM THE AUTHOR

Thank you for reading *A Kingdom Restored*. I hope you found the end of Heath and Merletta's tale satisfying! I would be so grateful if you would consider leaving a review on Amazon—it would really make a difference.

If you're looking for more adventure, fantasy, and clean romance, check out my upcoming release, *Song of Ebony*, a Snow White retelling which forms the first installment of a new series of fairy tale retellings.

And if you haven't yet read about what Rekavidur finds when he leaves Vazula to fly east, check out *The Kingdom Tales*, a completed series of fairy tale retellings in which our favorite yellow dragon features!

Join up to my mailing list at deborahgracewhite.com to be kept up to date on new releases, specials, and giveaways, such as bonus chapters. You'll receive some great freebies, too, including *An Expectation of Magic*, a novella which serves as a prequel to

The Vazula Chronicles, telling the tale of Heath's parents.

You'll also receive *Dragon's Sight*, an 8,000 word prequel to *The Kyona Chronicles* (a series set before *The Vazula Chronicles*, in the same world), told from the perspective of the dragon Elddreki (Rekavidur's father).

Again, thanks for entering the world of *The Vazula Chronicles*! I hope to see you back again.

ALSO BY DEBORAH GRACE WHITE

The Kyona Chronicles: YA Fantasy

The Kyona Legacy: YA Fantasy

The Vazula Chronicles: YA Fantasy

The Kingdom Tales: Fairy Tale Retellings

The Singer Tales: Fairy Tale Retellings
(releasing throughout 2023)

ACKNOWLEDGMENTS

So many people helped see *The Vazula Chronicles* through. As always, my first thanks go to my awesome husband Ray, my alpha listener. You're the best, and I love how much you've engaged with this series.

A huge thank you to my beta readers: Andrew, Adrian, Mel W, Mum, Tamara, and Berri. Your feedback and encouragement were invaluable.

Extra thanks to Dad for developmental editing.

Karri, this is my favorite cover of the series—I love it! And Becca, the map continues to be gorgeous!

To you, the reader, thank you for giving me the privilege of being an author.

And most importantly, to God, who alone can restore everything lost and broken and give it new life.

ABOUT THE AUTHOR

I've been a reader since I can remember, growing up on a wide range of books, from classic literature to light-hearted romps. The love of reading has traveled with me unchanged across multiple  continents, and carried me from my own childhood all the way to having children of my own.

But if reading is like looking through a window into a magical and beautiful world, beginning to write my own stories was like discovering that I could open that window and climb right out into fantasyland.

I cannot believe how privileged I am to actually be living that childhood dream and publishing my own novels. I do so from my hometown of Adelaide, Australia, where I live with my husband and our three little ones.

I've never outgrown my love of young adult stories, so the genre of young adult fantasy was always going to be my niche. Feel free to email me at deborah@deborahgracewhite.com and introduce yourself! Or subscribe to my mailing list at deborah gracewhite.com for free giveaways, sales, and updates.